“A compuls thriller.”

(starred review)

“Thriller writing of the highest order.”

—*Providence Journal*

“Patrick Lee’s imagination knows no boundaries . . . just when it seems clear what’s truly going on, another surprise appears.” —Associated Press

“Patrick Lee manages to build character and create an audacious premise without ever taking his foot off the throttle.” —*Booklist* (starred review)

“A suspenseful, action-fueled adventure filled with big mysteries and adrenaline-pumping sequences.”

—*Mystery Scene*

“*Dark Site* succeeds on all levels . . . a clever, smart story with the only disappointment being that it’s not twice as long.” —Bookreporter

ALSO BY PATRICK LEE

The Sam Dryden Novels

Runner

Signal

The Travis Chase Novels

The Breach

Ghost Country

Deep Sky

PATRICK LEE

DARK SITE

St. Martin's Paperbacks

Published in the United States by St. Martin's Paperbacks, an imprint of St. Martin's Publishing Group.

DARK SITE

For information, address St. Martin's Publishing Group, 120 Broadway, New York, NY 10271.

www.stmartins.com

Library of Congress Catalog Card Number: 2018055980

ISBN: 978-1-250-03080-1

Our books may be purchased in bulk for promotional, educational, or business use. Please contact your local bookseller or the Macmillan Corporate and Premium Sales Department at 1-800-221-7945, ext. 5442, or by email at MacmillanSpecialMarkets@macmillan.com.

Printed in the United States of America

Minotaur hardcover edition / May 2019
St. Martin's Paperbacks edition / August 2020

10 9 8 7 6 5 4 3 2 1

FOR PAT FERA,

AND IN MEMORY OF TONY FERA

CONTENTS

PART ONE

WITNESSES

SEPTEMBER 2018

CHAPTER ONE

The last decision Danica Ellis made in her ordinary life—the life in which stress meant playing chicken with the rent due-date, and wondering if going back to school was another slow-motion train wreck of a mistake—was whether to buy sixty-watt or hundred-watt light bulbs. As choices went, it wasn't exactly roads diverging in a yellow wood. The prices weren't a hell of a lot different, and probably the electric bill wouldn't be swayed much, either—a few dollars per month, maybe. But a few dollars could matter. It had come to that once or twice already this year, and probably would again before she had her new degree and—fingers and toes crossed—some kind of career related to it. She grabbed the sixties off the shelf and tucked them into her cart beside the ninety-nine-cent white bread.

It was two in the morning and she had Kroger almost to herself. She'd passed a single bored cashier on her way in, and had seen no more than three other customers making lazy rounds among the aisles. Even the stocking crew had finished up and gone home for the night.

Danica moved on from the light bulbs. She rolled her cart into the broad lane that ran the length of the store's back wall. At this hour the open refrigerated displays seemed to radiate a deeper chill than they would have during the evening rush. Maybe it was the absence of dozens of warm bodies.

Just ahead, a man stood looking over the orange juice racks. Danica had seen him browsing paperbacks a few minutes earlier. He apparently hadn't found one to his liking; he had nothing in his hands now, and no cart, either. He was lean and attractive, and well-dressed for someone buying groceries in the middle of the night. Maybe he'd just come from a party; he was thirty, give or take.

Ten years closer to the cradle than you are, sweetie.

Jesus, since when did checking out a thirty-year-old make her feel like a leering pervert? Being forty-one didn't qualify you as ancient, did it? Especially if everyone said you were a *young* forty-one, and everything that had been perky in your twenties was still pretty damned perky, thank you very much.

Tell yourself whatever keeps your confidence up.

As Danica passed the man, he glanced at her and acknowledged her with a quick smile. She returned it, then found her eyes going to his left hand to check for a ring. He wasn't wearing one. Past him now, heading for the produce section at the far end of the store, she wondered if he'd seen the glance and understood its meaning. The notion made her cheeks flush, the feeling distinct against the cold rolling off the open cases.

You're out of practice at all this. Way out.

No argument there. Before now, the last time she'd been single she'd been thirty-give-or-take herself. A lot had happened in the intervening decade. Very little of it had been good.

She took a head of lettuce from produce and made her way to the checkout. She'd just finished setting everything on the conveyor when the same young man stepped into place behind her with a small bottle of orange juice. It crossed her mind to wave him ahead of her, but then the scanner beeped as the checkout girl passed the first item over it.

Danica glanced at the man again. He reminded her of Jake Ryan from *Sixteen Candles,* a reference that made her want to cry. Though she'd only been seven when that movie came out, this guy would have been, what, negative four?

After the glance, she kept her eyes on the groceries on the belt, though in her peripheral vision she took note of the guy's body language. Something about it gave her the sense that he was nervous. He kept turning his head just slightly, maybe halfway toward her, like he wanted to say something but couldn't quite do it.

The implication—the possibility, anyway—hit her like a drug. Was *he* interested? It wasn't entirely unthinkable. She really did look young for her age. How many times had her friend Carrie told her she looked thirty, with just enough angst behind the compliment to give it credibility? The thing was, Danica *did* feel pretty good about her looks. Even these days, grinding along at rock bottom in terms of self-esteem, she was happy with the picture in the mirror. She liked her eyes—big and brown and unable to hide anything she felt. *Anime eyes,* Carrie called them, with that same angst. She liked her hair, too; she had spent the last twelve months growing it long again, ditching the pixie cut she'd worn for years. She got compliments on the new look all the time. So why *shouldn't* this guy be interested? And what if *he* looked younger than he was? What if he was thirty-five? What if he didn't care about the difference, anyway? Not every guy was obsessed with—

"Found it."

A woman's voice—more like a girl's voice. It came from somewhere behind and to Danica's left. The Jake Ryan lookalike turned, and Danica turned with him. The newcomer could not have been older than twenty-five, and she could've posed for any of the fashion magazines lining the rack above the conveyor. She had a plastic bottle of Midol in her hand. She crossed to the young man, reached past him to set the bottle next to his orange juice, then shut her eyes and leaned into him, seeming to block out the whole world beyond the shirt fabric covering his chest.

He kissed the top of her head and spoke softly. "You'll feel better by the time we get home."

The girl nodded against him. She put her arms around his waist and held on tightly. To Danica's right, the cashier scanned the sixty-watt bulbs and stuffed them into a bag.

The parking lot was seventy degrees and heavy with a night mist that wasn't quite fog. Beyond the lot's edge the land dropped away in shallow steps to the Pacific, three miles west of Kroger. Spread out across the sloped terrain between them lay the western expanse of Brookings, Oregon, its pink-orange streetlights spectral in the haze. Danica liked seeing the town from up here at night. Working double shifts and getting her groceries at two in the morning was almost worth it for this view. Even now it was helping her mood—a little.

She angled to her car, at first hidden by a full-sized van someone had parked beside it. She popped the trunk and set the grocery bags inside. Twenty yards behind her she heard the store's automatic door slide open—the young couple coming out. She finished stowing her things, pushed the empty cart to the corral two spaces away, and got back to her car just as the couple reached the van. There was an awkward instant when all three were clustered at the mouth of the channel between the vehicles. The young man, a pace ahead of the girl, halted and left the space open for Danica.

"You were first," he said.

Danica thought of letting them go ahead anyway, then just shrugged. Losing three seconds wouldn't ruin their night. She stepped past them, went to her door and put her key in the lock, and felt an explosion of pain beneath her ear as the man's fist slammed into her neck.

Her knees gave. She dropped. She thought to grab her side mirror for support, but her arms and hands were useless. The punch had hit some kind of pressure point, like a kill-switch between her brain and her limbs. She landed on her ass, the impact jarring her spine and clacking her teeth together hard. Her body pitched forward until her head thumped lightly against her door, and then she tipped all the way over on her side, on the damp pavement.

They were both standing over her now, crowded and hunched in the space between the van and car. The young man dropped to a knee and leaned in close above her.

"Don't fight," the man said. His tone was calm, as advising as it was threatening—as though he'd done this before. "Don't fight, you'll be fine."

Danica saw a gun in his hand, not quite aimed at her. He braced his other hand on the asphalt, pushed himself back up to a crouch and withdrew. He spoke to the girl. "Get her wrists. I'll cover."

The girl dropped into Danica's field of vision. She no longer appeared overwhelmed by menstrual cramps. In spite of her youth, she showed none of the vulnerability she had displayed a moment before. Her lean features only made her look hard now. She looked like a soldier.

It occurred to Danica that the van was blocking all of this from the cashier's view in the store. The same probably went for the security cameras. None of which was an accident.

"Do it," the young man hissed.

The girl pivoted on her ankles, reached up and slid open the van's side door. As she did, Danica felt the nerves in her arms and legs begin to reawaken, the skin of her hands tingling with little pinpricks. She risked just enough movement to confirm to herself she had control of them again. The girl reached into the van and took out a pair of plastic zip-tie handcuffs, the kind some police departments used. She held them in both hands and turned to face Danica again.

"Lie flat," the girl said. "On your stomach."

Danica stared up past her at the van's interior. Even with its dome light on, it seemed darker inside than the night air above the lot. Like a cave. Or a tomb. No question about it: whoever they were, whatever the hell they wanted, if she let herself be dragged into that darkness, nobody would ever see her again.

"Lie flat," the girl repeated.

Danica considered her odds of getting away if she struggled right now. They weren't good, but they were better than they would be in another five seconds, or at any point beyond that.

The girl made a face that said she was done threatening; she reached for Danica's shoulder to force her down flat on her chest.

The moment the girl took hold of her, Danica threw her own hand up, grabbed the girl's forearm and pulled her downward, off balance. In the same movement, Danica rolled to free up the arm beneath her, made a fist with that hand and swung it hard at the girl's face.

For a fraction of a second, she thought the punch would connect. Then the girl jerked her head to the side and Danica's fist only grazed her jaw. An instant later they were fighting, hands grabbing wherever they could, elbows hitting every boundary of the confined space between the vehicles.

"Fuck," the young man said, "let me in there."

"I've got her."

"You *don't*."

The girl was trying to hit her, but couldn't manage it in the cramped space. It was all she could do to keep her balance, squatting like that while Danica still gripped her other arm, pulling her down as hard as she could. The girl kept having to use her free hand to brace herself against Danica's car.

"Get out of the way," the man said.

In the weird, adrenaline-spiked clarity of the moment, Danica found her focus snapping to every detail that might matter. The man's tone of voice struck her now.

He was afraid.

More specifically, he was afraid for the girl.

Danica thought of their intimate display in the checkout lane. The PMS may have been bullshit, but the affection between the two had been real.

Hurt her. Badly. Make him tend to her while you escape.

Danica had just enough time to be jarred by the ugly thought, and then the girl pulled her forearm free of her grip, and drew back to lob a punch Danica couldn't possibly dodge.

Hurt her.

Badly.

Danica threw one hand out sideways, beneath the near edge of the van, and pressed it to the vehicle's underbody. She knifed her other hand upward and grabbed a fistful of the girl's hair just above one ear. The unexpected move startled the girl; her cocked-back arm faltered, as if she had some sense of what was about to happen to her. If so, she didn't react quickly enough to stop it.

Danica wrenched her hands toward each other—one braced below the van, the other clutching the girl's head—as if she meant to bring a pair of cymbals crashing together. The girl, off-balance in her crouch, arms in no position to catch herself, plunged sideways. Her body followed her head down through a tight little arc; her temple slammed against the steel framing at the bottom of the van's open doorway. The impact made a double sound—a dull *thud* and a sickening *crack*—and seemed to knock the life right out of the girl's body. She sprawled atop Danica like a cut-down scarecrow.

"Emma?" The young man's voice had more panic than fear in it now. Danica heard him scrambling in the darkness near her feet, pressing forward, still hampered by the narrow space. She drew her legs up, knees to her chest, got both feet against the girl—Emma, apparently—and heaved her toward the man. She heard him curse as the girl's body knocked him back, and heard the gun clatter on the pavement. She didn't wait to hear anything else. She twisted, got her feet under her, pushed against both vehicles and got upright, and a second later she was sprinting away across the parking lot.

She dismissed the store as a refuge almost at once. It would've worked fine at six in the evening, crawling with customers and staffed with two dozen employees. Right now it held fewer people than the young man's gun held bullets.

The better option lay south of the broad parking

lot: an undeveloped tract of woodland covering at least three acres. Danica had driven past it every time she shopped here; on the rare occasions she'd done so in daylight, she'd seen thick cedar bushes and ferns beneath the boughs of dense pines.

She looked back as she ran. Her car and the van were a hundred feet behind her, and in the darkness between the vehicles, the young man was still crouched over the girl, trying to rouse her. His fear-soaked voice carried across the asphalt, the words indiscernible but the meaning clear. The girl wasn't responding.

Danica kept running. Another three hundred feet to the woods now. She drew her phone as she sprinted. She would punch three little digits, and then simply hide until an army of police cruisers descended on this place. She had just switched the phone on when she heard the roll and slam of the van's door being shut, far behind her. She threw another look over her shoulder: neither the man nor the girl's body were outside the vehicle anymore. Through the van's windows, backlit by the glare of the parking lot, she saw the man's silhouette as he clambered into the driver's seat. An instant later the vehicle roared to life.

Danica faced forward again, still sprinting. For an ugly second she expected the van's headlights to swing around and wash over her from behind, casting her shadow out ahead as the vehicle ran her down. That thought made the distance to the forest look like a mile; the van could reach her long before she got there.

She heard its tires bark on the wet blacktop. Heard the motor rev and the power steering whine.

Then nothing—just the sound of the van's engine fading away fast, even as it accelerated.

Danica looked back again.

The vehicle was racing for the street exit. It crossed the lot in bare seconds, took the turn too fast and fishtailed, and then it was gone, speeding away down the two-lane road into the night.

Danica stopped running. She stood there on the wide open tundra of the outer lot, listening to the receding drone.

Her heartbeat felt like someone's knuckle rapping against her ribs. Her breathing kept pace with it, ragged and uncontrollable. She raised the phone again, and found her hand shaking so badly she couldn't tap the icon she wanted. After a few seconds she managed it; the phone's number pad came up on screen. She pressed nine, then one—

And stopped.

She stared again in the direction the van had driven. Even the sound of it was gone now. She stood listening to her pulse beginning to ease. She stared at her car, far away in the milky light from the storefront, its tires bald and its paint faded.

"Why me?" she whispered.

The tone of the question surprised her a little—not petulant or even scared, but simply analytical. Why *had* they wanted her?

They had put careful planning into their attempt. The placement of the van, meant to conceal the abduction from any witnesses in the store. The timing of their exit, with their simple purchases, ensuring they would leave the place just moments after she did. They must have followed her here to begin with.

She pictured the couple again: young, attractive, non-crazy—they had been perfectly rational at every step. The idea that they had simply felt like abducting some random person, for no good reason, was ludicrous.

What explanation did that leave?

That they were professionals?

That someone had *sent* them to kidnap her? Someone with a reason? Did that make any more sense?

She wasn't a star witness in some prosecutor's case against a crime outfit. There was nothing like that going on in her life. She had no enemies that she could think of. She had no relatives with enemies, either, or with the kind of wealth that might inspire a ransom plot—she had no living relatives at all. Even the collapse of her marriage had drawn little in the way of bad blood. It had simply ended—two people with washed-out careers and washed-out feelings toward each other, decoupled and drifting. There had been nothing to fight over, in the end. No kids, not even alimony; Jason was as hard up as she was. He was living in Boston now, working at his parents' restaurant, dating someone named Cammie. Danica was still friends with him on Facebook.

"Why me?" she said again.

Why would somebody want to abduct a dead-broke divorcée working two jobs to put herself through business school? Whether the young couple had been acting alone or for someone else—just why? Why any of it?

You're not going to figure that out standing here. Let the cops handle it.

She nodded to herself at that thought. Her finger remained in place above the number one. Hovering.

She thought of her father, dead almost five years. Though not a day had passed when she hadn't missed him, that empty place in her life made her feel especially lonely right now: her father had been an FBI agent, and an Army officer before that. She would be on the phone with him right now if he were still alivc. She would have called him before the police. Would have sought his advice, because—

Because whatever this was, it already felt bigger than a local police matter.

That notion seemed to slide over her like a chilly draft. Pressing through her clothes, into the skin. What exactly *would* the Brookings Police Department do about this? They would look at security footage from the store, inside and outside. Maybe the van's license plate would be visible, assuming the vehicle wasn't stolen. And if that didn't pan out, then what? Were they going to assign cops to stand guard outside her house while she slept? Escort her to her classes and both of her minimum-wage jobs? Something told her the response would be less proactive than that.

Her breathing was close to normal now. She could hear the night wind in the pines behind her. Far ahead in the inner lot, her keys still hung from the lock in her driver's side door.

She stared, thinking it all through. She shut her eyes.

There *was* someone else she could talk to.

You don't even have his number anymore.

She could just get in her car and go see him, though. She would be there by morning. Late morning, maybe. Getting the hell away from Brookings was probably a smart move anyway, at least until she knew more.

What would you say to him, after all this time?

"Help me," she whispered.

Even that much would be hard to work up to. And maybe he wouldn't be thrilled to see her. But—

But he's a better option than the cops, for something like this.

On that point there was no arguing.

She opened her eyes and looked at her phone. The nine and one were still on the display. She deleted them, slid the phone back into her pocket and ran for her car.

CHAPTER TWO

The house reminded Sam Dryden of a bad dream—the one recurring nightmare that had ever troubled him. The dream was simple: he was walking through a tunnel, deep underground somewhere. The tunnel was narrow, maybe three feet wide. Its walls and floor were poured concrete, the ceiling some kind of metal grid-work held up by steel beams that ran across from side to side. There were dim white lights set high in the walls every ten feet; they led away into the darkness ahead of him, like a line of streetlamps marking the route of a highway at night, straight as a chalk-line through some pitch-black landscape.

In the dream, he was terrified of whatever lay at the end of the tunnel, though he never reached it—never even glimpsed it. He just walked, feeling that irrational panic rising inside him, like nothing he'd ever felt in real life—certainly not in his adult life. It was a child-hood dread that engulfed him, soaked him to the bone.

He had *been* a child when he started having the dream, somewhere around age twelve. Now he was forty-one, and had spent a good chunk of his past in the United States military, experiencing things that were real-life nightmares by most people's standards. None of those things had ever come back to him in his dreams, though. Just the tunnel. Just the concrete walls and the metal beams and the weak lights leading away into the black. Two or three times a year, that place would interrupt his sleep, and he would wake in the darkness feeling cold, as if he had the stale air of the tunnel still trapped in his lungs.

"I told you it needed some TLC."

Dryden blinked and turned.

The realtor showing him the house, a guy in his fifties named Henry Caine, stood in the open entryway. Dryden, in the foyer, had just finished walking through the place by himself. In the five years that he'd been buying and fixing old houses for a living, that had become a custom of his: solo walk-through, no distractions, nothing but his initial gut feeling.

"Maybe even TNT," Caine added, "but I wouldn't go that far."

"Neither would I," Dryden said.

He'd caught his first glimpse of the house ten minutes earlier, driving up to it. He'd parked and just sat there staring for over a minute.

From the outside it was beautiful. A Spanish-style villa built in the 1920s for a silent film star Dryden had never heard of, the home overlooked the Pacific from a high, windy bluff half a mile inland. Though its yard hadn't been maintained in some time, the structure itself was holding up well enough: white stucco exterior, barrel-tiled roof, lots of wrought ironwork. To stare at the place was to experience a kind of ceaseless déjà vu; this house had probably served as a shooting location for any number of films and TV shows over the decades. He'd probably seen it on some episode of *The A-Team* when he was a kid. A living vestige of old Hollywood, way out here at the west end of Malibu.

That was the outside. The inside was a ruin. The house's current owner was Layla Cray, the twenty-four-year-old lead singer of an indie rock group called Horse Latitudes. She had bought the house two and a half years ago, in immaculate condition, and a month later she'd left to go on tour in Europe. During the England leg of the tour she had begun dating the vice captain of Manchester United, then moved in with him when the tour ended and, as the realtor put it, *pretty much forgot about this place.*

At the very least, she'd neglected to keep in touch with the company she hired to maintain the property. Her original service contract with them had only covered the three-month period of the tour. The company had tried in vain to get a hold of her when the contract ended. So had various local housing authorities, when the lawn started growing wild, but somehow Layla Cray had remained happily unaware of the whole situation until about a month ago, by which time the house had sat vacant for over two years.

It showed. Some enterprising soul had broken a window in back and looted the house for whatever valuables it contained: plumbing hardware, paintings, three wall-mounted televisions. The thief had been kind enough to leave all the food in the cupboards, where it had rotted and putrefied, the smell drawing in what appeared to be half the insect population of Southern California. The bugs, in turn, had attracted the birds; their nests occupied every bookshelf and hanging light fixture in the house. The worst to come in, though, had simply been the elements. Below the broken window in back, water had soaked the carpeting and subfloor with every rainfall; weeds had germinated and sprouted out of the carpet piles in that corner. The basement was worse: water draining through the flooring above had flooded everything down there, probably dozens of times. Though the space was dry at the moment, the air was thick with the odor of mildew and God knew what else. Even up here in the entry Dryden could still smell it—the scent that had dredged the tunnel nightmare up out of his memory. It had been months since he'd last dreamed it.

"So?" Caine asked. His eyebrows went up: *What's the verdict?*

"Tell you outside," Dryden said.

Caine stepped back to clear the doorway, and Dryden moved past him into the morning breeze.

He crossed the brick-paved motorcourt to a low stone wall at its edge. Beyond the wall was a ten-foot drop to a sandy slope covered with scrub brush and, farther below, dense pines. Down past those, Dryden could see the switchback road that led up from the Pacific Coast Highway. The ocean lay calm—glassy and dark blue to the horizon.

He stood breathing in the smell of the pines. His gaze settled on a car parked at the roadside, one switchback below the villa, midway between the gated driveways of two other estates. The car looked like something you could pick up for three hundred bucks at a discount lot. Through the sun-silvered windshield Dryden could see someone in the driver's seat, though he could discern little detail. Dark hair, shoulder length. Pale hands resting on the wheel.

Caine's footsteps came to a stop behind him. Dryden turned to him, then took in the front face of the villa again. Seen from this spot near the stone wall, the house stood framed by the high country of the coastal range behind it, deep green forest and baked-tan desert hills. Empty blue sky above it all, except for a few wispy cirrus clouds.

"You like it," Caine said.

Dryden nodded. "I need to crunch some numbers before I make an offer. *If* I make an offer. There's a lot of damage. Some of the stuff that's ruined is original artisan work from the twenties. Carved stone and trim. I don't imagine Home Depot's going to have replacements in stock."

"How much time do you need?"

He pictured the basement: the floor joists above it blooming with green and black mold; the wood already turning fibrous with the onset of dry rot, which had probably spread upward into the walls of the main level.

"Twenty-four hours and I'll know."

"Give me a shout," Caine said. He turned and crossed to his car, and a moment later he was gone, winding away down the switchbacks.

Dryden stayed where he was, taking in the house and the grounds. As a project, it dwarfed anything he'd tackled so far. A lot of work. A lot of unpredictability.

Christ, though. The house. Even now he didn't want to take his eyes off it.

From behind him came the low rumble of an engine, and tires crunching onto the pavers of the motorcourt. Maybe Caine had forgotten something inside.

Dryden turned. It wasn't Caine.

The worn-out car he'd seen on the switchback coasted to a stop beside his Explorer. He could still make out little detail through the glare on the windshield.

Then the driver's door opened, and a long-haired man with a pistol stepped out.

CHAPTER THREE

There was no move to make against the guy; he stood fifteen feet from Dryden. No possibility at all of rushing him, at that distance. He had the gun already leveled; he could pull the trigger half a dozen times in the seconds it would take to reach him.

The man was forty or so. Lean, almost gaunt. Dark hair, pallid features. His free hand held his car keys; he pressed a button on the fob, and his trunk latch disengaged with a metallic *thud.* The lid rose halfway up on spring hinges.

The guy pocketed the keys, reached back in through the driver's door and withdrew a set of zip-tie handcuffs.

"Turn your pockets out," he said. "Do it slowly. Then raise your shirt and show me your waistband."

Dryden made no move to comply.

"I can bring you in dead if I need to," the man said. "It wouldn't get me in trouble."

"Bring me in to who?"

"Turn your pockets out and show me your waistband. Now."

Dryden stared.

No move to make. Not *against* the guy, anyway.

The man said, “I’m not going to—”

Dryden didn’t hear the rest of it. He pivoted and threw himself back and to the side, over the low stone wall.

He expected to hear the gun go off behind him, but all he heard was a shouted curse.

The drop was ten feet, but he fell farther than that; he hit the slope another five feet downhill from the base of the wall, the shrubs and sandy ground only doing a little to cushion the impact. His training helped with the rest: he let his legs take some of the shock, then let his body take what was left, tucking and rolling to dissipate the momentum.

On flat ground he would have rolled once and stopped. On this slope—easily forty-five degrees—he simply tumbled, gaining speed. Below him, the pines were coming up fast. If he smacked his head against one of them, he would wake up handcuffed in that car trunk—if he woke up at all.

But he made no attempt to slow or control the tumble. The risk was necessary; he had to get under the trees as fast as possible. Had to get out of the gunman’s sightline.

Dryden passed into the shade beneath the pines maybe three seconds after first landing on the slope. He threw his hands and feet outward, made himself flat. His body flipped one last time, still sliding wildly on the dry ground and the carpet of needles—

He hit. The collision—his right thigh against a tree

trunk, with the impact force of a swung baseball bat—jarred his body and made the world seem to skip like a bad frame on a videotape. High up on his right leg, just below the hip joint, something cracked loudly.

In the stillness that came, his hands and knees pressing into the loose soil, he waited for the pain. Waited for it to flare out from the hip like a sheet of flame.

Nothing.

He lifted his right hand and felt for the injury, and understood. In its own strange way, the news was even worse than he'd thought.

He slid his hand into his jeans pocket and withdrew his phone: the screen was shattered, the unit itself snapped like a wafer right across the middle.

No injury to his body, but no way to call for help, either. No way to make the safest move: hide and wait for the cops to arrive in force.

He pocketed the phone again and got his bearings. He was braced sideways against the trunk he'd collided with, twenty feet inside the shadow of the pine grove. Above this shaded area, the exposed portion of the slope lay in sunlight all the way up to the stone wall.

From his position, Dryden couldn't see the top of the wall—the canopy of pine boughs blocked the view. He couldn't see the motorcourt, or either vehicle up there, or the gaunt man with the pistol. Presumably the guy couldn't see him, either.

No telling how long it would stay that way.

Dryden made a quick scan of his surroundings. The ground here under the trees was as steep as the stretch above, and the soil was even less stable; the carpet of pine needles had killed any grass that might have firmed it up. Walking on this terrain would be impossible.

The pine trunks offered the only way to move around under control. Spaced every five or six feet, they would serve as handholds, each just within reach of the next.

Dryden pushed off from the tree he rested against and got his hands around one just below and to its left. Through the boughs of the forest, he could see the switchback road fifty yards downhill.

The road wasn't an option: the gunman could already be in his car, coasting down to some vantage point from which to lie in wait.

Dryden looked sideways along the face of the slope. In that direction the screen of trees went on for at least a hundred yards—probably farther. At some point the grove would end at one of the other estates perched along the road. With luck there would be someone home who could call the police. If there wasn't, he could break a window and trigger an alarm, and the authorities would be there just as quickly. Cops tended to show up fast in neighborhoods like this.

Dryden moved to the next tree. Then the next. He'd just braced himself to move again when the gunman landed sprawling on the open slope above, exactly where he himself had dropped fifteen seconds before.

The man tucked and rolled, then tumbled out of control just as Dryden had done, though in this case the plunge seemed involuntary. The guy was trying to stop, but failing.

Dryden saw why: the man still held the gun, which left him only one hand with which to check his momentum. As Dryden watched, the gunman rolled into the shade of the pines, passing within twenty feet of where he himself now crouched, without stopping.

Thirty feet farther down, the guy's leg snagged a trunk that spun him out flat, all four limbs thrown outward like Leonardo's Vitruvian Man, but facedown.

The pistol got away from him. It skated five feet out of his reach, coming to rest under a bushy sapling.

The guy slid to a stop, and was up in a crouch half a sccond later, head turning fast, eyes going everywhere.

The tree Dryden was braced against had dense boughs all the way down to ground level. Their visual cover should be fine if he held still.

The man below swept his gaze upward, right past the spot where Dryden half knelt. No reaction. Not so much as a flicker of the eyelids.

A moment later, finished with his initial scan, the man dropped his focus to the space immediately around him. His head jerked left and right, his eyes darting over the carpet of needles.

Looking for the gun.

It was clear he would spot it in a matter of seconds. At the moment he was facing the wrong way—the sapling that partially concealed it was directly behind him—but he was already turning, ten degrees at a time, being methodical.

He was halfway there now. Three-quarters—

Dryden vaulted upright from his crouch, threw himself sideways from the pine trunk, and screamed.

It worked as well as he could have hoped: the man below him startled and snapped his gaze upward, the search for the weapon forgotten.

Dryden was thirty feet above and twenty feet left of the guy, angling down toward him as fast as his body could move. He made no attempt to use the trees as handholds now; he aimed between them, lunging sideways with each stride and letting the shifting soil take him downhill, faster and faster. A barely controlled fall. He was going to hit the guy at thirty miles an hour.

He had covered half the distance when the man's brain seemed to kick into gear again: the guy dropped his gaze, looking for the pistol with renewed speed. Almost at once his head snapped to the side, his eyes locking onto the weapon.

He dove for it, in the process throwing himself clear of Dryden's path.

Dryden jammed a heel into the soil, pitched himself sideways to correct his angle. No good—the body-slam wasn't going to work if the guy was flat on the ground.

In the last instant before he would sail right over the man, Dryden saw the guy's hands wrap around the pistol. Dryden dropped both his own hands, grabbed two fistfuls of the man's shirt, and wrenched him off the slope as he went by.

Tumbling again, the two of them bunched together in a single mass, the world going around in a blur. A tree trunk skimmed both of their heads, close enough that Dryden felt it pass through his hair. The gaunt man cried out; Dryden could see him reaching with one hand, pawing at the ground, trying to stabilize their movement.

Which left only one hand holding the pistol.

Dryden ignored the trees—necessary risk—and grabbed for the weapon with both hands. He felt the man respond, panicking, trying to pull it away.

Another trunk, big around as a telephone pole, went past them in the blur.

Dryden got his left hand around the gun's slide, gripped it tight, and tore it loose from the man's hold. Got his own right hand around the pistol grip an instant later. Shoved the barrel into the guy's rib cage and pulled the trigger. Five times—maybe six. The shots sounded flat and dampened, the body itself acting as a silencer.

Dryden let go of both the man and the gun. He flattened himself out again. He skidded to a halt in a cloud of needles and sand. He saw the body thud up against a tree, ten feet farther down, bent around it at the waist.

Silence.

The filtered light beneath the pine canopy was full of kicked-up dust and ground cover, settling out and drifting off in the breeze.

A blue jay called, somewhere in the branches high above.

Through the trees downhill, the switchback road was closer—thirty yards away.

Dryden sat still for another ten seconds, taking deep breaths, letting his heart rate slow.

The gaunt man's back was facing him. Three of the bullets had passed all the way through, centered high in the torso. Dryden slid down the incline and pressed a finger under his jaw for good measure. No pulse in the carotid artery. Dead.

He checked the man's pockets. No ID. No wallet at all. He found the car keys he'd seen before, and a cell phone—undamaged.

A second later it began to ring.

CHAPTER FOUR

The phone's display showed the caller's number. The area code was 110, a prefix Dryden wasn't familiar with.

He knelt there next to the body, thinking hard as the ringtone continued.

He had heard the dead man's voice, up in the motorcourt. There had been nothing unusual about it—no especially high or low pitch, no particular accent or cadence. A normal voice, for lack of a better term.

But answering the phone and trying to mimic the gunman wasn't going to work. Not a chance. Though Dryden's own voice was also more or less normal, he sounded nothing like the guy.

The ringtone cut out.

Dryden waited thirty seconds for a voicemail notification.

None came.

He opened the phone's call log and saw only four other calls on the entire list, all from the past twenty-four hours. All from the same number—the one that had just called. The phone was probably a burner, a cheap model meant to be used for a short time and then thrown away, for the sake of anonymity.

Whoever had just called was almost certainly the person who'd sent the gunman after him. Or some go-between. Somebody who was directly involved.

Dryden closed the call log and opened the phone's text message app.

There were no previous texts, either sent or received.

Dryden tapped the icon to compose a new text. In the TO: field he entered the number that had just called this unit.

He typed: *Can't talk out loud, close to Dryden, plan to move on him in 10 to 15 min. Why the call?*

He tapped SEND.

Ten seconds later a symbol appeared on the display, indicating that the other party was typing a reply.

Dryden waited.

Another ten seconds.

Then the message appeared: *theres something else I need you to do as soon as you have him.*

Almost immediately the message-in-progress symbol showed again. Dryden waited for the second part of the response.

More than a minute passed, and then a block of text popped up: *found a possible contact the woman might run to. her stepfather. lives in la area. if she is going there from oregon she would be there anytime now. i have third party people in the city i can send to watch his house and grab her but i would rather you do it. easier that way. go there and watch for her as soon as you have dryden. here is the address.*

The message ended with a street address in Thousand Oaks, on Stockton Canyon Drive. Dryden knew the area, roughly.

He stared at the text messages again. Tried to get his head around the situation—all of it, including what had happened here. He found himself thinking in bullet points, an old habit from a time when confusing, fast-moving conditions had been more common in his life.

Someone wanted him abducted.

Whoever that was, they were after a woman, too.

She had to be someone he had a connection to—but who the hell did he know in Oregon? With a stepfather in Thousand Oaks?

He stared into the trees, thinking hard.

Not a single name came to mind.

At the lower edge of his vision, he saw the message-in-progress symbol again.

A new text appeared: *can you do it?*

Dryden typed a reply: *No problem.* He clicked SEND.

He turned in place and looked up the sandy slope toward the house. Then he faced the other way, down toward the road below. Downhill would be faster: he could reach the pavement in seconds from here, and sprint up the switchback to his Explorer in probably less than a minute.

It would take no longer than twenty minutes to reach Stockton Canyon—and whatever answers might be there. Whether or not the woman was really going there, the stepfather would know something—the woman's name, at minimum.

A few answers. Some basic sense of what the hell was going on. He wanted to know that much, at least, before he went to the police and put his life in their hands.

At least there was time to work with—not much, but a little. Whoever was after him—and after the woman—would sit back for now and wait to hear the next update from this phone.

The soft tone of a new text sounded. He looked down.

whats with the caps? you a grammar nazi all the sudden?

Dryden stared at the words. A tight little picture of suspicion, right there in a grey word bubble.

"Shit," he whispered.

The progress symbol came back. Then the text: *what is my dogs name?*

"Shit."

The screen remained static for fifteen seconds. Long enough for the other party to put it all together. To put enough of it together, anyway.

The symbol came back. Briefly. The text that followed was word-for-word what Dryden expected:

who the fuck is this?

CHAPTER FIVE

Dryden watched the phone's screen.

The symbol didn't appear again. It wasn't going to, either; there wouldn't be any more texts. Right now the person on the other end was making a call instead—to the people he had mentioned in his earlier message. The third-party people he preferred not to use. He would get them moving now. Frantically.

Because he knew the clock was ticking, didn't he? He had already given Dryden the stepfather's address.

Way up in the canopy, the blue jay screamed again.

Dryden stood up from where he had knelt over the dead body. He stared down through the pines at the switchback road. Thought of the route to Stockton Canyon. Thought of the stepfather, waiting there, unaware of trouble coming down on him. Maybe the woman was there, too, whoever she was.

Twenty minutes' drive time from here.

Twenty minutes to get there and warn them.

He could be there sooner if he ignored the speed limit, within reason.

He thought about it for another five seconds.

Then he closed the text app on the phone, brought up the keypad and dialed 9-1-1.

Fifteen miles to the northeast, and four miles from Thousand Oaks, Danica Ellis pulled into the driveway of a house she'd hoped to never see again.

She *hadn't* seen it in, what, nineteen years?

She killed her engine and stared at the place.

Nothing about it had changed. The same green ceramic wind chimes hung from their brace next to the kitchen window. The same black lava rocks filled the planter beds along the front walk. The tan brick exterior was the same. The dark blue shutters were the same.

The man inside must have changed, at least on the surface. Carl Gilmore had been fifty-three when Danica had last seen him. He would be seventy-two now.

Staring at the house, replaying the last time she had walked out that door—slamming it behind her, hearing some knick-knack in the hallway fall and shatter, feeling deeply satisfied at the sound—she found her hand wanting to put the key back in the ignition.

He doesn't know you're out here. It's not too late to forget about this. Don't think of it as a wasted trip. Chalk it up to a long pretty drive down the coast.

Who else could she go to, though? The few friends she had were either office workers or B-school students. She didn't know any of them well enough to ask for their help with something like this. What help could they give, anyway?

Her stepfather, for all his flaws, was a different story. Carl Gilmore, alphabetizer of bookshelves, straightener of photographs stuck to the refrigerator, burner of high school yearbooks if you left one on the kitchen table overnight after he told you three different times to put the goddamned thing away, had also been an FBI agent like her father. Had, in fact, been her father's boss.

That last point had been a hell of a sore spot between Danica and her mother, all through the long, angry years of her teens.

Why stop there, Mom? Why not just cut off Dad's balls and float them in a mason jar on the mantle for everyone to see? That would at least be artistic.

She regretted those arguments now, on the rare occasions she thought about them. She still had no idea what had compelled her mother to leave her father, or to turn to a man with all the kindness of a marble bust, but she must have had her reasons. With hindsight—and her own sunken wreck of a first marriage under her belt—Danica felt bad for having twisted the knife so many times. Her mother had tried to make her happy, right to the end—which had come by way of breast cancer the summer after Danica finished college, twenty-two years old. That final, knick-knack-destroying blowup with Carl had happened within a month of the funeral.

She didn't put the key back in the ignition. She stared at the house, weighing things.

She thought of her father, probably for the fiftieth time since the attack in the parking lot. Thought of how differently she would feel right now, pulling up outside his house instead. The whole way down from Oregon, all night and all morning, nice little memories of him had drifted into her thoughts, like fireflies over a calm summer field.

Her father had been a protector—and not just of her. He had kept in touch with people he served with in the military, especially those who'd ended up needing help later on. The one Danica most remembered was a guy named Russell Moss. He'd left the service around the same time as her father, and ended up homeless almost immediately. Her father had tried over and over to help him get back on track—to get a job and some kind of roof over his head. It hadn't really worked, but his persistence had eventually gotten Moss away from the drugs and criminal contacts that would have taken his life. In the end, Moss had settled down in a kind of outcast community in the mountains near Flagstaff, Arizona—off the grid, mostly out of trouble. He was probably still there now, living out his life, able to do so because he'd known someone who genuinely cared about people. The world needed more of those.

"You're stalling," Danica whispered.

The green wind chimes swayed, tinking softly.

"He's going to tell you to go to hell," she said. "You're going to be sitting right back here, ninety seconds from now, asking yourself why you bothered. And then you're going to spend the rest of your life pissed off that you gave him the satisfaction."

She leaned back hard into her seat. The movement

set the bobble-head Chewbacca on her dashboard nodding. Subtle but sure agreement.

"I know," Danica said, then opened the car door anyway.

By habit, she reached for her phone in the console tray—but it wasn't there. An hour into the drive down from Oregon, she'd had a flash of paranoia: someone who could send people to kidnap her might also be able to get the GPS data from her phone. She had left it in the tall grass next to a freeway mile marker, wrapped up airtight in one of her plastic shopping bags, all the while telling herself she'd lost her mind. Feeling much the same way now, she got out of the car.

She rang the doorbell and stepped back to wait. She turned at the edge of the porch and let her gaze take in the street.

This stretch of Stockton Canyon, the land flaring out wide like a small lake along the path of a river, was full of mid-twentieth-century houses arrayed in a grid of streets. A little pocket suburb tucked away in the high country above Thousand Oaks.

The trees were bigger than she remembered. There was more shade. The wind sounded different, singing through the leaves.

Behind her, the front door clicked and swung open.

She turned.

Carl Gilmore wore the same glasses frames he'd had nineteen years earlier. The eyes behind them were different—bleary and yellowed, surrounded by folds of skin that had been smooth before. The eyes narrowed at her for a second. Then they widened.

"Dani?"

He didn't tell her to go to hell. He stepped back and waved her in. She slipped past him into the entry hall; her first breath plunged her right back to high school and all the summers she'd spent here during college. Every house had its smell, like a fingerprint. This one was a mixture of Pine-Sol and Gain and whatever Carl used to seal the leather couch in the family room. The couch was still there; she could see it from the hall.

Carl shut the door and turned to her. His mouth worked to say something, but he kept stopping.

"Can we sit down and talk?" Danica asked.

They sat on the leather couch and she went through it in detail—everything that had happened from the moment she'd walked into the grocery store in Brookings at two in the morning.

When she'd finished, Carl turned and stared at the fireplace, or maybe at thin air in the middle of the room. For thirty seconds he said nothing. Then he stood and went to the sliding door, and looked out into the shaded back yard.

"I thought you might still have contacts in the FBI," Danica said. "Someone I could talk to. Whatever this is that's happening to me, I just thought . . . it would be safer this way."

She watched him, in profile. Watched for any reaction. She wasn't sure he'd even heard her.

"Carl?"

"Can't be," he said. He seemed to be speaking only to himself.

Danica rose from the couch. She went to where he stood at the glass door. For a moment he didn't acknowledge her.

"After all this time," he whispered.

"What are you talking about?"

He looked at her, at last. In the indirect sunlight through the door pane, she saw a sheen of sweat on his forehead. It hadn't been there a moment before.

"Carl, if you know something—"

"Tell me again," he said. "These two people who tried to grab you, you didn't think they were doing it for their own reasons?"

"It didn't fit. I mean, if I were a teenage girl, and they were a couple of weirdos, that would be one thing. But I'm not, and these two looked like . . ." She hesitated, then plunged ahead. "They looked like a prom king and queen who tied for valedictorian and then went to med school. They looked professional."

"And you're sure there's nothing going on in your life that explains that—someone hiring people to abduct you. No ex-boyfriend who ripped off a drug dealer, no employer cooking the books—"

She shook her head. "There's nothing like that. There's nothing strange in my life. There never has been."

Carl turned away from her again. He squinted at the glare coming through the glass.

"There has," he said softly.

Danica stared. “What?”

“There has been something strange. In your life.”

In the silence, Danica could hear a lawnmower running, somewhere down the block.

“What are you talking about?” she asked.

Carl ran his shirtsleeve across his forehead. “Christ,” he whispered.

“Carl, *tell me*.”

He was quiet a moment longer. Then he shook his head. “I’ll show you.”

He nodded for her to follow, and moved toward the back hall that led to his bedroom.

When Danica had last seen the bedroom, her mother’s craft desk had been in the far left corner. Her final stained glass project, a half-finished tiger, had still been sitting there a month after she died. No sign of the desk now; the tiger was probably in a box somewhere. It was hard to imagine even Carl Gilmore throwing it away.

He crossed to the walk-in closet on the far wall, stepped in and disappeared beyond the doorframe. Danica heard him moving something around. Cardboard boxes, it sounded like.

She went to the doorway and leaned in. Carl knelt at the back wall of the closet. He had shoved aside a stack of file boxes, revealing the tall steel door of the built-in gun safe that had been there as long as Danica could recall.

He worked the combo with practiced speed and disengaged the lock with a heavy *thud.* He pulled the door open.

There were three long guns leaning upright in racks. Two shotguns and a rifle, if they were the same ones she remembered. Farther down was a handgun and several loaded magazines.

Carl ignored all the guns. He reached for a shelf at the very bottom of the safe—a shallow space stacked with documents. Probably legal papers that would be hard to replace in the event of a fire.

He took hold of a thick yellow envelope near the bottom of the stack, and pulled it free. It was nine by twelve inches, stuffed with pages to a thickness of an inch or better. He stood upright and held it out to Danica.

"This was your mother's," he said. "Your father gave it to her. It's information about . . . what happened."

Danica stared at it. It hovered there in front of her, a manifestation of the whole surreal episode.

"What do you mean?" she asked. "What *did* happen?"

"She made me promise to never show you this," Carl said. "Before she died. She worried you'd dig into it yourself, and touch some kind of nerve. That you'd wake up sleeping dogs, I guess. People who might want to find you, even all this time later. If they're after you now anyway, you might as well know."

Danica's eyes went to the ends of the pages sticking out of the envelope. Their edges had curled and yellowed. They had to be decades old.

"Carl, what is this? Tell me."

A sound cut him off before he could answer: a high-powered engine, racing hard, then downshifting fast. Then a quick chirp of tires braking on concrete.

Danica stepped from the closet and crossed to the window that faced the front yard.

A police cruiser had nosed into the driveway at an angle, right behind her car. It had VENTURA COUNTY SHERIFF'S DEPARTMENT on the side, and all its LED flashers were strobing.

Its driver's side door swung open and a deputy got out. He rounded Danica's car and started up the driveway toward the house, keying the walkie-talkie clipped to his shoulder. He was passing her front bumper when a fast series of loud cracks came from somewhere along the side of the yard—*pop-pop-pop-pop.* Danica had just enough time to register that this was the sound of real-life gunshots—more subdued than the movie kind, and more terrifying—and then the deputy made a kind of shrug with his whole body and dropped to the concrete, right in front of her car. There was blood coming out of his head.

CHAPTER SIX

Behind her, Carl was already moving. He grabbed her by the arm and dragged her away from the window. The last thing she saw, before he pulled her clear, was a bald man in a black sweatshirt running in from the edge of the yard, toward the fallen deputy. The bald man had a gun in his hand.

Then Carl was hauling her across the room, stopping only long enough to duck into the closet again. He came back out with the handgun and all three magazines. He pocketed two, then shoved the third into the gun. He worked the slide on top, heading toward the hallway as he did, nodding for her to follow.

"Come on."

She noticed only then that he had the thick yellow envelope tucked under one arm. He stepped fast out of the room, the gun raised, finger on the trigger.

Danica could hear neighbors yelling outside. A little girl screaming high and shrill, then a woman shouting at her to get inside.

Carl advanced along the hall, back into the living room. He swung the gun toward the big sliding door, covering it for a moment—nothing there—and then moving on, heading toward the front entry hall. Danica had taken only a step into the living room, following Carl, when a sound rattled across the house from the unseen front door: somebody trying the knob.

Carl halted in place, the gun still leveled.

The rattling at the front entry stopped; the door was locked. There was a second of silence, and then somebody kicked the door, hard.

By then Carl was pulling her back toward the slider, which faced the rear yard. They had taken only a step in that direction when a man bounded onto the patio. Not the bald man. This man had thick blond hair down to his collar. He crossed the patio in two strides, raised a gun and fired three times, low into the glass. Danica saw the bullets punch into the carpet in front of her. Felt the impacts reverberate through the floor. The glass pane shattered and rained out of its frame.

Carl swung his pistol toward the opening. The blond man saw it, flinched and threw himself sideways.

Carl fired. Two shots—deafening, like firecrackers going off against Danica's eardrums.

Neither shot seemed to hit the man. He disappeared past the edge of the open doorframe, crashing into something metal just out of view—maybe the same old grill that had stood on that spot when Danica was a kid.

Another thudding kick hit the front door. The latch held, but something wooden cracked and groaned.

"Dani, come on!"

Carl still had her by the arm, but he wasn't pulling

her toward the slider now. He was leading her across the room, toward the front of the house again.

"Carl—"

"Basement. Go ahead of me."

He still had his eyes on the empty frame of the slider. The gun, too.

He let go of her arm and jerked his head toward the basement door, which stood in the short hall between the living room and the front entry.

"Go," Carl hissed.

Danica moved past him. She crossed the room, almost running now, her movements feeling dream-slowed, her thoughts not much better. Passing into the entry hall, she saw the front door buffeted by another heavy impact. She fumbled for the knob of the basement door, got her hand on it, turned it and hauled it open. The basement stairs dropped away into pitch darkness before her, only the top few steps visible. There had never been any windows down there.

Behind her, Carl fired another shot toward the patio. Then he was right at her back, pushing her through the doorway atop the stairs, his free hand on her shoulder to keep her from falling. He used the wrist of his gun hand to flip the light switch above the steps. The exposed bulb at the bottom of the staircase flared to life.

Bare concrete floor, cinderblock walls, two-by-twelve pine stair treads running down. Everything the same as it had ever been. Danica was three steps down when she heard a shot from the living room. Carl made a grunting sound, like someone had punched him in the stomach, and Danica felt his weight suddenly fall against her. She saw the yellow envelope hit the stairs at her feet. It cartwheeled to the bottom, tearing open, papers scattering on the concrete.

"Keep going," Carl said.

She could hear it in his voice already—sluggishness, like it taxed him even to speak.

Danica took the next step, and the next, fast but careful, letting him rest against her as she went.

Above and behind her, footsteps pounded across the living room. In the same instant the front door burst in, crashing into the wall between the entry and the kitchen.

She felt Carl pivot against her, almost throwing her off balance. He fired again, three fast shots, and somebody upstairs cried out and hit the floor.

A second later Danica reached the bottom of the steps, Carl still keeping up with her—he was clinging to her now, one arm looped over her shoulder, most of his weight pushing down on her.

"I've got you," she said.

She led him away from the stairs, across the spill of papers, until they were out of sight to the open doorway at the top.

Someone upstairs was coughing, the sound thick and wet. After a few seconds it sounded more like gargling. A man's voice, somewhere up in the entry hall, said, "Which way?" Then: "How many?"

The basement was a single large space, rectangular, the stairs close to one end, the furnace and water heater at the other. There were deep plywood-and-two-by-four shelves running the length of the longer walls, full of tools and storage totes and stacks of old magazines. There was no place to hide or take cover.

Danica led Carl to the corner farthest from the stairs, a square yard of space between the furnace and the side wall. She eased him to the floor, getting her first good look at him as she did.

"Oh Christ." The tone of her own voice rattled her.

The back and side of Carl's shirt were soaked with blood. His face had gone pale in a way that Danica wouldn't have thought possible—very close to paper white.

He settled into a seated position, his back against the wall, his gaze focused hard on the stairs across the basement. He raised the pistol, but almost at once it sagged, pulling his arm down like it weighed fifty pounds.

Danica knelt in front of him, her eyes at the same level as his own. He looked at her, but even that seemed like a struggle. His eyes kept losing her.

Then he exhaled hard, seemed to force himself to focus. He looked down and felt for his pocket with his free hand. He slipped his fingers inside and came out with one of the spare magazines. He thumbed a release lever on the pistol, dropped out the existing magazine, and managed to slide the new one into the opening. It locked into place with a definitive *click*.

He pushed the weapon into her hands.

"Already one in the chamber," he said. His voice was barely more than a breath. "Just pull the trigger. Eleven shots." The last two words he could only mouth.

"Carl—"

The old man shook his head. He narrowed his eyes at her—the stern expression she'd hated so much in her teens—and pointed at the stairs. *Don't look at me. Look there.*

Danica nodded. She turned where she knelt, raising the pistol. She looked down the barrel, lined up the sights and centered them on the part of the staircase she could see—the bottom two-thirds. She had never held a gun in her life.

Up in the entry hall, the gurgling had stopped. There was no sound upstairs at all.

Danica risked a glance at Carl—and felt her breath catch in a spasm.

The back of his head rested against the cinderblock wall, his eyes open and looking right through her. Carl was gone.

She felt a tremor setting in everywhere—her jaw, her shoulders, her hands.

The top of the stairs creaked. She sucked in a gasp and swung her head back around, raising the pistol again.

The shaking was worst in her hands. It was hard to keep the gunsights lined up with each other—harder still to keep them steady on a target spot.

Another creak—the next step down from the top, still unseen from where she knelt.

She took another breath and forced herself to hold it. She counted to three, then let the breath out slowly, under control. It helped with the shaking.

She put the gunsights on the highest stair tread she

could see. It was probably the fourth or fifth down from the top.

She waited for the next creaking step.

Ten seconds passed.

Fifteen.

She felt her grip on the gun going slick with sweat.

Twenty seconds.

Then came a new sound—not the creak of a wooden stair. A metallic squeak instead. Hinges. The sound ended with the click of a latch. The man on the staircase had just closed the basement door behind him.

Cold bloomed over Danica's skin, a gut-level dread that her brain caught up to a second later.

Then the light at the bottom of the stairs clicked off, plunging the basement into perfect darkness.

CHAPTER SEVEN

For a terrible few seconds she tried to keep the gun aimed anyway. Tried to lock her arms and hands exactly as they were.

It was hopeless. Everything still shook. In the pitch-black it was impossible to tell if she had the weapon held straight at all, much less pointed at the stairs. Even her body swayed where she knelt. There was no reference point by which to keep her bearings.

She made her breathing as quiet as she could, letting it flow in and out through her mouth instead of her nose.

She waited.

Maybe the next creaking step would give her something to aim at. Maybe—

An avalanche of sound cut off her thinking: rapid footsteps descending the staircase in a flurry of motion, then the scrape of a shoe on concrete, the slap of a palm on the basement floor, the scuff of elbows and knees scrambling in some direction over the surface—the whole sound, from start to finish, lasting no more than a second or two.

Then nothing.

Just silence and darkness—in which she was no longer alone.

Stay still. Stay quiet. He doesn't know where you are. He doesn't have much time to look for you, either.

Which was true. *Had* to be true. Because other cops would be coming. The neighbors would have called. Dispatch might even know that the first cop had been killed—they would at least know he wasn't responding.

How much longer could it be before backup arrived? How long had it been, already, since the deputy had been shot?

She thought about that. Tried to replay all that had happened since that moment, when Carl had dragged her away from the window.

It hadn't been long at all.

Ninety seconds, tops.

Still, help was coming. Soon.

Please.

She kept the gun leveled. Cocked her head and listened for any hint of movement.

She heard something. A faint scrape against wood. Something being moved on one of the plywood shelves. The sound was so soft she couldn't pinpoint it. It might have been anywhere.

A second later it stopped, as suddenly as it had begun.

Silence.

Then came an explosion of sound, ten feet away from her, something like a toolbox bursting open against the wall.

She cried out, the sound involuntary as a flinch, realizing in the same instant what she'd done. What the attacker had meant for her to do.

Move. Now. Be anywhere but right here.

She threw herself forward—too late.

The man crashed into her, slammed her body against the corner of the furnace. She felt the air driven out of her lungs. Heard her gun skitter away on the concrete somewhere nearby. Then he was on top of her, a knee pressing down in her back, her arms being wrenched behind her. She realized she was screaming, loud and incoherent, an animal sound full of panic. He was screaming back at her, telling her to shut up. She felt an open hand smack the side of her head, rocking it sideways and making her ears ring. A second later she heard the tearing sound of duct tape coming off a roll. Felt him looping it around her wrists, again and again, working by feel in the darkness, binding them painfully together behind her.

He let go of her and clambered to his feet, and then the flame of a cigarette lighter cut through the dark. She craned her neck and looked up. It was the bald man from the front yard. He held the lighter out ahead of him, seemed to get his bearings, then sprinted away across the basement.

She heard him thud up the stairs as quickly as he had come down them. He opened the door at the top and flipped the light back on. Danica blinked a few times and then he was standing over her again, leaning down and gripping her upper arms.

"Get up. Come on."

She made no move to do so.

"Get the fuck up!"

She screwed her eyes shut. Waited for him to hit her again.

But all he did was clamp her arms tighter and begin to drag her across the concrete floor. She opened her eyes and saw his tennis shoes in front of her, pointed toward her as he walked. He was moving backward, leaning down and hauling her toward the stairs. He was halfway there when a gunshot sounded, loud as a bomb blast in the enclosed space.

His hands gave one last little squeeze of her arms, convulsively, and then he let go and dropped in a heap right in front of her.

One side of his head, above the ear, had been blown away.

Lying prone on the floor, Danica raised her eyes.

A man with a gun stood at the foot of the basement stairs. Not a cop. Not anyone she had seen before now. He was her age, give or take. Dark eyes and dark hair. Lean build. He lowered the gun, tucked it in his waistband and crossed to where she lay. He knelt and put a hand on her shoulder.

"Are you okay? Are you hurt?"

She found it hard to answer. Hard to say anything at all. She knew the term *sensory overload;* some rational part of her brain was repeating it now, again and again. The rest of her thoughts were simply spinning, getting away from her—dry leaves in a windstorm.

"You're safe," the man said. "The police will be here in a few minutes."

He reached behind her, got a hold of the duct tape around her wrists and tore it across from one edge. He peeled it from her skin and threw it aside.

She got her hands under her, pushed herself upward and got into a sitting position on the floor. She felt her mind begin to settle.

The man stepped back and sat on one of the treads at the bottom of the stairs, giving her space.

She looked around. Took in the basement. The bald man, dead on the floor beside her. Carl, back by the furnace, his eyes open and staring at nothing.

Somewhere far away, the keening of a siren. A couple minutes out, maybe.

"Do you know what this is about?" the man asked.

She turned and looked at him. She thought of Carl in the bedroom closet, trying to tell her something. The memory was hard to make sense of now. Part of the overload.

She shook her head.

"What's your name?" the man asked.

"Danica. Ellis. Danica Ellis."

He was staring at her more intensely now, as if looking for something in her features.

"I've never seen you before," he said. "I've never even heard of you."

Before she could respond to that, he said, "I'm Sam Dryden. Have you ever heard that name? Have you seen my face? Even in a picture?"

She shook her head again.

He kept his eyes on her a moment longer, then looked down at his hands in his lap.

"I don't get it," he said softly, maybe to himself.

Danica sat forward. "Who are you?" she said. "I mean—are you from next door, or—"

She realized the man's posture had suddenly changed. He was still looking down, but not at his hands anymore. His focus had gone to the spill of papers at the foot of the stairs, next to the torn-open envelope.

He leaned down, reached for one of the sheets, then stopped. His gaze went to a different page, close by. He tugged it out from under a pile that half covered it, and held it in front of himself, in the light.

"How the hell . . . ?"

His tone sounded different than a moment before. He sounded unnerved.

His eyes went back and forth over the sheet, rapidly. Then he stopped and tilted his head, listening. The incoming sirens were louder now. He seemed to be gauging their distance.

"What is it?" Danica asked.

He didn't answer. He slid off his seat on the stair tread and knelt down over the scattered papers. He looked from one to the next, as if trying to study them as much as possible in bare seconds.

He spoke without looking up. "Where did these come from?"

"My stepdad—Carl. He had them."

The man named Sam looked up at her. "He had them here in this house?"

Danica nodded.

"Where did he get them?" the man asked.

For a second the question threw her. Then she remembered. "My mom. He said she was—" She cut herself off. "I don't know. I really didn't understand."

"Anything you can tell me—"

"I don't *know* anything. I just got here. I don't know."

He turned his attention back to the papers. He looked as stressed as anyone Danica had ever seen. He glanced up the stairs, into the daylight shining down from the open door at the top. He seemed to be focusing on the sirens again. Coming to some decision. He sat that way for two or three seconds, and then his expression hardened. The stress seemed to vanish, leaving resolve in its place. Whatever choice he'd been weighing, he'd made it.

He shoved all the papers together into a rough stack, got a hold of them, and stood. He turned to her.

"How much can you trust me for now?" he asked.

"What?"

He pointed at the bald man, lying in a spreading pool of blood. "I'm obviously not with him, and if I wanted to hurt you, I could have done it by now. Can you accept that much, for a start? That I'm not going to hurt you?"

She thought about it. Nodded.

"Then I need you to trust me on something. That we have to leave here, right now. That we can't stay and wait for the cops."

"What are you talking about?"

"The people who are after you, they came for me, too. I don't know who they are, I don't know why they want us, and I don't know how you and I are connected." He held up the stack of pages. "But I know what this is. I know some of it. And I know it's not something the police can deal with. Not even close. If we go into their custody, we're going to be helpless. We have to get out of here. Right now."

He crossed to where she sat. He held out a hand. "Can you trust me enough to do that?"

She stared at him. There was something in his expression that wasn't quite fear. It was concern, she thought—concern for her.

"Yes," she said.

CHAPTER EIGHT

It was two minutes later before Dryden spoke again. He had the Explorer doing exactly the speed limit on Stockton Canyon Drive, a mile uphill from the house. In the rearview mirror, he could see the distant cluster of emergency vehicles around the place; they had begun arriving less than thirty seconds after he and the woman left.

Danica Ellis, she had called herself. He glanced at her; she sat in the passenger seat, hugging her arms close to her body. Even in bright sunlight, after the dim space of the basement, he was sure he had never seen her before. He had a good memory for faces, though he was pretty certain he would have remembered Danica's regardless: her eyes looked like an artist's exaggeration, meant to convey kindness—at least on any normal day. Right now they conveyed only fear. That still left them beautiful.

"How much do you know?" Dryden asked.

She didn't quite flinch. She blinked and turned to him. "I told you. I don't know anything. I don't understand this at all."

"You were running from these people," Dryden said. "Even before you went to that house."

She stared at him.

"Why don't I tell you what I know first," Dryden said. "Then you can tell me your part."

She considered it for a moment, then nodded. She stared forward at the road, its route climbing now into the high country of the upper canyon. "Okay."

Dryden spent two minutes covering everything that had happened to him, starting with the gaunt man pointing a gun at him in Malibu, and finishing with his own hell-bent drive up to Thousand Oaks—even after calling the cops. He'd done twenty over the limit the whole way, every instinct telling him seconds might count.

When he finished speaking, Danica told him her side of the story; it took even less time than his. Afterward she sat staring ahead through the windshield. She had the stack of papers from the basement in her lap. She looked down at them, then glanced at Dryden.

"So tell me what these are," she said.

Dryden took his eyes off the road for a second and studied the pile. The sheet on top wasn't the first page—everything had gotten scrambled when he'd gathered the stack together—but it looked like all the others he'd seen in those few seconds at the bottom of the stairs: typewritten text, double-spaced, just enough distortion to show that it had been photocopied from some original source material. The stack of pages added up to a single thick document.

The visible page was covered with redaction marks,

blotting out easily half the text in bits and pieces, all over the sheet. The whole document was probably like that.

Of the text that remained clear, Dryden had read almost nothing. There hadn't been time.

Danica was still looking at him. Waiting.

"I don't know its details," Dryden said. "But I know what it is. I know what kind of document it is."

He reached over and tapped the very top of the page, where a string of text made up a header. He'd seen the same line at the top of every sheet:

WITNESS NULLIFICATION [C43-YANKEE]—PERSONS 2855 & 2856

"It's called a scrub file," Dryden said. "I've heard of them, but I've never seen one myself until now. I wasn't sure they really existed."

"What's a scrub file?"

Dryden thought about it. There were only so many ways to say it. There was only so much he knew in the first place.

"Jesus," he whispered. It was still hitting him—the gravity of the thing. And what it must mean, in terms of what they were involved in here.

Danica watched him.

"I used to be in the military," Dryden said. "I heard about scrub files and witness nullification back then, but only as old stories, rumors. It was something the government used to do, way back. Cold War stuff. They quit doing it long before I was ever in the service."

"But what was it?"

"It was a way of dealing with people who accidentally learned things they weren't supposed to . . . when you couldn't justify killing them. Like innocent bystanders who happened to see something classified. The textbook version I always heard about went like this: what if there was a fire at some civilian office building that was actually a CIA safe house? What if local firefighters showed up and went in, before the government could secure it, and what if they saw something that had to stay secret, at all costs? What are you supposed to do, kill them? Kill people who were just doing their job?"

Danica looked down at the stack of papers. She ran a fingertip over the header line.

"Witness nullification," she said. "How did it work?"

Dryden followed the road through a sharp curve. Dense forest on both sides of it now, high in the hills above the canyon. The road would lead over the pass and come back down on the other side, somewhere at the west end of the San Fernando Valley.

"Drugs," Dryden said. "A combination of them—a cocktail. The idea was to permanently damage someone's memory going back weeks or months beforehand. If it worked, the witness wouldn't remember the thing they'd seen. Problem solved."

"They forced people to take the drugs?"

Dryden nodded. "Forced them, ordered them, tricked them, whatever. It wasn't a pill, if that's what you're picturing. This would have been chemicals in a drip bag. And it wasn't anything that went through FDA trials for safety. There were people who died from it, going by the stories I heard. Even when it worked, it was major brain trauma, with weeks of recovery. Christ, it was *supposed* to be brain trauma. That was the point of it. It wasn't some careful thing they spent years refining; it was just a class of drugs that had memory damage as a side effect. Pretty simple, really. And it was the lesser evil. It was better than killing somebody, that's all."

He indicated the stack of papers and continued: "A scrub file is a write-up of whatever the witness knew, before taking the drug. Like a snapshot of the memories that were about to get erased."

They rode in silence for thirty seconds. The pine forest gave way to a region of blackened trunks where a wildfire had burned through, probably a year or two before. Dense green grass covered the forest floor beneath the dead trees, dotted with yellow and purple flowers.

Danica held up the pages. "Is this tied to something from your time in the military? Is that why these people are after you? Do you think someone used drugs like that on you?"

Dryden shook his head. "Like I said, they stopped doing that stuff way before my time. And even if someone *had* done it, I'd know. Trust me. People who had this done to them, they knew it. It wasn't anything subtle at all. You'd have weeks or even months missing from your memory. There's no gap like that from my time in the military."

Danica was quiet for a long moment, looking at the stack.

"My father was in the Army," she said. "He got out when I was a kid, junior high." She looked up at Dryden. "That man back at the house, the older man—my stepdad—he told me this document was my mom's. He said my dad gave it to her. He said she never wanted me to see it, because—" She paused, maybe piecing together whatever she'd heard. "He said she was afraid I'd dig into it and wake up sleeping dogs."

The burned trees fell behind. A broad stretch of sandy, barren ground opened up on both sides of the road.

"What did your father do in the Army?" Dryden asked.

Danica shrugged. "He always called it logistics. He was stationed at Los Alamitos here in L.A. I remember him coming home every night like it was just another office job. We didn't live on base or anything. It all seemed pretty normal."

A silence played out. Dryden could feel them both thinking the same obvious thing.

"No, I don't remember him recovering from brain trauma," Danica said. "Or forgetting some big chunk of time that'd just happened. I think I would have noticed a thing like that, if it happened anytime after I was four or five. Before then, who knows?"

"What was your father's name?"

"Richard Ellis." She said it with a little rise at the end—a statement and a question at the same time. *Does that ring a bell?*

"Never heard of him," Dryden said.

Danica looked up and watched the road coming at

them, flanked by the arid land. After a moment she dropped her eyes to the page again.

"Persons 2855 and 2856," she said. "So this is, what, a scrub file for two people? *If* one of them was my father, I don't even have a guess who the other was."

"Guessing is all we're doing so far," Dryden said. "Let's just read it." He pointed to the lower right corner of the visible page. "They're numbered. It shouldn't take you long to put it back in order. If you don't mind reading it out loud, I'll just keep driving, keep us moving until we have some idea what the hell we're dealing with."

She nodded and began working her way through the pages.

"It has to tell us something," she said.

Dryden glanced at the sheets as she thumbed through them, every page half covered by redaction lines. He thought of other sensitive documents he'd seen, years back, their content blocked out in the same way.

Redaction tended to be thorough, for obvious reasons. He'd seen hundred-page reports cut down to text that included not a single name or location or date.

"It has to," Danica said.

No it doesn't, Dryden thought.

PART TWO

ECHO HOUSE

JULY 1989

CHAPTER NINE

For Sam Dryden, it started on a calm summer night.

He was standing at the screen of his bedroom window, staring out into the dark. It was two in the morning, the first hours of Tuesday, July 18th. He couldn't sleep. There were lots of things on his mind.

The bedroom itself was one of those things: this was his first night in it. Its window looked out on a pitch-black field of tall grass, sloping down toward the quiet storefronts and streets of Ashland, Iowa, population 428. The town was half a mile away, a little island of soft light surrounded by nothing but dark, wide-open countryside. The only things visible farther out were the porch lights of distant farms, most of them swallowed up in the night haze. That was the view from Sam's new bedroom. His old one had overlooked Los Angeles from twenty stories up.

He pulled one of the movers' boxes to the window and sat on it. He rested his chin on his hands, and his elbows on the windowsill. He studied the town. It was no more than a little grid of streets, like a tic-tac-toe game with random extensions growing from it. Two primary roads crossed through its heart, reaching away in four directions to the empty farmlands beyond.

Hardly anyone lived downtown, Sam guessed. The businesses were all dim and closed up. Nothing moved in the pools of streetlight glow. The residents were all up here in the subdivision, built on level ground atop this rise. Sam's house stood at the suburb's edge, facing south. He could see none of the other houses from his window.

The sounds of the country were alien to him. No rumble of traffic. No car horns. Just the rhythmic song of insects and frogs, maybe a few million of each out there in the dark fields. The house had unfamiliar sounds, too. There was something behind the back wall of his closet that went *click, click, click, hum* every so often. He'd heard it twice since they'd arrived this evening. Probably a loose flap of metal in an air duct. A *house noise,* Sam called it. The kind of thing you noticed at a friend's place, but ignored at your own. Hopefully he'd be ignoring this one within a few days.

He shifted forward on the box and let his forehead touch the screen. Out at the western outskirts of downtown, he could see the school he would be attending in the fall: a long rectangular building flanked by vacant grounds. His dad had driven him past it earlier. Sam wondered how many kids would be starting seventh grade with him. Maybe just a few dozen, he guessed, all of them close friends since kindergarten. No doubt he would be the only new kid.

At least it was only July. School was several weeks away.

He closed his eyes and exhaled softly.

New house.

New town.

New school.

New life.

Heavy thoughts, all of them.

But they weren't the reason he couldn't sleep.

Two weeks earlier, back home in L.A., he had also been staring out his bedroom window screen. The view had been a little different: Century City from two hundred feet up, Santa Monica, the 405, Venice Beach out in the marine fog—those things and a thousand others that made up the backdrop of his world. He had stood there trying to soak it all up—to appreciate it before he lost it.

Thirsty, he had turned from the window and stepped out of his bedroom. He passed his parents' room, darkened with the door not quite shut. Only his dad was in there tonight; his mom was in San Diego, visiting her sister—saying goodbye before the big move to Bumfuck, Iowa. She had made no secret of her feelings on the whole matter. She was happy in Los Angeles, thank you kindly. That the family was moving because of Mr. Dryden's job—new corporate office in the burgeoning city of Brenner, five miles north of Ashland, gotta have our best legal guys there to get things off on the right foot—had caused more than a bit of friction between Sam's mom and dad in recent weeks. He happened to be thinking about that very thing, returning with his bottled water, when he passed their doorway again. He was three steps farther when he heard his father speak, just above a whisper.

"*Of course* we don't tell Sam. Jesus, Audrey. He's got enough to deal with right now. We're not dumping this on him, too."

Sam stopped. He turned and moved two steps back toward the cracked-open door. In the silence, he heard the tinny monotone of someone's voice over a telephone earpiece. His mom, speaking from San Diego. No way to make out her actual words, but something of her tone came through. She sounded mad.

Mad about whatever it was they weren't dumping on him.

And what the hell might that be?

The question had hardly taken shape in Sam's mind before a pretty obvious answer came to him.

Are you kidding me? Are you fucking *kidding me? Are you two breaking up? How's joint custody going to work? Am I going to shuttle back and forth between L.A. and Green Goddamned Acres every two weeks?*

He felt his hand tighten around the water bottle. He had always liked to think of himself as a pretty worldly kid. He'd been to movie premieres a few times, whenever one of his father's Hollywood clients was on the red carpet. He'd had dinner at Spago with his parents and Gene Hackman and the movie producer Arnold Kopelson. Why any of that should make him tougher than other kids when it came to heavy emotional stuff, he wasn't sure at the moment, but he had imagined himself to be thick-skinned for a twelve-year-old.

Holy hell, though, if he was guessing right about this—

"Audrey, listen to me. I'm not worried about the new house, and you shouldn't be, either. I understand it's unusual, what happened to the guy . . . *whatever* happened to the guy . . . but there's no reason to think the house had anything to do with it."

Sam took another step closer, listening. What exactly *was* this?

In the bedroom, he heard his mother's voice over the phone again. She spoke for only a moment before his dad cut her off:

"You don't have to repeat the details to me. I've been over them. Yes, it's creepy. I'm not ignoring that. I'm sure it's the reason other buyers have passed on the house. But being creeped out is a gut reaction, and we're rational people. Whatever this was that happened to the last owner, it was more than a year ago. It's history, okay?"

For the next twenty seconds only his mom talked. When his dad spoke again, all he said was, "If Sam hears about it anyway, we shrug it off. Tell him we're not worried. Which we shouldn't be. I know. Love you, too."

The phone settled back into its cradle in the darkened room. Sam stood outside the door for a long moment, listening to his father breathe.

He could hear him breathing now, too—sound asleep in his new bedroom across the hall from Sam's own.

He and Sam had made the drive here over the past two days, arriving this afternoon about an hour before the moving van. Sam's mom would be flying out next week, after squaring away a few last things with her own job in L.A.

Sam opened his eyes again and stared out over Ashland. The haze had begun to gather into wisps of fog. He watched them drift like ghosts through the cones of light under the streetlamps. Out of the darkness and back into it.

At last he stood, crossed to his bed and lay down. Reliving the overheard conversation wouldn't get him any closer to sleep. Neither would wondering what the hell had happened in this house a year ago—what had happened to its last owner.

He shut his eyes. He listened to the night sounds out in the dark, and felt sleep finally starting to edge in.

He woke at noon. His dad was gone—it was his first day on the job.

In daylight the landscape outside Sam's window lay in orderly squares of crop fields, framing the cluster of buildings downtown and reaching away into the humid distance. The broad stretch of tall grass just beyond the back yard, sloping half a mile to the town's edge, lay green and damp in the summer air. The slope was empty except for a picnic table someone had abandoned way out in the middle of it. Over the swaying tops of the weeds, the table looked like a boat that'd slipped its moorings and gone adrift.

Sam took a shower, had some peanut butter toast,

then dragged his bike out of the garage and headed out to explore the subdivision.

The place wasn't new; that was his first impression. Much of it lay in shade beneath the canopies of huge maples that lined the streets. The trees had to be forty or fifty years old, planted all at the same time by whoever had created the subdivision. Here and there, gnarled roots had pushed up the sidewalk slabs from below, setting them at odd angles.

The suburb's streets were laid out in three big arches, each tucked inside the next. On a map it would've looked like a sideways rainbow, attached to the primary road that ran south to Ashland and north to Brenner. Within the subdivision, shorter streets here and there connected the three arches to one another.

At the north end of the sideways rainbow, butted up alongside the main road running north and south, was a park—Nash Park, according to the carved wooden sign at the entry drive. Sam rode in past the sign and coasted to a stop.

There was a merry-go-round. There was a teeter-totter with faded red paint. There was a swing set—four black-rubber swings hanging from chains, the ground furrowed into a long crater beneath each.

A girl about Sam's age sat on the farthest of the four swings, her bike close by on the grass. Otherwise the park was empty.

Sam stood there, astride his bike. The girl hadn't noticed him yet. She sat with her head down, not swinging, just kind of swaying there, tracing a little circle in the dirt with her shoe. She had long brown hair that blew around in the breeze. Her hands looked small and delicate, holding the steel chains. Her fingernails were pink, matching her shirt.

Sam had talked to girls often enough at his old school. A couple of his friends were girls, even. It had never been a big deal, really. But there was talking to girls and then there was *talking to girls*. He really hadn't done much of the latter. Hadn't just walked up to one at a dance, or in the hallway, and introduced himself. That seemed to be one of those skills you needed years and years to get good at. From what he'd seen, even some guys as old as twenty hadn't quite mastered it.

Watching this girl on the swing, it occurred to him that he could probably turn around and ride away without her knowing he'd been here. He didn't really feel like doing that, but still—

She looked up and saw him, and flinched a little. He saw her hands tighten around the swing chains.

"Sorry," Sam said. "I was just riding around—I wasn't—I mean—"

Jesus, dude. Chill.

The girl managed a smile. "It's okay." Then, before Sam could reply, she said, "You're the kid that just moved in, right?"

Sam nodded.

"I live down the street," the girl said. "I saw you. And . . . your dad?"

"My mom," Sam said, "and she's really self-conscious about her looks, alright?"

He had no idea where the joke had come from, and

no idea if it was the least bit funny. His brain had just whipped it up and shoved it out there.

For a second she almost seemed to take it seriously—then she scowled and shook her head. “Funny, smartass.”

But she laughed, too, and for some reason the sound of it blew away about ninety percent of the tension that had coiled up in Sam’s chest the moment he’d seen her.

“You want to sit down?” the girl asked. She indicated the swing next to hers.

“Yeah,” Sam said. He pushed his bike onto the grass and dropped it, and crossed to the swings. He sat beside the girl.

“I’m Sam Dryden,” he said.

The girl touched both of her feet to the ground, turned herself toward him and offered a handshake. “Dani Ellis,” she said.

CHAPTER TEN

It was crazy how quickly the talking became easy. Even after a minute or two, there was nothing to it. Who would have guessed?

He kept making her laugh, which felt amazing.

He kept looking at her eyes, too. They were big and brown and alive in some way he hadn't seen in many other people. He tried not to look at them too much—tried not to look when she happened to be looking back. He hoped it wasn't obvious. The whole eye-contact thing was tricky, although it helped that they were on swings. Most of the time they were both just looking forward, across the road at the open farmland, or else at their feet trailing aimlessly in the dirt beneath them.

Neither of them got the swings moving. They just sat there talking. There was something cool about that—just sitting there. It felt a little grown-up, Sam thought. Maybe that was it.

Dani was twelve, like him. She had lived in Ashland for only the past three months. She and her parents had lived in L.A. before that, a fact that triggered a whole rush of things to talk about. Dani had grown up in Long Beach, which really wasn't anywhere near Sam's old home in Century City, but they had a ton of common references anyway. They had both been to Griffith Park, and Disneyland, of course—Dani's favorite thing at Disney was New Orleans Square. Sam had never given it a serious look, but he found himself rethinking it now, hearing the way she talked about it.

Each of them had also been to the Forum a handful of times with their parents. Both were duly pissed about the NBA finals the month before. The whole playoffs had been perfect before that: three shutout series, one after another. Then the finals—against Detroit, of all teams; it was going to be like a revenge movie. Everyone said so. *When Magic pulled his hamstring I thought my dad was going to kick in the TV,* Dani said. *Out for the rest of the series, I couldn't believe it.*

Sam asked her what it had been like living here for the past three months, after being used to L.A.

She said it had been better than she expected, for one reason: she'd met a girl named Lauren who moved in around the same time as her. Lauren was from D.C., which was about as different from L.A. as a place could be, but the two of them had clicked instantly.

"It was great," she said. The words came out soft. Sad.

"Was?"

She nodded. "Lauren and her dad moved back to D.C. last week. I've been bored out of my mind ever since."

A silence settled in. It was the first time in ten minutes that Sam couldn't think of what to say. *Sorry to hear about that* would sound fake, he thought. Or cliché, or whatever. He gave it ten seconds, but nothing good came to mind.

"That sucks," he said.

"It really sucks," Dani said. "Thanks."

Sam nodded.

They were quiet again, but it seemed like an okay sort of silence. He let it go on. High above them, the chain connectors creaked lightly with the small movements he and Dani made, side to side, forward and back.

"Can I ask you something?" Sam said.

"Sure."

"The house I just moved into. Do you know about something weird happening to the last guy that lived there? Like a year ago?"

Her eyes lit up, pushing away the gloom that had settled in them. "Mr. Pierce," she said.

"I didn't know his name."

Dani was nodding. "That was him. All the kids around here know about it."

"What happened to him? I mean, all I know is that it kept other people from wanting to buy the house, all this time. Like it was something really creepy."

Dani's eyebrows went up and she nodded again. "Yeah, you could say that."

"The suspense is killing me," Sam said.

Dani laughed. She chewed on her lower lip, thinking it over.

"I don't know much about Mr. Pierce himself," she said. "Not even his first name. The way kids tell it, he's always just Mr. Pierce. I know he didn't have a wife or kids, but apparently he was a nice guy, normal, whatever. Always said hello to people. And then one day last summer . . . he just disappeared."

Sam felt the metal of the swing chains seem to radiate a chill into his hands.

"At first, nobody noticed," Dani said. "He could've just been out of town, for all anyone knew. Then, after enough time, some far-off relative couldn't get a hold of him, so finally someone here went into the house to check it out. They said everything looked fine, at first. His car was gone, like he'd taken a trip somewhere, and the house was just how you'd expect it to be, if that's all that happened. Clothes in the hamper. Shades down. Nothing weird or anything. Then they checked the mailbox. *That* was a little strange. They found like ten days' worth of backed-up mail inside it. If he was going to be gone that long on purpose, it seemed like he would have told the post office to hold the mail for him."

Sam pictured it: Pierce's mailbox jammed full of flyers and envelopes. The mailbox he himself had ridden his bike past, half an hour ago when he left the house.

"So something happened to him," Sam said. "Probably wherever he went on his trip. There must have been a record of things he did. Like hotels he stayed at, or times he used a credit card. Stuff like that."

Dani shook her head. "They did a computer search for all those things, and came up empty. No record for any of it. They figure he just went on a road trip someplace, and paid cash everywhere. And his car never turned up, so . . . no one even knows which direction he went. It's like he drove out of Ashland and right off the face of the Earth."

Sam's mind was already far away from the conversation. It was back in his house, across the subdivision. Pierce's house. He envisioned it a year ago, empty, waiting for its owner to come back.

"After about six months they declared him officially dead," Dani said. "His relatives put the house up for sale. But like you said, no one wanted it. I guess the whole situation weirded people out."

She'd been staring off as she spoke. Now she met Sam's eyes, and a flicker of concern crossed her face, like she'd just remembered that Sam lived in the house she was talking about.

"But that's stupid," she said quickly. "Whatever happened to the guy, the house wasn't part of it."

"Yeah," Sam said. He didn't think he sounded convinced of that fact, though.

"Change of subject," Dani said. "Do you like riddles?"

The question caught Sam off guard. He shrugged. "Yeah, I guess. Why?"

"I've got one for you. A hard one. And there's a reason I'm asking it, but you won't understand that until you've figured out the answer."

He wondered where she was going with this. It sounded like a game, but she also looked pretty serious about it.

"Let's hear it," Sam said.

Dani shook her head. She planted her feet and stood up from the swing.

"It's not something I can tell you," she said. "I have to show it to you. If you're up for a bike ride."

CHAPTER ELEVEN

They rode out of the park—its entry drive came in from the curved subdivision street—and then Dani led the way to the nearby two-lane road that ran north and south into the countryside—Truman Avenue, according to the street sign.

Truman was tightrope straight in both directions as far as Sam could see. Half a mile to the north it cut through a long band of forest that ran east to west. To the south, Truman went straight through the heart of downtown Ashland, and beyond into the wide-open farmlands.

Sam studied the road. Since the age of seven he'd been riding around on sidewalks and city plazas with his friends, but he couldn't remember ever riding on anything like Truman Avenue: two-lane blacktop with no sidewalks, just gravel shoulders flanked by deep, weed-choked runoff ditches. A road with a speed limit of fifty-five miles per hour, and drivers who probably didn't obey it. On the plus side, there hardly seemed to *be* any drivers. Right now there were none in either direction. And when they did come along, they'd be visible a mile away. It wouldn't be hard to watch for them.

Dani pedaled out onto the road, south toward downtown. Sam followed. A moment later they had passed the entirety of the subdivision and were riding side by side, picking up momentum down the long slope between the suburb and the little town below.

Out away from the shaded residential streets, the afternoon was bright and hazy, the flatlands running away to vague horizons maybe twenty miles out. The sky was full of tall, billowy clouds cut off flat on the bottoms. Those cloud bottoms made their own sort of landscape, upside-down, planing away to their own horizon out in the haze.

Ahead was the town, a few low-slung blocks hugging the terrain. It swam in the heat ripples coming up off the pavement. So far, Sam had only seen the town up close from his dad's car while passing through—a trip that took about twenty seconds. He really hadn't gotten a good look at the place yet.

"Is that where the riddle is?" Sam asked. "Downtown?"

Dani shook her head. "It's way out past it on the other side. Southwest, out in the country."

They rode for a while without saying more. After a minute they reached the edge of town. Truman Avenue served as Main Street. They passed the first buildings—a general store on one side, and some kind of grain storage on the other: a round, two-story structure made of corrugated metal, with a domed roof and a small funnel at the top. Tractors and huge rolling bins were parked around it.

They passed other storefronts along the main drag. A sandwich shop with an old woman behind the counter and no customers. A hardware store that didn't look much busier. A post office whose clerk was sitting out front on a bench, sipping a glass of lemonade. She waved as Sam and Dani went past. Sam couldn't tell what the rest of the buildings were. Farming-related places, he imagined.

A minute later he and Dani were through the town and back out in the country. The downslope was behind them now, and to their left and right, level cornfields extended for miles. The shoots were bright green and maybe knee high, sticking up out of the ragged soil. The only plants taller than that were a grove of pines off to the east: a city-block-sized vestige of whatever forest had once covered these lands.

Dani pointed ahead and to the right. Sam followed with his eyes and saw a tiny structure far out on the plain. It looked like a single-room house, faded yellow with a black roof. No garage. No vehicles parked near it. Not even a mown yard. Just a weed-filled lot surrounding it, and then more cornfields. It was probably a mile and a half away, line-of-sight. By road it was farther.

"That's where we're going," Dani said.

"What is it?"

"You'll see."

The rest of the ride took eight minutes. They came to the tall weeds surrounding the house, and lay their bikes down.

Sam stood staring at the place. Up close it was more impressive than he'd expected. The yellow exterior was brick. Maybe at one time the yellow had been vivid, but decades of sunlight had bleached it to nearly the color of sand. The roof was covered with black stone shingles. Clearly the place had been built to last.

Yet for all that, it was a standing ruin. The window frames were just square, empty holes in the exterior wall, with little bits of rotted wood clinging to grooves inside the edges. The glass panes were long gone. The front door, a red-painted slab of iron or steel, sagged a few inches open in its rusted casement. Huge portions of the door's paint job had flaked away, bit by bit, leaving the remaining paint in complex patterns that looked like continents and islands. The door might have been a map of an alien world.

"This is Echo House," Dani said. "That's what everyone calls it, anyway. It used to have a different name."

She took a step forward and used her foot to push aside a section of weeds, revealing a stone marker set in the ground. It looked like a tombstone, except for what was engraved on it:

ASHLAND TOWNSHIP SCHOOL
FUNCTIONAL 1847–1938

"An old one-room schoolhouse," Dani said. "According to this, it's been here almost a century and a half."

Sam stared at the marker, then looked at the school again. Through the window cavities he could get only a rough sense of the dim interior. The space was probably about the size of the two-stall garage at his new house. He tried to imagine himself attending this place a hundred years ago, when suddenly Dani clapped her hands three times, loud and fast.

Sam spun to look at her, but before he could ask what she was doing, he heard a set of answering claps from somewhere far away to the west. The same pattern of three claps in rapid succession.

He looked past her, west along the road, and saw a huge barn a quarter mile in that direction. Its long side was probably a hundred feet wide and forty feet tall. It was a giant, perfectly flat surface, facing the schoolhouse as directly as a movie screen faced an audience.

Sam offered a dry smile. "If you dragged me all the way out here to ask me where the echo comes from, you're slacking in the riddle department."

Dani returned the smile. "Yeah, yeah. Everyone knows where the echo comes from."

"So what's the riddle?"

For a moment she didn't answer. She walked farther into the overgrown yard, until she was halfway between the road and the schoolhouse. Then she turned back to Sam, and raised her arms in a sweeping gesture that took in everything around her. Echo House and all of its surroundings.

"Lauren and I used to come out here all the time," she said. "No reason. It was just a place to hang out. A place to ride our bikes to. We'd stay for an hour, sometimes longer. We'd probably been here half a dozen times before we finally noticed something about it. Something . . . weird."

"Weird?" Sam said.

"*Really* weird."

"What is it?"

"That's the riddle. See if you can spot what's weird."

Sam frowned. "*Lots* of things about it are weird. No one cuts the grass. The door's falling off. The roof's made of stone."

"Lauren and I didn't need half a dozen visits to notice those things."

"Well, is it something inside or outside?"

Dani shrugged, smiled, and mimed zipping her mouth shut and locking it.

Sam shook his head and turned his attention on the schoolhouse.

"What's the penalty if I don't figure it out?" he asked.

"I think you'll get it. And I'll go easy on the scoring. Lauren and I took forever to see it. But then again, we didn't know we were looking for it."

For the next hour Sam studied every detail of the place. He and Dani talked about random things—movies, books, Nintendo—but he didn't ask for any more clues to the riddle. He also didn't call out every little thing he saw that seemed potentially weird enough, hoping to hit on the answer. Better to play it cool until he was sure he had it right.

He scrutinized the outside of the structure first. He

saw lots of things that drew his attention, but none of them seemed especially weird. There were two bricks missing, side by side on the back wall, about waist high. There was a bird's nest tucked up under one of the eaves, dry and crumbling like it'd been there for years. There was an old lever-action water pump in the side yard, with OMAHA VALVE CO. imprinted on the handle, and spiderwebs strung from the spout.

After checking everything he could see outside, Sam went to the door. It opened without much effort, though it ground against its frame with a metal scream. He heard the sound ricochet off the distant barn even as he stepped into the schoolhouse.

For a few seconds, as his eyes adjusted, he worried about stepping on rotted floorboards and falling through to some kind of basement. Then the details resolved, and he saw that there was no basement at all. The floor was made of flagstones set in cement. In fact, he'd already seen the floor from outside, he realized. It extended right under the walls and beyond, by about six inches on all sides. That made it a very simple foundation: a broad stone platform slightly larger than the building that rested on it. None of which qualified as weird. Sam moved farther inside, and heard Dani enter behind him.

Seen from the interior, away from the glare of the summer afternoon, the schoolhouse was actually pretty bright. The windows were small by modern standards, but there was more than enough light to compensate.

Sam looked around. Here, again, lots of things

caught his eye, but none of them struck him as unusual. He saw metal candleholders built into the walls every four feet. Most were empty, but melted stubs remained in a few of them. In the back left corner there was an iron potbelly stove. Its door was long gone, and its chamber was full of weeds and sticks where some animal had made a home, maybe over the winter. For a moment the stove itself seemed like a possible answer to the riddle: it had stood out here unattended for over half a century since the school shut down, and nobody had come along and stolen it. That was at least *a little* weird. Then Sam saw the reason: each of the stove's legs flared out at the bottom, like the business end of a trombone, and the edges of each flare were trapped securely under the flagstone slabs of the floor. The stove had been set in place first, and then the floor had been laid down around it, permanently locking it in position. Clever idea. But not weird.

After a while Sam felt desperation setting in; he was running out of places to look. Already he'd studied every object and surface, inside and outside the schoolhouse. Now he went over everything again, looking closer. He checked the water pump in the yard. He crouched and looked up into the spout. Nothing there but a fat spider. He ducked and looked into the waist-high hole in the back wall. He saw only the darkness of the wall's interior cavity. He eyeballed every candleholder inside the schoolhouse. He knelt and studied every grout-filled seam between the flagstones that made up the floor. He noted how the individual stones at the room's edge really did continue beneath the wall to the outside: the color and grain matched up perfectly on both sides of the wall. He bent down and peered into the potbelly stove, past the nest of weeds inside. Nothing important in there. He leaned behind the stove to look at its backside, but all he saw was a tiny engraving, stating that the stove had been forged in St. Louis in the year 1885. Last, he checked the schoolhouse door, front and back. He spent a couple minutes staring at the pattern of flaked-off paint. Maybe some part of it would look like Elvis if he squinted just right. Maybe that would count as weird. But no amount of squinting revealed anything.

He glanced at his watch. 4:30. He should probably be home when his dad got there, sometime after 5:00, if only to avoid worrying him.

"We can take off if you need to get back," Dani said.

Sam nodded. "But I'm not giving up. I'll come back tomorrow and keep looking. I'll figure it out."

Dani smiled. "I don't think you'll have to. I'm betting you'll figure it out tonight, just by thinking about it."

"Why do you say that?"

"Because you've already seen what's weird. You looked right at it. Give it time, and it'll hit you."

"You know *weird* is kind of a loose word, right?" Sam said. "It means different things to different people. Like, scale of one to ten, ten being bigfoot in a Ferrari . . . exactly how weird is this thing?"

"Let's call it a nine-point-five," Dani said. "It's *weird.* It's *lose-sleep-over-it* weird." Her expression faltered. She suddenly looked very serious. Maybe even a little scared. “And then I can tell you the real reason I brought you out here, and why this is more than just a riddle.”

CHAPTER TWELVE

They were in Dani's driveway fifteen minutes later; her house was four doors down from Sam's, on the same side of the street. Sam stayed on his bike as Dani opened the entry next to the garage door, and rolled hers inside. She came back and stood at the threshold.

"Let you know first thing tomorrow if I figure it out," Sam said.

"You will."

"Thanks for welcoming me to the neighborhood."

She smiled, but beneath it Sam saw that scared edge again. "Wait til you know the neighborhood a little better before you thank me."

He spent the next half hour at his bedroom window, looking south beyond downtown at the distant, pale yellow speck of Echo House. He ran it all through his head again: everything he'd seen.

The potbelly stove kept coming back to him. He wasn't sure why. Maybe it was just the most interesting thing about the place—maybe it had nothing to do with whatever was weird.

He kept thinking about the flagstones, too, and how the ones at the edges went right under the schoolhouse wall, from one side to the other. But again, there was nothing especially strange about that. Lots of places had probably been built that way, back in the old days.

Maybe he was overthinking the problem. Maybe the answer was something big and obvious, and he was focusing too hard on small details to see it.

His dad got home at twenty after five. Sam asked how his first day had gone. He said it'd been great, though Sam caught stress in his voice. Probably normal, for a new job.

They went out for dinner at a burger place in Brenner. The town was noticeably larger than Ashland. Busy restaurants. Chain stores and banks. A used car lot. Still tiny by the standards Sam was used to.

Over dinner he said nothing about the day's events, beyond riding around the suburb on his own. Part of him wanted to talk about Dani, and Echo House, and all that was on his mind. A bigger part of him didn't. Maybe he just wanted to understand it all better, before saying anything about it.

More than just a riddle, Dani had said.

Whatever that meant.

It was half an hour past midnight. Sam lay in the dark, in his room, his dad asleep across the hall. The window was open, the sounds of the night coming through the screen.

Echo House.

He'd been thinking about it for hours. He felt no closer to solving the riddle.

The potbelly stove.

The flagstones.

Both kept rising to the surface of his thoughts, whether he wanted them to or not.

An hour slipped by. He heard the *click, click, click, hum* sound behind the closet again. The house sound. Apparently he hadn't learned to ignore it yet.

After a while he felt sleep pulling him down, right to the edge of consciousness, half in and half out of dreamworld.

He found himself in the tall grass outside the schoolhouse again. He stood before the stone marker in the yard, with the weeds blocking his view of its engraving. He felt a sudden urgency to read what was carved there, though he couldn't say why. It was only the school's name. What did it matter?

But the urgency persisted. He had to see it.

Only he couldn't. He was unable to move in the dream. Unable to step closer. Unable to stoop and swing his arm to clear the way. The weeds swayed in the summer wind but offered no glimpse of the stone.

Then a hand came into view. A slender hand with pink fingernails. It swept the weeds aside, revealing the stone marker in full.

Sam sat up in the darkness of his room. His heart was beating just noticeably faster than usual.

He sat very still and thought through the details. The answer to the riddle wasn't one simple thing. It was a combination of things. Like a little jigsaw puzzle. He let it fall together in his mind, and considered it from all sides until he was sure he had it.

Dani had been telling the truth: it was very, very weird.

He didn't sleep after that. He sat awake for another hour, thinking about Echo House.

Then he heard footsteps outside the window.

He tensed and held his breath. The nearest crickets went silent.

The footsteps came closer. Someone approaching across the yard, moving carefully through the dark.

A sudden, irrational panic came to him:

It was Mr. Pierce.

Somehow he'd found his way home after all this time.

Then the footsteps came to a stop, right outside the window.

"Sam?"

Dani's voice, just above a whisper.

He breathed out, shaking his head at himself. *Stupid.* He pulled off the covers, stood and crossed to the screen. Dani was just outside, barely visible, a silhouette against the lights of town.

"Yeah," Sam said.

"You figured it out, didn't you."

"How'd you know?"

"Because you answered just now. Which means you were wide awake. Which means something was *keeping* you awake."

"Yeah, I figured it out."

"Can you come outside? I don't want to wake up your dad."

"Sure, hold on."

He pulled his shorts and a T-shirt on, then found his socks and shoes. It took him a moment to find the screen's release tabs, by feel. He pulled them and eased the screen outward until it came loose from the frame. Dani took hold of it and set it down against the outside of the house. Sam slipped out onto the dew-damp grass.

"This way," Dani whispered.

He followed her across the yard, into the high grass beyond, out onto the open stretch of the slope. He saw within seconds where they were going: the abandoned picnic table he'd seen before. It was probably a hundred yards out past the edge of the lawn. They'd covered half the distance when Sam happened to look up.

What he saw brought him to a dead stop. He nearly lost his balance.

"Holy shit . . ." he whispered.

Dani stopped and turned back. Sam heard her laugh softly.

"They look pretty good," she said, "when you get away from city lights."

Sam could only nod. He could think of no other reply. The sky had all of his attention.

He'd never seen the stars look like this.

He'd never imagined they *could.*

"You didn't get out of L.A. much, did you?" Dani said.

"Not really."

On vacation once, with a friend's family north of Santa Barbara, he had experienced nights this dark—but the house had been in deep woods, up in the hills, and he'd never gotten a look at the sky. The only other trips he'd taken were to visit relatives, all of whom lived in other big cities. He had an uncle in Philadelphia he'd visited a few times, who'd taken him fishing in the Pine Barrens east of town. It was almost this remote out there, but Sam had only been there in daylight.

In Los Angeles, even on a clear night, he might have seen five or six bright stars through the light-pollution. Out here there had to be thousands, scattered like tiny chips of broken glass across the ink-black night. The bright ones looked great, but the fainter ones were what left him in a daze: there were just so *many* of them. Thousands everywhere he looked. How had he gone his whole life without seeing this?

"Come on," Dani said. "It's better lying down."

Sam stared up for another few seconds and then followed her the rest of the way to the table. Up close, he saw that the thing was huge. Not a standard rectangle-shaped table, but a big square one with seats on all four sides. The top surface was probably six feet by six.

Dani climbed on and lay on her back, on one half. Sam took the other.

He saw at once what she meant. Lying down was the way to look at the stars. No strain in your neck from craning it upward. No need to think about your balance. Best of all, no horizon. His field of view was entirely filled up with sky.

For at least a minute neither of them spoke. They

just lay there under the vault of stars, the night sounds of the open country all around them, the humid breeze pressing against them, sliding past.

"When I first moved here," Dani said, "and I got my first look at this, I thought I was going to be happy here. Between this and Lauren, I really believed it. That was before I learned certain things about this town."

He waited for her to go on, but for a long time she didn't.

Then he heard the scrape of her shoulders on the tabletop, and turned to see her sliding closer. She stopped six inches away, and pointed at an especially bright star above them.

"That's Vega," she said. "It's twenty-six light-years away. When you look at that star, the light hitting your eyes is fourteen years older than us." She pointed to another bright star, close to Vega. "That one's called Deneb. It looks about the same as Vega, but it's not. It's a supergiant, and it's more than thirty-five hundred light-years away. That light you're looking at is older than the Romans. It's hard to think about stuff like that, but I like it."

She went quiet again. Sam heard the wind brushing the grass stems against the table's legs.

"I came out here every night for the first couple weeks," Dani said. "I'd lie here for hours. I got so into it. I got an astronomy book from the school library and memorized stars and constellations. I was excited. I really was happy."

Another silence settled in. Sam listened to the sound of her breathing, softer than the breeze moving over the field. Then he heard her turn toward him on the table.

"So tell me what's weird about Echo House," she said.

He turned to face her, too. He could just make out her shape against the sky.

"It's the stove," he said. "And it's the floor. And it's the building itself. It's all three of those things, together."

"What about them?"

"The stove is trapped in place by the floor," Sam said. "Which means the stove was there first. They set it there and laid the flagstones down over its feet."

"Right . . ."

"Then they built the school on top of the floor. They must have, because the stones go under the wall. So the order goes like this: stove first, then the floor, then the school. And that's all great . . . except the stove is about forty years *newer* than the school. The engraving on the back says the stove was forged in 1885. But the stone marker out front says the *school* was built in 1847. It doesn't add up. It's not even possible. How could the stove have been set in place before the school was constructed, if the stove didn't even *exist* yet?"

For a moment Dani said nothing. The insect chorus filtered across the darkness.

Then she said, "I knew I had you pegged as a smart guy." And though Sam couldn't see it, he could tell by her voice that she was smiling.

"So how could they build it like that?" he said. "How is it possible?"

"It's not. It's fake."

"The stove is fake?"

Dani shook her head. "The *school* is fake. It's like a stage prop. It wasn't built in 1847. My guess, based on other things I've seen, is that it was built sometime in the last fifty years. It was never a working school at all. It's just there for looks."

"That doesn't make sense," Sam said. "Why would someone build a fake old schoolhouse, just to abandon it? If it's for looks, why doesn't someone cut the grass?"

"Because it's not there to look *good.* It's supposed to look *real.* A real schoolhouse would probably be just like that, abandoned and left to rot. It's just one little part of the big illusion."

"What illusion?"

She was silent a moment. Then she said, "The illusion that Ashland is a real town."

CHAPTER THIRTEEN

"What?" Sam said.

"It's not real."

Sam drew his elbows against his sides and pushed himself up to a sitting position. Dani did the same. Sam stared past her silhouette at the dimly lit streets of Ashland, down at the base of the slope.

"Of course it's a real town," he said. "It's right there."

"I know it *exists*. What I'm saying is that it's fake."

"How can a town be fake? If it has shops and restaurants, and all these houses . . . if people *live* here . . . doesn't that automatically make it a town?"

"Does a cowboy hat automatically make someone a cowboy?"

Sam started to say more, but stopped. Maybe she was messing with him. Maybe this was a joke people around here played on new kids.

"Okay, forget *how*," he said. "*Why* would someone build a fake town? Even if they could."

"It's camouflage," Dani said. "It exists to hide what really goes on around here."

"Which is?"

Dani didn't answer. Sam saw her look away, and heard her tapping her fingertips lightly on the table.

"I don't think I can make you believe it just by talking," she said. "I thought I could, as long as you'd seen Echo House, and figured out the weird thing for yourself. I thought that would be a good enough starting point. But now that I think about it . . . everything I want to tell you is just going to sound stupid. I've never had to describe it for anyone. Lauren and I discovered all of it together; neither of us ever had to bring the other one up to speed."

"What are you talking about?" Sam said.

Dani drummed her fingertips a moment longer. Her silhouette turned toward him in the darkness.

"I swear I'm not trying to get you in trouble," she said, "but can you come and look at something with me? It's a place. If you see it, then you'll know I'm not kidding. We can be there and back in about two hours, on foot."

"You mean right now?"

"Yeah. We have to go at night. In daylight someone would catch us."

Sam imagined his dad waking up and finding him missing. If it happened right now, it wouldn't be the end of the world. Sam was close enough to hear him if he yelled through the open window, and he probably wouldn't get grounded just for coming out here to stargaze. But if he actually *went* somewhere—an hour's walk on foot—things could turn out quite a bit worse. He and Dani might return from their trip to find a dozen police cars parked in the street. His dad wasn't one to panic, but finding his son missing in the middle of the night might do the trick.

"It's two thirty in the morning," Dani said. "What time does your dad get up for work?"

"Not by four thirty, I know that."

"Does he have a habit of checking in on you during the night?"

Sam thought about it. He was pretty sure neither of his parents had done that in years, but there was no guarantee his dad wouldn't do it tonight, so soon after moving to a new place. He might just lean in through Sam's doorway after using the bathroom or something. If he did, the glow from the alarm clock would be enough to give away the empty bed.

"We *have* to go at night?" Sam said.

"Yes. It'd be crazy to try it during the day. Trust me."

For a moment Sam said nothing.

"It's okay if you don't want to do this," Dani said. "I understand. It's just that you'll never believe what I need to tell you, if you don't see this place for yourself. *I* wouldn't believe it, if I hadn't seen it."

Silence, except the sounds of the night. Seconds passed.

"Okay, let's go," Sam said.

"Good." Dani slid off the table and stood. "I need to get something from my house. I'll be back in two minutes."

"I need to do something, too. I'll meet you here."

She nodded and disappeared into the darkness

toward her own yard. Sam turned back for his. Less than a minute later he was in his room, silently opening his top dresser drawer and feeling for a pen and a notepad. He took them both to his nightstand, and used the soft pool of light in front of the alarm clock to write a message:

OUT WITH A FRIEND. NOTHING DANGEROUS, I PROMISE. BACK BY 4:30.

By no stretch was it going to keep him from being in deep shit, if his dad actually discovered him missing. At best it would keep his dad from calling the cops—at least until 4:31.

He left the notepad open on his pillow, then slid back out the window into the night. He closed the window behind him. By the time he reached the picnic table, he could see Dani already standing there. She held something out to him.

"Flashlight," she said. "Don't turn it on yet. Not until we get there. Not until we're inside."

He took it. Dani had one, too.

"This way," she said, and started off along the face of the slope, straight toward Truman Avenue.

At the road, Sam expected Dani to lead him south toward town, as she had that afternoon. Instead she turned north, and for the first few minutes of their walk, they had the subdivision beside them, sprawled out to one side of Truman, a zone of pale streetlamps and porch lights shining out through the maples. On the other side of Truman was empty farmland, vast and black.

The country to the north, directly in front of them, was also black. Sam tried to recall how it'd looked in daylight. It was pretty flat, he knew. The land only sloped between downtown Ashland and the edge of the subdivision. Both north and south of that stretch, it was flat everywhere. The only other thing he could remember was the long band of forest that crossed Truman half a mile north of the suburb.

They walked in silence for a while. Sam thought of asking Dani to explain what she'd said—about Ashland being a fake town, about it being camouflage for something else. Instead he kept quiet. Whatever place she was taking him to, obviously she wanted him to see it first, and then tell her story. A story he wouldn't believe any other way, apparently. Maybe she was right about that. He didn't believe it so far.

The suburb fell farther and farther behind them. There was nothing around them now but dark open fields, and the stars arching overhead. Sam could hear the low corn shoots rustling like paper in the breeze. It was hard to judge distance in the dark, but he guessed they were about halfway to the forest, when he heard the far-off whisper of tires on pavement somewhere behind them. He and Dani turned at the same time, and he saw the road to the south crowned with light, where the land dropped at the crest of the slope. A car was coming up the hill, still just below the top, out of sight.

"In the ditch," Dani said.

She led the way off the road, past the gravel shoulder and into the thick weeds. Just inside them, Sam felt the ground drop away sharply. The ditch was a lot deeper than it looked. Four feet, if not more.

"Don't go all the way down," Dani said. "There's water at the bottom. Get a handful of the weed stems and just hold on."

Sam couldn't see anything, but it was easy enough to follow her instructions by feel alone. He got his hands around a dense clutch of weeds, thick as a heavy rope, and braced his feet and knees against the steep wall of the ditch. He heard Dani doing the same, right beside him, and within a few seconds they were both holding still, well hidden in the deep grass, their heads just below the surface of the road.

At that moment bright light washed over the tops of the weeds. The car had crested the slope. As it drew nearer, the light and sound intensified. The dew-soaked weeds caught and scattered the glow. Sam realized he could see Dani clearly.

"Never did this in L.A.," he said.

"Me either. What are the odds?"

A second later the car rushed past above them. The weeds turned from bright white to fading red, and the smell of exhaust filled the air. Within moments the night was quiet again.

It took them another ten minutes to reach the forest, and a couple more to pass through it, back into the clear beneath the stars. They'd gone another quarter mile when Dani stopped and faced west. Sam could just make out some kind of gravel track in that direction, leading inland off the road. It was bordered by the weeds of an undeveloped lot on its south side, and an open cornfield to the north. Far out across the cornfield stood a farmhouse. Sam would've missed it, if not for a mercury light on a post in the yard.

"Whatever you do," Dani said, "*do not* turn on your flashlight now."

She led him onto the gravel track, walking carefully, quietly. Sam followed her example.

"See that farmhouse?" Dani whispered.

"Yeah."

"During the daytime, there are always lots of people there. Half a dozen cars parked out front. People sitting at desks near the windows, working on computers. They come and go in shifts. Not like people that live there. More like people that work there."

"You don't think it's really a farmhouse?"

"I think it's some kind of office. And I'm pretty sure there's a night shift, too. Lauren and I watched the place from the woods one day, way up in a tree. Some cars show up right around dark and stay for a few hours, or even all night long. It's a busy place."

"Is that what we came here to look at?"

"No."

They continued along the track. After a while they were due south of the farmhouse—or whatever it was. Sam guessed they were passing it at a distance of about a football field. None of its rooms were brightly lit, but he got a sense of some faint illumination from inside, like from TV screens. Some kind of screens, anyway.

A few hundred yards farther on, Dani veered to the right, off the gravel track and into the open space of the cornfield.

"Only step between the planted rows," she whispered, "where the ground is packed hard. If you step where it's soft you'll leave prints."

He saw what she meant; the distant mercury light was just bright enough to give away the denser soil between the corn shoots. He felt exposed out on the open ground, though he knew nobody watching from the house could see them. In daylight it would've been a different story. It would've been impossible for someone *not* to see them.

They followed a diagonal path across the field for two hundred feet and then Dani stopped. They were now very far from the road and the house, way out in the empty darkness of the cornfield. At first Sam couldn't tell why Dani had stopped here. Then he leaned to the side and saw what was in front of her.

At a glance it was only a cluster of weeds and tangled shrubs. A little island of untended ground, ringed by big rocks that had probably been cleared from these fields a century and a half ago. The whole formation wasn't much bigger than Sam's bedroom.

But there was more to it. There was a shape hidden within the undergrowth, Sam saw. It looked like a dark rectangle lying flat among the weeds. He stepped up beside Dani for a closer look, and realized the big rectangle was actually a hole in the ground. In fact it was a staircase, leading down below the surface of the field.

"What the hell?" Sam said.

"Lauren and I first saw this the day we staked out the farmhouse. From the road, you could drive past this field every day, your whole life, and not know this was anything more than a patch of weeds. But from up in the trees, you can just make out the opening. We took a closer look at it that same night."

"Where do the stairs go?" Sam asked.

"To the place you need to see to believe. Come on."

Dani moved forward and set her foot carefully down onto the first step. Then she descended easily into the darkness. Sam followed. As soon as he was below the surface, he could see nothing at all. He made his way down the stairs by feel, running one hand along the wall—it felt like rough, cold concrete—to keep his balance. He'd gone down about twenty steps when he heard Dani's voice, just ahead and below, telling him to be careful, and then he felt her hand reach up and take hold of his wrist.

"I'm at the bottom," she said. "Take the last few steps slow, or you'll walk into the door."

A second later he was standing on a flat surface, right beside her. She let go of his arm.

"Don't turn on your light yet," she said.

Then he heard a *click,* and her own flashlight came on, though very dimly. She had her hand clamped over its lens, so all that shone out was a pink glow through the skin of her fingers. She moved the light forward and Sam saw a door right in front of where they stood. There was no knob—just a heavy steel handle, spotted with rust. The door was painted black, but it, too, was rusted, and the paint was coming off in flakes. Above the handle was a keypad with twelve buttons laid out like those on a touch-tone telephone. Ten numbers, along with an asterisk and a pound sign.

"Don't tell me you know the code," Sam said.

"Five sevens in a row. Same as all the other abandoned stations."

"The what?"

"I'll explain it all in a minute."

With her free hand she pressed the number seven five times, and Sam heard a *thud* as the lock disengaged. Dani took hold of the handle and pushed, and the door swung inward heavily. Sam helped her, and together they shoved it open enough to slip around it and inside. As they did, Sam saw in the glow of Dani's light that the metal door was three inches thick, like that of a bank vault. It fell shut behind them with another *thud* and a *click*.

The darkness was absolute beyond the clamped lens of Dani's light. Then she took her hand off of it, and the beam entirely lit up the space they'd entered.

They were in a short corridor of some kind. Its floor, walls, and ceiling were lined with grey ceramic tiles. It was four feet wide and maybe ten feet long. They were standing at one end of it, with the heavy door at their backs. The hallway was featureless except for another door capping the far end, and a huge block of text that had been stencil-painted, in black, onto one of the side walls. It read:

UNITED STATES D.O.D.
ASHLAND-STATION 14

LIMA 4 CLEARANCE REQUIRED
BEYOND THIS POINT

"You do have Lima four clearance, right?" Dani asked. She laughed softly.

"What the hell *is* this place?" Sam said.

"You haven't seen anything yet. Trust me."

"But are there *people* here? Are we going to get caught?"

Dani shook her head. "It's abandoned. Probably for decades."

Sam started to ask more, but stopped. His gaze went back to the writing on the wall. He watched as Dani trailed her flashlight over the letters *D.O.D.*

"Department of Defense," she said.

"Is this what I had to see to believe?" Sam asked. "That this town is full of these abandoned places? Whatever this is."

Dani shook her head. "Only some of them are abandoned. And Ashland isn't a town. It's a military base."

CHAPTER FOURTEEN

Sam stared at her. "Come again?"

"It's a military base. This entire area. The stores downtown, the suburb, these farms all around it. It's all part of the base."

"Military bases have fences around them. They have guard shacks, patrols—"

"Not this one."

"Wouldn't people know? How would all those people in the suburb not know they're living on military property?"

"They do know," Dani said. "All those people are in the military. The grownups, anyway. My dad. Your dad, too."

Sam almost laughed. "My dad's a lawyer for Kamen and Ross. They're one of the biggest firms in the country. He moved us out here because they set up some new office to handle companies in the Midwest."

"I'm sure it all makes sense on paper," Dani said. "But I promise you, your dad works for the military, at least as of today. They need lawyers too, right?"

"This is ridiculous," Sam said. He could hear the

pitch of his voice rising. He knew it was disbelief—but a faltering disbelief. Because whatever Dani was telling him, clearly it *wasn't* just some prank to play on the new kid in town. His eyes kept going back and forth from her face to the stenciled text on the wall. This place was real. Whatever the hell it was, it was real.

"I know it's hard to accept," Dani said. "But let me ask you something. Do you believe there are men and women in America doing secret work for the government?"

"Sure. Somewhere."

"Do you think their kids know about it?"

Sam considered that. The concept had never crossed his mind before. It was such a random notion.

"Probably not," he said.

He imagined his face must be stone blank. He wanted to ask her how she could know any of this, but the question stopped in his throat. Obviously the *how* was part of the story she'd brought him here to tell him.

"I know," she said again, seeing his expression. "It's hard. And weird. It was the same way for me. Let me show you the rest of this place, and I'll tell you the whole thing from the beginning. It won't take long. There's only so much I really know."

She nodded to the door at the far end of the corridor, and crossed toward it. Following her, Sam felt dizzy in a way that had nothing to do with his balance. He absently switched on his own flashlight as they reached the second door. Like the first, it had a handle instead of a knob, but there was no keypad above this one. Dani pulled it open and Sam slipped through after her.

The space on the other side was a stairwell. It was clean and simple and plain, not much different than any stairwell Sam had ever seen. The walls and steps were poured concrete. Sam and Dani were on a landing at the very top of the space. Only the first flight of stairs was visible, descending to the next landing down. Dani led the way.

"How far down do the stairs go?" Sam asked.

"A hundred twenty steps. And every step is ten inches high—yes, I measured. So twelve hundred inches, total. That's exactly a hundred feet. Add the twenty feet of stairs leading down from the weeds, and this stairwell bottoms out a hundred twenty feet below the surface of the cornfield."

"What's down there?"

"Two doors," Dani said. "One of them is locked, with another keypad, but punching in the five sevens doesn't open that one. Lauren and I only tried it once. We were scared to try again, in case it might set off an alarm or something. But the other door, no keypad. You just open it and walk through."

"What's on the other side?" Sam asked.

"You'll see in a minute. If there's a word for it, I don't know it."

Sam said no more. He continued descending the stairs after Dani. They took each step carefully in the swinging glow of the flashlight beams.

"So here it is from the beginning," Dani said, "starting three months ago when I moved here. Lauren and I were both new in town. We met, we clicked, we rode our bikes all over the place. We found Echo House, and out of habit we went there practically every day. We noticed the problem with the stove, and the dates. We told our parents about it—my parents and Lauren's dad. Her mom died when she was born. We told all of them about Echo House, and their response was so odd. They didn't want to hear about it, but it was almost like . . . like they were holding something back. And when we pressed it, they'd get mad at us. Like, *Stop talking about it, girls, it's nothing.* Strange, right?"

They rounded a landing and continued downward. Sam had already lost count of how many flights they'd descended—maybe three or four.

"By this time we'd met plenty of other kids around the subdivision, and at school," Dani said. "We told a few of them about Echo House. They reacted like our parents had. *It's nothing. Who cares?* They just flat-out refused to talk about it. It was as if every last person in this town had been . . . *trained.* And maybe that's a weird way to say it, but it's true. It was like they'd all gotten used to the idea that you just didn't talk about certain things. And they'd hush up anyone who tried to."

Sam noticed the echo of her voice changing as they descended. When they'd first entered the stairwell, the reverberations had all come from below. Now they seemed to be coming from high above. They must be getting near the bottom.

"By the end of that first month," Dani said, "Lauren and I could see exactly how this town does that to people. How it trains them. It's almost an automatic thing. It comes from every conversation. Every time someone tells you to keep quiet for your own good, every time they cut you off midsentence, and look around like they're afraid someone overheard . . . every moment like that, you feel yourself getting a little more scared, too. Wanting to just keep your head down and not make trouble."

They rounded one more landing, and Sam saw a final flight of steps, and at the bottom a concrete floor maybe fifteen by fifteen feet.

He saw the two doors, facing each other across the square space, one on the left wall and one on the right. The left door had the keypad. The other had nothing but a handle. They descended the last few steps and made their way to the right-side door.

"We almost gave in," Dani said. "We really almost did."

She looked up and met his eyes.

"Come on," she said at last, and pulled the door open.

Sam followed her through. A second later he felt his thought process come to a dead stop.

Somewhere in the back of his mind, it occurred to him that people often used the word *stunned* to describe their feelings. If a baseball team came from behind to win in the ninth, or some celebrity couple split up, people said they were stunned by it. He himself had probably used the word lots of times. But now, standing in the space beyond the stairwell door, it was clear as pool water that he had never been truly stunned by anything.

Until now.

The chamber they'd entered had a ceiling as high up as that of the gymnasium in his school back in L.A. Sixty feet up, maybe. The width and length of the chamber, however, put the gymnasium to shame. He wasn't even sure he could gauge the size of this space. It extended hundreds of feet in both directions, the vastness terminating at what looked like concrete walls, way out in the gloom where the flashlights could barely reach. Their two beams were grossly outmatched by the size of the place. They might as well have been penlights.

Sam moved his beam along the massive steel trusses that held up the ceiling, supported every fifty feet or so by upright columns. He saw complex triangular framing, like the supports of a railroad bridge. He tried to imagine the weight of soil pushing down on the ceiling from above—there were another sixty feet of dirt on top of this open space.

After a few seconds he lowered the light and swept it over the chamber's vast floor. It was bare concrete, like the surfaces of the stairwell, and it was mostly empty. Mostly. Here and there, random shapes stood frozen in the near-dark: metallic structures, some as small as children's toys, others larger than pickup trucks. The shapes were completely foreign to Sam; he had no idea what they were, and none were close enough to see clearly in the limited flashlight glow.

"By then," Dani said, "the end of that first month, Lauren and I still had no idea what was really going on in Ashland. We only knew *something* was."

She waved him forward, and together they moved out onto the open floor. As soon as the wall fell away into darkness behind them, Sam was struck by the sensation that they weren't indoors at all. In the cavernous space, with their flashlights shining only on the ground ahead, it felt exactly as if they were out in a parking lot in the middle of the night.

"We started looking around for whatever answers we could find," Dani said. "We studied the town. Looked for anything else that was strange. Which turned out to be pretty much everything. Remember the sandwich shop on Main Street?"

"Yeah."

"No customers."

"I noticed."

"There are never customers," Dani said. "Never. I have a telescope in my bedroom, and from my window you can see the front of that restaurant. One time Lauren and I watched the place all day, ten hours, taking turns. The old woman behind the counter showed up at eight in the morning. Nobody else went in, the whole day long. She came out at six and drove away. That was that."

"There would have to be *some* customers," Sam said. "Aren't there ever just . . . tourists passing through?"

"We're sixty miles from the freeway. This is probably the exact middle of nowhere. Nobody passes through. But the sandwich shop did have a customer one time. Me. I walked in and ordered a turkey sandwich on rye."

"What happened?"

"The lady stared at me like I was trying to sell her some cookies. Then she went into a back room and bumbled around for five minutes, and came back out with a sandwich: bologna on white bread. She said they were out of turkey and rye."

"*Everything* is fake in this town? Literally everything?"

Dani shrugged. "The cornfields have real corn in them. I think that's about it."

They were moving toward one of the metal shapes—one of the larger ones. It was only a dozen yards away now, but Sam still had no sense of what it was. Just the discarded ruin of some strange machine.

"You might imagine," Dani said, "that Lauren and I were going a little crazy by that point. We knew the whole town was some kind of . . . mask, I guess. But why? A mask covers something. What was being covered here? And then it occurred to us that our parents must know a lot more than they were letting on. They'd chosen to move here, after all. Maybe they knew everything. So with that in mind . . . we did something pretty bad."

They reached the metal structure. Both flashlight beams played over it, and at last Sam saw what it was: an old Army Jeep, like something out of a World War II movie. He also saw why it'd been hard to recognize at a distance. It was smashed. Crumpled in on itself from all sides, as if a giant had picked it up and crushed it between his hands.

Then Sam directed the flashlight over the finer details of the wreckage, and realized that words like *smashed* and *crumpled* were a little off the mark. There were no stress-fractures in the metal. No jagged edges. No break-points. All the damage was smooth and curved, even rippled. It looked the way a plastic toy Jeep might look, if someone dropped it into a campfire for a minute or two. This thing hadn't been crushed. It'd been melted.

Sam's light beam found one of the Jeep's doors, where black stencil-painted text had been applied, apparently *after* the damage. The writing was identical to what he'd seen in the corridor upstairs, though smaller. It read:

MK-II HYENA
NONGUIDED THERMOBARIC ORDNANCE GS-820
BRAVO TEST-18 APRIL 1964

Beneath the blocky stencil text, someone had added with a grease pencil: *NICE AND TOASTY!*

"The bad thing we did was to eavesdrop on my dad," Dani said. "I know it's totally wrong. If I ever have kids, and they do that to me, they're grounded for a month. But it was all we could think of."

"Eavesdrop how?"

"Have you ever seen a microcassette recorder?"

"Sure."

"I used to use one at my old school in Long Beach," Dani said, "for taking notes. It's tiny, and it's the kind that you can set to be voice-activated. It only records when it's picking up sound."

Sam nodded. There had been kids who used them at his old school, too.

"My dad has a briefcase he takes to work every

day," Dani said. "He leaves it in the den every night, under the desk. I found a way to peel back thc inner lining and hide the recorder inside. I didn't know if it would work—if it would pick up any sound at all, from in there. And most of the time it didn't. I was lucky to get even two or three minutes of conversation in a whole day. I think it all depended on how close people happened to be, to the briefcase. But yeah, I heard a little—my dad talking to people he works with."

Dani stepped back from thc half-melted Jeep. She turned and slowly trailed her flashlight across the wide-open floor, from one metal wreck to another. Sam saw that they were all target vehicles, or the wasted remains of them. Not all of them were melted. Some were just blown apart. One, an old tank of some kind, had been shattered into pieces like a glass sculpture. All that remained was the gun turret, resting tilted on a pile of jagged metal shards. Sam couldn't even guess what could've done that.

But the room itself he didn't have to guess about. This place had been some kind of proving ground for weapons. Very secret, very dangerous weapons.

"After the first week of hiding the recorder," Dani said, "Lauren and I understood pretty much everything. There were random little details, like the door code for these abandoned stations, but mostly what we got was the big picture—the part I already told you. That the adults in this town work for the military. And the town itself is one big camouflage tarp to cover it all. Fake shops. Fake old schoolhouse. Fake history. Fake everything."

Dani finished her slow turn with the flashlight, coming full circle.

"But why would they bother doing that?" Sam asked. "The military has regular bases all over the country. They have places way out in the desert, surrounded by minefields and armed guards. When they want to keep things secret, they can do it there. Why would they need Ashland?"

"I wondered that, too. All I could think of is something that scares me."

"What?"

"What if they're keeping other kinds of secrets here?" Dani said. "Not just important things, but . . . illegal things. Like things you can't be *officially* working on, at some ordinary base."

Sam didn't answer. He felt a chill as if a breeze had suddenly blown over his skin, though the air in the chamber remained as still as it must have for decades.

"My mom told me once that I was shaping up to be an idealist," Dani said. "I think she's probably right. I had a report I was supposed to do in history, at the end of sixth grade back in L.A. The teacher gave us a list of topics to pick from, and I picked the Tuskegee Airmen. Have you heard of them?"

"Red tails," Sam said. He'd gotten into model airplane building over the past couple years—part of a growing obsession he seemed to have with all things military. He'd started out with modern warplanes like the F-14 and the B-1, but soon fell in love with World War II aircraft. You couldn't get very far into that subject without learning about the Tuskegee Airmen, the all-black fighter squadron that had turned out to be just about the best bomber escort group in the whole war. Sam's favorite model, packed carefully in a box in his bedroom right now, was the P-51 Mustang flown by Lee Archer: *Ina the Macon Belle.*

"When I went to the library to do my research on them," Dani said, "I found something else Tuskegee is known for. It probably wasn't something my sixth-grade teacher wanted a report on. Have you heard of the Tuskegee syphilis experiment?"

"Gotta go with no on that one."

"You know what syphilis is, though."

"Yeah," Sam said. As awkward as sex ed had been, the material was pretty much impossible to forget.

"Well, in Tuskegee," Dani said, "the United States government ran an experiment to measure what that disease could do to people if it went untreated for a really long time. You know how they did that? They brought in hundreds of men who had the disease, and told them they were going to treat them for it. And then they didn't. They didn't even tell them they *had* syphilis. They gave them some b.s. diagnosis so they wouldn't know enough to go get treatment somewhere else. They kept them clueless for forty years, suffering from the disease, probably passing it to their wives or their girlfriends. Forty years, and at any point along the way they could have given them ten days' worth of penicillin and cured them. There ended up being six hundred victims of that experiment, and every last one of them was black. Think about that. This really happened. And recently. It only ended in 1972, after somebody told a reporter about it. That's only five years before we were born. That's what I mean by other kinds of secrets."

There was a little tremor in her voice, just detectable. In the indirect flashlight glow bouncing up off the concrete, Sam could see a sheen in her eyes. She blinked and turned away, sweeping her beam quickly over the smashed ruins of vehicles in the chamber.

"I could be worried about nothing," Dani said. "Maybe all that's going on here is stuff like this—old weapons, or whatever. And if that's it, then someday I can burn all the notes I've made from those tapes, and forget the whole thing, and never tell another soul. But if it's secret because of something else . . . something *wrong* . . . then I want to know. I want to know so I can tell somebody and put a stop to it."

She faced him again. Her eyes still had the film of moisture in them. For a second she seemed embarrassed by it; she reached to wipe at her eyes, but stopped and lowered her hand instead. She stood there in front of him, looking as vulnerable as anyone he'd ever seen, all defenses down.

"If you're wondering," she said, "yes, this scares the shit out of me. It was scary enough when I had a friend in on it with me, and for the past week, on my own, I've been more afraid than ever. I'll understand if you don't want anything to do with this, and I'm sorry for dragging you in, but I couldn't help it. I didn't want to be alone with it anymore."

She sniffled, blinked, looked down at her watch.

"We should get back," she said. "Don't decide yet. I want you to think about it."

She turned and moved off, back toward the stairwell door.

They didn't say much on the walk home. The stars wheeled overhead in the pitch-black sky, Vega and Deneb and however many billion others. Sam thought of what he'd seen in the underground chamber. He thought of his dad, waking up in a few hours to go to work, and do . . . what, exactly? What was his job now? What was *he* now?

Something he can't tell me, anyway.

He thought of Mr. Pierce's disappearance; everything he'd heard about it stood in new light now, throwing new shadows, and still making no sense at all.

He thought of Echo House, and the empty sandwich shop downtown—the downtown of a place that wasn't a town.

They passed the little park on the north edge of the subdivision. The empty swings moved in the night wind, creaking softly.

Three minutes later they were at the south end of the sideways rainbow of streets. There were no police cars waiting in Sam's driveway. No lights on in the house. Good signs. He and Dani moved past the street, out onto the slope, and came up to Sam's house from the back side. His screen still stood where he'd left it, leaning below the window. The two of them stopped a few feet away from it.

Dani turned to face him.

"There's something you should know," she said, "before you decide if you want to get caught up in all this."

He waited for her to continue.

"The past few days, in the recordings from my dad's office . . . it sounds like there's something going on. Something bad, I mean. Some kind of problem here in Ashland, happening right now."

"Like what?" Sam asked.

Dani shook her head. "I don't know. I only get to hear bits and pieces, but . . . it scares them, whatever it is. My dad sounds scared. So do the people he talks to. It's like there's something going wrong. And I think it's something big."

She was quiet a moment, then added, "It wouldn't be fair if I didn't tell you about that, before you make up your mind. And I meant what I said before: I won't blame you, if you want to stay the hell away from this stuff. I'll see you tomorrow."

She turned to go, even as she finished speaking.

"Hey," Sam said.

She stopped. Turned back to him.

"I'm with you," he said. "On all of this. Anything you do, I want to be part of it."

It was hard to see her face in this light—there was only the sodium-orange glow of the streetlamps downtown, half a mile away—but he could see her blinking fast. Then she took a deep breath and stepped forward and hugged him—tight. She held on, saying nothing. He could feel her shaking a little. Not quite crying, but just holding it back. He could hear it in her breathing, too. He held on to her, and they just stood there, and if there had ever been a better moment in his life, he couldn't think of it now.

"Thank you," she whispered.

"You're welcome," he said. It didn't come out sounding as tough as he wanted. He forced a laugh and said, "Hey, it's only treason, right?"

Dani laughed, too. She sniffled and finally let go. She drew back only a foot, and met his eyes. She managed her own forced-tough look.

"We're twelve," she said. "What can they do to us?"

PART THREE

THE MAN IN SHIPROCK FOREST

SEPTEMBER 2018

CHAPTER FIFTEEN

There were three college kids and a dog playing in the surf at Point Rojo. Dryden had the Explorer parked in a public lot overlooking the beach. There were a few restaurants clustered at the ends of the lot, to the left and right. It was mid-afternoon, and beneath the overcast sky the ocean was slate grey. There was nobody around but the kids and the dog—a big black Lab.

Dryden sat at the wheel. Danica was in the passenger seat. They had the windows down and the cool wind rushing through. They could hear the surf crashing, and the dog barking, jumping up after a Frisbee the kids were throwing back and forth.

Dryden shut his eyes and leaned back into the headrest.

They had driven for three hours after leaving Thousand Oaks. In the San Fernando Valley Dryden had gotten on I-5 and taken it north into the mountains, finally cutting west and coming out at the Pacific Coast Highway, far north of Los Angeles—far north of his home in El Sedero, too. Three aimless hours, staying mobile, while Danica read aloud the redaction-laced scrub file.

It was almost entirely meaningless. For page after page, the fragmented material told them nothing.

Which was no coincidence. No surprise, even.

Early on, they had stopped in West Hills and bought a notepad on which to jot down the bullet points—any scrap of useful information they found in the scrub file, anything that might help identify Persons 2855 and 2856, the two people who'd had their memories bleached out with narcotics.

That notepad had stayed empty until five minutes ago, when Danica reached the very end of the file: a single short paragraph that dropped like a lead weight in their laps.

She had read it out loud twice, the second time carefully, as if slowed by the drag-force of what the words implied.

Then she'd simply written it down on the notepad, verbatim. The sole bullet point. The one thing they could make sense of in the here and now.

Dryden had pulled into the lot overlooking the beach while she wrote it. He'd buzzed the windows down and killed the engine, and now they were just sitting here, letting it all crash into them like the breakers in the surf, over and over.

> *-Page 149. Full dosage was contra-indicated for both subjects (Person 2855, Person 2856) due to their age (subjects are 12, one male, one female) but on authority of the C.O. on scene, full dosage*

was deemed safe and was administered, with emergency personnel ready to intervene in case of adverse reaction.

Dryden read it, then read it again. He felt his own internal voice slowing down on the second pass, as Danica's real voice had done. Taking it all in. What it said. What it meant.

Finally he just stared through the windshield again.

Two of the college kids were sitting on the beach now. The other was still out in the waves, throwing the Frisbee for the dog to chase.

"I was in a car accident the summer after sixth grade," Dryden said. "July 1989. I was with my dad, and supposedly we got T-boned by some guy who fled the scene—they never caught him. My dad came through it unharmed, and I spent two weeks in a coma. When I woke up I couldn't remember the accident, or even the car ride. Actually it was worse than that. My memory going back even weeks and weeks before the accident was pretty much gone. I remember a doctor telling me that was normal, after what I'd been through."

The kid with the Frisbee threw it one last time and then headed in to the beach. The dog chased it down and plucked it out of the foam of a breaking wave.

"In those first days after I came out of the coma," Dryden said, "I remember asking my parents what had happened in those months I couldn't remember. The end of the school year, the whole first half of summer. All that stuff was blank. I remember my dad telling me we'd actually been planning to move, because his firm wanted to transfer him to some regional HQ somewhere. He said we were already at the new place, living there for a few days, when the car accident happened. In the aftermath of it, he and my mom decided against the move. Decided to come back to L.A. and let me recover there. They told me all that in passing, like the move was no big deal. They didn't really seem to want to talk about it. It was like, *Don't think about any of that stuff. Just focus on getting better. That's all that matters.* I remember friends saying, *Yeah, you left, we had the whole going away party and everything.* But compared to the accident itself, compared to almost dying, I hardly thought about the move at all. After the coma I spent a month mostly in bed, my brain still about halfway fogged over. By the time I was past all that, I don't think the subject of moving away ever came up again. My parents sure as hell never brought it up. It was just this weird little detail that came and went."

"Do you remember the name of the place? Where you moved to?"

Dryden shook his head. "If I ever heard it, it would have been during those weeks when my head was still cloudy. I don't remember ever asking about it, later on. After a while I never even thought about it."

His eyes trailed over the jotted bullet point again.

"Three or four months," he said softly. "If I had to pin it down, I'd say that's how big the gap in my memory was. Like early April to late July that year, 1989. I can remember looking back and trying to get a fix on the last thing I could recall before the coma, and it was spring break. After that there was nothing."

He looked up from the notepad and met Danica's gaze.

"When I saw this scrub file this morning," Dryden said, "none of this even occurred to me. All my life, I never once questioned whether that accident really happened. Why would I? And this morning it never even crossed my mind as a dot to connect to all this."

Danica looked away through the windshield. Dryden could still hear the dog barking, splashing around.

"Someone must have given my parents the same script they gave yours," she said. The disbelief was still there in her voice. "Hit and run accident, July 1989. Coma, screwed-up memory for the few months leading up to it. Everything from Easter to late July . . . gone. Like a bunch of pages torn out of a book."

Her eyes narrowed as she thought about it.

"My family moved to some new place, too, during the time I couldn't remember. For my dad's job. But I think I was actually there for a while—not just a few days. More like a few months. I remember my parents telling me we'd lived there almost the whole time I couldn't remember. They seemed kind of hung up on that, actually. Like they really, really wanted to know if I could remember any of it. In those weeks when I was recovering, they asked me about it all the time."

"*Did* you remember any of it?"

Danica shook her head. "Nothing. And they were weird about telling me anything, whenever *I* asked *them* about it. I remember finding that so odd. On the one hand, they wanted to know if any of it was coming back to me, but they never wanted to answer any of my questions about that place. They acted like none of it mattered. They might have even said what your parents said, word for word: *Focus on getting better. That's all that matters.*"

"They never told you the name of the place?"

"If they did, I don't remember. I really doubt they did, though. It's funny how things like that can work: if people keep dodging a subject long enough, you feel uncomfortable bringing it up. So it just . . . goes away. It did go away. I think after a while I just thought the subject bugged them because they'd almost lost me. It made sense, even. What parent wants to dwell on something like that? And I never really got to ask my old friends about it, because when we moved back to L.A., it was to a different area. I'd grown up in Long Beach, but we lived up in the valley after that summer. And then my parents got divorced, and my mom married Carl, and we lived in that house in Thousand Oaks. I don't think I ever talked to my friends from Long Beach after the coma. The whole thing was like a dividing line in my life. There was before, and there was after. And four months of nothing in between."

For thirty seconds neither spoke. They sat there, staring at the handwritten bullet point and the stacked pages of the scrub file.

Danica trailed her fingertip over the header. *WITNESS NULLIFICATION [C43-YANKEE]—PERSONS 2855 & 2856.*

"You and me," she said softly. "I guess we met back then, for however long. And neither one of us was in a traffic accident."

"I don't imagine we were," Dryden said. "No, somebody strapped us down on a gurney and pumped our veins full of that shit. Twelve years old. Jesus Christ."

"So we . . . witnessed something?" Danica asked. "You said that was why they used to do that, right? Because people saw something they weren't supposed to?"

"Yeah."

Danica rested a hand on the scrub file again. The pages and pages of redacted nothingness.

"What the hell did we witness?" she whispered. "What and where?"

"And why is someone trying to kill us over it now, after twenty-nine years?"

Dryden stared at the pages and tried to think of anyone who could help them look into it. Any old contact from his time in the military, who might be familiar with this kind of thing—any loose thread to pull on.

No one came to mind. Anyone old enough to have been involved in something like this—somebody with that level of clearance back in 1989—would probably be retired or dead by now.

"I don't know how we're supposed to dig into this," Dryden said. "I don't even know where to start."

Danica looked up through the windshield again, at the ashen water and the overcast.

"I might," she said.

CHAPTER SIXTEEN

Forty miles shy of Flagstaff, the mountains rose out of the desert like a shallow-sloping coastline above the sea, visible from the freeway in the light of a three-quarter moon. The slopes were covered with dense pine forest, marked here and there by the snaking routes of switchback roads leading upward, disappearing into the folds of the landscape.

It was just past ten o'clock at night. Dryden was driving. Danica was asleep in the reclined passenger seat; she had drifted off half an hour earlier.

Before that, they had talked for hours, all the way across California and a good chunk of Arizona. The talk had been practical at first: the specifics of where they were going, and who they hoped to meet there.

The *where* was Shiprock National Forest, not far ahead now, south and west of Flagstaff in the mountains that butted up against I-40.

The *who* was a man named Russell Moss. He had been a friend of Danica's father, years back, when they served in the Army together. Both men had left the service in the summer of 1989, a timeframe that was, at the very least, interesting. Danica's father, Richard Ellis, had become an FBI agent after his time in the Army. Russell Moss had become a vagrant. The way Danica understood it, her father had spent years trying to help the guy straighten his life out, strong-arming him into rehab programs and calling in favors to get him employment. Eventually Moss had gotten clean, socked away a bit of money, bought an old trailer and moved to Shiprock Forest, where there was some kind of encampment of like-minded people—those who, for whatever reasons, wanted the world to leave them alone.

Danica had met Moss herself once, in her early twenties, when she'd taken a road trip with her father. They had stopped for a few hours at the camp in Shiprock, located way off the beaten track; it was at the end of a Forest Service road, in a place called Somber Valley.

He didn't seem crazy or anything, Danica had told Dryden. *No one else there seemed crazy, either. They just seemed like people who'd figured out what made them comfortable, and for them, it was living out there, away from the rat race.*

Whether Moss would know anything useful about the summer of 1989 was the big question. Beyond the suspicious timing of his leaving the service, there wasn't much to pin a hope on. This was just the only move they had, right now.

Dryden glanced at Danica, still asleep. The two of them had spoken of other things during the drive, besides their present circumstances. They had talked about their lives. Danica had been married for most of her thirties, and had gotten divorced just over a year ago. She was taking classes at a satellite campus of Oregon State now, going for a business degree.

With the marriage behind her, she was on her own in the world—a handful of friends, but no relatives. She'd lost her mother almost twenty years back, and her father not quite five years ago. In the last year before he would have retired from the Bureau, the man decided to get his pilot's license. A few months into his new pastime—and a few months shy of his last day on the job—he rented a little Cessna 150 for a night flight out to Santa Catalina, twenty miles off the coast from Los Angeles. Halfway there, he dropped off of LAX's radar and stopped responding to radio calls. The Coast Guard eventually found parts of the plane—the pieces that could float—but, as expected, they never recovered Richard Ellis's remains.

Danica spoke of it in tight little sentences, the brushstrokes of someone long-since worn out by a subject. Then she talked about her plans for the new degree. Getting her feet back under herself, career-wise. Doing some traveling, maybe in a few years. She struck Dryden as someone trying hard to keep her focus aimed forward and not back—someone determined to be happy again, and working toward it as best she could.

He told her his own story, in broad terms. His time in the military. His life afterward—the good and the bad. When he talked about his wife and daughter, he heard himself lapse into the same tight brushstrokes

Danica had used a moment before. It was always hard to tell someone about Trisha and Erin. There was no way to say that your family had died, without making that person feel miserable for you. He said it and then moved past it; he talked about the last five years, flipping houses in little beach towns up the coast from L.A. The feeling of making things beautiful again—of enjoying nearly every day, even the hard ones, because you were always making headway, getting things done. He told her about the big Spanish villa in Malibu, and the work it would take to bring it back to life. When he described it, Danica looked as if she were picturing the place, taking it in.

Shc shifted in her sleep now. She rolled her head to the left, facing him, her eyes still closed. A lock of her bangs hung past one side of her face, moving a little in the air from the dash vents.

He tried to remember the last time someone had had this much of an impact on him, this quickly. He'd been in relationships, on and off for a few years now, trying to restart that part of his life. When he'd begun dating again, he hadn't expected to find the kind of connection he'd had with Trisha—they had met in high school—and so far, that expectation had been borne out. The relationships had all been fun enough, had all seemed worth trying, had all been just . . . fine. And with each of them, in the end, the lack of depth had been a mutual feeling. Every one of them had ended with a kind of shared shrug. *This was nice. Take care.*

There was something different about Danica Ellis. He had felt it right away, even through the adrenaline rush of those first minutes in Thousand Oaks. The feeling had persisted all day, pulling his attention to little details about her: the way her lower eyelids went up when she was focused on some thought; the vertical line that showed up in the middle of her forehead—not quite centered—when her eyebrows knitted together. Lots of things like that. He wondered if she had noticed him noticing. Wondered if she felt any connection at all in return.

Don't bring it up. Focus on living through this. Ask her about it later, if there's a later.

He glanced at her again, then let it go and studied the mountains coming up to meet them in the pale light.

She woke twenty minutes later. She yawned and stretched and rubbed her eyes, and stared ahead through the windshield at the change of scenery; she had fallen asleep with empty, dark desert around them, and now the headlights lit up a gravel road hemmed in by dense pines.

"Almost there," Dryden said.

Before Danica could reply, a pair of headlights rounded a curve in the narrow road, two hundred yards ahead through the trees. There would be just enough room for the two vehicles to get past each other, if they both slowed—but Dryden saw almost at once that the oncoming vehicle didn't mean to pass. It braked and came to rest in the center of the dirt road, its high beams blazing. Behind it, the red glow of its taillights lit up the encroaching trees, against which the vehicle's shape stood out in hard contrast—a midsize sedan.

Dryden brought the Explorer to a stop well short of the car. He shoved the selector into reverse instead of park, though he kept pressure on the brake pedal for the moment. If need be, he could gun the Explorer backward, make a J-turn and floor it in the other direction.

"Welcoming committee, I guess," Dryden said.

Danica nodded. "This happened when I came here with my father, too. I think they get nervous about outsiders."

Up ahead, both doors of the sedan opened. Against the taillight glow on the pines, Dryden made out the shapes of two men—big guys—getting out. A moment later they were moving through the glare toward the Explorer. Dryden could see their hands; they weren't holding any weapons at the moment. They wore light jackets, though, which might conceal shoulder holsters or guns stuffed into waistbands.

Dryden had two pistols in the Explorer: the one he'd taken from the gaunt man in Malibu, and the one Danica's stepfather had owned. Each was loaded, with a round in the chamber. He had one in the glove box and one in the center console tray, a few inches from his right hand. He took hold of the latter and tucked it out of view beneath his right leg—he could still get to it in an instant.

"Let's not assume the worst," Danica said. There was tension in her voice.

"Always be ready for it, though."

Twenty feet from the Explorer the two men split up, one moving toward each side of the vehicle.

Dryden buzzed his window down. He rested his right hand on the outside of his thigh, an inch above the grip of the concealed pistol, and waited.

The man that came to the driver's side door was in his sixties. He had close-cropped hair, which was bone white, and a goatee centered on a weathered face. He wore glasses that were about twenty years out of style.

"Folks lost?" the man asked.

"Doesn't look like it," Dryden said.

The guy stared at him for a moment, processing that answer. Finally the man said, "What's your business up here?"

"Russell Moss."

The man's eyes narrowed. "What do you want to see him about?"

"That's between us and him."

"Not yet it isn't. Not while I'm in your way."

Dryden started to reply to that, but Danica set a hand on his shoulder before he could speak. She leaned across him to look at the older man. He stooped down to see her through the open window.

Danica nodded toward the distant car. "Is that a C.B. antenna?"

Dryden looked. Danica had good eyes; the slender mast of the antenna was just visible, centered on the vehicle's roof.

"Yes, ma'am."

"Can you call the camp and talk to Moss?"

The man frowned. "Want to tell me what this is about?"

"Tell him Richard Ellis's daughter wants to see him," Danica said. "That should be good enough."

The guy frowned, thinking it over.

"Please," Danica said.

The man's gaze went back and forth between her and Dryden for another few seconds, and then he stood upright and walked back toward the sedan. The other man followed. The two of them got back into the vehicle and shut the doors, and for a long time nothing else happened. Dryden imagined the radio call going through. Imagined the reply, and whatever exchange followed it.

Five long minutes passed. Neither he nor Danica spoke. They just sat there, waiting, watching the road beyond the parked car.

Then the distant trees caught the glow of a new set of headlights—another vehicle coming along the road from up ahead. It rounded the curve and coasted to a stop behind the sedan. Its driver's door opened, and a lone man stood up from it. He strode past the car and angled across the field of its headlight glow, toward Dryden's side of the Explorer.

Dryden still had the window down. The guy came abreast of it, stooped and looked in at the two of them.

"Danica," the man said. Not a question.

Danica nodded. "Russell."

The man gave a single nod in reply.

Russell Moss was younger than Dryden had expected; the guy was in his mid-fifties, give or take. He had a lean face and thick brown hair. He wore jeans and a blue flannel shirt. He looked like a guy in the middle of a camping trip, which maybe he was, in a sense. His eyes, direct and unblinking, went back and forth from Danica to Dryden.

"This is Sam Dryden," Danica said.

Something passed through the man's expression at those words, if only for a second. It might have been simply a reaction to an unfamiliar name, though Dryden's gut told him there was more to it than that.

Moss looked at him, nodded quickly again, then looked back at Danica. "What's this about?"

"Can we sit down and talk with you?" Danica asked.

"You're sitting now. I'm fine standing."

"You know what I mean." Danica nodded ahead along the road. "Let us in. We need to talk."

Moss shook his head. "I'd just as soon get it settled right here, and then you can be on your way. Camp gets a little spooked when strangers show up."

"I'm not a stranger," Danica said. "My father—"

"Your father was a friend of mine. You're not. So whatever you want to talk about, talk about it. Here and now's good enough."

Dryden considered informing the guy that this was actually public land, despite whatever territorial pissings he and his friends had marked it with. He also considered grabbing him by the hair, hauling him halfway through the open window and ramming his face into the steering wheel three or four times to knock some politeness into him.

Instead he locked eyes with the guy and spoke

evenly. "Tell us what happened in the summer of 1989. Tell us what happened to *us*."

Dryden saw the same reaction he'd seen earlier, at the mention of his own name. It looked like recognition and surprise mixed together, and then a forced calm meant to hide both.

"I don't know what you're talking about," Moss said.

"Bullshit," Dryden said.

Moss had been leaning down with his hands on the Explorer's door. Now he pushed off and stood upright, backing off a pace. "It's time for you to leave," he said. "I can't help you, and I'm not going to be talked to like this."

He turned away without waiting for a reply, and set off back toward his vehicle.

Danica cursed under her breath and shoved open the door on her side. Dryden did the same, leaving the pistol where it lay on the driver's seat. By the time he'd stepped around his own open door, he could see Danica already running to catch up to Moss. The man stopped and turned to face her.

Far beyond the two of them, the guys in the sedan got out again, but for the moment they made no move to get involved.

"Listen, we came a long way to see you," Danica said. "The least you can do—"

"It's not my problem where you came from."

Dryden caught up to where they stood. He stopped three feet from Moss, forming the third corner of a triangle.

Danica had a look on her face Dryden hadn't seen there yet. Her eyes were intense and her cheeks were a little flushed. She was pissed off. Like all expressions, he liked how it looked on her.

Facing Moss, Danica said, "Let's talk about where *you* came from. Let's talk about the gutter you were crawling around in before my dad pulled you out of it. You'd be dead by now if it weren't for him."

"Yes," Moss said. "So what?"

"So you owe him. But he's gone now, so you owe me instead."

Moss actually laughed: a low, sharp breath that conveyed what he thought of that logic.

"Have a good night," he said, then turned and started walking again.

"People are trying to kill us," Danica said.

Moss stopped. For a second he stayed facing away, as if deciding whether to turn back to her or just keep going. Then his shoulders sagged. He turned in place and looked at her again.

Danica nodded toward Dryden. "We have a document that says we witnessed something twenty-nine years ago, in the summer of '89. And now somebody wants to kill us over it, whatever the hell it was that we saw, and you're the only person in the world we can think of to ask about it." She took a step closer to him, and when she spoke again her voice was softer. "You know something. I could see that in how you reacted a minute ago. You know what happened back then—or some part of it. You know *something*. Don't tell me you don't."

Moss held her gaze for another two seconds and then looked away, into the night.

"Help us," Danica said. "We're in the dark against these people. We don't know who they are, we don't know what they want, we don't know anything at all. We're going to die if we don't get some answers."

Moss shut his eyes tight, and rubbed the bridge of his nose with his finger and thumb.

Danica took another step toward him. "We were just little kids when this happened to us. Twelve years old, and they gave us a drug to fry our fucking brains. It could have killed us, and they did it anyway. Those are the kind of people we're up against."

Moss opened his eyes and looked at her. "You're wrong about that part," he said, his own voice going soft. "The people who are after you didn't give you the drug."

Danica traded a look with Dryden, then stared at Moss again. "What do you mean? How can you know that?"

"I know because I'm the one who drugged you," Moss said.

CHAPTER SEVENTEEN

For a long moment there was no sound except the idling engines. The wind picked up through the pines, cold at this altitude.

"Both of you," Moss said, turning to look at Dryden as well as Danica. "I administered the drug to both of you. Same time and place. July 1989. Ashland, Iowa."

Danica mouthed the name of the town, glancing at Dryden as she did. "I've never heard of it," she said.

"You have," Moss said. "You just don't remember."

Dryden searched his own memory for anything about a town with that name in Iowa. Nothing came to him. Which was no surprise, really.

"That must be where our families moved to," Dryden said, looking at Danica. "Mine and yours."

She nodded, thinking it through.

"You wanted to sit down and talk," Moss said. "Alright. Follow me. I'll tell you every part of it that I know, but I won't promise it'll be enough."

The sedan pulled to the edge of the road to let the Explorer past. Beyond it, Moss's vehicle—an old white

F-150 pickup, covered with rust—backed up and made a three-point turn and lumbered off down the gravel lane. Dryden followed.

The road climbed for half a mile, wandering back and forth with the terrain, and then descended sharply through a series of switchbacks. Through the open window, Dryden could feel the air outside change, becoming more humid as they made their way down. Somber Valley had a microclimate of some kind, the landscape channeling the prevailing winds in some particular way.

They followed the F-150 through one last switchback, and all at once they cleared the trees and saw the camp. It lay a quarter mile ahead, spread out along the banks of a river at the bottom of the valley. From this distance it was just a spill of lights—low-wattage bulbs and campfires flickering in the darkness. Danica buzzed her own window down as they drew closer; the course of the dirt road would take them along the near edge of the camp.

A minute later the first structures of the settlement went by: an old Airstream trailer probably from the 1950s; an RV a few decades newer than that, with a big awning unfurled over a picnic table; something that looked like a Quonset hut cobbled together atop a cinderblock foundation. Beside nearly every home, people hunkered around campfires in little groups, cooking hot dogs or burger patties. Every pair of eyes followed the Explorer as it went by. In the firelight, every face looked wary: men and women, mostly middle-aged or older.

Moss pulled in next to an old camping trailer. It had wheels, but at the moment its frame rested on squat piles of bricks. It appeared to be his home; there was no other structure on his lot.

Dryden pulled in behind the F-150 and killed the Explorer's engine. He and Danica got out, and Moss gestured to a firepit next to the trailer, with plastic lawn chairs scattered around it. There was a bed of embers burning low under a metal grate across the fire, where Moss had probably cooked his dinner sometime this evening.

"Let's talk," Moss said.

They sat in the plastic chairs, and Moss set a few pieces of firewood onto the embers in the pit. He watched until they caught, and flames licked up through the metal grate.

"Hungry?" Moss asked them. "Thirsty?"

Dryden and Danica both shook their heads; they had hit an Arby's off I-40, just before Danica fell asleep.

Moss stared at the fire for a long time, looking focused. Trying to assemble the details, maybe.

"Can you start with what happened?" Danica asked. "Whatever we witnessed in that town—Ashland, you called it?"

"It wasn't a town," Moss said softly. His gaze stayed fixed on the flames. "Not really, anyway. I guess it looked like one. It was supposed to."

Danica glanced at Dryden, confused. He could only shake his head; he had no idea what the man was talking about.

Danica said, "I'm not sure I follow—"

"Ashland was an R & D site," Moss said. "For black-budget defense stuff. Maybe illegal stuff. I wasn't privy to the specifics. But on the surface it just looked like some little town. Like nothing special. A dark site—that's the term I heard for it."

"Are you saying it was a military place?" Danica asked.

Moss nodded. He leaned closer to the fire, holding his hands out to it.

Dryden started to ask something, then stopped himself. He stared absently at the heat-rippled air above the metal grate, thinking.

All afternoon and evening, since he'd first understood that he and Danica were the witnesses who'd had their memories scrubbed, the obvious question had troubled him: how could he have witnessed anything in the first place? How could he have been within a thousand miles of government secrets, when he was twelve years old?

For Danica the connection had seemed clearer: at least her father had been in the military.

For Dryden it was a different story: his mother had served on the boards of a handful of charities, and his father had been an attorney for his entire professional life—a very successful one, working for corporate clients in Los Angeles, including a few movie producers and actors.

But if his father had moved the family to Ashland, Iowa, because his job demanded it, and if Ashland was a military post—

Did that mean his father had actually worked for the military? Without Dryden ever finding out?

On the face of it, the idea seemed ludicrous. The image of Ben Dryden in a uniform, going through weapons training, crawling in the mud under razor-wire during a live-fire exercise—none of it matched the bookish, manicured mental picture Dryden had of the man.

Of course his father wouldn't have actually had to be *in* the military to work for them. The armed forces did business with civilian contractors all the time, including lawyers.

He thought about it a moment longer and then pushed it away for the time being. He turned to Moss.

"What exactly did we witness there?" Dryden asked.

It took a while for Moss to begin speaking again. He once more took on the look of someone revisiting old knowledge—sorting photos in some shoebox in his head.

"There was an accident," the man said. "Something they were working on, out there . . . it went bad. Real bad. It was a mass-casualty event, some number of deaths, a huge number of injuries. Whatever it was, it happened the night of July 20, 1989."

"You don't *know* what it was?" Danica asked.

Moss shook his head. "Maybe you misunderstand—I wasn't actually stationed at Ashland. I wasn't cleared for that kind of work. I was a twenty-six-year-old corporal based at Fort Leland, fifty miles east of there. About an hour before dawn on the twenty-first, they woke up everyone on my base and trucked us out to Ashland—or close to it, at least. They had us man the roadblocks that were going up by then. They set up what they called an exclusion zone around the accident site, at a radius of three miles from Ashland on all sides. They blocked every road. Nobody got in or out without clearance."

Dryden took in the words. Tried to get his head around the implications—the scale of an accident that would require that kind of response.

"Jesus," he whispered.

"My unit was assigned to a roadblock straight north of town," Moss said. "I think it was the major county road that went right through Ashland. I couldn't see the town from there, and for a while there was no word at all, as far as what had happened. Then some of the higher-ups put together a kind of headquarters right there, near that blockade, in a field next to the road. A whole bunch of tents, generator trucks, comm equipment. I overheard just a bit of what was happening inside the town. They said there were buses going in to bring out the wounded and the dead, and taking them to triage sites on the southern boundary of the exclusion zone."

Dryden watched Danica's reaction to all of it. It seemed to match his own: a struggle to take in the magnitude of the thing.

"I asked one of the men in charge if I could be transferred down there," Moss said, "to where they were treating the casualties. I was the medic for my unit; I'd been through med school on a military scholarship. I'd actually just finished up my required time in the

Army, for that scholarship, which meant I could quit if I wanted to. But as of that morning, I was still planning to stay in for a while. A few more years, maybe. Anyway, they told me to stay put on the roadblock. They didn't need any help, thanks."

Far away across the camp, a handful of people laughed. A joke over a fire somewhere. Dryden barely heard it. He kept his focus on Moss.

"For a long time not much else happened," Moss said. "We got those little bits of news, like drips out of a faucet. Nothing more. Finally, a couple hours after sunrise, two MPs in an open Jeep came up the road out of Ashland, and parked. When they got out, I could see the back seat. That's when I saw you two."

At last the man lifted his gaze from the firepit. He looked back and forth between Dryden and Danica, maybe trying to reconcile their faces with those of the two children in his memory.

"You weren't hurt," Moss said. "Not physically. But you looked awful. You looked like you'd been through something no little kid should ever go through. I remember thinking you had the thousand-yard stare that soldiers talk about. Shell-shock."

A couple in their sixties wandered past on the dirt road, with a small dog on a leash. Moss nodded at them; he waited for them to pass by before he spoke again.

"The two MPs from the Jeep went and talked to some of the higher-ranking guys in the tents. I didn't hear what they said, but pretty soon after that, the two of you were taken inside those tents, somewhere out of sight. And around that time, the whole atmosphere around that little command center seemed to change. I could tell, even from outside. There was a lot of activity, a lot of tension. At one point a chopper touched down, and the crew offloaded a bunch of medical equipment cases. Mostly what I remember, though, was the body language of the people in charge. The whole thing just had this panic-mode feel to it. Like a lot of very powerful people were sweating something, and whatever it was, the two of you were in the middle of it."

Moss drew away from the flames and sat back in his chair. The move darkened his features, putting his face mostly into shadow.

"That's when I got dragged into it," he said softly. "One of the senior officers came out to the roadblock and pulled me aside, asked me to repeat my medical credentials. Then he took me to one of the tents, and inside I saw the two of you strapped down in restraints, with all that field hospital gear from the chopper set up and running next to you. You were looking at me like I was some monster, there to kill you."

Moss's gaze hardened on the last few words, his eyes fixed on the firepit again. From where Dryden sat, the reflection of the flames made it look as if Moss's eyes were actually burning.

"I'd heard of witness nullification," Moss said. "It was like an urban legend in the service, especially among medics. I didn't think it had been done for years and years—and maybe it hadn't. But they had the drugs right there, alongside all that equipment they'd flown in. They ordered me to administer them, and then watch over you both in case things went bad."

Moss looked down at his hands, which were interlaced atop his knees.

"I could have refused the order," he said. "And if they ordered someone else to do it, I could have gone up the chain of command and ratted them all out. Only . . . how far up would I have to go? The decision to use those drugs had probably come *down* from somewhere up there. I thought about picking up a phone, instead, and calling a reporter. But in the end, I didn't do any of that. I was too chickenshit to step out of line and disobey."

He breathed out slowly, his eyes still cast down.

"There should have been a whole team of doctors and nurses watching over you two," he said, "after I gave you the drugs. But it wasn't like that. It was all just kind of thrown together, jury-rigged. It felt like . . . like none of it was official. Like it couldn't afford to be. So no team of doctors and nurses. No, it was just me there. For the next thirty-six hours I was in that tent, monitoring your heart rates and breathing and everything else."

Moss looked up at Danica, and Dryden saw that his eyes had filmed over.

"Three hours in, Danica, you went into V-fib—cardiac arrest. I had to use the defibrillator on you two different times. I didn't think there was a chance in hell you'd get through that first day."

He glanced at Dryden. "You seemed to respond a little better, but it was still touch-and-go for a while. I didn't start to feel confident about either one of you until midway through the next morning. Finally, when you were both in the clear, they took you away somewhere, and that was that. They gave me a nondisclosure form to fill out, and told me I'd face capital punishment if I ever talked about what happened. I signed the form, and then I turned in my resignation. I told myself I could put all this shit behind me, go be a doctor like I always planned, and not let the memory get under my skin."

He wiped at his eyes with the knuckles of one hand, blinked a few times, breathed out through his teeth.

"I should've asked them to use those fucking drugs on *me,*" he said.

"I should've asked them to use those fucking drugs on me."

Not quite a mile away from Russell Moss's campfire, by line-of-sight, a man in a dark green coat listened to those words through his headset.

The man was looking down on the encampment in Somber Valley from a pine-covered hillside to the east, his elevation maybe six hundred feet higher.

The audio was coming to him by way of a Wraith 406 quad-rotor drone, tricked out with surveillance hardware; the drone was the size of a Saltine cracker and not much heavier. It made zero sound, and it was engineered so that the draft from its rotors would cool all the working components to ambient temperature; even high-end thermal cameras could not detect it in flight. At the moment, the Wraith wasn't in flight anyway: five minutes earlier, the man in the green coat had landed it on top of Russell Moss's camper.

The man had been stationed up here in the pines all day long, and now into the night; he and his team had been sent to recon this place soon after Danica Ellis evaded her second attempted kidnapping, this morning in Thousand Oaks, probably with help from the other target, Dryden.

The man in the green coat had been given those orders by his employer, whose name he didn't know and never would—*nobody* knew that guy's name.

I put their odds of showing up there at better than fifty percent, the employer had said. *It's a logical place to look for answers, and it's plausible the Ellis woman would think of it.*

The man in the green coat had positioned his team carefully after arriving this morning. He had put his spotters high above the single road leading into the valley, and set himself up right here for the stakeout, far from the sprawl of campers and trailers and cobbled-together shacks below.

Now he simply watched. And waited. He had a pair of Zeiss binoculars which he trained on Moss's lot every few minutes, while he listened through the headphones. When Dryden and the Ellis woman left, he would easily see and hear it. His cell phone already had the word *Now* entered into its texting app; he needed only to switch it on and tap SEND, and the message would reach his spotters—no longer high above the exit road but tucked down right next to it, three miles away from the makeshift encampment along the river.

Get them alive if possible, the employer had said. *Dead if it's all you can do. And take the warnings about Dryden seriously—his military background is considerable. There's a six-year chunk of it even we can't get access to.*

The man in the green coat shut his eyes and listened to the crackling campfire over the headset. He wasn't worried. His men would have every possible advantage, and yes, they would be careful. They knew all about being careful.

For over a minute, none of the three spoke. Dryden replayed in his head what Moss had told them. He understood it well enough, though coming to grips with it was a different matter.

Danica looked up across the fire at Moss. "Did my father serve with you at Fort Leland?"

"Richard? No, he was based right there at Ashland."

Danica seemed confused. "But I thought you two served together. I thought you were old friends."

Moss shook his head. "No, ma'am. I never met him at all until about two years after the incident there. By then I was in a detox place in Phoenix, trying to get clean, and he was an FBI agent. He tracked me down, came to visit me, said he knew I was the one who'd given you the shots. For a minute I thought he might be there to kill me, but he told me not to worry about that. He said as far as he was concerned, I'd saved your life. If they had given my orders to somebody else, that person might have lost you."

"He tracked you down just to tell you that?" Danica asked.

Moss shook his head again. "No, he had a lot more

on the agenda than that. He wanted information. Anything I could remember about that day outside the accident site. Names of people in charge, things I'd overheard them say. Everything. And yeah, he knew it would mean breaching my nondisclosure agreement."

Dryden said, "You mean he wanted to know who gave the orders to drug us. The people who almost killed his daughter. Was he hoping to expose them?"

Moss rubbed a hand over his chin. "Not exactly. I'm sure he would have liked to see those people behind bars, or worse, but what Richard wanted was more basic than just settling a score. He wanted to know what the hell happened that night, in Ashland."

"He didn't already know?" Danica asked. There was incredulity in her voice. "He saw it with his own eyes, didn't he? Wasn't he there when it happened?"

"He was there," Moss said. "To hear him tell it, just about every survivor of the accident came away only half understanding it. Like it was all chaos at the time it went down—whatever it was. As for the parts he *did* know about, I never asked him to tell me. By that point, years after the event, I didn't want to know any more about it. I wanted to get it behind me, if I could."

"But Richard wanted to know all of it?" Dryden asked. "Is that what you're saying? He had part of the picture, and he wanted to fill in the gaps?"

"That's not quite what I mean," Moss said. "Richard was after something specific. He wanted to know what *you two* saw."

Danica glanced at Dryden, then back at Moss.

"What *we* saw?" The question in her tone spoke for itself. She watched Moss and waited for him to go on.

"There were three or four hundred people living in Ashland when the accident happened," Moss said. "But the government didn't use the memory drugs on any of them. Just the two of you. Whatever happened the night of July twentieth, 1989, all those people were witnesses to it. Whether or not they understood it, they saw it. But you two got drugged because you saw something else that night. Something a lot worse."

CHAPTER EIGHTEEN

Dryden could see a thousand questions in Danica's eyes—probably the same thousand he wanted to ask.

To Moss, he said, "What are you talking about? What would be worse than a mass-casualty event?"

"I don't know," Moss said. "Neither did Richard, but he knew that was the reason they used the drugs on you. He got that from more than one source, later on. You two witnessed some specific event—something none of the rest saw. Whatever it was, it was worse than the accident. The military sure as hell thought it was worse—or more important to keep secret, anyway. They were willing to risk your lives to hide it."

"When you say this was . . . something no one else saw," Danica said, "you don't mean some totally unrelated thing, some other event that happened by coincidence—"

Moss shook his head. "No, it was part of the accident itself. That's how Richard understood it. Some terrible little wrinkle of the thing, that had to stay secret at any cost. And getting to that secret—that was what he wanted. He was obsessed with it, I think. He was taking big risks looking for the answers, talking to anyone he hoped he could trust. People like me, and people he'd served with in Ashland. That went on for years. Sometimes he'd come here just to show me a personnel photo he'd gotten hold of, and ask me if I'd seen that face at the command center, near that roadblock. He'd do anything just to get one more little scrap of info."

Dryden saw something settle into Danica's expression. The weight of some ugly idea that had just come to her. She shut her eyes like someone fighting a headache.

"You alright?" Dryden asked.

She nodded, opening her eyes again. "I just always thought—" She turned to Moss. "I thought my father helped you get back on your feet because you were a friend. But the way you make it sound . . ."

She trailed off, as if she didn't want to say the rest.

Moss seemed to understand.

"Please don't get me wrong," he said. "I think your father was a good guy. He probably *would* have done that for a friend, just to help. But I wasn't a friend. I was a source. I'd like to believe he helped me turn things around as some kind of, I don't know, repayment for the information I gave him. But if I'm being honest with you, I think he just found me useful, and it would have run against his interests if I overdosed in a ditch somewhere."

The impact those words had on Danica was subtle but unmistakable—like a shove off balance, but taken in stride. Some heroic image of her father had just been put in stark relief, revealing imperfections. She blinked a few times and seemed to move past it for the moment.

Dryden turned to Moss. "Did Richard ever tell you things he'd learned? About this other thing Danica and I saw?"

Moss shook his head. "Like the rest of it, I didn't want to know."

"Can you tell us what he asked you about?" Danica said. "Anything you remember might help us."

Moss thought about it. "There was an Army investigation into the accident. I knew that much, from his questions. It's no surprise; there'd *have* to be an inquiry, after a mess like that. After a while, it seemed like Richard was focused on that investigation more than anything else. He seemed desperate to learn whatever he could about it. Was it still an open case? What were the names of those working on it? What information did they have? I guess that made sense. If he wanted answers, that was the basket with all the eggs in it."

Moss made a face—the equivalent of a shrug. "And that's it," he said. "Now you know as much as I know."

A long silence played out. To Dryden, it felt as if they were parked and idling at a dead end.

"Does any of this tell us why someone would be after us now?" Danica asked. "It feels like it could still be anyone."

Dryden nodded but said nothing.

"Could it just be the military trying to finish the job?" Danica asked. "As in, they drugged us twenty-nine years ago to shut us up, and now they're saying, 'Screw it, let's be thorough and just get rid of them.'"

"Seems like a stretch," Dryden said. "Even for people like that."

"Then who?" Danica asked. "And why?"

"Those are always the most important questions," Dryden said.

But he had no answers. No solid guesses, even. For another long moment, no one spoke.

Then Moss seemed struck by something. He looked at Danica.

"You were the next of kin, right?" he asked. "When your father died?"

"The only kin."

"So you must have gotten all his stuff."

"Yes," Danica said. "Why?"

"Was there a three-ring binder? It would have been blue leather, about the size of those little day-planners people used to carry around. Like five by seven inches."

Danica thought hard about it, then shook her head. "I don't remember anything like that."

"He brought it with him every time he came here," Moss said. "It was full of his notes. I remember thinking, *I bet that's the only place he writes any of this stuff down. I bet there's not a word of this on any computer, any place someone could be recording keystrokes or getting into his files.* That binder would contain everything he ever learned about the accident, whatever that amounted to."

Danica still looked like she was trying to remember. Her eyes seemed focused intensely on empty space in front of her. But she could only shake her head again.

"I just can't remember ever seeing it," she said.

"Even the one time I came here with him—although I'm pretty sure I took a long hike in the woods by myself, while you two talked."

She went quiet, frowning. "No," she said at last. "There was no binder like that in his house when he died. I would have looked through it. And I'm pretty sure the contents would have jumped out at me."

Dryden turned to Danica. "What if he didn't keep it in his house? When you told me he died, you said he was still with the Bureau. He hadn't retired yet."

"Yeah."

"So maybe he kept the binder at work. Secure storage in an FBI field office would be safer than his house."

"But I still should have seen it. The Bureau sent me a box of his personal belongings from the office, everything he—"

She stopped herself, looking almost embarrassed.

"Right," she said.

Dryden nodded. "They would have checked all of his things before giving them to you. For any agent, there could be sensitive material there. And in his case, if they found a binder of notes about all this stuff—the things we're talking about . . ."

He trailed off, thinking. He imagined Richard Ellis's superiors going through his personal effects after he died. Saw them finding that binder: pages and pages of military secrets he had gathered, off-duty and against the law, all while he had worked under their supervision as a federal agent. What would they have done?

He could see Danica thinking about it, probably

along the same lines. Possibly coming to the same conclusions—or guesses, anyway.

"Look, maybe they never saw the thing," Dryden said. "Maybe your dad kept it in a safe-deposit box, and it's still sitting there. But if his superiors *did* find it, it should have scared the hell out of them. They should have worried that if anyone found out about it, they'd get dragged in front of Congress and grilled. *Why was one of your agents digging into stuff like this? Why didn't you know what he was up to?* They'd probably expect to get fired just for being there, so the public could see a few heads roll. That stuff happens all the time."

"So what would they have done with it?" Danica asked. "Burned it?"

"Maybe. Or just sat on it and hoped no one ever came looking for it. Either way, it wouldn't be hard for us to figure out who could have seen it, inside the Bureau. Anyone assigned to review your father's belongings would need to have at least his level of clearance, and they'd have to know his caseload. I'm guessing it would just be his boss, or his boss's boss."

"I'd say that was Carl, my stepfather," Danica said, "except he retired years before my dad died. I don't know who any of his superiors were, at the end."

"We could sure as hell find out," Dryden said.

"Are you saying we should go to the FBI?" Danica asked. "Tell them everything, and put ourselves in their hands?"

Dryden thought about it a moment longer, then exhaled deeply; the sound of it betrayed his own anxiety.

"Christ," he said. "I don't want to. Without knowing who's after us, it's like chaining ourselves to a stake."

"Would the FBI even take us seriously?"

"They already are," Dryden said. "Or at least they're taking *you* seriously."

Danica looked puzzled.

"They've got a crime scene with four dead bodies in Thousand Oaks," Dryden said. "One of those, your stepdad, is a former FBI agent. Another one's a cop, and the last two are hired killers who probably have damned interesting records. Then there's your car outside, with out-of-state plates, and no sign of you. Right there, I can think of at least two reasons the FBI would take charge of that scene, and I'm sure you're at the top of the list of people they'd like to speak with."

She was nodding, taking it in.

Dryden went over the logic of it himself—the idea of showing all their cards, and entrusting their lives to the FBI. Earlier in the day, when he had first seen the scrub file in that basement in Thousand Oaks, his instinct had been to run—he simply hadn't believed the police could handle the situation, whatever the hell it was. It had seemed suicidal to go into their custody while someone out there—someone powerful and connected enough to know about scrub files—wanted them dead or captured. It had made sense to stay mobile until they had more information.

Now they had it. They knew about Ashland, and they had the date of the accident in 1989. They knew there had been a military investigation. They knew about the binder, and they could push for the names of whoever might have seen it, within the Bureau.

All that stuff added up to strings that could be pulled—but he and Danica couldn't pull any of them. The FBI could.

He looked at her and saw her wrestling with the idea. She looked up and met his gaze.

"What if the people after us are *in* the government?" she asked. "We're both wondering it. What if they have friends in the FBI?"

"Then we die. This move is risky as hell. Trust always is."

Danica looked nervous but in control.

"As if we're not taking a risk being on our own, right?" she said.

"There's an FBI field office in Phoenix," Dryden said. "We can be there in a couple hours."

Danica nodded, then pushed her fingers through her hair and lowered her head. She sat there like that, her hands encasing her head as if she were about to scream.

But she didn't. She spoke quietly instead. "Tell me the best-case scenario if we do this. I just want to hear it."

"Best case is a hundred FBI agents with guns watching out for us. I'll take those survival odds."

"Best case is a hundred FBI agents with guns watching out for us. I'll take those survival odds."

The man in the green coat smiled, then couldn't stop himself from laughing softly.

"Worst-case scenario coming your way," he whispered.

CHAPTER NINETEEN

Danica stared through the windshield as Dryden backed the Explorer out of Moss's lot. She could see the lights of the encampment all along the river; most of them had gone out for the night, and the fires, too. She and Dryden both had their windows down, and the damp, smoky scent of wet embers came drifting through the vehicle. It reminded her of camping trips with friends, years ago.

Dryden cut the wheel and braked and put the vehicle in drive, but kept it still for a moment. He looked at Moss, standing a few feet away.

"We won't mention your name," Dryden said.

"If you have to," Moss said, "go ahead. I've hidden from this long enough."

"Richard Ellis was right, you know," Dryden said. "About you saving our lives. If you'd refused to give us those drugs, they would have gotten someone else to do it. And we'd have probably died."

Danica watched Moss's reaction to the words: something like a shrug and a nod that seemed to say, *Thanks, whether or not I deserve it.*

Dryden gave him a quick wave and then let off the brake, and a moment later they were rolling past the scattered lights and fires that still glowed.

The image of long-ago camping trips was still in Danica's head. How long had it been since she'd last done that? Ten years? More? All at once she pictured herself and Dryden camping somewhere, just the two of them, after all of this was over with.

You like him. Admit it to yourself, anyway.

Yeah, she liked him. She was pretty sure that feeling had been there almost from the moment he'd shown up in Carl's basement. He had saved her life in about as dramatic a fashion as someone could, so there was one reason not to trust her emotions just yet. And really the adrenaline rush of those first moments had only halfway faded, even now. The situation had persisted—the life-and-death aspect of it all, hanging over them like a blade. None of that lent itself to clear thinking when it came to sorting out feelings. Nor should it, obviously. It wasn't the time to think about that stuff.

Alright, stick a pin in it for later. But you do like him, and it's not the adrenaline talking.

She glanced over at him, then looked away again.

They were five minutes from the camp. Outside the open windows, there was nothing but pitch-black woods going by. In the headlights, the gravel lane began climbing into the high country above the river, skirting the face of the valley wall. On the right side of the road, the ground angled upward into the dark at forty-five degrees, the slope choked with pine trunks. On the left side there was simply a drop-off: a perfect black void with a few treetops hovering in it.

"I wish I could remember us as kids," Danica said. "I mean when we knew each other. Even if it was just a few days."

Up ahead, the road curved sharply. Dryden slowed, coming toward it. He seemed about to reply, and then the vehicle made the turn and its headlights washed over a fallen pine thirty feet away, entirely blocking the road.

Dryden locked up the brakes; the Explorer's tires bit into the loose gravel and then slid, bringing the vehicle to rest just shy of the deadfall. Out in front, dust from the road swirled upward into the headlight beams.

For maybe a second, everything was silent. It was enough time for Danica to think, *Maybe it's nothing, maybe it's a coincidence, maybe it just happened to fall—*

And then through her open window she heard movement—in the darkness just to her right, somebody scrambling fast down the wooded slope. Coming right toward the vehicle.

She felt panic rising inside her, her pulse thudding in her ears. She turned to Dryden and saw him staring straight ahead into the dust. He didn't look panicked—not even caught off guard. There was nothing in his eyes but concentration. He looked like someone doing a math problem in his head—rapidly.

Then he took a fast breath, in and out, and reached for her with his right hand. For a second she had the crazy impression that he meant to hold hands with her—but all he did was take hold of her seat belt and snug it tightly against her chest.

"Sam—"

She didn't get to finish it. In the next instant, Dryden hauled left on the steering wheel, took his foot off the brake and slammed it down on the gas pedal.

"Sam, wait—*SAM*—"

The vehicle lunged forward through its turn, the headlights sweeping out into the darkness above the drop-off—the void full of hovering treetops—and then the front wheels went over the edge and Danica felt the world drop sickeningly out from under her.

She was aware of herself screaming. Aware of her seat suddenly tipping impossibly downward, like the scoop of an earth-mover dumping its load. Both of her feet shot forward reflexively, jamming hard against the wall of the footwell beneath the dash. For a moment she screwed her eyes shut, and then by some compulsion she opened them again, and saw nothing but pine boughs rushing at her. They bent and rode up over the Explorer's hood, scraping past the windshield. Some of them—the bigger ones—jarred the vehicle and sent it skidding left or right.

They're slowing us down, she thought, *but we're still going fast. We're going very fucking fast and—*

The impact.

Like the end of the world in half a heartbeat.

The airbags exploded around her, and the seat belt slammed across her chest like a two-by-four. She felt the Explorer's back end throw itself upward and then come crashing back down, the movement threatening to crack her head against the underside of the roof—but the seat belt held her fast. A second later, everything came to rest, the transition almost as jarring as the impact had been. She was still in her seat, held in place by the belt, the world around her almost impossibly calm.

She sucked in a breath and immediately started coughing—the air was thick with gasoline fumes, coming in through the empty frame of the windshield.

And smoke. From where, she couldn't tell.

She was still coughing when she felt Dryden's hands take hold of her—felt them patting down her arms and then her upper legs.

"Are you hurt? Can you feel everything?"

She blinked and looked up and saw him right there in front of her, leaning across the console and facing her.

"Is anything numb?" he asked. His speech was quick, urgent.

Danica shook her head. "Don't think so."

Dryden unlatched her seat belt and she tilted forward into him; he got a hold of her and guided her across the console toward the open door on his side.

"You're doing good," he whispered. "Come on, we have to move fast."

He helped her past the steering wheel, and the hanging shreds of airbags, and the pebbles of tempered glass that covered everything. The light inside the vehicle was chaotic: warning lights on the dashboard flashing out through the wispy smoke—strobing reds and blues and greens.

He held on to her as she stepped outside; her foot

came down onto tilted ground, slipped a few inches, came up firm against a tree root.

From somewhere right behind her, beneath the vehicle, came a guttural sound—like a gas grill igniting.

"Go," Dryden whispered.

He guided her away from the vehicle along the face of the slope, straight out from the driver's door. A few seconds later, the forest around them bloomed with bright orange light. Danica felt the radiant heat of the fire—like sunlight on a hot day. She and Dryden were nearly running now; it was easy to see the ground and the trees, all of it alive and jittering in the light of the flames. Danica glanced back and got her first good look at the wreck: the Explorer was pointed downhill on the slope, its front end compressed around the trunk of a pine. The entire vehicle was ablaze.

In the same moment she heard a man's voice, high above in the dark woods, calling out to someone. Another distant voice answered, though the words were indiscernible.

Danica faced forward and kept running, keeping up with Dryden over the steep ground and exposed roots.

As they ran, she found herself holding on to a single hope: that they could outrun the light. That if they could cover even fifty yards before the attackers made it down the slope, she and Dryden would simply be invisible in the dark. After that, they could just keep moving—all night long if need be.

The idea had hardly formed when the faint light around them suddenly flared brighter—almost absurdly so.

She looked back again and saw why: the pine boughs directly above the Explorer were now burning, too. Brilliant flames curled upward into the higher branches, which themselves were beginning to catch. Even at this distance, Danica could hear the pine tar cracking and popping. That was the sound she was focused on when the first bullet went by.

A high, buzzing whine, like a bug going past her ear at a thousand miles an hour. The crack of the gunshot followed right on top of it, in the same tiny part of a second.

Dryden was already ducking, turning in place, pulling her down. As they slid to a stop, he shoved one foot against the slope, propelling both of their bodies behind a giant trunk. A second and third gunshot sounded, coming from the same place as the first—the direction of the burning vehicle a hundred feet behind them. At least one of the bullets tore into the trunk behind Danica's head.

In the dimness behind the trunk, Dryden reached for his waistband. Danica saw both pistols tucked into it: the gun he had taken from his attacker in Malibu, and the one that had belonged to Carl.

Dryden took hold of the latter; it held the full magazine Carl had loaded into it before he died.

Dryden put his mouth to her ear and spoke urgently: "See the shadow of this tree? Out ahead of us?"

He pointed, and she followed the shadow with her eyes: a broad swath of darkness projected across the wooded slope, like a pathway.

Danica nodded quickly—and even as she did, she

heard footsteps somewhere behind them, running, scrambling this way.

"Stay in it," Dryden whispered, "and stay ahead of me. *Now go!*"

She pushed off from the tree and ran.

Immediately the sensation felt all wrong: running on dark ground, *choosing* dark ground, where every landed footstep felt like a guess.

She could feel Dryden right at her back, sometimes almost pushing her forward. They had covered no more than ten yards when another bullet ripped through the trees close by. Then she heard Dryden turn in place right behind her—and fire.

Four shots in fast succession—yet they sounded deliberate, careful. They sounded aimed.

Far back in the darkness, a man screamed and went sprawling in the dry soil.

Danica kept running. The surrounding forest was at last growing dim again, with distance from the burning Explorer and tree. Still it was *only* dim—not half dark enough to conceal them.

Behind them, the voices were shouting now, either in alarm or anger, or both. Then came a volley of their gunfire, more shots than Danica could count. She heard the buzzing-insect sound again, so close to her right ear that she cried out and almost lost her balance.

Dryden turned again and opened fire—not as carefully this time, maybe not aiming at all, though it halted the gunfire that was coming their way.

"Keep going," he whispered. *"Fast as you can move."*

Farther into the dark now—the shadow of the big tree was no longer even discernible against the space around it.

Yet the running footsteps were still there behind them. The crashing of bodies through small branches and undergrowth.

"Dammit," Dryden hissed.

Danica took her eyes off the ground in front of her and glanced back at him.

He was looking at the pistol in his hand, holding it up to the light as he ran.

The slide was locked open. Danica had never owned a firearm, but she knew what that meant: the weapon was empty.

She faced forward again, scrutinizing her route through the trunks and low boughs. Behind her, she heard Dryden stuff the gun back into his waistband and draw the other.

Then Danica's foot hooked on something—a root jutting up farther than it had appeared to. Her breath rushed out and her arms pinwheeled, and for a second she was certain she was going down.

Then the snared foot came free and she threw it forward, jammed it hard into the soil in front of her, the movement just enough to let her catch her balance while she kept running.

"Jesus Christ," she hissed.

"I know, I know. This is no good."

He could obviously see the same thing she could: the darkness wasn't enough to hide them yet, but it was more than enough to conceal the next jutting obstacle on the ground.

Suddenly he thrust an arm over her shoulder, pointing to something ahead and just upslope from them: an enormous fallen trunk, like a low wall that was easily two feet high.

"I see it," she said.

"Get down behind it."

"What?"

"There's no choice. Do it."

She nodded and made the turn—partly running and partly scrambling now, grabbing saplings for handholds as she made her way upward on a long angle toward the deadfall.

From behind them came another salvo of shots, a dozen or more. She heard the bullets zipping into the dirt and ricocheting off limbs, no more than a few feet away in the gloom.

She reached the downed trunk and vaulted over it without stopping, pressing herself flat to the arid soil and scattered pine needles behind it. Half a second later Dryden landed just beyond her—face to face in the near-dark.

He was still holding the second gun. He brought it up in front of his chest, took a deep breath and forced it out, then sat up fast and leveled the weapon.

Danica heard someone gasp, forty or fifty feet away, in the instant before Dryden fired.

A single shot, and then he threw himself flat beside her again, and even before he landed she could hear someone coughing and choking. It sounded wet. Like a near-drowning victim trying to force water out of his windpipe.

She heard other voices cursing and dragging the injured man over the ground.

"How many of them left?" Danica asked.

"Two."

"And how many bullets?"

Dryden thumbed a lever on the side of the pistol and dropped the magazine out of it, then felt the open top of it with his fingertips.

"Shit," he whispered.

"You're out?"

He shook his head. *"One in the chamber."*

He raised his head just enough to see over the sideways trunk. His gaze darted back and forth over the slope beyond.

"Got a plan?" Danica asked.

Dryden nodded. *"Drop the closer guy, rush the body and get his gun."*

"Is that going to work?"

"We'll see."

His eyes were narrowed, watching the dark woods. He turned his head just slightly, listening.

Suddenly he threw himself down, and the deadfall came to life with bullet impacts, ripping into the bark, shredding the top edge of it. Danica could smell the burned wood where the shots had hit. She could hear the gunfire coming from both shooters, though they sounded like they were in separate positions now. As if they had split up.

The shooting stopped again. In the silence there came the metallic sounds of weapons being reloaded—wherever they were.

"They're going to try to get around us," Dryden said.

"What the hell do we do?"

For a few seconds Dryden didn't answer. He looked at the gun again, considering it.

"Sam?"

"When I rush them, you go that way." He nodded along the slope, the direction they'd been running earlier. *"Run and don't look back."*

Danica shook her head. *"No, this isn't going to work—"*

"If you get enough lead distance it will. They'll be busy with me for at least—"

"I'm not talking about me. What you're *going to do isn't going to work—"*

"There's nothing to argue, and no time anyway."

"Sam—"

"On three. One—"

"Listen to me—"

"Two—"

A jackhammer explosion of sound came out of the darkness, from somewhere high up the slope—above themselves and the two remaining attackers. It sounded like automatic rifle fire.

Dryden jerked his head around toward the noise.

Danica did the same, and saw a pair of muzzle-flashes through the trees, thirty yards up—pulsing like high-speed strobe lights.

"Those are M4s," Dryden whispered.

A second later the gunfire stopped, and from the same direction came a man's voice, loud and sharp:

"Weapons down, now! Get them down! Show us your hands!"

A second voice followed: *"Do it! We will fucking kill you! Do it right now!"*

Though it seemed clear the commands were not aimed at herself or Dryden, Danica saw him set the pistol aside on the ground. He rested both his hands on the bark of the deadfall, up in plain view, while keeping the rest of himself shielded by it. She rolled toward the trunk and did the same.

A moment later she heard boots scraping and thudding as the newcomers made their way downhill. She heard a soft hiss of static and then a voice, speaking quietly as if into a radio headset. "Subjects contained. All teams to my position. Twelve-eight."

The static hissed again and then cut out.

Dryden sat up slowly into full view, raising his hands to shoulder level. Danica followed his lead. She stared over the fallen trunk at the wooded slope, back across the expanse she and Dryden had traversed in their sprint.

From this direction she could see everything clearly—the forest stood in silhouette, backlit by the burning SUV and the tree above it, maybe a hundred yards off along the hillside.

The two surviving attackers were fifty feet away, both of them on their knees with their empty hands raised.

The men with the automatic rifles descended into view in careful steps, keeping the weapons trained.

In the glare of the distant firelight, Danica could just make out certain details of the newcomers: men in their twenties or thirties, lean and fit, wearing dark blue windbreakers. As they came to a stop just above the subdued attackers, the nearer of the new arrivals turned and surveyed her and Dryden where they sat.

"Either of you hurt?" the man asked.

They shook their heads.

The guy made a quick nod and then returned his full attention to the men on the ground. In doing so, he pivoted just enough that Danica could see the back of his jacket. In big letters just visible in the indirect light of the flames, it read *FBI.*

Seconds later, bright flashlight beams speared the darkness from somewhere up near the road. Three lights, then half a dozen or more.

More voices, too, and a clamor of footsteps coming down.

Danica turned to Dryden, and found him ignoring the FBI men entirely. He was staring at the two attackers on their knees, his expression still tense with focus. He regarded them as if they were every bit as dangerous as they'd been a minute before.

Danica found her own gaze pulled back to them.

The men knelt there, staring up into the barrels of the M4 rifles, their hands still raised. One of the two had a dark beard, trimmed short. The other had short blond hair.

Something about the bearded guy drew Danica's

attention. Something in his manner. She stared a moment longer and realized what it was: his jaw was clenched and he was breathing fast, and his hands made little convulsive movements.

Like he was psyching himself up to do something.

It came a second later, and happened so quickly she hardly had time to flinch.

The bearded man's hand shot to his waistband, where his shirt hung untucked. An instant later the hand was swinging up again, holding a small pistol. Danica could see the FBI men reacting, their rifles centering on the guy. The bearded man twisted on his knees and swung the gun to one side—toward the blond man kneeling next to him. He shoved the barrel against the man's temple and fired. In exactly the same moment both M4s roared, and the bearded man's chest was torn open by autofire.

A second after that there was only silence—the quiet of a forest in the middle of the night.

CHAPTER TWENTY

It was thirty minutes later. Dryden stood with Danica beside a black Chevy Suburban, which was parked on the grass in an alpine meadow. The Suburban was one of eight SUVs and sedans idling at random angles in the field, headlights blazing, LED strobes flashing from their grilles. Men and women in FBI windbreakers milled around, talking on phones or hunched together over tablet screens.

The meadow was half a mile up the road from the fallen pine that had blocked the way earlier—half a mile farther along in the direction Dryden and Danica had been driving, before everything happened.

From where he stood, Dryden could see over the woods that ranged down the hillside below the open field; he could see far out over the Arizona desert, where I-40 stretched away into the night, its course marked by the headlights of sparse traffic.

And sirens—lots of them, threading their way along the interstate in this direction. Police and fire units, no doubt. The big pine down on the slope was still burning, though the FBI personnel didn't seem worried about it. Over one of their radios, Dryden had heard mention of a chopper en route with a water bucket.

Otherwise, he and Danica had been told very little. A young guy with some kind of medical training had shone a penlight into their eyes to check for dilation, then asked the standard raft of emergency questions about pain, double-vision and light-headedness. Finally a man in his fifties had asked them to stand here and try to relax—someone was coming to speak to them soon.

Now they were waiting.

Danica looked around at the FBI vehicles and the gathered agents.

"So the guys who dropped that tree onto the road must have been watching us in the camp," she said, "and they were waiting to get us on the way out. And these FBI people were . . . watching *them?*"

Dryden nodded. "One way or another."

He pictured the attackers staking out the encampment with spotting scopes, and the FBI watching the attackers with a high-altitude drone—a Global Hawk or a Reaper with a million-dollar thermal camera, looking down from three miles up in the darkness. Maybe these agents had been staged right here in this meadow, far back from the road, waiting for a surveillance tech a thousand miles away to start yelling *go* into their headsets.

All of which meant one thing for sure: both the FBI and the bad guys knew about Shiprock Forest, and that it was a good place to watch for at least Danica to arrive.

“All this for a missing person from a murder scene in Thousand Oaks?” Danica asked. The skepticism was evident in her tone.

“Seems a bit much, doesn’t it? Usually they put your picture on the news and flash a tip-line number.”

“Then what’s really going on? What is this about?”

“Something a hell of a lot bigger than either of us,” Dryden said.

As he finished saying it, he heard the sound of distant rotors—a helicopter coming in from somewhere to the south. He turned and saw its winking lights just rising into view over the treetops along the meadow. He guessed it was the fire chopper finally arriving; then it got closer and he saw that it was a standard-sized utility type, the kind that news channels and police forces used. It came in low over the field, its rotor-wash whipping the grass and stirring dust up into the headlight beams. It was black with *FBI* in big white letters on the side. Dryden watched it touch down twenty yards north of the assembled vehicles.

A rear door opened and three men emerged: two younger guys in windbreakers, like the personnel already on-scene, and then a man who might have been sixty. He was black, with greying hair at his temples; he wore a dress shirt, suitcoat and jeans with no tie. He surveyed the clustered vehicles for only a moment before his gaze settled on Dryden and Danica. He came to them, the other two men in tow.

“Sam Dryden and Danica Ellis,” the man said. He shook their hands. “I’m Jack Grace—SAC from the field office in L.A.”

"How do you know my name?" Dryden asked; he had not identified himself to any of the personnel present.

"We know a lot," Grace said. "I'll be glad to explain all of it, but I need a few answers from the two of you first. I know you've already spoken to Russell Moss. I assume he told you as much as he knows?"

Behind Grace, one of the two men who'd landed with him took a phone call. The guy cupped the phone to his ear and wandered a few paces away to speak.

"We don't want Moss to be in any trouble," Danica said. "If you need to involve him—"

"We'll be speaking to him," Grace said, "but he's not in trouble, and he's not a high priority. We already have his information."

"The blue binder," Dryden said. "You have it, don't you?"

For the first time Grace looked surprised. Then he simply nodded. "Ms. Ellis's father left it in his secure locker at the field office, five years ago. I only learned of it this morning, but I wish to hell I'd seen it before now."

"Why?" Danica asked. "What's happening? Why are these people after us?"

Before Grace could answer, the guy with the phone stepped back to him and spoke quickly. Dryden heard urgency in his voice—or outright fear.

"The team in Boston wants to be looped in as soon as we learn anything," the man said. "Same for New York."

Grace was already nodding. "Tell them of course," he said.

The guy paced off again.

"What is this?" Dryden asked. The low-burning dread in his own voice surprised him.

Instead of answering, Grace said, "I imagine Moss told you about Ashland, Iowa."

Dryden nodded.

"What *exactly* did he tell you?" Grace asked.

"That it was a military R & D site," Dryden said. "For off-the-books stuff, some of it possibly illegal."

"Probably *all* of it," Grace said, as if to himself. He glanced away over the parked vehicles, then turned his gaze on Dryden and Danica again, going back and forth between them.

"We know you were drugged, as children. We know that was done because you witnessed something there at Ashland." He stepped closer to them, and his eyes took on a look that was close to pleading. "Is there *anything* you can remember from your time in Ashland? Anything at all?"

Dryden shook his head.

"Nothing," Danica said.

Grace kept his eyes on them. The pleading look was still there. "You're absolutely certain?"

"Can you tell us what this is about?" Dryden asked.

"Please," Danica said. "Why does all this old stuff matter? Why is someone after us *now?*"

Grace exhaled slowly and looked away again. He ran a hand over his chin, the movement awkward and rough. In the glare of the headlights, Dryden saw a sheen of sweat on the man's face.

"They're after you now because it *matters* now," he

said. He turned and looked at them again. "The accident on the night of July 20, 1989, involved a weapon system that was developed at Ashland. We have no information at all about this weapon—who designed it, what it could do, what became of it later. It could be chemical. It could be a bio-agent. We don't know. But we have very good reasons to believe someone has managed to reconstitute it, and that it's about to be used in an attack on a civilian target. We think that attack is coming somewhere inside the United States, anytime in the next twelve hours."

Danica put a hand to her chest and took a deep breath. Dryden felt his stomach tighten.

"The people behind this attack are the same people who've been trying to get to you," Grace said. "The fact that *they're* worried about you is the reason we think you can help us. Like whatever you saw back then, all those years ago, there's some way it points to these people right now. *They* seem to think so."

Dryden heard Russell Moss in his head.

You two witnessed some specific event—something none of the rest saw. Whatever it was, it was worse than the accident.

"You're all they're scared of," Grace said. "That has to mean something."

"*But we don't remember,*" Dryden said. "Christ, we just don't, and there's no way to change that."

Grace looked back and forth between the two of them again. "Actually there is," he said.

PART FOUR

THE CLOUD CHAMBER

JULY 1989

CHAPTER TWENTY-ONE

The morning was hot and humid. The house had air-conditioning, but Sam had it turned off for now. He had most of the windows open to let the breeze blow through. It came in from the south, over the tall grass that covered the slope below the subdivision. He had the house to himself; his dad was at work, wherever that was. *Whatever* that was.

More than a full day had passed since Dani had let him in on the truth about Ashland—the walk to Station 14 had happened the night before last. They had spent much of the time since then together. She'd shown him the written notes she'd made from nearly two months' worth of audio recordings—the conversations she'd managed to capture by hiding the microcassette recorder in her dad's briefcase. The notes were in a yellow legal pad that was about halfway filled up with her handwriting.

There were lots of details in the notes, though most of them didn't make much sense. As Dani said, it was like listening in on dentists or car mechanics on the job, hearing just bits and pieces. But it all added up to the big picture clearly enough: the talk was strewn with military terminology—phrases like *lieutenant* and *chain of command.* Plenty of evidence about what Ashland *was*—just not much about what was actually happening here.

Not until the past week, anyway. That was when the notes started getting interesting.

Dani had caught the first sign of trouble five days ago. A man in her father's office had spoken of something called *the problem.* In the notepad, Dani had underlined those two words, and in the margin she had written, *He says that like it means something, like it's something my dad is supposed to understand.*

For the next minute, the two men had spoken of *the problem,* but from the words on the page, there was no way to tell what any of the talk meant. Like most of the conversations Dani had written down, there were too many unknown references, things that were hinted at but not explained.

In fact, this conversation was worse than most of the others. Reading it, Sam had gotten the sense that these two men were speaking very cautiously about *the problem.* Because maybe they weren't even supposed to be talking about *the problem.*

Whatever it might be.

Dani had caught a second conversation about it two days later, between her father and a different man. This other guy said he'd shown his twelve-year-old son how to load and fire the revolver he kept in his home office—just to be on the safe side. Just in case *the problem* ended up being as dangerous as it sounded. Dani's father had told him not to sweat it, that nothing bad was going to happen, but this time Dani had written in the margin, *Never heard my dad sound like this. Is he scared?*

That was it, so far. Just those two oddball conversations about *the problem.* Sam and Dani had talked about it all afternoon yesterday, and then he'd lain awake for what felt like half the night before finally crashing out.

It was just past nine in the morning now. Sam had already showered and dressed, and had just finished breakfast. He had the TV on in the living room, though he wasn't paying much attention to it. The people on *Good Morning America* were talking about the Moon landing, which had happened exactly twenty years ago today: July 20, 1969.

Sam was in the kitchen, rinsing his cereal bowl in the sink, when someone knocked on the door. A small hand, pounding hard. He set the bowl down and shut off the faucet and dried his hands. He stepped out of the kitchen into the front entryway and saw Dani through the narrow window beside the door.

Her eyes were red, like she'd been crying. She saw him through the glass and waved him toward her. He crossed to the door at almost a run and pulled it open.

"What happened?" he asked.

"Yesterday's tape," she said. "You need to listen to it. Can you come over right now?"

He got the front door key from its drawer in the kitchen, locked up, and followed her back to her house. He could hear a hitch in her breathing as they walked. She kept wiping at her eyes.

"Dani, what is it?"

"I want you to hear the tape first. I want to see if you think the same thing I do."

The day before, she had described the exact process she used for sending and retrieving the tapes. She actually had two recorders, and she had lots of leftover tapes from the previous school year. Her approach was simple, and was designed to minimize the risk of her father catching her in the act.

Every night, once both her parents were asleep, she went into the den and opened the briefcase. She pulled the recorder out of its hiding place inside the lining, popped out the tape and put in a different one, then hid the recorder again and closed the case. The whole thing took less than thirty seconds, from the time she left her bedroom until she was back in it. She could do it in almost perfect silence, and without turning any lights on. Best of all, she could hear her parents' breathing the entire time; if either of them woke up, she would know instantly. She would have plenty of time to simply close the briefcase and slip back to her room, and try again later in the night.

The rest of the process was a cakewalk: she simply waited until both her parents left in the morning, then listened to the previous day's tape using her second recorder. Most days, the tape contained just a few minutes of audio. She would listen once, then listen again and try to write everything down, then listen a third or fourth time and make sure she had it right.

Sam recalled how he'd felt, hearing her describe it all. Her mind worked exactly like his. She was methodical and careful. She was okay with taking risks, but only when they were necessary, and she took them in the smartest possible way. She wasn't fucking around.

He followed her into her house; it was the first time he'd been inside. The place was about like his, but more broken-in. There were no movers' boxes stacked along the walls. It had the feel of a house where everyone had found their little rhythms and patterns over the course of a few months. Things were put away and arranged and settled.

Dani led him down the hall to her room. They passed the den, and a bedroom that must belong to her parents. When she'd first mentioned that both her mom and dad had jobs, it triggered an obvious question: did her mom work for the military, too?

Dani didn't know. Her mom claimed to work in an office in Brenner—some local company that sold farm equipment. Maybe that was the truth. There was no way to check on it—no way to hide the microcassette recorder in her purse without her finding it.

The whole idea raised another question for Sam: what about *his* mom? In L.A. she had worked part-time on the board of a charity organization. From what Sam had heard, she was planning to still do some of that work by phone, after moving to Ashland. It didn't sound like she planned to have a job locally. The question was simply how much she knew about all this. How much did she know about her husband's new line of work?

She had to know some of it. How far in the dark could his dad hope to keep her about something that big? And for how long? It was one thing to pull the wool over your kid's eyes, but your wife? Sam thought of the strange tension that had been in the air between his parents, for the weeks leading up to the move. It had been understandable enough at the time, but it made more sense now.

Dani pushed open her door, and Sam followed her in.

The room was like the rest of the house: settled, moved into. Still, it wasn't at all the way a kid's room should be. It wasn't plastered with posters or photos, or overflowing with any of the hundred little things that marked a room as really *belonging* to someone. Dani hadn't claimed this space as her own. Maybe she had started to do that, in those early weeks when she didn't know the truth about this town. Had started to and then stopped. The thought of it crept under Sam's skin. Another little tap of the hammer, driving home the reality of his new world.

There was a bed, and a nightstand, and a dresser, and a desk. The only pictures in the entire room were on top of the dresser: three photographs in standing frames. The first showed a much younger Dani, eight or nine years old, smiling with two friends, probably somewhere in L.A. The second photo was more recent, but still at least a couple years old: Dani with the same two friends at a public aquarium.

In the third picture Dani looked exactly the way she did now, down to the haircut. She was standing arm in arm with a girl her age, on the lawn in front of this very house. The other girl could only be Lauren, the friend who'd moved away last week. She had blond hair and green eyes. Both girls were smiling in the photo, but the expressions were half smiles at best. In contrast with the carefree happiness in the other two pictures, Dani's and Lauren's smiles looked almost forced. Their eyes seemed to say, *Who the hell are we kidding?*

Dani went to the desk. Sitting atop it were a microcassette recorder and the yellow legal pad Sam had already seen. It was open to the last partly filled page, and there was a date written for a new entry: yesterday's date. But Dani hadn't written anything there yet.

"Here, have a seat," Dani said.

Sam sat in the chair in front of the desk. Dani picked up the recorder; through the machine's plastic window, Sam could see she'd already rewound the tape.

"You'll hear two men talking," Dani said. "One has a really deep voice, and the other's just normal. The normal voice is my dad. The deep voice is some guy named Trent. He's someone pretty high up—one of the people in charge, I guess. I've heard him four or five times before, on these tapes. You saw his name in some of my notes yesterday."

Sam nodded. The name was familiar.

"Okay," Dani said. "I won't say anything else. Just see what you think."

She pressed PLAY.

Sam stared at the recorder and listened carefully.

At first there was only silence, except for the low hum of the tape deck running. Whatever sound had triggered the machine to begin recording, yesterday in Dani's father's office—a spoken word, a closing door—it had ended by the time the machine kicked on.

Five seconds passed. Then a man cleared his throat, and spoke, his voice deep and slow—Trent, obviously.

Trent: *"I need to talk to you about this thing with Coleman."*

Dani's father: *"The problem."*

Trent: *"The problem."*

Dani's father: *"Is there news?"*

Wooden chair legs scraped on a floor. Sam pictured someone sitting down.

Trent: *"In a way, yes. I just got off the phone with division. They're scared. I get the feeling this thing is about to go very bad, in a very big way, and I don't think they're telling me everything."*

Dani's father: *"Why would they hold back?"*

Trent: *"I think they're getting ready to cover their own asses, if the worst outcome happens. I think it'll be a few of us here who take the fall. Me, for sure."*

There was a silence. A few seconds.

Trent: *"I'm speaking with all the department heads here, starting with you, because I want to know as much as I can. Anything at all you've heard, anything you even suspect, I want to know."*

Dani's father: *"I don't think anything I know is related—"*

Trent: *"Let me tell you what I know, first, and then if you can build on it, I'd appreciate it."*

Dani's father: *"Of course."*

Trent: *"First there's Pierce. Gone without a trace,*

one year ago. Now there's Coleman, missing under identical circumstances. None of his relatives can account for him, no sign he's using his credit card or hitting ATMs. Nothing at all. He's just gone, like Pierce—into thin air. We dug into both of their work histories, tried to find anything they had in common. We came up with exactly one thing. An old project called Rigel. You know it?"

Dani's father: *"Rigel . . . No, what is that?"*

Trent: *"I know very little beyond the names of a few people involved . . . and how it started and ended. It was a black-budget thing, quite a while back now. Pierce established it, right here on-base, almost ten years ago. He worked on it for five years. He had a handful of people off-site doing peripheral work on it—people at labs in D.C., and a few out west. Whatever they were developing, after those five years Pierce himself pulled the plug. He flew to D.C., went before some closed-door Senate panel, and told them they should kill the project. His own project. He said it should be disinvented, if possible. Burn the files, scrap the equipment, everything. Like it never existed."*

Dani's father: *"Jesus."*

Trent: *"Pierce was that scared of it, whatever it was. And the government followed his advice. They erased Rigel right out of the books. You can imagine, then, that it raised a few eyebrows when Pierce disappeared last year. It was possible someone had grabbed him to learn about Rigel. All the files were already long gone, but obviously he still had important information in his head."*

Dani's father: *"So now with Coleman missing, too—"*

Trent: *"Exactly. The guys at the top are ready to pull their hair out. Whatever Rigel was, it's plausible that someone out there is gathering up the people who could restart it. That's pretty much where it stands right now."*

One of the two men exhaled. Even in the rough recording, Sam could hear a shudder in the breath.

Trent: *"If there's anything you know about Pierce or Coleman, any rumor, anything at all, I need to hear it now."*

A long silence drew out. Sam waited for the recording to cut off; there must be some point at which the machine would have stopped itself, if it weren't picking up any sound.

But then came another sigh, this one quick and sharp.

Dani's father: *"I can't think of a thing."*

Trent: *"Alright. If you* do *hear something—"*

Dani's father: *"I'll come straight to see you."*

Trent: *"Good enough."*

The chair scraped again. Footsteps scuffed on tile. A door opened and shut.

A much longer silence set in, and after ten seconds Sam heard a *click:* that portion of the recording had come to its end.

The tape continued to turn, apparently playing whatever the machine had happened to record later on—the next thing that had triggered it to start taping.

It didn't sound like anything important. Just someone tapping away at a keyboard—an electric typewriter or a computer.

Sam glanced up from the recorder and saw Dani standing at her dresser. She was staring idly at the framed pictures—especially the third one showing herself and Lauren.

"I already listened to the rest of the tape," Dani said. "It's just ten minutes of random office noises, off and on all day. Most of the tapes come out like that."

She finally turned from the dresser and met Sam's eyes.

"Can you describe what you just heard?" she said. "I just want to hear someone else say it. So I know I'm not going crazy."

Sam nodded. He went back over it for a moment, in his head, and then began:

"Somebody else is missing," he said. "Someone named Coleman. It sounds like he just disappeared in the past few days. He had a connection to Pierce: an old project called Rigel . . . and Rigel sounds scary as hell. The government shut it down, because Pierce asked them to, and now . . . people in charge around here are worried someone is trying to start it up again. Someone who could have kidnapped Pierce and Coleman to find out what they know."

He tried to think of anything more, but finally just shook his head. "That's it."

Dani nodded. "That's what I heard, too," she said, and all at once her voice cracked. She didn't cry, but she was on the brink. Her eyes looked a little redder than they had a moment before.

The reaction struck Sam as odd, but only a little; it was scary stuff to hear about. He stood from the chair and put a hand on her shoulder.

"You're not alone with this stuff anymore," he said. "It makes sense to be scared. There's nothing wrong with that."

"I'm not scared for me," Dani said.

Before Sam could say anything back to that, Dani turned to the third framed photo again. She pulled it closer to her, and stared into it.

"Coleman is Lauren's last name," she said. "It's her father that disappeared. And so did she."

CHAPTER TWENTY-TWO

The room went silent except for the cassette recorder, still playing random office sounds. Sam could hear a dot-matrix printer screeching and droning somewhere in the background.

"I thought Lauren and her dad moved away," Sam said.

Dani nodded. "They *were* moving away. They were packed and ready. I helped Lauren box up her room and put everything in their van, the last night I saw her. They were leaving the next day, but she said she'd come over before they left. I mean, obviously. It wasn't like she was going to leave without saying goodbye."

A tear finally overspilled her eye. She wiped at it, looking miserable.

"And then she *did,*" Dani said.

"What?"

"She did leave without saying goodbye."

The tears were in her voice now. He could hear her pitch rising, her throat tightening. She took a deep breath and forced a bit of control.

"That's what I thought," Dani said. "I woke up the

next morning and walked down to her house, and the van was gone. I knocked on the door. Nothing. They'd just . . . taken off. No goodbye. And you know what? It made sense after I thought about it. I imagined Lauren lying in her bed that last night, so relieved to finally be getting the hell out of here, getting all this behind her, and I imagined her thinking, *Do I really want to stay connected to all this shit? Do I want to stay in touch with Dani? Do I want to call, or write? Don't I just want this over with?* I imagined her walking outside that next morning, and looking down the street toward my house, and feeling bad just for a minute . . . and then getting in the van and not looking back. That's what I thought, until I heard this tape twenty minutes ago."

On the recording, the dot-matrix printer finished. The sound of the keyboard came back in.

"That morning when I thought they left," Dani said, "that was four days before I met you. Which is two days ago now. So six days. That's how long ago they disappeared. Six days I thought she was off in her new life, starting over, my phone number already in the trash. But she wasn't. She *isn't.* She's in trouble somewhere right now, and what am I supposed to do?"

Even as he watched her try to hold it together, Sam found his thoughts locking onto the underlying idea: that someone had abducted Lauren and her father on the very day they were planning to leave. He couldn't help but recognize the genius of it: nobody would have noticed them missing right away. It could have been a day or more before anyone realized something was wrong—the time it would have taken them to reach their new home, wherever it was.

A smart move on the part of whoever had grabbed them. Damned smart.

"I should have known something might happen to her," Dani said.

Sam looked up. "Why? How were you supposed to know?"

She turned away from the dresser, crossed to her bed and sat on the edge.

"There were things she wasn't telling me," Dani said. "For the last month, at least. I suspected it at first, and later I was pretty sure."

"What made you think that?"

"She was just . . . dodgy about certain things. Things she would ask me about, but then she didn't want to say why they mattered to her."

"What kind of things?"

Dani nodded to the yellow legal pad next to the recorder. "Stuff I heard on the tapes, and wrote down."

"Like what?"

"A place called Station Nine," she said. "One of the abandoned ones."

"Like Station Fourteen? The one we went to?"

"I don't know if it's like that one," Dani said. "I mean, I know it's abandoned, but I've never seen it. Station Fourteen is the only one Lauren and I ever actually found. There are half a dozen others somewhere around here. We've heard them mentioned in these recordings, but never anything about where they are."

"And Lauren was interested in Station Nine?" Sam asked.

Dani nodded. "She said she overheard her father talking about it, on the phone in his den. She eavesdropped on him like that, whenever she could. He didn't have a briefcase for us to hide a recorder inside. Anyway, Lauren said she heard him talking about Station Nine. She said he mentioned its location—that the entrance to it was 'inside the baron's,' whatever the hell that means."

"Baron's, like the Red Baron?"

Dani shrugged. "I guess. And if there were a Baron's Burger Hut downtown next to the sandwich shop, it would have made sense, but there's not. Lauren and I tried for hours to figure out what it meant. We looked up last names in the phonebook, looked up the name of every business, everything we could think of. There's nothing around here that even sounds like *the baron's.*"

On the cassette tape, a phone rang. Dani's dad answered: *"Three-six, go ahead."* After a long pause, he continued: *"Yeah, that's fine, you can send the paperwork here. Use the secure fax."*

The phone's handset clattered back into its cradle.

"To me," Dani said, "it was just another random thing that didn't go anywhere. We'd heard lots of stuff like that on these tapes. But Lauren was obsessed with Station Nine. She wanted to find it. She would read the few notes we had on it, over and over."

"What do those notes say?" Sam asked.

"Nothing at all. Just random mentions of the place, in the middle of conversations."

"Then why would Lauren care about it so much?"

"Because I think when she heard her dad talk about it, she heard more than just the location. Whatever the rest of it was, it's the reason she was so stuck on finding it. And it was something she didn't want to tell me. The few times I pressed her on it, she said it was nothing, no big deal. But you can tell when someone's holding back. Why she would do that, though . . . I don't know."

"Maybe it scared her. Maybe it was something that bad."

"Maybe," Dani said. "No matter what, I think it has something to do with her and her dad's disappearance. Which would mean Station Nine is part of all this. Part of . . . the problem. Part of Rigel, whatever that is."

Before Sam could ask anything else, a new sound came over the recording on the cassette player. He flinched and spun toward it. In the corner of his eye he saw Dani startle at the movement.

"What's wrong?" she said.

"Play that back. That sound."

"It was just the secure fax in my dad's office. It goes off all the time."

"I need to hear it again."

Without waiting for her, he picked up the device, stopped the tape and rewound it a few seconds. He pressed PLAY.

Dani stood from the bed and came up beside him.

Sam turned one ear toward the tape deck, waiting.

Then the sound came again:

Click, click, click, hum.

CHAPTER TWENTY-THREE

Two minutes later they were standing in Sam's bedroom, staring into the closet.

"You're sure it's the same sound?" Dani said.

"Positive."

Sam began pulling out the few movers' boxes he'd set in the closet the other day. Dani joined in, and within another minute they had the space cleared, the back wall exposed all the way to the floor.

"I've heard it a bunch of times," Sam said, "starting the day we moved in. I thought it was some random noise the house made. Like the hot water heater or something."

He stepped to the closet's threshold and studied the back wall. It was painted flat white, and was featureless except for wire shelves at chest and head height. There was no way to access the space behind the wall without simply cutting into it. Sam leaned into the closet and looked up at its ceiling. There was a narrow hatch there, which led to the attic.

"We need something to stand on," he said.

There was no ladder in the house, but the end table next to the couch was tall enough to do the trick. After sliding it into the closet and climbing onto it, Sam could reach the ceiling hatch easily. He shoved it up and off to the side, and a moment later he was sitting in the dim space of the attic, his feet hanging down through the opening. He reached back down and helped Dani up. She clambered into a seated position next to him.

It was easily ninety degrees up here, and thick with humidity, and though the attic was empty, it still managed to feel cramped. Shallow-angled roof beams made up its ceiling, and four-by-eight-foot chipboard sheets comprised the floor. The air was heavy with the smells of wood and dust and something like glue—probably roofing tar.

Sam studied the piece of chipboard beside the hatch, directly above the space behind the closet. At a glance, it looked no different than the rest of the sheets. Then he looked closer.

This board had no nails holding it down, like all the others did. It was just resting in place.

There was a gap at the near edge of the chipboard sheet: an inch of empty space between the board and the wooden frame that surrounded the hatchway. Sam got his fingers through the gap and took hold of the board, and found he could tilt it up easily. Dani got a grip on it, too, and together they shoved it aside.

The exposed rectangle where the board had lain was spanned by heavy structural beams. Sam realized he was looking at the living room ceiling from above. The spaces between the beams were filled with insulation—except one. The nearest one. In that space there was only darkness, leading down to a cavity behind the closet wall.

Dani leaned over it.

"Light switch," she said. She reached down into the dark and flipped a switch that had been crudely wired into place near the top of the wall, and the hidden chamber was bathed in white fluorescent light.

It was exactly the size of Sam's closet—but without the doors. The walls were the same white-painted drywall, and at one end there was a built-in ladder made of two-by-fours. It extended to a floor covered with the same carpet as the bedroom and closet. Other than the ladder, the space contained only two things: a small table, and on top of it a fax machine. It looked about like every fax machine Sam had ever seen. Whatever made it *secure* was probably just some special circuitry inside it.

Sam noticed that the broad, rear wall of the hidden space had tiny holes in it, where screws or bolts had been removed. The holes formed lines about three and six feet above the floor. They corresponded exactly with the heights of the closet's shelves.

"This *was* the closet," Sam said. "Originally, I mean. When Pierce first moved in, this space must have been the closet for this bedroom. He built a new closet in front of it—he even moved the shelves."

Dani nodded, then directed her focus to the fax machine. So did Sam. He saw a phone line and a power cord sticking out the back. Both were patched into the house's wiring through a ragged hole in the drywall.

Sam stared at those details for only a second, then turned his attention to the machine's receiving tray, and the stack of faxes piled there.

"I wonder what those are about," Dani said.

"Let's find out."

They descended the two-by-four ladder and crossed to the machine. Sam was immediately struck by how few faxes there were. From high above he'd assumed the stack was half an inch thick—the things had been piling up in the tray for at least as long as Pierce had been missing.

But it wasn't half an inch thick. It had no thickness at all. Sam picked up the pages and separated them; there were only two.

"That's impossible," he said. "There would have to be *at least* all the ones I heard arrive, which must be half a dozen by now. But really there should be hundreds, if it's been getting them since last summer."

"Look at the date on it," Dani said.

She pointed to it, written in tiny digits along the edge of the most recent page: *July 13, 1988*—last year.

For a moment Sam didn't understand. And then he did. He reached under the hinged receiving tray and lifted it. Below was the feeder tray for blank paper. It was empty.

"It must've run out within days of when he disappeared," Dani said. "All it had was two blank sheets left. So these messages are a year old."

Sam nodded. Then he rearranged the faxes to put the earlier one on top, and together they began to read them:

STATUS UPDATE
FROM: Anonymous_Watchdog_Member
TO: All

Satellite images updated for the following risk areas:
Pauini, Brazil-NO OBSERVED RIGEL ACTIVITY
Pangar Djerem, Cameroon-NO OBSERVED RIGEL ACTIVITY
Uzo, Indonesia-NO OBSERVED RIGEL ACTIVITY
St. Andrew Island, Australia-NO OBSERVED RIGEL ACTIVITY

Anyone at/near these locations should remain cautious and follow all safety procedures. Protect yourself.

No further information at this time.

STATUS UPDATE
FROM: Anonymous_Watchdog_Member
TO: All

Satellite images updated for the following risk areas:
Mubendi Preserve, Uganda-NO OBSERVED RIGEL ACTIVITY
Wells Town, British Virgin Islands-NO OBSERVED RIGEL ACTIVITY
Bharanpala Lake, India-NO OBSERVED RIGEL ACTIVITY

Anyone at/near these locations should remain cautious and follow all safety procedures. Protect yourself.

No further information at this time.

Sam finished the second fax and looked up at Dani. She glanced at him, then returned her eyes to the page, her forehead furrowed.

"What the hell are we caught up in?" she said softly.

She traced the fax's header with her fingertip. "*From Anonymous Watchdog Member . . . to all.* It sounds like these faxes are being sent to lots of people at once."

Sam nodded. "I guess that's why this machine is still getting them, even when Pierce has been gone all this time. The messages are just going out to . . . some kind of group, I guess. And he was part of it."

"Watchdog," Dani said.

She was quiet for a long moment, her eyes narrowed.

"Watching for Rigel activity," she said, "whatever that is."

"I wonder if Watchdog is Pierce and the other people who worked on the project with him," Sam said. "I mean, it almost has to be, doesn't it?"

Dani thought about it, nodding.

"In that recording we just listened to," she said, "Trent told my dad there were people in D.C. and out west who worked on the project, too. So there could be lots of these people out there."

"I don't get what they're doing now, though," Sam said. "I mean, they're watching these places all over the world for something that has to do with Rigel, but . . . why are they doing that, if the project got shut down five years ago? Pierce himself told the government to pull the plug."

"What if he didn't trust them to really do that?" Dani asked. "What if he and the others wanted to keep an eye out, just in case someone started it up again?"

Sam trailed his eyes over the two lists of locations in the faxes. The *risk areas.* He'd heard of the countries, but none of the specific places were familiar.

"There's some reason these places matter," Dani said. "Why, though?"

Sam thought about it, but came up empty.

"We'd have to know more about what Rigel is, to understand any of this," he said. "I still feel like we're at square one."

"We can refill the tray in this machine, at least," Dani said. "Then when the next new fax comes in, we'll get it. With everything that's been going on lately, the other members of Watchdog might be doing some serious talking."

Sam looked up sharply. "Other members."

For a second Dani looked confused. Then she got it. "Lauren's dad."

Sam nodded. "He worked on Rigel along with Pierce. He was probably part of Watchdog, too."

"With his own hidden fax machine."

CHAPTER TWENTY-FOUR

Lauren's house wasn't far away—like Sam's and Dani's it stood along the southern edge of the subdivision, overlooking the grassy slope and the downtown storefronts half a mile away.

Dani took a spare key from a hiding place beside the porch—a fake rock—and unlocked the front door.

It took less than three minutes to find the hidden room; the setup was almost identical to Pierce's. A false wall at the back of the den closet, a narrow space behind it, accessed through the attic.

But the fax machine was gone. There was only a crude hole in the wall where the electrical and phone lines must have come through.

No surprise, really.

"They were moving," Sam said. "I guess he would have unplugged it and packed it away by that final night."

Dani said nothing. She just looked defeated.

They climbed back out through the attic, into the den, and walked the rooms of the house. The air was hot and stale; the place's windows had been shut for a week, and the air conditioner hadn't been running.

Sam watched Dani take in the space. She must have a ton of happy memories of hanging out with Lauren here, and now the place was stripped bare except for a few big pieces of furniture: bedframes and mattresses, a couch and a table, a big green recliner.

The one place that had a few personal touches left was the basement, which appeared to have been a rec room. It was carpeted, and contained a pool table and a few arcade games. There was a dartboard on the end wall, along with three movie posters: *Superman, Rambo: First Blood Part II,* and *Lethal Weapon*. There were darts stuck into two of the posters—one into Superman's navel, the other into Rambo's navel. Maybe that was some inside joke on Dani and Lauren's part.

The last thing Sam noticed was a wall-mounted display box, a little bigger than a medicine cabinet, filled with autographed baseballs—sixteen of them. The display box had a Philadelphia Phillies logo across the top. Sam moved closer and tried to read some of the signatures on the baseballs. He recognized two of the names: Mike Schmidt and Steve Carlton. The rest he either couldn't read or hadn't heard of.

"Why is Lauren's dad a Phillies fan?" Sam asked. "I thought he and Lauren came here from D.C."

"Her dad grew up in Philadelphia," Dani said. "He talked about the Phillies all the time. He said they're the oldest team in the country."

She sat down on the floor against one of the arcade machines. She leaned back into it, shut her eyes and sighed. The opposite of hope, captured in a single sound.

Sam crossed to a bay window near the pool table. The Colemans' back yard was one story lower than the front yard, allowing for the full-sized window. Sam stood there looking out; the view was about the same as from his own bedroom: south over the grassy slope and downtown Ashland.

"I remember them packing up, that last night," Dani said. "They got everything done but these last few things down here. They were going to grab this stuff in the morning. The posters, the baseballs. That was going to be it."

Sam found his thoughts sticking on the baseballs again, for some reason he couldn't quite pin down. He wondered if Lauren's dad had ever played the game.

Sam had played, back in L.A. Three years in Little League. His batting was only above average, but he could pitch with the best of them. His fastball topped out at seventy-three miles per hour, and the Junior League coaches had shown up to watch him practice a few times. They'd said he had promise. One more aspect of his old life that wasn't going to matter around here.

"I wonder when it happened," Dani said. Her tone was flat and detached. The voice of wrung-out, frayed nerves.

Sam turned to her. "When what happened?"

"The abduction. Like . . . later that same night, after I left? Or maybe the next morning."

"No sheets or blankets on the beds upstairs," Sam said. "Were they still on, when you were here that night?"

She narrowed her eyes, going back in time in her memory.

"Yeah," she said. "So . . . they were kidnapped in the morning. They got up and took the sheets and blankets off and packed them away, and it happened sometime after that."

"I guess," Sam said. He wasn't sure why she was dwelling on those things.

"It means they were awake," Dani said. "It wasn't like somebody picked the lock and came in at three in the morning. Lauren and her dad were already up and around . . . and someone just came in and took them."

"Okay," Sam said.

"What if Lauren was down here when it happened? Getting ready to pack up this last stuff?"

For the first time since they'd found the fax machine missing, Dani's voice had perked up again. Her eyes, too. They were alive. Intense.

"How could we know that, either way?" Sam asked.

"We can't, but . . ." Dani pushed up off the floor and stood. She crossed to the movie posters on the far wall. "But this doesn't make any sense," she said.

She was pointing at the two darts, stuck into the posters.

"You guys didn't do that?" Sam asked.

Dani shook her head. "We never played darts at all. And I know for a fact these weren't stuck here the last time I was in this room. Besides, it's just not something Lauren or her dad would do. Not just out of the blue, for no reason. It's weird. I mean, if you knew them . . . trust me, this is weird."

Sam went to her side. He stared at the darts, each stuck into a navel in the images—the only two navels visible on any of the posters.

"What if Lauren *was* down here when everything happened?" Dani said. "She would have heard her dad confronting whoever it was that came to grab them. What if she heard something important—somebody's name, something like that? And if she had even a little bit of time before they came down here and found her . . . she could have tried to leave some kind of message behind. It's exactly the kind of thing she would do."

"You mean . . . the darts are supposed to be a message?"

Dani rubbed her forehead. She seemed perfectly aware of how strange the idea sounded. Yet her eyes remained focused on the posters.

"Look, I could be wrong about the *why* part," she said. "But the darts have to mean *something*. There can't just be no reason for them being like this."

Sam pointed to a small notepad and pencil, tucked into the shallow wooden cabinet that held the dartboard on the wall.

"If she wanted to leave a message, she could have just written one," he said.

He went to the notepad and picked it up. Several pages up front had been torn out, probably over months or years. None of the existing pages had anything written on them. He flipped through them quickly to make sure.

"Okay," Dani said. "But she'd have to hide the note, or else the kidnappers would have just taken it when they grabbed her." Her gaze went from the notepad back to the posters. "So what if that's what the darts are about? Like . . . a red flag . . . or a hint."

"About where she put the note?" Sam asked.

For a long moment Dani didn't answer. Then she turned and leaned back into the wall and shut her eyes tight. Her hands made little fists at her sides.

"I don't know," she said. "Maybe my brain is making stuff up to keep from going nuts. What do you think?"

Sam turned in place and swept his gaze over the basement. He looked at the bay window, and briefly wondered why Lauren wouldn't have just escaped through it, if she had really been down here when the kidnappers arrived. She could have run to a neighbor's house and called the cops. Then he saw that there were no latches on any of the windowpanes; none of them could be opened. And the glass was double-layered. Lauren might have been able to shatter it, but not quickly or quietly; anyone upstairs would have heard it and come running.

He turned back to Dani.

"I think there are only so many places to hide a note down here," he said. "So let's look."

Dani opened her eyes again.

"Thank you," she said.

They spent half an hour searching. They peeled the posters off the walls and looked behind them. They checked behind the dartboard, and behind its wooden cabinet. They took the baseball display case off the wall. They opened it up and studied every baseball from all sides, in case the message had simply been written on one of them. They looked under and behind and on top of the arcade games. They went into the laundry room below the stairs, and checked inside the washer and dryer.

No note from Lauren. Nothing at all.

Their only find was something that deepened their confusion: in each of the six pockets of the pool table, there was another dart. They were crammed way down in, out of sight to anyone not standing right above them and looking down.

"Okay," Sam said, "so the darts are definitely supposed to mean something. But what?"

Dani looked as lost as Sam felt. "Belly buttons and a pool table," she said. "If there's a connection, I'm missing it."

Sam thought about it for more than a minute, but got nowhere.

"Stumped," he said softly.

Dani made no reply.

Sam went back to the bay window and stared out into the late morning sunlight. The tall grass on the slope moved in long, rolling waves.

He found his gaze drawn to the block-sized pine grove, far away to the southeast, beyond the cluster of buildings downtown. He had seen those pines two days before, on the way to Echo House with Dani. He didn't know why they drew his attention now, except for the obvious fact that they were almost the only trees visible south of the subdivision.

He looked at Dani. She was sitting against the arcade machine again. She had her knees pulled up close to her, and her forehead resting on them.

He wished there were something he could say to her. Something to make her feel better. He watched her for a few seconds and then went back to staring out the window.

Staring at the distant pines.

All at once he blinked and turned again. He looked at the baseball display case—he and Dani had left it on the floor after searching it. He stared at the team logo across the top of the case's front.

"You said Lauren's dad grew up in Philadelphia," he said.

Dani answered without looking up. "Yeah."

"You ever been there?"

"No."

"I have," Sam said. "My uncle lives in Philly, on the east side. The New Jersey side."

"Okay."

"There's a big pine forest up there, just a few miles from my uncle's house. It's a thousand square miles of wilderness, right there in the middle of Jersey. But people who live around there . . . people who grew up there, like Lauren's dad . . . they don't call it a forest. They have a different word for it. You know what it is?"

Dani finally raised her head. She met his eyes. Her expression had taken on an edge of hope—she could see he was going somewhere with this.

"They call it the Barrens," Sam said.

CHAPTER TWENTY-FIVE

On their bikes it took only a few minutes to reach the pine grove, after stopping at Dani's house for two flashlights. The woods, maybe twice the size of a football field, filled out the northwest corner of a square-mile section of farmland. They stashed their bikes in the ditch and stepped into the trees. Inside, the air was cool and clean-scented. Shafts of green-tinted sunlight shone through. The ground was dry and sandy and carpeted with dead needles.

Sam had imagined the entrance to Station 9 would be the same as that of Station 14: something like the access stairs to a subway platform. But before he'd even begun scanning the ground for anything like that, Dani leaned close to him and pointed ahead through the trees.

Just visible through the trunks and low pine boughs, forty or fifty yards away, stood a small wooden structure. They wove their way through the trees until they were standing in front of the thing.

It was a shack, abandoned for what must be decades. The thing was made of rough-sawn planks tacked together with nails. It leaned heavily to the left, the wall beams on that side rotted and falling apart. There was a wooden door on the front, latched shut with an iron lock that had long-since rusted itself into a single fused lump. Which didn't matter, anyway—there were broken-out openings in the walls that were large enough to step through.

Sam went to the nearest of these and leaned in with his flashlight on. Dani stepped up to another, to his right.

The air inside the shack smelled like mildew and decayed wood and damp earth. There was no floor—just a dirt surface overgrown with ferns and a few other plants. Things that thrived in darkness. The brush filled the space except for a long, empty rectangle in the middle: a set of stairs like the kind at Station 14, leading down.

For the next minute, everything else was the same as Station 14, too. The stairs. The black steel door at the bottom. The keypad next to it.

"Five sevens in a row," Dani said.

She punched them in, and the lock thudded open. The two of them pushed the heavy door inward and stepped past it.

The space beyond was instantly familiar: a short corridor lined with grey ceramic tile, and black stenciled writing on the wall:

UNITED STATES D.O.D.
ASHLAND-STATION 9
LIMA 6 CLEARANCE REQUIRED
BEYOND THIS POINT

"Lima six," Sam said. "We're moving up in the world."

Dani crossed to the opposite door, which no doubt led to a flight of stairs going down. She opened it and stepped through ahead of Sam—then gasped and flinched and jumped back, crashing into him.

"Jesus Christ," she whispered. She put a hand to her chest, like her heart had suddenly kicked into overdrive.

Sam shone his light through the door and saw the reason.

There was no flight of stairs there. Just a room, ten feet by ten, with a square pit dead-centered in its floor. The pit was probably five by five, and plunged out of sight into pitch-blackness.

There was no railing around it. Another step and Dani would have gone over the edge.

"I don't imagine safety codes were around when they built this place," Sam said.

"You'd think basic common sense would do."

"You'd think."

She took another few seconds to catch her breath, then shook her head and stepped through the opening again. She moved to the edge of the pit, carefully, and dropped to a knee. Sam knelt beside her, and they aimed their flashlights down into it.

The hole was a concrete-lined shaft dropping away straight down, with a metal ladder bolted to one wall. The shaft's depth had to be two hundred feet. Their light beams didn't actually reach the bottom, but they could see the bottom anyway—the pit had its own light source down there, some kind of bulb that shone as simply a bright orange pinpoint.

"How abandoned could it be if the lights are still on?" Sam asked.

He realized he'd whispered it.

"Very good question," Dani said—also whispering. Then: "What do you think we'll find down there?"

"Your question wins," Sam said.

Dani managed a nervous laugh. "I'm not big on heights, you know."

"Good motivation to not fall," Sam said. He turned off his flashlight, pocketed it, and took hold of the top rung.

The shaft turned out to be 240 rungs deep, whatever that came to in feet. Thirty rungs up from the bottom, the shaft's four concrete walls flared out to form a pyramid-shaped open space. The ladder continued straight down through the middle of that space, to where its footings were anchored in the floor. Sam reached the bottom and stepped off, followed by Dani a second later.

The orange bulb they'd seen from above was right there at the ladder's base: a plastic-shrouded safety light set into the concrete. The floor of the chamber was twenty by twenty feet square. The space was featureless except for a single door on the west wall, and a block of text beside it, in the now-familiar stencil font:

THIS STATION DECOMMISSIONED
NO ENTRY PERMITTED WITHOUT
CASE-SPECIFIC AUTHORIZATION

The stern warning was backed up by a set of heavy-duty steel locks and beams across the door. There were no number pads or keyholes to be seen—whoever had barricaded this door had wanted it to stay shut forever.

But it hadn't.

Someone had drilled and cut their way through every one of the locking measures. The metal shavings were strewn at the foot of the door, which itself hung an inch open in its frame. Sam could just make out a hint of light from beyond it, milky white instead of orange. It flickered erratically, like an old fluorescent bulb running down.

Beside him he saw Dani shiver.

For the longest moment neither of them moved. Sam listened for any sound of activity—any sound at all—from the other side of the door. He heard nothing.

He took a step toward it, Dani moving just behind him. It was easy to be silent on the concrete. Three more steps put him right beside the frame. He leaned forward and put his ear directly to the inch-wide gap in the door. He listened for thirty seconds.

Silence, as dead as he'd ever heard it.

He drew back and glanced at Dani. Her eyes were full of the same uncertainty he felt. Then her eyebrows made a shrug: *now or never.*

He nodded, put his hands to the door and began to push it open—slowly.

An inch per second.

For the first five inches it moved smoothly, with no resistance or sound.

Then one of the hinges groaned.

In any normal place, full of background noises, the sound would've escaped all notice. In the crypt silence of Station 9, it might as well have been a stack of dinner plates shattering.

It echoed through the shaft around Sam and Dani—and also through the unseen space beyond the door.

Both of them froze.

They locked eyes and didn't breathe.

They waited.

Ten seconds passed.

No sound of a response.

Twenty seconds. Thirty.

Nothing happened.

Sam eased the door inward another few inches and took a deep breath, then put his head through the gap and got his first look at the space on the other side.

He stopped worrying about making noise.

CHAPTER TWENTY-SIX

The place was deserted.

And destroyed.

Sam stood there a moment with his head through the door, then simply opened it all the way and stepped through. Dani followed, and for a long time they held still, just inside the threshold, staring.

The room they'd entered was good sized, maybe thirty feet by thirty. Three doorways opened off the left-side wall. None of them had doors—they were just empty steel frames—but from his angle Sam couldn't see into any of the rooms beyond. On the far wall of this first room was a counter lined with computers and equipment that reminded him of the biology lab in his old school. All of it was smashed to pieces. The computers, too. Fragile inner components had been carefully removed and broken to crumbs with a hammer—the hammer was still lying there among the debris.

At one end of the counter stood a wire-mesh garbage basket. A few spaghetti-like strands of shredded paper lay in the bottom, atop an inch-thick mound of ash.

Sam's eyes covered all of those things in a few seconds, and then he forgot them almost entirely. The room's right-side wall grabbed his full attention.

It was lined with cages.

Each took up a cubic yard of space.

Each contained a dead animal.

They looked like monkeys of some kind. They were big—the size of a large dog—with slender arms and legs, long snouts, and deep-set, close-together eyes. And jagged teeth—fangs and pointed incisors like those of a cat. They were almost certainly baboons. Sam had seen them on TV, and at the San Diego Zoo when he'd gone with his cousins.

There were eight cages in all. The baboons in the first seven lay crumpled at the bottoms, in various stages of decomposition. Leaked bodily fluids had pooled around them, mostly dried and crusted, but some still gleaming in the stuttering fluorescent light. Sam saw tufts of blood-stiffened fur stuck to the cage bars here and there, and deep gashes on the animals' forepaws. The baboons in the first seven cages had fought desperately to escape before they'd died.

The baboon in the eighth cage had succeeded.

Its corpse lay sprawled halfway across the sill of the enclosure's door, which hung fully open, its lock mechanism warped and broken. It looked as if the animal had managed to free itself, only to die of exhaustion before it could take another step.

But after a few seconds Sam realized that wasn't the case. Ragged, bloody footprints, originating from the open cage, crisscrossed the entire room. Distinct trails led into each of the three doorways on the left side, and wound their way among the ruined machinery strewn about the place. The baboon had escaped and explored the abandoned station, and then for some reason—maybe just familiarity—had returned to its cage to die.

The last thing Sam noticed was a kind of electrical control box bolted to the wall, just shy of the nearest cage—it was only a few feet from where he and Dani stood. It had the word *ElectroBolt,* like a company logo, across the top, and it had rows of plastic buttons below that. The first eight of those were labeled with stickers that read CAGE 1, CAGE 2, and so on through number eight. Just above all of those, though, was a big red button labeled MASTER RELEASE/ALL LOCKS. That button was covered by a clear plastic dome on a hinge, to make sure nobody pushed it by accident.

Crude wiring ran from the control box to the floor, and then down the row of cages, where the door locks all had the same ElectroBolt logo on them.

Sam took it all in—the smashed equipment and the cages and the dead animals. And the smell. With every breath, he caught more of the rancid atmosphere of the room. It was like a bathroom stall where some-one hadn't flushed, combined with the rusty scent of blood.

"Someone was working in this place," Dani said.

Sam nodded. "Recently."

He felt his thoughts automatically retracing the things he and Dani had learned earlier. The bullet points, any-way.

Project Rigel, whatever it was, had started ten years

ago and ended five years later—its own creator, Mr. Pierce, had pulled the plug, out of fear.

Then Pierce had apparently formed a group called Watchdog, to keep an eye out for anyone trying to restart the project.

For reasons Sam couldn't guess, that group was watching places all over the world, in countries like Brazil and India.

Maybe that search had been aimed at the wrong places.

"We figure the bad guys are people trying to get Rigel going again," Dani said. "Right? That they kidnapped people who originally worked on it, to use what they knew."

Sam nodded.

"So what are we seeing here?" Dani asked. "I mean . . . did someone try to relaunch Rigel *right here? In Ashland? Right under the military's nose?*"

Sam tried to get his mind around the absurdity of it. For a moment he considered another possibility: that the military itself was trying to relaunch the project.

That idea fell apart almost at once. No, he and Dani had already heard what the military thought of all this, in the tape-recorded conversation in her father's office. The government was losing its shit trying to figure out what was going on. Besides, if the military *had* wanted to restart some old project like Rigel, they could have just done it. Officially. They wouldn't need to sneak around kidnapping their own people to work on it. They could *order* them to work on it.

Dani's eyes suddenly narrowed. "Wait . . . if the work

happened here . . . then the people they kidnapped would've been here, too."

She thought about that for another second, then took a deep breath and cupped her hands to her mouth.

"Lauren!"

The screamed word echoed off the strange geometry of the underground rooms.

Nobody answered.

Dani screamed it again, and then a third time.

Nothing.

She turned back to Sam. She looked more afraid than she had even a moment earlier, before Sam had opened the door from the shaft.

He understood why. The bad guys were gone. Whatever they'd been working on here, they'd finished it. They hadn't needed their equipment anymore, so they'd destroyed it. And if they hadn't needed the captives anymore—

Dani seemed to read what he was thinking. Her jaw shook.

"Let's just take it one room at a time," Sam said softly.

Dani nodded, and together they crossed to the first of the three doorways.

The room beyond was no larger than a walk-in closet. It seemed to have been someone's office. There was a computer set up on a card table, with a plastic lawn chair in front of it. The computer, like all the others, had been taken apart and methodically destroyed. Yet the room bore signs of more careless destruction, as well—marked by the bloody paw prints and claw scrapes of the baboon. The thing had smashed the plastic chair into three pieces, and pounded a deep bow into the front edge of the card table.

All that had survived the damage was a section of newspaper, lying folded between the computer monitor and the tower case. Sam pulled it out and let it fall flat atop the table. It was called the *Wells Town Post.* Sam recognized the town's name at once, and turned to Dani. She was nodding—she'd made the connection, too.

"Wells Town, British Virgin Islands," she said. "One of the places Watchdog is keeping tabs on."

They studied the front page together. The lead story was about a boating accident that'd injured four people. It was accompanied by a big photo of a tropical harbor, and someone being carried from a boat on a stretcher.

"Look at this one," Dani said. She pointed to a smaller story in the lower corner. Sam leaned over it and began to read:

More 'bailarines terribles' reported by hikers

Three more reports were filed with Wells Town Royal Police this week by hikers claiming to have witnessed the so-called 'bailarines terribles' in the hill country outside of town, far from populated districts or even footpaths. Authorities were quick to dismiss the sightings as either misunderstandings or hoaxes. This year's spate of reports are the first of their kind in over sixty years in the British Virgin Islands. Most experts reject even the much older reports, which range from the early twentieth century back to pre-colonial times. For several hundred years, as the stories go, the dense jungles around Wells Town were plagued with the 'bailarines.' To modern readers, these accounts sound like something out of a film directed by George—

CONTINUED ON D18

"Ah hell," Sam said.

He flipped through the rest of the section, but only the *A* pages were there. He and Dani scanned the room, but the remainder of the paper was nowhere to be seen. Its ashes were probably among those in the burn basket in the next room.

Sam glanced at the top edge of the section's front page. The date was from over a year ago, in the early springtime.

"This paper was printed a few months before Pierce disappeared," Sam said. "Maybe around the time these people got started trying to reactivate Rigel."

"These reports out of Wells Town must be connected to the project, somehow," Dani said. "According to the faxes we found, Watchdog was monitoring that location, and all the others, for something called *Rigel activity*. I'm guessing the term *bailarines terribles* is another name for that same activity."

"But this says the old stories go back centuries," Sam said. "Rigel obviously wasn't around all *that* time."

"What if Rigel is a project based on something that

was already happening in real life?" Dani said. "Something rare, like whatever this article is talking about. Rigel could have been . . . I don't know . . . some project to study it and use it. Like for a weapon."

Sam nodded. "That would be a good reason for Watchdog to keep an eye on places like Wells Town. Places where the real-life version might happen. They could watch for it, and if they ever saw it, they could try to prevent anyone from using it to relaunch the project."

Sam's eyes tracked over the article stub again.

"*Bailarines* sounds Spanish," he said. "The terrible *bailarines,* whatever that means."

"Ever take a Spanish class?" Dani asked.

"I had a semester in fifth grade. I don't remember much of it. How about you?"

Dani shook her head.

Sam's gaze dropped to the article's cutoff point.

"It'd be a nice clue to know what movie director they're talking about," he said. "George Lucas is the only George I can think of, but it doesn't make much sense."

"Not unless there used to be Jedis and robots running around in the jungle outside Wells Town. For hundreds of years."

Sam shut his eyes and thought about it. There had to be at least a few other directors named George, but for the moment nothing was coming to him.

They stepped back out of the room and proceeded to the next one—the second of the three doorways in the big first room.

Beyond that doorway, they found a short corridor

that ran twenty feet to a heavy glass door, which stood wide open. The glass door was two inches thick, and its edges were lined with dense black rubber; if you closed it, it would form an airtight seal. The two of them stepped through it, and Sam felt his breath catch. He heard Dani's do the same.

The room beyond was probably the strangest one he'd ever seen. Stranger than the vast open space of Station 14. At floor level, this room was normal enough: it was big and square—about the size of the entry room with the cages—and its floor and walls were concrete like the rest of the place.

But not the ceiling.

There *was no* ceiling—at least not in any usual sense.

Instead the tops of the walls flared outward to an empty space above the room. A *colossal* empty space. It was fifty feet across and maybe a couple hundred feet tall, reaching above their heads almost all the way back up to the floor of the pine forest. Dozens of orange lights, like the one out in the ladder shaft, lit the space at regular intervals. Staring up into it, Sam had to concentrate on his balance to keep from falling. The sensation was surreal—like looking up at the opposite of a skyscraper. An emptiness with the dimensions of a high-rise.

After a moment Sam let his gaze drop to the floor space around them. It was littered with more broken machinery, along with the wooden crates it'd all been packed in. No doubt the bad guys had carefully destroyed this stuff, but Sam could see telltale signs that the baboon had been in here, too. Every broken panel of wood had been marred by blood splatters and scratches.

On the right-side wall there was another block of stencil text:

MC3—CLOUD CHAMBER

Beneath the text was a complex array of what looked like nozzles for air hoses. Sam counted thirty of them. Each one had a little valve atop it, like the spigot for a garden hose. Each valve capped a narrow pipe that vanished into the concrete wall. Sam stared back up into the mammoth chamber and saw, after a moment, that pipes of the same size and color emerged from its smooth walls here and there, at varying heights. He guessed they were the other ends of these same pipes down here in front of him, and tried to imagine what this place was for. If someone wanted to, they could attach a tank of any kind of liquid—or maybe a gas—to these valves at floor level, and pump it through the pipes to a spot high up in the empty space above. For what reason, he couldn't guess.

Whatever the case, one thing was certain: this room was what made Station 9 special. This was the reason the bad guys had needed to do their work here, and no place else.

Sam turned his attention back to the ruined crates and machinery. He and Dani made a quick search, but found nothing of interest. No shipping labels. No documents. No further sections of the *Wells Town Post*.

One room left.

They returned to the entry area, with the cages and the three doorways. Sam went to the third and looked through it into the final room.

There was a dead man lying on the floor.

CHAPTER TWENTY-SEVEN

Sam stared and didn't move. A long time passed. In his peripheral vision he saw Dani appear beside him, not quite positioned to see into the last room.

"What is it?" she asked. There was fear in her voice, clamping it down like a shaking hand.

Sam glanced at the dead body again.

"Do you know if Mr. Pierce had black hair?" he asked.

Dani shook her head. "Lauren's dad does—oh my God—"

Her fear forgotten, she came forward and stepped past Sam into the room. She all but ran to the dead man—Lauren's father, apparently—but when she got there she didn't know what to do. She started to kneel, and then didn't; started to reach for him, but pulled back. She plowed her hands through her hair and just stood there, shaking.

Sam went to her. He stared down at the body on the floor. The man lay on his back with his eyes closed, his face bruised purple and deeply gashed. One of the bruises had a patterned edge, matching that of a boot's sole. The bad guys had beaten him to death and left him here.

The baboon had been in this room, too—its bloody tracks were everywhere—but it seemed to have left the body alone. There were no scratches or bite marks on the skin. Lauren's dad must've been dead by the time the thing got loose.

Sam looked at Dani. He was trying to think of what to say, when suddenly she flinched hard and drew back from the corpse, just barely suppressing a scream. Sam followed her stare to the body.

Its eyes were open and looking up at Dani.

A second later the man coughed, and shifted his focus back and forth between the two of them.

"Oh my God," Dani said. "Oh my God . . . we need to get him help . . . an ambulance . . ."

Sam was nodding, already backing toward the doorway. "If you want to stay with him, I'll ride to town and call 9-1-1."

"Do it."

But before Sam could turn to run, the man shook his head violently from side to side.

"No," he croaked, his voice hardly stronger than a whisper.

Sam hesitated. He traded a look with Dani. Then Dani knelt and took hold of the injured man's hand.

She spoke gently. "Mr. Coleman, you need a doctor."

The man coughed again. He drew a breath, which seemed to require all the effort he could muster.

"I'll be dead either way," he whispered.

"We have to try," Dani said.

Mr. Coleman shook his head again. "You have to listen."

His voice was getting weaker by the word.

Dani looked at Sam, then back at the dying man.

"But Mr. Coleman—"

He suddenly gripped her hand harder. His frail arm shook with the exertion.

"If you care about Lauren . . ." he whispered, "*listen.*"

Dani stopped protesting. She met the man's stare and nodded.

Sam returned to Dani's side and knelt down next to her, and waited for the man to speak again.

Mr. Coleman's eyes defocused as he considered what he had to say. Sam guessed he was trying to put it in the fewest words possible. He only had so many left.

"Is it still Thursday?" the man whispered.

Sam and Dani both nodded.

"What time?"

"A little after eleven," Sam said. "In the morning."

Mr. Coleman seemed relieved by that answer. He gathered his thoughts for another few seconds, then said, "There's a barn. Out by the old schoolhouse."

"Echo House?" Dani said. "The barn near there?"

Mr. Coleman nodded. "Tonight. Two in the morning. You have to be . . . watching."

By the last few words he was barely audible. Both Sam and Dani were leaning close above him, straining to hear.

"You want us to watch the barn near Echo House

at two in the morning?" Dani said. "Is Lauren going to be there?"

Mr. Coleman nodded.

"Can we just call the police and get them out there?" Dani said. "Or get a message to someone in charge around here?"

The dying man shook his head. "Police defer to . . . federal authority here. And forget . . . anyone in charge."

Dani looked confused and frustrated. "But *why?* Mr. Coleman, what *is* all this? What is Rigel? What are these people going to do tonight at the barn?"

Mr. Coleman shut his eyes tightly. He looked despondent, and Sam knew the reason: the man was simply out of time. There was way too much to say.

He opened his eyes again and fixed his stare on Dani.

"*You* can save her," he whispered. *"You."*

"How?" Dani asked.

His next two words were so quiet he was almost mouthing them: *"You'll see."*

Then he broke into a coughing fit that made his whole body convulse. Dani continued gripping his hand in hers.

When Mr. Coleman went quiet again, Dani leaned very close to him.

"I'm sorry to keep you talking," she said. "But please, can you tell us why we can't get someone to help? I'm sorry. I'm so sorry . . ."

Mr. Coleman took another breath. Sam had a feeling it was nearly his last.

"Insiders," the man whispered.

"Insiders?" Dani asked. "You mean people working with the bad guys? People here in Ashland?"

Mr. Coleman nodded. "One for sure . . . maybe more . . ."

"Who's the one?" Dani asked. "Do you know the name?"

Mr. Coleman nodded, and then he let go of Dani's hand, took hold of her shoulder and pulled her down to him. She turned her head and put her ear directly to his mouth, and Sam heard him gasp one final word. He couldn't make out what it was.

If Dani understood, she didn't show it. For a second she didn't move or even blink, and then she raised herself up, and Sam saw that Mr. Coleman's face had gone slack. His eyes stared at nothing above him. His hand had fallen limp at his side. He was gone.

For a while neither of them spoke. Then Sam turned to Dani to ask if she'd heard the last word. But before he could speak there came a sound from elsewhere in the station. A wooden crate falling over.

Both of them jumped as if electrically jolted, and stood up fast. They turned to the doorway, through which they could see some of the cages along the far wall of the big room. On a hunch, Sam sidestepped to get a view of the last cage. The one with its door open. The one whose occupant had lain across the threshold. Dani did the same, and let out a low, scared breath.

The baboon was gone.

CHAPTER TWENTY-EIGHT

They heard the thing scream a second later. A high-pitched, ragged cry that reverberated through the complex. Dani grabbed Sam's arm. She was shaking. So was he.

The scream came again, accompanied by the sound of splintering wood as the baboon attacked one of the crates—all of which were in the Cloud Chamber, next door to this room.

Sam looked around. It took almost no thought to grasp the trouble they were in. There was no door they could shut to close this third room, and no place within the room to shelter them. No place to even hide. The room was bare except for Mr. Coleman's body.

The big entry room outside was no better: it had the counter along the back wall, but no cabinets beneath it. Just empty space.

The Cloud Chamber had a door—but the baboon was already in there.

Could the two of them run to that door right now and throw it shut, trapping the animal inside the chamber?

Sam pictured them trying it—trying to swing that

heavy, two-inch slab of glass closed before the baboon saw them and lunged at them.

He shook his head; it wasn't even worth thinking about.

That left one more room to consider: the little one with the card table and the wrecked computer. Useless.

Sam stepped to the doorway. Dani moved with him. They could hear the animal still ransacking the crates inside the Cloud Chamber. They stared across the larger room at the steel door leading back to the ladder shaft. The thirty-foot distance to it looked more like a hundred yards. Even if they could reach it, get through and slam it shut from the other side, there was no way to latch it. All the locks had been drilled out. They'd just have to stand there holding it shut against the force of an enraged, hundred-pound animal on the other side.

Another wild scream. Another crash of breaking wood.

How long before it lumbered into this room? A minute? Even that much time felt like wishful thinking.

"What the hell do we do?" Dani whispered.

Sam didn't answer. He didn't know.

He stared at the distant door, the ladder just visible in the orange-lit chamber beyond. Running for it could get them killed, but it was all he could do to keep from trying it anyway. Just grabbing Dani and propelling her forward as fast as they both could go.

Instead he swept his eyes across the rest of the big room—and saw what they had to do.

The only thing they *could* do.

He whispered it to Dani. She looked at him like he was crazy. Then the baboon shrieked again, and she nodded, fast and frantic.

They each took a deep breath—and ran.

Not for the door to the shaft.

For the open cage.

The instant they left the smaller room, Sam felt like he was in the nightmare where your limbs seemed to weigh a thousand pounds each, and you could barely run, while the monster had no such difficulties.

Dani was a step ahead of him. At fifteen feet, the open cage was maybe four running strides away. The rational part of Sam's mind told him there was no reason to assume the worst. No reason to think the baboon was already behind them, coming after them. It was busy demolishing crates in the Cloud Chamber. It might not even become aware of them until it heard the cage door slam shut, with them inside it. It made sense. He *needed* it to make sense.

Then Dani tucked into a crouch at the end of her last step, dropping and slipping through the cage door without even touching the sides. Her momentum carried her to the back of the cage, giving Sam all the room he needed to get in. In the same movement, Dani pivoted, whipping her head around and looking back.

For maybe a tenth of a second her eyes focused on Sam.

Then they focused past him.

Just past him.

Dani screamed—but Sam didn't hear it. The sound was lost beneath the scream that came from behind him: the baboon's shriek, so close he was sure he could feel its breath on his skin.

An instant later he dropped low, crouching in the same movement Dani had made to enter the cage. He reached for its door with one hand and got his fingers around its gridwork. Slipping through the opening now, turning and yanking on the door as hard as he could. He'd pulled it only halfway closed when the weight of the animal crashed into it, slamming it the rest of the way shut, knocking Sam backward into Dani, both of their bodies compressing against the cage's rear wall.

Sam got his hands under him, got himself positioned to grab hold of the door, expecting the animal to pry it open and come in after them—

But by then he could see what had happened. The baboon's impact had warped the door, tucking the top corner inside the frame while the bottom corner remained outside. The warping had jammed the door in place—for now, at least.

The baboon was standing a foot away from the cage, staring in at them. Blood ran from its mouth and eyes. For a moment it just stood there, breathing rough, staring.

Then it lunged forward and attacked the jammed door with a flurry of movement, pounding it with cat-quick forelimbs that made the entire cage shudder and groan.

Dani threw her arms around Sam and held on tightly. He kept himself between her and the animal, for whatever symbolic good it could do. If the door gave, he guessed she'd survive about three heartbeats longer than he would.

The assault went on for twenty or thirty seconds. Then the baboon drew back from the cage, its deep-set eyes glaring but losing their aggression. It lumbered forward and gave the door one last bash, and then it loped over to the room with the card table and set to work demolishing it further.

They waited. Ten minutes passed. The baboon tore apart what remained of the computer that sat on the card table, then focused its rage on the table itself, pounding it and tearing at the plastic surface with its claws. After a while the animal lost interest. It staggered back into the large entry room. It looked weary. It looked sick. The blood was running in streams now from its nose and eyes. Its shoulders spasmed and jerked.

"What the hell did they do to it?" Dani whispered.

"Rigel," Sam said. "Whatever Rigel is, that's what they did to it."

"Some kind of drug, you think?"

"I don't know," Sam said. It seemed possible. Lots of things seemed possible.

One thing was certain: whatever work these people had been doing here, to re-create Rigel, they had finished it. Now they were out there somewhere, with their results in hand.

The baboon collapsed again a few minutes later. It sank to the floor in the middle of the entry room, ten feet from the cage Sam and Dani were holed up in. It rested its head on one arm and shut its eyes, and its breathing softened until they could no longer hear it.

They waited another five minutes. The thing didn't move. They looked at each other and nodded, and Sam eased forward to get a look at the jammed door of the cage. He could see easily enough what it would take to open it: contorting the cage itself, by pushing against one corner or another, to take the pressure off the spot where the door was wedged.

He worked at it slowly—quietly. He kept his eyes on the baboon as he did. A minute later the door slipped free of the frame.

The climb up the ladder shaft seemed to take forever. They both stared down the entire time, watching the orange light shrink away below them, and hoping like hell they didn't see a shape suddenly block it out.

They reached the top, clambered out of the pit and hurried into the room beyond—the short corridor with the grey ceramic tiles and the stenciled writing on the wall. They crossed to the far end and pulled open the steel door that led out to the staircase, and slammed it shut behind them.

Dani took a step back and lost her strength. She sat down hard on one of the concrete stair treads and put her head in her hands.

Above them, the confining walls of the staircase rose like the sides of a tight hallway with no ceiling to cap it off. Instead it opened to the dim, humid interior of the abandoned shack overhead. Sam could smell the ferns again, and the dirt, and the rotted wood—all of it like heaven after the air inside Station 9.

Dani still had her face buried. Sam sat down beside her, his shoulder against hers. She was shaken up pretty badly. Sam could feel the same reaction in himself, his arms thrumming like tuning forks—adrenaline on a delay timer.

"You'll feel better in a minute," he said softly.

Dani shook her head without looking up.

"I won't." She sounded sure of it, for some reason.

"Why not?" Sam asked.

"Because of what Mr. Coleman said. At the end. The name of the insider."

"You heard it?"

Dani nodded. "All he said was the last name, but it was clear enough."

"What was it?"

She raised her head at last, and looked at him in the murky sunlight filtering down from the shack.

"Ellis," she said.

Sam thought about it. "That sounds familiar to me."

"It should. You heard it two days ago when we shook hands. It's my last name. And my father's."

PART FIVE

IN THE RUINS OF ASHLAND

SEPTEMBER 2018

CHAPTER TWENTY-NINE

Dryden watched the meadow full of FBI vehicles drop away below him, their headlights once more filling up with dust in the downblast of the rising chopper. He was seated at the back of the passenger bay, next to Danica. Jack Grace and the pair of agents with him were belted into the remaining seats, which faced backward toward the two of them. Through the window, Dryden could see the stream of incoming emergency vehicles winding their way along the valley road.

The chopper reached the height of its climb, rotated in place, then pitched down at the nose and set off in a line toward the south.

Grace pointed to a pair of wired-in headsets hanging on the bulkhead behind Dryden and Danica: big firing-range-style ear protectors, each with a built-in microphone sticking out the front. Grace and his men were already wearing their own. Dryden and Danica put theirs on, and Grace spoke into his mouthpiece.

"We've got a plane waiting at an airstrip north of Phoenix. We'll be there in twenty minutes, and on the ground in Iowa by five thirty in the morning local time.

Another chopper ride puts us in Ashland right around sunrise."

Even with the dampening effect of the headset, and the thrum of the turbine engine underneath it all, Dryden could hear the tension in the man's voice. To him, the few hours it would take to reach Iowa probably felt like the last few grains slipping through the neck of an hourglass.

Grace had already told them, before takeoff, the reason they were going to Ashland. There was a plan—Grace had called it a Hail Mary option. To Dryden, it had sounded like a literal Hail Mary rather than the football version. It sounded like something to try on faith alone.

It was also the only move they had left—so they were doing it.

Now, facing them in the dim interior of the chopper, Grace said, "I'd like you both to run through everything that's happened, since the first time these people tried to abduct you. Try to include every detail you can. You never know what might end up mattering."

The agent seated to Grace's left took out a spiral-bound notebook and a pen, and sat waiting to write.

"When you're done," Grace said, "I'll tell you everything *we* know. Wish I could say it'll take me a while, but it won't."

Dryden and Danica took turns with the story—everything from her attempted abduction outside the supermarket to the arrival of the FBI agents on the wooded slope. They finished as the chopper slowed to

a hover above the airfield: a desolate strip just beyo
the northernmost suburbs of Phoenix, surrounded b
industrial parks and black desert hills. Dryden could see the plane already waiting—a light business jet parked right at the runway threshold, its strobes flashing and its door open.

They set down thirty yards from the plane, got out and ran for it, and two minutes later they were in the air again, banking and climbing, the enormous sodium-orange sprawl of Phoenix sliding by outside. The plane settled into its northeast heading, out over the desert, and Grace began his story.

It started four years back, with the emergence of a new arms dealer on the global stage. A very smart arms dealer, who was uncannily good at staying invisible. He—assuming it was a he—seemed to know every trick the FBI and other agencies had at their disposal. Like a mouse that knew how to spring traps.

So far, the Bureau had never picked up a single useful fact about him: age, description, nationality, accent—anything. There was nothing on which to base even a nickname, so he never got one—agents just referred to him by his investigation handle, Whiskey Four; he was the fourth manhunt assigned to Task Force Whiskey at Quantico. After a while, the handle itself became a kind of nickname for the guy—everyone just called him Whiskey.

The only evidence that he existed at all was the merchandise he sold; for four years now, all over the world, government raids of terror cells and crime syndicates had been finding the shit, and it wasn't den-variety—the guy wasn't selling Kalashnikovs cheap knockoffs of Stinger missiles. No, Whiskey was selling classified U.S. military hardware, some of which had never actually been deployed in the field. In a few cases, the stuff had never even been approved for production beyond a few prototypes, which should have been kept under lockdown at secure R & D sites.

How the guy was getting his hands on that kind of stuff, nobody knew. He had to be cutting deals with insiders, manipulating them with carrots and sticks. But if he could do that, it meant he knew his way around the inner workings of the military, just as he did with the FBI.

When that fact became apparent, the hunt for Whiskey Four got shifted into the highest possible gear. Congressional committees met with high level FBI and CIA people behind closed doors, and cut them blank checks with a single, wire-taut string attached: *find him and stop him, right fucking now; if the rules get in your way, let us know and we'll bend them around you.*

None of it helped. The money and the blanket-approval made no difference at all. There were simply no tracks in the soil. Whiskey was a ghost—the rumor of a ghost—and in the past four years, the picture of him had become no clearer.

It had become scarier, though—just under a week ago now. That was when chatter started coming in, from informants in half a dozen criminal organizations around the globe. Those scattered reports all said the same thing: Whiskey had gained possession of a weapon system unlike anything ever used in battle before—a weapon that would stun the world. To prove this to potential buyers, he promised to demonstrate it against a civilian target inside the United States. That would happen on a set date, before noon Eastern Time.

The informants providing these leaks had all been reliable in the past. Their handlers were vouching for them at present. The analysts at Langley and Quantico who broke down the data, compared it to other intel, and ran it through the confidence protocols all came back sweating and pale. The threat looked real—as real as anything else that had ended with helicopter footage on CNN and Fox.

That was when the higher-ups went back behind closed doors with the congressional committees, and asked about bending the rules a bit further, or breaking them, or putting them through a wood chipper.

A lot happened in the next twenty-four hours, and none of it was pleasant. In far-flung places all over the world, doors got kicked in and people got dragged from their beds or kitchen tables or showers—anyone even vaguely suspected of doing business with Whiskey. They ended up in the custody of American allies who weren't bound by American limits on interrogation.

In the days that followed, in nice offices overlooking the Potomac, people paced and waited for news from ugly little rooms that didn't overlook anything. When that news finally came—two days ago now—it was just five words, coughed out by a man to his captors:

Rigel. It's something called Rigel.

The statement raised lots of eyebrows—mostly in confusion. What the hell was Rigel? A fast computer search of Pentagon databases returned two hits: there was an infrared camera built for AWACS aircraft called a Rigel FLIR, and there was a suite of navigation software for Coast Guard interceptor boats called Rigel Nine Seven. Neither of those sounded especially dangerous.

At that point, with time running out, the investigators opted for crowdsourcing. They put the word out to all FBI field offices, CIA stations, and military investigative units: *If you know what the term* Rigel *means, in the context of classified military systems, get in touch with us right now.*

"That's when I came into the picture," Grace said. "I got the memo about thirty-six hours ago. As head of the L.A. field office, they wanted me to ask around in the ranks, especially among guys with military backgrounds. I talked to a couple dozen of them in a few hours; none of them had heard of anything called Rigel. It wasn't until the next morning, *this* morning, that I decided to talk to my old boss, the guy who was SAC in that office right before me. I called him at his place in Florida and ran it by him, and he got quiet as soon as I said the word *Rigel*. Then he said, *There's something you need to know about.*"

"The blue binder," Danica said.

Grace nodded. "Just he and two other men had seen it. They found it five years ago in your father's office, after he died. It was in a secure safe in the wall. It jolted the hell out of them, reading that stuff. He must've broken twenty different laws to get that information, and they were probably breaking a few of them just reading it. But they read it anyway. Then they put it in a safe-deposit box and decided to keep their mouths shut about it, and cross their fingers no one ever came around asking about the damned thing."

Grace shifted in his seat. He glanced out the window beside him. Nothing out there but darkness now—probably the New Mexico Rockies.

"He put me in touch with the other two men," Grace said, "and I had the binder in my hands thirty minutes later. It names both of you right away, and the term *Rigel* shows up soon enough, but there's no description of what the hell it is. Anyway, I was only a few pages in when I called the guys in D.C. who'd sent that memo around. I told them this was the lead, for sure, and that we needed to find the two of you right away. But we'd barely gotten started on that search when the word came in from Thousand Oaks: the murder scene with your car out front, Danica. That's when we were sure beyond a doubt—we were on the right track."

"These people," Dryden said, "Whiskey's people . . . they came after the two of us because the crowdsourcing tipped them off. Right? When the FBI put the word out to other agencies and the military, asking about Rigel, Whiskey got wind of it."

Grace nodded. "He has deep connections inside the military. It's how he does business in the first place. So yes, he would have found out we were getting closer. If he was afraid we might eventually find out about you two, it would make sense to grab you first. Like I said before, the fact that he's worried about you gives me hope—the only hope I have right now."

"That binder," Danica said, "wasn't there anything else in it that could help? Beyond the name *Rigel*?"

Grace shook his head. "The book is mostly scattered notes your father took down from people he met with, in the years after the accident in 1989. Friends he'd served with at Ashland, who he trusted. He cobbled together what they knew, and somewhere in there he got the name of that weapon system, but whoever he got it from didn't know anything else about it. In any case, your father seemed to be . . . obsessed with learning what happened that night, and he seemed to have a real fixation on the military's own investigation of it."

"Moss mentioned that," Dryden said.

"It's not unheard of," Grace said. "That sort of victim mind-set. The man almost lost his daughter, and here was the military pretending it never happened, keeping all the answers for themselves. I think it may have been that simple. It just pissed him off, and he couldn't let it go. He wanted to find out what the hell they knew."

A long silence played out. Dryden listened to the deep drone of the engines, and the whisper of thin air over the jet's skin.

Then he looked up at Grace. "Why can't *you guys* find out what the military knew? You're the FBI, and you've got the whole government backing you on this thing. You've probably got the president weighing in."

"More than weighing in," Grace said. "I've talked to him twice already today. This is all he's focused on right now."

"Then why no results?" Dryden asked.

"I don't think I've made it clear just how deeply the military buried what happened in Ashland. That investigation the Army did? They destroyed their own files on it after they finished it. They did the same for any documentation of what Rigel was about, which is why the Pentagon's database didn't have anything useful in it. They also wiped out the personnel files for Ashland: everyone who worked and lived there, everyone in D.C. who was connected to it, everyone who took part in the investigation afterward. Twenty-nine years later, we simply don't have their names. We'd have to interview thousands of ex-military people to stumble on a few who worked at that site, and hope they could point us toward a few others. In weeks, we could do it. Not in hours."

"What about the names in the binder?" Danica asked. "People my father knew there."

"We got through to some of them. Out of seven names, four had passed away, two were retired and willing to speak to us, and the last was Russell Moss, who never even served at Ashland. The two we interviewed weren't much help. They're both in their eighties now. They gave us a handful of names, other people they worked with in Ashland, but the ones we could track down were all dead of old age. Same for the guys who ordered Moss to drug you, at that roadblock north of town. Everyone old enough to be in charge, back then, is gone now."

Grace was quiet a moment. Then: "There was one other name in that binder. We think it was a civilian, because it doesn't match any military ID from 1989.

Someone named Lauren Coleman. Does it ring a bell with either of you?"

Dryden thought about it, but could only shake his head. He saw Danica do the same.

"What does the binder say about her?" Dryden asked.

"Only a few lines," Grace said. "Questions, really, like mental notes Richard Ellis jotted down for himself. He wrote, *What happened to her? If she survived, where is she? Relocated somewhere?* Whoever she was, it sounds like Ellis knew her before the accident, and then never found out what became of her. Beyond that, we know nothing about her—not even her age at the time. Right now there are over three hundred Lauren Colemans in the United States. And if she's still around somewhere, she could be married and going by a new name. Like anyone else from Ashland, we might track her down in the long-term, but not today."

Grace sighed and rested his hands in his lap. "No, you're it. We're trying everything else we can, I promise. There are people on the phones right now, chasing every half-assed thing they can think of. But it's not going to work—not in time. So it's down to you. I'm sorry, but it is."

Dryden stared out into the darkness below, and thought of the Hail Mary plan again—the reason they were going to Ashland. It rested on an idea—an awkward fact the American intelligence community had started running into, a few years back:

Some of their nullified witnesses from decades ago—the people who'd had their memories scrubbed with those drugs—had ended up remembering a thing or two. Sometimes a lot more than that.

The first known case was a man named Kurt Reyher, an East German intel officer who defected to the United States in 1967. He escaped by meeting with American agents inside the Bode Museum in East Berlin, who then smuggled him out of the country. They brought him stateside and the CIA spent two months interviewing him, learning everything they could. Then they used the drugs to blank out his memory of that time, so he would never know exactly what he'd revealed, or who'd questioned him. That was a precaution in case his own people ever got him back. But they didn't get him back. He settled in a suburb outside Houston and got married and had two kids, and everything was fine—until one day in 2008, when he and his wife were vacationing in Berlin, and they decided to check out the Bode Museum. The moment Kurt Reyher set foot in that place, the memories started coming back—vague at first, and then vivid.

As far as we can tell, Grace had said, *it was the setting that did it: being back inside that place, which hadn't changed much in all the years since he was there.*

The museum, with its distinct look and feel—maybe even its smell—had pulled up Reyher's memories like a salvage tug hauling part of a shipwreck out of the murk.

Which meant the nullification drugs probably didn't erase memories at all—they just buried them under a ton of silt. And if you could get a hold of something down there and pull it up, you might bring a lot more with it. In Kurt Reyher's case, he eventually recalled the names of the operatives who'd helped him escape East Germany, and some of those who'd interviewed him afterward. All those lost memories were tied together, like the hubs and spokes of a Tinkertoy assembly.

That last part made sense, Dryden thought. Even ordinary memories were connected like that. How many times had he recalled some long-ago experience and found it linked to others? A high-school dance, a fight in the hallway afterward, a friend joking around later with an ice pack to his cheek. Memories strung together in a daisy chain.

"What does Ashland look like now?" Dryden asked. "If it was supposed to mimic an ordinary town in 1989—"

"It's been fenced off and abandoned ever since the accident," Grace said. "The parts above ground probably won't look familiar now, after almost thirty years of decay. We'll have you look at them anyway, in case they spark something. But according to the binder notes, there are underground complexes on-site, and it indicates that you two may have been inside some of them, one way or another. Those parts of the facility won't have changed at all since then."

"Like the Bode Museum," Danica said.

Grace nodded.

Outside and far below, Dryden saw details of civilization sliding into view again. A few midsized cities along the dull orange artery of a freeway. He realized his jaw had tightened, involuntarily. He let it relax, and turned away from the window.

Danica was watching him. "Something wrong?" she asked.

He started to answer, but cut himself off, unsure of how to say it. Unsure of what he felt, even.

"What is it?" Danica said.

Dryden looked at her. "I hope we remember as much as we need to. But—"

He stopped again. He didn't want to say the rest—didn't want to admit it. He exhaled hard. *Fine, what the hell?*

"That other thing we witnessed," he said. "The thing that was worse than the accident itself. There's a part of me that hopes we don't remember it at all. A part of me that's scared shitless to find out what we saw. And I don't know why."

Danica stared at him a few seconds longer, then blinked and looked away. "I thought I was the only one," she said.

CHAPTER THIRTY

Dryden was staring at Ashland for close to a minute without even realizing it. From five hundred feet up in the chopper, looking out over the landscape in the breaking light, the enormous green circle out ahead of him might have been just another crop field with a radial sprinkler system. He had seen them all his life from the windows of airliners, dotting the country like checkers on a grid. He could see a dozen of them now, off to the left and right; the crops had already been harvested and the fields were brown and vacant, but their perfectly round outlines remained.

That circle out ahead was nobody's farmland, though: the thing was six miles across. And it sure as hell hadn't been harvested. It was wilderness land, its details coming into clearer view with each second as the chopper drew nearer. The dark green that filled the circle was tall prairie grass, choked everywhere with random scrub brush and groves of hardwood trees, some of them probably fifty feet tall. Their leaves showed the first traces of autumn color setting in. Here and there among them, the standing ruins of farmhouses and barns jutted up out of the grassy sea, like beached relics in a tidal basin.

Where roads had once been, there were now just faintly indented lines in the wavy surface of the weed tops, hinting at root-fractured asphalt and runoff ditches hidden below. All of it looked ghostly under the pink sky, in the sidelong light of dawn.

Far out ahead, at what Dryden judged to be the center of the circle, stood the clustered remains of the town itself. He could see two separate patches of decaying sprawl: a roughly square shape that might have been a small downtown, and a half-moon shape just north of there. He guessed the half-moon had been a residential subdivision, because the whole thing was densely overgrown with tall trees—much taller than the random groves that had sprung up everywhere else. Which meant they were older. Probably they had been full-grown shade trees even twenty-nine years ago, spreading over the neat sidewalks and back yards of Ashland.

The chopper was closing in now, coming up to the southern boundary of the circle. Dryden swept his gaze slowly left to right one last time, taking in the vastness of the thing.

They set up what they called an exclusion zone around the accident site, Russell Moss had said, *at a radius of three miles from Ashland on all sides.*

Now as the chopper went into a hover and began to descend, Dryden took in the chain-link fence that marked the boundary between the circle and the land around it. In the fields that butted up against the fence from outside, tractor furrows and short-chopped corn stalks extended right to the boundary itself. Local farmers weren't letting a square foot go to waste. In the gleam of sunlight, Dryden saw tangles of razorwire arrayed along the top of the fence, spooling away in both directions as far as he could see.

He found himself doing the math, regarding the fence: the circle was six miles in diameter, and six times pi was just under nineteen.

Nineteen miles of chain-link and coiled wire.

"Jesus," he whispered.

He glanced at Danica, sitting beside him. She was staring out the window, too, taking it all in with wide eyes. She turned and met his gaze. Her eyebrows went up and down in a little shrug, as if to say, *We'll see what happens.*

"Welcome back," she said.

The chopper set down on the blacktop of a county two-lane, thirty yards from where the fence cut it off. This road was exactly centered on the southern border of the circle.

Dryden climbed out into the morning air; it was crisp and cool and he could smell the damp earth of the tilled fields. Grace came around the front of the chopper carrying two FBI windbreakers; he handed one each to Dryden and Danica. Dryden slipped his on, turning and taking in the small army of FBI personnel that had already massed along the road. There were black SUVs and open-top Jeep Wranglers, maybe a dozen of each. There had to be a hundred men and women standing among the vehicles, dressed in black and carrying M4 rifles.

"Abundance of caution," Grace said, seeing both Dryden and Danica take in the firepower. "Whiskey's smart enough to predict us showing up here."

Dryden nodded; the same thought had crossed his mind more than once already.

Behind Grace, two agents climbed into the open passenger bay of the chopper. They strapped themselves in right on the threshold, their legs hanging outside and their feet braced on the skids. Both carried handheld spotting scopes. A moment later the chopper powered up and lifted off again, climbing out over the circle. The two spotters were already surveying the wide open space within it.

Dryden turned his attention to the fence, where agents with torches were hard at work. They were cutting away a section as wide as the road, shoulder to shoulder. As they worked their way up from the bottom, Dryden's focus went to a big metal sign fixed to the fence, dead-centered above the roadbed.

NO TRESPASSING BEYOND THIS POINT!
VIOLATORS WILL BE PROSECUTED
UP TO FIVE YEARS IN PRISON / $250,000 FINE
RECLAMATION ZONE FOR THE STUDY OF
NORTHERN SAVANNA GRASSLAND ECO-REGION
IOWA DEPARTMENT OF NATURAL RESOURCES &
IOWA STATE UNIVERSITY

A moment later, the torch work completed, the men at the fence pulled the cutoff section down and dragged it across a ditch into the dormant cornfield.

Dryden stared at the open gap in the fence line, the now naked boundary between the outside world and Ashland. The effect was more jarring than he had expected. Where the road crossed the margin, everything changed: smooth, well-kept blacktop on one side, crumbled asphalt shot full of weeds on the other. Where the section of fence had stood, the three-foot-high grass now appeared compressed against thin air, holding the shape of the chain-link like a casting from a mold.

Dryden turned as the first of the open Jeeps rolled up beside him. He looked back along the line of vehicles; the armed agents had all taken their seats inside them, ready to roll.

All at once he felt the pressure settling onto him, all the weight of the moment concentrated onto a space the size of his shoulders. He pictured tactical teams just like this one, in cities all over America, saddled up and ready, waiting for news from right here—from himself and Danica.

Dryden had been under that kind of pressure before—his old line of work had offered a steady supply of it. But in all those cases, there had at least been something he could *do.* Some action he could take, however steep the odds against success. The responsibility on his back had also been in his hands.

This situation was different. The world was waiting for him to do something that wasn't even up to him—the memories would come or they wouldn't.

At the edge of his vision, Dryden saw Danica draw a hand across her forehead. Maybe the same pressure was landing on her.

On the far side of the Jeep, Grace was reaching for the front passenger door when he stopped, seeing their expressions. He came around the back and stood facing them.

"Hey," the man said. His tone was even, though he couldn't hide the stress behind it. "I know this is a crapshoot. There's no precedent for how to do it, and no guarantee it'll work. Anyplace we look at, in there, if you feel like you're getting something back . . . I don't want you to force it. Not if that's going to screw it up. We need this fast, but we also need it right. So—" He cut himself off, thinking. He glanced back down the caravan of waiting vehicles, then looked at Dryden and Danica again. "Don't feel hurried. But hurry."

He turned and went back around the Jeep and got in.

Dryden traded a look with Danica, and then they climbed into the back seat.

A moment later the vehicle had crossed the boundary into the tall grass, and was rolling through it at forty miles an hour.

It felt more like being in a boat than a Jeep. The weeds hissed around and beneath the chassis like water. Behind it, strung out in a long line, came the motorcade of other Jeeps and SUVs.

Dryden stood up from his seat and leaned forward against the roll bar. The view before him was wide open, unobstructed. Beside him, Danica stood and did the same. They watched the distant ruins of the town close in toward them, and waited for something to click.

"Hold up," Dryden said.

The driver brought the Jeep to a stop.

They had come almost two miles north from the fence, and had just passed a line of low, scrubby hardwoods on their left—to the west of the road. As the grove had slid past, it had revealed a small house standing half a mile away, all alone in the rippling grass. The thing was sun-bleached yellow, with a dark grey roof. A quarter mile farther west stood an enormous barn, broadside to the yellow house. The barn's roof had partly caved in from rot, but the exterior walls remained intact.

Dryden realized his breathing had changed—had gone just noticeably shallow. He turned to Danica and saw her staring at the house and barn, too—raptly.

Grace turned in his seat and looked up at both of them. "You got something?"

"I don't know," Dryden said. "Maybe."

"Call it a strong maybe," Danica said.

"Is it the house or the barn?" Grace asked.

Dryden shook his head. "I can't tell. Might be both."

Grace turned to the driver. "Take us over there."

The Jeep got moving again. Up ahead, the telltale impression of a crossroad cut through the weeds. The driver made the left, and a few seconds later the Jeep was accelerating straight west toward the two derelict structures.

The moment Dryden climbed out of the vehicle, in front of the small house, the sense of déjà vu intensified. The exterior walls were made of brick, and the roof was slate. Dryden realized he had already known that, even before they were close enough to see those details—he had been thinking of it as a brick house from the moment it slid into view past that grove.

Danica got out behind him. In his peripheral vision, Dryden saw the Jeep's driver start to open his door, but Grace leaned across and stopped him, making a gesture that said, *Leave them to it.*

Dryden glanced down at the weeds in front of him, looking for the near edge of the runoff ditch that flanked the road. Instead he saw what must have been the entry drive to the yard, long ago: a gravel lane that crossed the ditch, just visible now in the deep grass. Dryden followed it. He had gone only half a dozen steps beyond when his foot smacked against something rock solid. He cursed softly and caught his balance, then stepped back from the thing.

He saw a low, squat shape under the weeds. He knelt and pushed them aside, revealing what at first appeared to be a tombstone. Then he read the engraving:

ASHLAND TOWNSHIP SCHOOL
FUNCTIONAL 1847–1938

"I'm getting a really strong vibe from this," Danica said. There was a hush in her voice—some mix of wonder and fear. "How about you?"

Dryden nodded. "I've seen this before. I know it."

He stood again and considered the building—the schoolhouse. The front door hung a few inches ajar, and partly detached from its frame. It was mostly bare metal, rusted all over, but a few chips of red paint held on here and there, like tiny islands on a map—

A map of an alien world.

The phrase seemed to shove itself into his mind, from out of nowhere.

He crossed the yard to the cracked-open door, took hold of it and pulled. It swung outward with a protest of grinding metal, sharp and high-pitched. Two or three seconds later he heard that sound again, from far away to the west.

He and Danica turned in place. Dryden considered the barn, a quarter mile away, its giant side wall facing the schoolhouse.

Before Dryden could say anything, Danica brought her hands up in front of her and clapped them together—three times in a fast cadence. The staccato sound came back to them across the field, dampened and hollow.

"Echo House," Danica said, seeming to think of the words even as she voiced them. "That's what we called this place."

As the house itself had done, the name immediately struck Dryden. Danica was right about it—no question of that.

He stared at the distant barn a moment longer, then turned and stepped into the dim interior of Echo House.

He saw a flagstone floor, and candleholders set into

the walls, and a potbelly stove in a back corner of the single room. Every bit of it pinged his recognition.

Danica stepped in through the doorway and came up beside him. They stood staring at the place.

"It clicks," Danica said. "But . . ."

"But that's *all* it does. I don't feel it connecting to anything else."

Danica shook her head. "Nothing like that. Not yet."

Dryden took in the room a few seconds longer, waiting for something else to come to him. Nothing did.

Don't feel hurried. But hurry.

"Let's look at the barn," Dryden said.

From up close, the barn's vibe was harder to put a finger on than Echo House's. Standing in the overgrown yard before the giant building, Dryden studied the details of its exterior. Behind him, the sun was just above the horizon, glaring off the weathered wood of the structure. Dryden moved from place to place, trying to find an angle that looked familiar. None did.

"I can't explain it," Danica said. "I could swear we were here, but . . . the sight of it doesn't trigger much of anything, for me."

Dryden could make no sense of it, either. He felt the same certainty that the two of them had been here—even a vague intuition that they had watched this place, for some reason, maybe for hours. Yet its features, clear and sharp in the direct sunlight, stirred no recognition at all.

After a moment Dryden lowered his gaze to the

huge rolling door on the front of the barn, which stood open a few feet. Thc space beyond was dim but not dark; the partly collapsed roof let in plenty of light.

He and Danica crossed to it and stepped inside. They stood there for ten seconds, saying nothing. Dryden saw giant rough-hewn timbers, and scattered debris from the roof, and bird nests and hornet nests and three decades' worth of wood rot.

"I don't feel anything at all in here," Danica said.

"Same."

Behind them, outside and far away, Dryden could hear the rotors of the chopper beating the air. Like a ticking clock running at triple-time.

"Let's go," he said.

The long motorcade returned to the north-south road and continued toward downtown. They reached it a minute later; the Jeep's driver slowed to a crawl. Dryden swept his eyes over what remained of the place: a line of storefronts and other businesses running up the main drag, across from the rusted shell of an old grain elevator. Every building had sagged and decayed. Here and there, walls had tilted or fully collapsed.

None of it struck a chord with Dryden, though that didn't surprise him; nothing here looked remotely like it would have in the summer of 1989.

Out ahead, beyond the last of the storefronts, a broad grassy slope led up to the subdivision, which lay entirely east of the road—the half-moon shape, as it had looked from the air. From here, Dryden could see that he'd been right: it was all houses up there, tucked in under the canopy of huge shade trees, the space beneath them cluttered with second-generation growth. Only the houses at the outer edge of the subdivision were visible now, like watchmen just inside the forest, staring out over the open field below.

The procession sped up again as it left the downtown behind, climbing the rise with open land on both sides. Dryden watched the subdivision come up on his right; a moment later they were beside it, slowing again, he and Danica staring into the dark reaches of the woods. The shapes of houses drifted by, deep in the trees, silhouettes backlit by murky sunlight.

The lead Jeep came to a stop at the far end of the woods—the northern edge. Dryden looked back along the length of the motorcade, stretching down to probably the midpoint of the forest.

He heard the chirp of a two-way radio, and turned toward it: Grace had it on his belt, the microphone clipped to his shoulder. Now a man's voice came through the speaker: "*Air to point, over.*"

Grace keyed the microphone. "Go ahead, air."

"No sign of any access point to the underground. We're going farm by farm now, checked about half of them so far."

Dryden looked around and found the chopper, two miles away to the west. It was flying in a slow, tight circle above a distant barn and its outbuildings.

"Alright, keep on it," Grace said. He let go of the key switch, then opened the door and got out. He waved to one of his men, coming forward from the next Jeep.

"Get everyone on foot," Grace said, then nodded

at the woods. "I want a sweep of the whole subdivision, three agents to a house, fast and thorough. We're looking for any means of access to the underground complex. We'll check here and then we'll look downtown. Go."

The agent turned and ran back to his Jeep, waving others toward him.

Dryden climbed down out of the back seat, along with Danica. Grace met them, then turned his focus in toward the nearest houses, barely visible through the screen of underbrush.

"Any chance you'll spot the ones you lived in?" Grace asked.

Dryden considered the nearby homes. Like the storefronts downtown, they were rotted and falling apart. From outside, much of the recognizable detail was obscured by tree limbs. On the insides, there was probably little left but exposed framing and piles of collapsed drywall.

I'm not sure I'd know mine even if I could *remember it,* Dryden thought, but didn't say.

To Grace, he said, "When in doubt, try like hell."

The man nodded, appreciating it but unable to make himself smile. He clapped Dryden on the shoulder, then moved off quickly to take charge of his people.

Together, Dryden and Danica made their way into the trees. They could hear the FBI teams mobilizing, off to the south.

After the first twenty feet, the dense ground-level brush ended and the space opened up, as Dryden had hoped it would; this far in under the canopy, there wasn't enough sunlight for small plants. There was only a carpet of dead leaves and pine needles, probably several years' worth.

They had just passed into that space when Danica stopped and turned toward something off to the left. Dryden followed her gaze, and saw the remains of a small playground. It stood at the farthest tip of the forest, snugged up against the road. There was a merry-go-round and a teeter-totter and a swing set, all hopelessly tangled in dense shrubs and strangler vines.

Dryden found his focus drawn especially to the swings, though he couldn't say why. He glanced at Danica and saw her staring at them, too.

A thought came to him, as fleeting as the transient sunlight through the trees: not all of the lost memories would have been bad ones. That hadn't occurred to him until now; he had been too preoccupied wondering what sort of nightmare he and Danica had experienced all those years ago. But they had been children, after all—there would have been nice moments they shared, in those few summer days. Maybe something good had happened right here in this little park. Something they both would have liked to remember.

Dryden stared at the swings a few seconds longer, but nothing more came to him. Danica turned and met his eyes.

"Keep moving, I guess," she said softly.

Dryden nodded, and they continued on toward the nearest houses.

They moved south through adjoining yards, and across short inner streets that tied together the longer, arching ones. Here and there, a stretch of pavement or sidewalk showed through the layer of dead leaves.

They met FBI people in tight groups, moving fast from house to house. There had been no luck yet finding an underground access point.

They were getting closer to the southern edge of the woods—Dryden could see the trees thinning, maybe a hundred yards farther on—when they found something that made them stop: a pine tree with a yellow Ford Escort leaning against it. The car was pitched nose-up at forty-five degrees, its front bumper resting against the tree trunk, its back end braced on the ground.

Stranger still, the tree itself seemed to have been deformed by the weight of the car. Though the pine's trunk was as thick as a telephone pole, its bottom curved sharply as if bowed under the mass of the Escort's front end. Then, once it cleared the bumper, the trunk pointed straight upward as normal. The tree had simply grown that way.

"I might have thought the car was here first," Danica said, "and the tree grew up afterward and lifted it, but . . . it doesn't work like that. I mean, that's not how a tree grows. It wouldn't have done this."

Dryden was nodding; she had it exactly right. A growing trunk didn't push upward over time, like the magic beanstalk in the old story. A tree just kept adding new length at the top, while the lower parts of the trunk stayed put. A young tree that sprouted beneath this car would not have lifted it like this, even if it could have borne the weight. It would have grown out around it, seeking the light, or simply died for lack of it.

Dryden thought of those things, but only with a small part of his attention; all the rest was consumed by the same feeling he'd had at Echo House.

"I've seen this car," he whispered.

Even now, staring at the thing, the feeling seemed to grow. It was stronger than any vibe he'd felt so far. There was more to it than déjà vu. There was—

Dryden flinched and took a step back. Danica turned to him, startled.

"What is it?" she asked.

"I don't know. Just for a second, I felt . . . panicked. I can't explain it."

"Do you think it's a memory coming back?"

Dryden was quiet a moment, trying to find the feeling again. Seconds passed. Nothing there.

"I don't know what it was," he said at last. "What about you? Are you getting anything from this?"

She stared at the vehicle for a long moment, narrowing her eyes.

"Nothing," she said.

Dryden stepped closer to the car again, studying it. Of all the vehicles they had seen in the subdivision, it was the only one with all its windows intact. Its windshield had a big spiderweb fracture on the driver's side, but the glass was still in one piece; ditto for the window above the hatchback. Every other car and truck they had seen, either parked in driveways or garages, had been damaged by falling hardwood limbs or collapsed sections of ceiling. This Escort, for whatever reason, had been left in somebody's back yard; the two nearest houses both had rear decks pointing this way.

Dryden took hold of the door handle and pulled, half expecting the door to be fused shut with interior rust.

Instead it opened immediately. The hinges groaned, and because of the car's angle, the door had to be lifted as it swung out, but otherwise the thing moved easily. The air inside the vehicle wafted out, stale and dry, as if undisturbed for years. Dryden leaned in and studied the interior: the front and back seats, the footwells. Nothing there. He released the door and let it fall shut.

"I don't know," he said again.

The sense of recognition was still there, but whatever else it was tied to had come and gone.

They continued south past the next line of homes, onto a street that turned out to be the last one. The houses beyond it formed the outer edge of the subdivision; they were the same houses Dryden had seen facing out over the slope above downtown Ashland.

"Wait a second," Danica said.

There was something in her voice—a rush of excitement, Dryden thought.

He looked at her; she was focused on one of the outer-edge houses, across the street and down a ways. She stared a moment longer, then broke into a sprint toward the place. Dryden ran after her.

They came to a stop in the house's front yard. Like every other home they had seen, it had weathered the years badly. Most of the windows were broken, and one corner sagged deeply where an upright beam must have rotted through.

Yet the overall shape of the structure still held, and the vinyl siding, dark green with white trim, remained intact.

"Was it yours?" Dryden asked.

For a moment she didn't answer. Her expression was one of searching, trying to dial in on what she felt.

"I don't think so," she said at last. "But it's so familiar . . . like I was here all the time."

"Maybe it was a friend's house."

"Maybe."

Dryden studied the place more intently, waiting for it to stir any impression. If he felt anything, it was only fleeting—vague enough that he might be imagining it.

Danica took a step closer to the house. "This is the first time I've felt like there's something else trying to come to the surface."

She crossed the yard to the front door, which was intact but warped in its casing. She put one foot against it, right beside the knob, and simply pushed. With a sound like a bundle of twigs breaking, the frame gave way around the latch. The door swung inward.

The moment they stepped inside, Dryden gave up on the place. Whatever spark Danica had felt about it from outside, the inside wasn't going to ring any bells. Every wall surface had either blackened with mold or fallen away from the studs. There were a few pieces of furniture—two bed frames with bare mattresses, a table, a couch, a recliner—but even those could have looked nothing like they had when Danica last saw them. All the cloth had darkened or else been chewed away by animals. There were dried-up bird nests embedded in the couch's foam backing. It was like standing in the skeleton of somebody's home, with the rotted bits of a few organs left behind for good measure.

They came to the basement last. It was a soggy ruin like the rest of the house—at the foot of each wall, the floor was heaped with crumbled sheetrock that had once covered the uprights. Mold and even ferns and mushrooms had sprouted from some of the piles.

But unlike the upstairs, the basement contained things that had weathered the decades intact—things that had kept their shape, anyway: a row of arcade machines along one wall, a bay window looking out onto the slope, a pool table centered in front of it.

Since they'd entered the house, Dryden had been watching Danica for a sign that she recognized something. Now he felt a jolt of familiarity himself—it flickered like a candle, then flared bright in his mind.

"Holy shit," he whispered.

Danica turned to him, but before she could ask anything, Dryden stepped past her and crossed to the pool table at almost a run. His eyes were locked onto the nearest pocket, even before he could see down into it. He stopped at the corner of the table, shielded his eyes against the glare of sunlight, and looked down into the pocket's depth.

"Don't tell me," Danica said. That earlier sound was back in her voice—the edge of a thrill.

Dryden looked up and met her eyes. He could see her focusing, letting it come to her.

"It's a dart," she said. "A plastic dart."

Dryden reached into the pocket and lifted it out: a red plastic dart with its metal tip still attached.

For a few seconds they both just stared at it. Then Dryden rounded the table, from one pocket to the next, retrieving another dart from each.

"They were supposed to mean something," Danica said. "I can remember that much, but that's all. The darts were . . . what? A riddle?"

"A message," Dryden said. "From who, I don't know, but it was definitely a message. You and I were supposed to figure it out."

Danica was nodding, making the same connection herself. Still, she looked frustrated as hell. Her eyes screwed almost shut as she tried working through it.

Dryden set the six darts on the pool table's surface; the felt had rotted away in places, exposing dull grey slate.

"It was important," Dryden said, the thought and the spoken words arriving almost together. "The message. Does it feel like that to you, too? Like it ended up being something critical. Life and death. We really had to figure out what it meant."

Danica opened her eyes and looked at him. "Did we?"

Before Dryden could consider that, someone called to them from outside. It was Grace, yelling through the broken windows upstairs.

Dryden took a last look at the darts, willing his mind to connect the next dot. Then Grace shouted again; there was urgency in his tone.

"We should go," Danica said.

Dryden nodded. He turned from the pool table and followed her up the stairs.

Grace was standing a hundred feet away in the street, with a dozen agents around him. Others were running in from elsewhere in the subdivision. When Grace saw Dryden and Danica coming, he broke from the group and sprinted toward them. The two of them ran to meet him halfway.

"Chopper found something," Grace said. "A set of stairs going down underground, out in the middle of a field. It's a couple miles north of here."

Grace was already turning, leading them north and west toward the side of the forest where the vehicles were parked. He waved one of his men over and spoke hurriedly.

"Tell Ramirez to get the hydraulic jack ready on the drive up. There's going to be some kind of door we need to get through. I want the shaped charges ready to go, too—not wired up, just ready. We make every second count now. If this—"

A sound cut him off—the default tone of an iPhone receiving a text message. Still walking, Grace reached for his pocket.

But in almost the same instant, Dryden heard that tone coming from everywhere around him—a rapid, clustered repetition of the sound, like an echo rebounding in a mirror maze.

Every FBI agent within earshot had gotten the text message in unison, whatever it was.

En masse, the group came to a stop. They traded fast glances as they withdrew their phones: *What the hell is this?*

Dryden watched their faces as they looked at their screens. The message had to be something short; every man and woman reacted to it in a glance.

"You son of a bitch . . ." Grace whispered.

Dryden stepped closer and looked at the man's phone.

The sender's number was a line of asterisks, and the message fit in a small word-bubble:

Too late to stop me. The attack happens one minute from now.

CHAPTER THIRTY-ONE

For the longest time, no one said a thing. It was quiet enough that Dryden could hear those around him breathing.

Then the radio on Grace's belt beeped, and the chopper pilot's voice came through the speaker, high-strung and almost shouting.

"Air to point, air to point, we got a problem up here!"

Grace keyed his shoulder mike. "Go ahead."

"It looked like a bunch of quad-rotor drones, eight or ten of them. They just went right under us, moving fast. They're coming toward your position." Over the radio, Dryden could hear at least one of the two spotters yelling something in the background. The pilot listened, then spoke again. *"Yeah, my guys are saying ten. And it's not little camera drones. These were big heavy-lift types, like fifty pounders. They were carrying some kind of canisters. You need to get back to your vehicles right now."*

Dryden turned in place; he watched the realization hit each person standing there, all at once, the same way the text message had:

The attack was coming here.

Right here, and right now.

An instant later, Grace and his people were sprinting full-out. Grace was screaming at them to move their asses, to not stop for anything. In the middle of it all, he turned and looked for Dryden and Danica; the two of them were keeping up, no more than ten feet behind him.

They had gone only another fifty yards, though, when the sound came to them: a high, frenetic buzzing, coming down through the treetops to the north.

"Don't stop!" Grace shouted. *"Move, move, move!"*

But Dryden was already doing the math. The distance to the vehicles—easily a quarter mile to the nearest of them. The time before the drones arrived—seconds now. Whatever was in the canisters, the air in this forest was going to be saturated with it long before anyone reached the safety of the motorcade.

Grace kept shouting, looking around for his people, like a shepherd. Maybe he knew it was hopeless—he *had to* know—but he wasn't giving up. Dryden admired that, though it changed nothing: these people were not going to make it. The whine of the drones was almost on top of them now.

Without breaking stride, Dryden took Danica's hand and veered hard to the right, northeast while the others ran northwest.

"Come on!" he said.

"What are you doing?"

"You'll see."

She made no attempt to pull away. They sprinted

together, ducking low limbs and boughs, the FBI people already lost to sight.

Then Dryden heard a sharp metallic impact, like a saucepan landing on concrete, somewhere far to his left. From the same direction, voices cried out, full of alarm. The sound came again a second later, not far from the first.

Then something came skittering down through the canopy just fifty feet to Dryden's right. It thudded dully into the dirt, kicking up dead leaves and needles. Dryden turned his head as they sprinted; he caught a glimpse of a red metal tank the size of a beach ball, with a black valve assembly attached. An instant later, thick white vapor began surging from it under pressure. In a matter of seconds the cloud was twenty feet across and growing, carried on the steady breeze that blew among the tree trunks.

Dryden faced forward again. Beside him, Danica was looking around, too.

"It's everywhere," she said.

A dense screen of pines extended across their path, dead ahead. Dryden hoped like hell he was right about what lay beyond. They crashed through the boughs without stopping—and saw the tilted yellow Escort fifty feet ahead of them.

Dryden sprinted harder as they crossed the last of the distance; he let go of Danica and reached the vehicle two steps ahead, slamming to a stop against it. He pulled the handle, took hold of the door and hauled it upward, stepping back and clearing the way for her to get past him. She was already there, reaching up and in, grabbing onto whatever she could and hoisting herself into the car. As she did, Dryden risked a look over his shoulder: the white gas had already enveloped the screen of pine trees.

He pivoted around the door, reached into the car and grabbed hold of the steering wheel. He pushed off the ground with both legs and landed in a sprawl in the driver's seat; the door slammed shut beside him, and not even a second later the world outside the car simply vanished. It looked as if white paper had been stretched over all the windows. Pale light came through, but no detail at all. Even the car's hood was lost in the murk.

They sat there, breathing fast and hard, awkwardly spilled in their seats. Dryden found his focus going to the edges of the windows, then the floorboards, scrutinizing each place for a gap where the gas might enter.

He looked up and scanned the roof for rust holes; there weren't any, though he'd seen plenty of rust on the outside of the vehicle. He watched the cracks of the spiderwebbed windshield, then turned in his seat and looked at the back window, which was fractured in the same way.

Nothing came through.

He watched a moment longer, then faced forward again. He stared into the blank white void that had replaced the forest outside the glass.

"Rigel," Danica said softly.

Dryden nodded.

She looked at him. "What do you think it is? Nerve gas?" Fear laced her voice on the last two words.

"It could be anything. It's supposed to be something no one's ever seen before."

"Except us. Twenty-nine years ago."

He nodded again. He thought of Grace and the others. They were somewhere out there right now, with their lungs full of this stuff—whatever it was. He found himself reflexively staring out the side window, as if he could peer through the gas and look for them. But there was nothing there. Nothing but milk-white vapor filling the air.

Dryden scanned the floor and the window seams one last time, then leaned his head back into the tilted seat and shut his eyes.

"It's clearing out," Danica said.

Dryden opened his eyes and looked around. He could see the Escort's hood, and the dark shape of the pine trunk rearing up above it. A few seconds later, details of the nearest boughs began to resolve. The gas was dissipating quickly.

He guessed three or four minutes had passed since they'd gotten into the car. He looked out through the window on his side, in the direction they had come from—the direction in which Grace and his people must be.

Dryden could see the wall of pines he and Danica had run through. He watched as they grew clearer and sharper. After thirty seconds, he could see no trace of the gas in that direction. He turned and looked through Danica's window; out that way, just a haze of the stuff remained, moving off fast in the wind.

"How long should we wait to get out?" Danica asked.

"If the others can be helped, minutes probably count."

Danica nodded, took a deep breath, steeled herself.

"Let's go," she said.

Dryden shoved open the door.

They found the first of the FBI personnel a minute later: a woman with short black hair, lying on her side in the dead leaves. Her M4 rifle lay a foot away.

Dryden knelt fast and put a finger to her carotid artery pulse point.

Her pulse was strong and regular.

So was her breathing; her chest expanded and contracted in the steady rhythm of a sleeper.

"I see some others," Danica said.

Dryden stood and followed her gaze: there were three men down beside the nearest house. He and Danica ran toward them, but they had covered only half the distance when Dryden saw Jack Grace off to the right, thirty yards away. He had collapsed sitting upright, his back against a standing section of picket fence.

They sprinted to him and dropped to his side. Like the woman, he was breathing well with a strong heartbeat. His rifle lay across his lap, and his open windbreaker exposed a holstered Glock.

The radio on his belt beeped, and the chopper pilot's voice came through. *"Air to point, say again, please acknowledge. Anyone on this channel, please respond."*

Dryden could hear the chopper somewhere close by,

maybe hovering above the northern edge of the subdivision. He unclipped Grace's shoulder microphone, pulled it toward himself and keyed the switch.

"This is Dryden. All FBI personnel are unconscious but alive. No idea of their condition. You need first responders in here as fast as you can get them."

"Already in contact with dispatch. First emergency units are twenty minutes out."

Still holding the microphone on its cord, Dryden stood up and scanned the woods. From this position, he could see at least a dozen other fallen agents, spread out roughly along the route they had been running on before the gas hit them: a line leading northwest toward the parked motorcade. All the rest must be somewhere farther along in that direction, lost to sight beyond the intervening trees.

Dryden keyed the microphone to respond to the pilot, but froze—somewhere out of view, far away along the scattered line of unconscious bodies, a man had begun screaming. The sound was high-pitched and primal—maybe expressing pain, or simply fear.

Danica stood up fast, her body going rigid.

The scream came again, followed by a burst of automatic rifle fire.

PART SIX

LOS BAILARINES TERRIBLES

JULY 1989

CHAPTER THIRTY-TWO

Sam stood waiting in the darkness next to the picnic table, on the grass-covered slope below the subdivision. All around him, the weeds moved in the night wind. He was staring south past the lights of downtown Ashland, into the miles of open farmland beyond, where Echo House stood. He couldn't see it at the moment. He couldn't see the barn down the road from it, either—the barn that made the echo. The barn Lauren Coleman's father had spent his last few breaths talking about.

Pant legs swished in the weeds. Sam turned. Against the streetlight glow of the subdivision, Dani's silhouette came toward him and stopped.

It was just past midnight. Sam's father had fallen asleep twenty minutes before. Sam had waited another ten, to be sure, then slipped out the window.

Dani had a pair of binoculars hanging from her neck. Sam had his own; it was his dad's pair, scrounged from one of the movers' boxes this afternoon.

"Ready?" Dani asked.

"Yeah."

It was the first time they had spoken since returning from Station 9, early in the day. They had agreed to meet here as soon after midnight as possible. Then they'd hidden their bikes out in the grass of the slope, and Dani had gone back to her house alone, maybe to go ballistic and scream and break things—Sam thought he might have done that, if he were her. He had tried to imagine, all day since then, what it would feel like to learn your own father was involved in your friend's abduction. To know he was part of something dangerous and illegal in all the worst ways, and that he would spend the rest of his life in prison when this was over with.

"How are you holding up?" Sam asked.

"Like I'm made out of toothpicks." Dani's voice sounded strained.

"Does it help to know you're more of a badass than anyone I ever met?"

"No," she said. Then: "Maybe a little."

It was tricky riding down Truman in the dark, as opposed to walking down it as they had a few nights before. At bike speed, it took focus to keep from straying off the pitch-black pavement.

Downtown was deserted. The hanging streetlights swayed in the breeze. The two of them slipped past the storefronts and through the muted light, and in moments they were out in the deep night south of town.

It felt like an hour, but it actually took less than fifteen minutes to reach Echo House. Sam checked his watch as they rolled into the weed-choked yard: 12:18.

Whatever Mr. Coleman had wanted them to watch for, it would happen an hour and forty minutes from now.

They dropped their bikes and stood staring west toward the barn. Sam remembered thinking it was about a quarter mile away, when he'd seen it in daylight. Right now he couldn't see it at all. The barn was completely dark, inside and out.

Or seemed to be.

As he stared, Sam thought he could make out vague traces of light. Tiny slivers of it here and there, like the outlines of windows or doors.

"Are you seeing that?" he asked.

Dani nodded.

They trained their binoculars on the place; it was hard to dial in the focus, with nothing obvious to use for a reference, but after moving the binocs around for a moment, Sam found one of the faint slivers—it slipped past his frame of view, a blurry scratch of light. He found it again and adjusted the focal depth, and resolved it.

It was the outline of a window, faintly rimmed with a glow.

"The lights are on inside the barn," Sam said, "with the windows covered."

Dani nodded. "You think someone's in there?"

"I don't know."

For a long time they just stared, moving their viewpoints over the dark surface of the building. Sam made out the shapes of three windows and a giant door—the kind of door a tractor could fit through.

"I think we should get closer," Dani said.

Echo House's weed-covered lot was surrounded by cornfields for hundreds of yards, including the entire quarter mile distance to the barn. Sam and Dani left their bikes hidden in the ditch near Echo House, and set out into the cornfield on foot. It felt like a risk, but Sam knew it didn't actually make a difference. If it came down to running for it, the bikes would be no help on the soft earth of the cornfield, and even less help on the road, against bad guys who almost certainly had a car.

They made their way across the open field as quickly as possible. As they'd done a few nights before, on the way to Station 14, they stayed on the compacted ground between the planted rows, where the soil would take no footprints.

The barn was due west of Echo House, but they angled slightly southward, row by row, as they went. They finally stopped at a point directly southeast of the barn, where the corn stalks gave way to a field planted with some dense, grasslike crop that Dani said was alfalfa. The alfalfa didn't grow in rows; it covered the field in one flat mass, eight or ten inches high, providing an open view all the way to the yard that surrounded the barn.

Sam and Dani sat down just inside the corn. They were fifty yards from the barn's nearest corner. This close, the haloed shapes of its windows and door were more discernible, but only slightly so. A passing driver would have thought the place was dark and deserted.

Sam looked at his watch.

12:30.

Ninety minutes to go.

Forty-five minutes slipped by. Nothing happened. The fields were full of insect sounds, and the whisper of the corn shoots. Sam stared at the long arc of the Milky Way overhead. From time to time an airliner passed high above, its wingtip lights strobing in the darkness. After a while he saw something else moving in the sky: an unblinking speck of light, no brighter than a faint star, tracing a straight and slow path across the night. It couldn't be a shooting star—those had to be much faster. He pointed it out to Dani.

"It's a satellite," she said. "You see a lot of them if you watch long enough."

Sam watched until it faded out of view, far to the east.

"Those first couple weeks after I moved here," Dani said, "when I got into stargazing, Lauren did, too. On Friday or Saturday nights, or any night after summer vacation started, we'd go out to that picnic table and just lie out there with a bag of chips and a six-pack of soda, and watch the sky for three or four hours. You know you can see shooting stars even when there's not a meteor shower? Any ordinary night, if you keep watching, you see three or four of them an hour. You see a satellite every five or ten minutes. I know it might sound boring, but it wasn't. They were some of the coolest nights I ever had. While they lasted."

At twenty minutes past one in the morning, the big door on the side of the barn opened. There was a few seconds' warning—a heavy metallic *thud* as some kind of latch was released—and then the door lumbered aside on its rollers, casting a harsh light out into the darkness. It opened only partway, to a width of five feet. The light streaming out projected a long, trapezoid-shaped glow across the bare ground of the barnyard, and though the direct light came nowhere near the two of them, Sam felt a moment of panic—even their own spot at the edge of the cornfield seemed brighter now than it had before. It felt as if anyone stepping out of the barn would see them at once.

Then he thought about it, and relaxed a little. Someone coming out of the barn would have eyes adjusted to its bright interior—the surrounding fields would look pitch-black from that point of view.

Hopefully.

Anyway, there was no point thinking about it. There was nowhere to run now if things went bad.

Sam looked at Dani. She had her binoculars to her eyes, every ounce of her attention fixed on the open barn door.

Sam raised his own and centered them on the opening. In the magnified view, the doorway looked like it was no more than twenty feet away from him.

Still, he couldn't see much inside the barn: just a slice of the space within. An ancient wooden floor, crusted with dirt. The rough beams of a wall on the far side. The front end of a car, just peeking into view. No sign of Lauren Coleman.

Sam wondered, for probably the hundredth time, what exactly they were supposed to be watching for. What had Mr. Coleman meant by *you'll see*? Had he known for sure that there was a way to save Lauren? Or had his last words been just a desperation move by a dying man, sending the two of them here in the hope that they only *might* see a way to rescue his daughter?

Sam spent a moment thinking about that, and then a man walked out of the barn, followed seconds later by another. It was hard to make out much detail; the men were just silhouettes against the lit-up humidity of the barnyard.

Then somebody called out from inside the building. A man's voice, loud and commanding.

The two men outside stopped and turned back to face the doorway—they were thirty feet from it now.

Sam swung his binoculars back to the opening, but no one else appeared there.

The men outside said something back to the unseen speaker in the barn. The conversation went back and forth for a moment; Sam couldn't discern any of the words.

Then a hand gripped the heavy sliding door from inside and hauled it shut again, plunging the barnyard back into darkness.

The men outside were still talking to each other, though more quietly now. Their footsteps scraped on the ground, but it was impossible to get a sense of their direction. Then there came the sound of a chain being pulled free of something, and a door creaked open and banged loudly—wood against wood. Sam pictured the men entering some kind of equipment shed—he was sure he had seen some sort of outbuilding near the barn, the other day. A few seconds later there came a clatter of metal: heavy tools being jostled around.

"What do you think they're doing?" Dani whispered.

"I'm not sure."

The rummaging sound lasted a moment longer; after that there was only silence.

A minute passed. Then two. Sam began to feel nervous. It put him on edge not knowing where the two men were, or what they were up to.

Then he realized he could hear something. It was very faint—he could almost miss it under the sound of the wind. He tilted his head, putting an ear toward the barnyard, where the noise seemed to originate. As he did, he saw Dani doing the same. The sound was soft and rhythmic. A kind of hissing that came in beats, almost musical, once every few seconds.

"What is that?" Dani whispered.

Sam shook his head. He had no idea.

And then it stopped.

Immediately afterward there were footsteps again, thumping across the ground toward the barn.

All at once the big door slid back open. Sam started to raise his binoculars, along with Dani, but then she gasped and dropped them back to her lap.

Sam saw the reason.

"Oh Christ . . ." he whispered.

The two men slipped into the barn, but by then neither Sam nor Dani were looking at them.

They stared instead at the place where the two men had been standing out in the dark—and working. It was obvious now what the sound had been: the hiss of metal against soil. Fifty feet away from the barn door, centered in the light that spilled from it, was a waist-high pile of dirt with two shovels stuck into it. And next to the pile was a long rectangular hole in the ground.

The two men had just finished digging a grave.

CHAPTER THIRTY-THREE

Dani's reaction was overwhelming. She fell backward from where she sat, just managing to catch herself with her arms behind her.

"No," she whispered. *"No . . . no . . ."* She kept repeating it, shaking her head. Her voice shuddered. *"No . . ."*

Sam felt the acid rise in his stomach. Was *this* what Mr. Coleman had wanted them to do? Simply witness Lauren's burial so they could report it to someone? So she wouldn't spend eternity in an unmarked grave? Was that all the man had been able to ask for, in the end?

"No . . ." Dani whispered. The word came out through clenched teeth. She was losing it.

Sam turned to her. There was nothing he could possibly say. Instead he just put his arms around her and pulled her against himself tightly. She responded, hugging him back and burying her face in his shoulder. He felt her tears through his shirt. He had his head just above hers, facing the barn. He had to keep watching. He had to know.

Ten seconds later the two men came out again. They were carrying a body between them; without the binoculars it was hard to see it clearly.

And then it moved. It jerked and twisted in their arms.

"Dani," Sam whispered. "Look."

She let go of him, wiped at her eyes and turned them on the barn.

The body kept fighting, but by its movements it was obvious that its wrists and ankles were bound.

"Oh my God," Dani said.

Her hands were still shaking, but she managed to get hold of her binoculars again. Sam raised his own, and got them centered on the two men and their victim; he tracked them until they stopped beside the grave, at which point they dropped the body on the ground.

It landed diagonally, relative to Sam and Dani's position. By chance, that angle made it easy to see the victim's features—there was just enough light from the big door shining onto the face.

It wasn't Lauren.

It was a grown man. He was tall and skinny, with blond hair receding from his forehead. Sam guessed he was around forty years old. The binds holding the man's wrists and ankles were heavy wraps of duct tape.

"That's Mr. Pierce," Dani whispered. "There's a picture of him in the hallway at school, from when he helped with the science fair a couple years ago."

Sam stared at the man's face through the binocs. The face nobody had seen in almost a year.

One of the men who'd carried him walked away,

back toward the barn. The other man stayed where he was, standing over Pierce's helpless form.

In the magnified view Pierce's mouth moved, and across the darkness Sam could hear his voice. His words were lost to the distance, but their tone and meaning weren't. He was begging for his life.

"Oh my God," Dani said again. "They're going to bury him alive. They're—*oh!*"

The man standing over Pierce had just kicked him in the ribs. They heard Pierce cry out and cough in pain. Then the man braced a foot on Pierce's shoulder, and shoved him roughly sideways—right to the edge of the grave. The man stepped forward and braced the foot for another shove.

Then he stopped.

He drew his foot away and turned to face the barn. Someone was calling out to him from just inside the door.

Sam swung his binoculars to the opening; a hand appeared there, holding some small dark object.

"Is that a walkie-talkie?" Sam asked.

"I think so."

The man at the door waved the handheld unit as if saying, *You have a call.*

The man outside looked annoyed. He left Pierce lying there and stalked back to the barn. He went right in through the door, grabbing the walkie-talkie as he did, and suddenly there was no one outside at all. Pierce lay unattended at the graveside, wrists and ankles still bound. Clearly no one was worried he'd make a run for it.

Sam looked at Dani. She looked back at him. Her eyes were wide and scared.

"You're wondering the same thing as me," Sam said. "Aren't you?"

She nodded quickly. "What happens to Lauren if we save him?"

Uncertainty twisted her expression. She turned her eyes back to Mr. Pierce.

"Shit . . ." she whispered. "I don't know. I don't know . . ."

"If we're going to help him, we have to go *right now.* Seconds are going to count."

"I know, I know . . . but . . . what *about* Lauren? If they lose track of Pierce, and they panic . . . oh God . . ."

"She might die," Sam said. "But if we sit here, Pierce *definitely* dies. Right in front of us."

Dani's breathing accelerated again. "I just don't know . . ."

Seconds draining away. Fast, fast, fast.

Suddenly Pierce raised his bound hands to his face, pressed his palms together and mouthed something to the sky. A prayer.

"Oh hell . . ." Dani whispered.

"I'm in, if you are," Sam said. "Now or never."

Dani sucked in a last deep breath. *"Now."*

She lunged to her feet, and a second later the two of them were sprinting for the barnyard, the night air streaming past their ears. Sam felt his heart slamming against his ribs, for reasons that had nothing to do with running. His eyes kept darting back and forth between the grave ahead and the barn door off to the left. The doorway stayed empty. For the moment.

He was a step behind Dani, sprinting in single file, their feet leaving a ragged path through the alfalfa. A moment later they passed beyond it, onto the hard-packed ground of the barnyard. Pierce was only twenty yards ahead. Then ten.

They hardly stopped when they got to him. They slid to a halt, reached down and took hold of an elbow each.

"Forward," Sam hissed. "Take him to the road."

Dani nodded, and like that they were moving again, the two of them dragging Pierce along over the hard-pan dirt.

Sam looked back as they went, scrutinizing the ground behind them.

They were leaving no tracks at all. Not even drag marks where Pierce's legs trailed over the dry soil.

Farther behind them, he saw the near edge of the alfalfa field, just visible in the light from the barn door. He could see the crushed, single trail he and Dani had made as they crossed it.

A wild hope flickered in him, at the sight of it. He pushed it away and turned his attention forward again.

He and Dani were twenty or thirty yards from the road yet, which lay in the darkness beyond the light spilling from the barn; for the moment, the three of them were still inside that light—bugs on a white tablecloth.

Sam craned his neck to look at the open door again, willing it to stay vacant a little longer. So far, so good.

They reached the edge of the bright zone and slipped beyond it, into the cover of dark. No more than five seconds later, a man's voice shouted angrily behind them. Sam looked back again. One of the others had re-emerged from the barn. The man was staring at the empty ground beside the grave, where Pierce should've been.

"He doesn't see us," Sam whispered. "Don't slow down, whatever you do."

The man at the doorway called back inside for the others, his words laced with curses Sam could just make out.

He and Dani kept moving. Dragging Pierce deeper into the darkness. Closer and closer to the road.

Now there came footsteps behind them. Pounding the hard ground. Men scattering from the barn and splitting up to search the night.

Sam and Dani reached the road, right where the barn's driveway led onto it. They kept going, crossing the pavement, Pierce's clothes scraping softly on its surface.

"Ditch," Dani said.

"Definitely."

An instant later they reached the far shoulder of the road, just shy of the weed-filled drop-off. Behind them, Sam finally heard the sound he'd been expecting: a car's engine roaring to life. He risked a final look back, and saw headlight beams shining straight out from within the giant barn door, which had now been pulled open to full width.

"Come on," Dani whispered.

Sam nodded, and together they descended into the ditch, easing Pierce down with them. With his hands bound in front of him, Pierce was able to grip the dense weeds for himself. Within seconds all three of them were below the level of the roadbed; hardly a breath later the weeds above them bloomed with headlight glare. The car had come out of the barn and turned toward the road.

Sam waited for it to rev up and pull out onto the pavement, but it didn't. Instead its engine continued growling in low gear, and then the headlight glow on the weeds slid away toward the east. The three of them turned and watched it go. It moved like a carefully controlled spotlight. Sam realized what was happening: the car was turning in a circle right there in the barnyard, sweeping its high beams over the surrounding fields. No doubt the rest of the men were watching the light, eyes peeled for any glimpse of Pierce.

Dani turned to the man and whispered frantically. "Is there a girl in the barn?"

Pierce glanced back and forth between the two of them, still shaken and probably confused as hell. Sam tried to imagine the guy's mind-set. Tried to imagine what it all looked like through his eyes—to have been dragged away from his own grave by two strangers who turned out to be kids. And now Dani was asking about a girl in the barn, which meant they weren't just random kids who'd seen him in trouble. It meant they knew things. Sam watched Pierce's expression in the faint light of the ditch. Watched the guy try to make the pieces fit.

"Is there a girl in there?" Dani repeated.

Despite his confusion, Pierce nodded.

"Lauren Coleman?" Dani asked.

Pierce stared at her, then nodded again.

Dani's breath came out in a rush. She looked past Pierce to Sam. "What do we do now?" she asked. "What's going to happen to her?"

Instead of answering, Sam dug his feet into the side wall of the ditch and pushed himself upward. He raised his head just above ground level, still mostly concealed by the weeds, and stared across the road at the barnyard.

He could see the car still making its slow turn in place, scanning the fields with its headlights. The beams were pointed east at the moment, gradually tracking southward.

There were three men on foot in the barnyard, all of them staring at where the headlights shone.

The men's eyes, still adapted to the lit-up space inside the barn, probably couldn't make out what Sam had seen a moment before. But they would—a few seconds from now, when the headlights came to it.

"Take a look at this," Sam whispered.

Dani climbed to the edge of the ditch and lifted her head above it, next to Sam's. She followed his gaze.

The car's lights were pointed almost exactly southeast now, moving like a ship's searchlight over a pitch-black ocean.

Then the beams froze in place.

One of the men shouted something and bolted forward. The others followed. They closed in on what they had seen: the trampled-down path through the alfalfa, which stood out in stark contrast in the headlights.

"We didn't leave any tracks coming from the grave to the road," Sam said. "But we left that single line through the alfalfa."

Dani was nodding, putting it together. "It looks like a path leading *away* from the grave, toward the cornfield we came from."

"And we didn't leave tracks in the cornfield either," Sam said. "We were careful. So these guys . . ." He was quiet a moment, thinking it all through. Then he nodded, sure of the logic. "These guys are going to think he just broke the tape on his ankles and ran away by himself. They're going to think he's out in that corn somewhere. What else *could* they think?"

All at once Dani seemed to understand what he was getting at. She turned sharply toward him.

"If they go out there to search for him," she whispered. "If they *all* go . . ."

Hope lit up her eyes. She turned and stared at the distant searchers for another second, then let go of the edge and slid back down to Pierce's level.

"How many men are in the barn?" she asked. "How many bad guys?"

Pierce's earlier confusion, still present, seemed to reach a kind of tipping point. He shook his head, staring at both Dani and Sam.

"Who are you?" Pierce asked. "How are you—how can you be here?"

"We'll tell you," Dani said, "but I have to know how many people are in the barn."

"Are you *with* someone?" Pierce asked. "Are there . . . grownups with you?"

Dani shook her head. "It's just us. Please, how many—"

"But you're just kids—"

"How many fucking people?"

Pierce didn't quite flinch, but Dani's tone silenced him. He stared. Then he looked away, as if thinking hard.

"Five," he said. "Five men."

"You're sure?" Dani asked.

Pierce nodded. "I'm sure."

Sam turned to look at the car and the searchers again. In the bright light streaming out of the barn, he could see the interior of the car easily. There was nobody in the passenger seat. Just the driver.

Plus the three men on foot.

That left one still unaccounted for.

Dani climbed back up next to him and took in the scene for herself.

At that moment the driver shoved open his door and got out. One of the three men in the field turned, cupped his mouth, and shouted something. Sam couldn't make it out, but the driver nodded, rounded the car and sprinted to the open barn door. He disappeared inside.

"Bring the last guy out with you," Dani whispered.

The man reappeared ten seconds later—still alone. He had a small bundle of objects in his hands.

Sam raised his binoculars and sighted the guy in.

He was carrying flashlights.

"Oh come on," Dani whispered. She was still watching the open barn door. "Come on . . . One more . . ."

The doorway stayed empty.

The driver sprinted to the three other men in the field and handed out the flashlights. A moment later there were four beams out there, scanning the darkness, moving away into the knee-high stalks of corn.

No movement at the doorway. No sign of the fifth man. Nothing at all.

"Keep watching," Sam said, and slid back down to Pierce.

He took hold of the wrapped duct tape around the guy's wrists, and felt for the leading edge. He found it after a few seconds; he got a fingernail under it and started peeling it up.

The guy still looked like a mess. The shock of nearly dying was probably part of that, but Sam guessed it was mostly the confusion that was getting to him.

"We listen in on things we're not supposed to," Sam said. "And we go places we're not supposed to. We've been inside some of the abandoned stations, like number fourteen, north of town. We know what Ashland really is."

He got the end of the tape strip loose enough to pinch it between his thumb and fingertips. He began pulling it free in loops, unraveling it from around Pierce's wrists.

The guy was staring at him intently now, processing what he'd just heard.

"We know there was a project called Rigel," Sam said. "We know you started it ten years ago, and pulled the plug five years later. We found Station Nine this morning. We were able to speak to Mr. Coleman—for a minute or so."

Pierce reacted, drawing in a sharp breath. "Coleman? No, that can't be right, he was—" Pierce cut himself off, still staring at Sam. "They killed him. They beat him to death. I saw them do it. They would have killed me down there, too, but they needed me for a few more things."

"He lived," Sam said. "At least a while. He told us to come to this barn at two in the morning. He said Lauren would be here. He said if we watched, we'd see a way to save her."

Pierce looked up at Dani—she was still focused on the barn, her expression tense and unchanging—then dropped his gaze to Sam again.

"Did Coleman say anything else?" Pierce asked.

Dani spoke without looking down. "We asked him if we could just call the Army. If we could send them here to save Lauren. He told us not to. He said there were . . . insiders. People who might tip off the bad guys in advance. Meaning we could end up getting Lauren killed if we did that."

Sam pulled a final loop of tape from Pierce's wrists. Freed from the binds, the man's hands shook just noticeably.

"What insiders?" he asked. "Did he give you any names?"

"One name," Dani said. "Ellis. *My* last name. And my father's."

Pierce looked up at her again, though her own gaze

stayed fixed on the barn. Finally the man lowered his eyes to the ditch wall in front of him. He didn't look as confused as he had a moment before, but his mind seemed to be racing.

"Hey," Sam said. "Do *you* know how we're supposed to save Lauren? Do you know what Mr. Coleman meant, when he said we'd see what to do? You were with him. You should know whatever he knew."

Pierce turned to him, still deep in thought. After a second he shook it off. He ran a hand through his hair.

"Oh Christ," Pierce said. "Yeah, I know what he meant. But I don't think it'll work now."

For the first time, Dani turned and looked down at the man.

"What do you mean?" she asked.

Pierce sighed, his head resting in his hands now. He looked like he had ten things to say, and didn't know which one to start with. At last he looked up, his eyes going back and forth between Sam and Dani.

"I don't know how much you know about Rigel," he said, "but as of right now, the people in that barn have a working version of it. Actually they have three. They moved them out of Station Nine last night, three trips by car to this barn. They were getting nervous, staying down there any longer than they had to. There was always some chance the military would reinspect that place, especially after Coleman's disappearance last week. The Army would have known for sure there was something going on with Rigel, and Station Nine was the original fabrication point."

Pierce reached down and felt for the tape at his ankles as he spoke. "These men moved the Rigel units here, and tonight at two in the morning, they've got a vehicle coming to transport all of them out of Ashland."

"How does that help us save Lauren?" Dani asked. "What did Mr. Coleman want us to do?"

"You wouldn't have had to do anything," Pierce said. "These guys were never planning to kill her. She wasn't any threat to them. She didn't know anything that could be used to track them down later. Coleman and I knew that stuff, but not her. Their plan was just to leave her behind in the barn, at two in the morning. Maybe someone would come and find her, maybe not. They didn't really care, but they definitely weren't going to kill her. No need."

Sam traded a look with Dani.

You'll see, Mr. Coleman had said.

"We could have just walked in and gotten her," Sam said.

Pierce nodded. "But with me getting away . . . all bets are off. When these guys don't find me in that field, they're going to assume I'm running for the nearest phone to call base security. There are twelve active stations under Ashland, with more than a hundred armed officers guarding them. I can have half of them surrounding that barn within minutes of making the call."

The last of the duct tape around his ankles came loose with a rip. He wadded it and dropped it in the weeds.

"Which is exactly what I need to do now," he said. "It's time to slam the lid down on all of this."

Dani looked unsure. "If there are people on the inside who can tip them off—"

Pierce shook his head. "We're past that now. These guys already know the clock is ticking."

He gripped the weeds and climbed up until his head was above the ditch, alongside Dani. Sam did the same, and the three of them stared across the pavement at the barnyard.

The four flashlights were far away to the south now, and more spread out, sweeping the vast darkness of the field.

The barn door remained wide open and empty.

"It wouldn't matter if the last guy *did* come out," Pierce said. "The girl isn't just tied up in there. She's locked in a room—some kind of storage for tractors or something. It's got a heavy wooden door with a steel lock. You'd be five minutes with an axe, breaking through it. They'd hear you."

"But if the Army comes in and surrounds this place," Dani said, "it's going to be a standoff with Lauren in the middle of it."

"Yes," Pierce said. "It will. And she could die. I'm not going to b.s. you about that. If I call in the military, Lauren might die." He took his gaze off the barn, turned and looked at Sam and Dani. "But her odds are even worse if I don't make the call."

"What do you mean?" Dani asked.

"I mean if I had to bet, I'd say the last guy in the barn is on the two-way right now, relaying a message to the transport vehicle. He's saying screw two o'clock, get here as fast as you possibly can. Because minutes count now, and even if they get out of here early, the military might be after them by then. And in that case . . . if I were these guys . . . I'd damn well want a hostage with me. Wouldn't you?" He turned and stared at the barn again. "My gut says if these guys get away, they take the girl with them . . . and no one ever sees her again."

Sam watched the idea settle over Dani. She closed her eyes tight, as if she could wish it away.

"It's not that I'm asking for your agreement on this," Pierce said. "I'm calling them, regardless. I'm only trying to explain it so you'll understand why. You saved my life, it's the least I can do."

Dani opened her eyes. She looked about as rattled as Sam had ever seen her. She met his gaze for a moment, then finally turned to Pierce and nodded. "Okay. I want you to call them." She pointed east along the road. "We left our bikes in the ditch down there, near the old school. We should be able to reach someone's farmhouse in a few minutes."

Pierce thought about it, staring east into the dark.

"We can do better than that," he said.

CHAPTER THIRTY-FOUR

Dani's bike had a banana seat just big enough to fit both her and Sam; Pierce rode Sam's bike. From Echo House they followed Pierce east to Truman Avenue, which led north toward downtown Ashland and the subdivision beyond—but they didn't go to either of those places. They rode only half a mile north on Truman before Pierce turned off the pavement onto the gravel driveway of an old farmhouse.

The house stood perched atop a slight rise amid the acres and acres of planted corn. There was a dim yellow porch light shining over the front yard, under the dense canopies of sixty-foot maples and oaks.

Pierce rode up to the porch steps and got off the bike. Sam and Dani stopped behind him.

"Do we just knock?" Sam asked.

Pierce shook his head. "No one would answer if we did."

He climbed the steps and crossed to the door. There was a doorbell button next to it, glowing soft orange in the darkness of the covered porch.

Pierce didn't press the button. Instead he took hold

of the casing that surrounded it, and pulled one edge outward. The casing opened on a hinge, revealing a keypad that looked like the ones in Station 14 and Station 9, only newer; the buttons were backlit, glowing faintly blue.

Pierce entered a number. Sam didn't catch what it was, but it sure as hell wasn't a string of five sevens in a row. A second later the door's latch clicked; Pierce turned the knob and shoved it inward.

Sam and Dani got off the bike, climbed the steps and followed Pierce through the door.

At a glance, the inside of the place looked normal enough. Sam had never been in an old farmhouse before, but if he'd pictured one, it would have looked something like this. In the indirect glow from the porch light outside, he saw a kitchen that looked like something from an old movie: dinged-up wooden counters, a small stove with iron grills on top, a big round-edged refrigerator that was light green or blue—it was hard to tell in the dim light.

Past the kitchen was a dining area that opened to a living room at the back of the house, with a set of French doors on the far wall. Through the panes set in the doors, Sam could see a deck that looked out over the pitch-black fields—a western view, which meant the barn near Echo House should be visible from the deck.

There was an old roll-top desk along one wall of the living room. Pierce went to it and raised the cover, revealing some kind of instrument panel. It had lighted buttons with abbreviated labels Sam could make no sense of. Its central feature was a computer screen with a keyboard in front of it. Pierce pressed a power button and the monitor flared to life—a black screen with green text flashing by too quickly to read.

"Is this place . . . a station?" Dani asked. "An active one, I mean?"

She was looking around as she spoke. Sam guessed she was picturing the same thing he was: a staircase somewhere leading down, not to a basement but to an underground complex like the others they'd seen.

Pierce shook his head. "Nothing like that. Just base office quarters. Most of the farmhouses are set up like this."

The sequence of flashing text finally stopped. For a second the screen stayed blank, and then a single line appeared in the upper left corner: *ENTER SUPERVISOR PASSWORD:* _____

Pierce leaned over the keyboard and typed *PIERCE-471826,* then pressed ENTER.

The screen dimmed, as if the machine were considering his request, and then a new line appeared: *ACCOUNT ADDRESS (SENDER):*

"Ever heard of electronic mail?" Pierce asked.

Sam shook his head, along with Dani.

"Give it a few years," Pierce said softly, his attention mostly focused on the screen.

He typed, *pierce@ashland.arpa.mil,* and pressed ENTER again. A second line appeared beneath the first: *ACCOUNT ADDRESS (RECIPIENT):*

Pierce typed **all*@ashland.arpa.mil,* and once more hit the ENTER key.

A final slug of text appeared: *MESSAGE:*

Pierce's hands hovered over the keys for only a second or two, and then he began typing rapid-fire:

> *Request immediate armed response half a mile west of intersection of Truman and Cedar, old barn near schoolhouse. Live samples of weaponized bioagent Rigel are in play. All personnel must wear Level A respirators. Hostiles are five men in/around barn. Secure location as quickly as possible. I advise scrambling air support from ANG Willow Bluff in case hostiles leave their current location; they may do so at any point. Be advised they have a hostage, a young girl. Take all precautions to save her.*

He pressed ENTER a final time, and the text on the screen vanished. The word *SENT* appeared up in the corner.

"That message will go to every active terminal in Ashland," Pierce said. "Anyone on-duty, sitting at their desks, is getting it right now."

Sam looked at his watch, just visible in the glow of the desk panel.

1:35. The original deadline was twenty-five minutes away. He imagined the people in the barn moving fast, rushing around, preparing to move out even sooner. He imagined their transport vehicle—a van, a big truck, whatever it turned out to be—racing down some dark two-lane right now, doing thirty over the speed limit, shaving off whatever time it could.

He imagined the active stations all over Ashland, too. Alarms blaring, soldiers running for weapons lockers, then maybe elevators and vehicles. Pierce had literally called in an army. The only question now was whether it would arrive in time.

"There's a secure bunker downstairs," Pierce said. "It's not much bigger than a closet, but it's safe. I'd like both of you to wait in there until this is over with."

Dani shook her head. "I'd go crazy wondering what's happening out there. I need to watch."

She crossed the living room to the French doors, turned one of the lever knobs and pulled the door inward. She stepped through onto the deck and went to the rail.

"We're safe enough here," Sam said. "If trouble comes this way, we'll have time to react."

Pierce frowned, but said nothing more. Sam turned and followed Dani onto the deck. In the darkness, the boards creaked under his feet. The wind felt stronger than it had earlier; he could hear it moaning in the leaves above the yard.

Dani had her binoculars raised and aimed at the barn, far off to the southwest. Sam stared at it; the still-open doorway appeared as only a bright rectangle standing upright, nearly a mile away across the dark fields.

Sam raised his own binoculars and managed to get them sighted in. The magnification brought the barn door a lot closer, but the image shook and wavered; it was impossible to see anything clearly. He knelt on the deck surface and set the binoculars onto the flat board atop the railing, then angled them left and right until he once again had the barn door centered in his view.

The image was rock-steady—and far more detailed than he had expected. He could easily resolve the shapes of men moving in and out of the barn, carrying boxes, setting them down in the dirt just outside the door. Getting ready to leave.

There was no sign of Lauren Coleman.

Sam heard Dani stoop down beside him; she braced her own binoculars on the railing and sighted them in.

Behind them, the deck boards creaked again. Pierce had stepped out through the French doors. He wandered to the railing off to Sam's right, and stood staring off at the distant barn.

For thirty seconds, nobody spoke. Sam watched the men in the barn going about their frantic work. Beside him, Dani did the same. At last Sam took his eyes from the binoculars and stood. He turned to Pierce, barely a shape in the darkness.

"What is Rigel?" Sam asked. "What is it *exactly*?"

Next to him, Dani gave up on her own binoculars and stood. She turned and stared at Pierce, too, waiting for the answer.

"You don't want to know," Pierce said. "Kids shouldn't have to think about things like that."

"We've already seen what it can do," Dani said. "We were in Station Nine. We saw the baboon—the one that was still alive."

"We saw the newspaper, too," Sam said. "The article about the *bailarines terribles,* in the jungle outside Wells Town. We know Rigel is based on something that goes back hundreds of years."

"Millions of years," Pierce said. "And you haven't seen half of what it can do. Just leave it at that. The rest of it would only scare you more."

"We're already scared all the way," Dani said. "We want to know the whole story."

"It's technically a crime to tell you. State secrets. They hand out capital punishment over those."

"That's a strange thing to say to people who saved your life," Sam said.

Pierce exhaled, not quite laughing. He leaned down and braced his hands on the deck rail, and lowered his head.

"You really want to know?" he asked.

"Yes," Dani said.

"Start with the *bailarines,*" Sam said. "What are they?"

Pierce straightened up again. He turned his head and looked at the two of them. "If you ask the locals in Wells Town, the *bailarines* are the living dead."

CHAPTER THIRTY-FIVE

Sam stared. Pierce was still looking his way, but after a moment the man turned and gazed out over the cornfields again, first toward the barn, and then north, in the direction of downtown Ashland and the suburb—and presumably most of the active stations. The direction from which the military response would show up, hopefully anytime now, maybe as a mass of headlights streaming down every country road for miles around.

"I'll take it from the beginning," Pierce said. "It starts with a disease. An extremely nasty one called neocortical malaria. It works like other kinds of malaria: mosquitos spread it from host to host. In this case, the disease seems to favor certain species of tropical birds—and sometimes people."

Pierce turned his back to the railing and leaned against it. Sam and Dani kept their eyes on the barn—and the still-empty horizon to the north.

"I'm sure you know about regular malaria," Pierce said. "It's caused by a parasite, and it's one of the worst diseases in the world. It kills millions of people every year. Compared to that, neocortical malaria is almost unheard-of. It's never infected nearly that many. It hardly ever infects people at all, because the parasite doesn't live long inside the mosquito; usually it dies before the mosquito can go from one host to another—unless the hosts are very close together, like birds in a nesting colony. That's the good news. The bad news is what happens to the unlucky people who *do* get infected. The symptoms of neocortical malaria are nothing like the other forms of the disease. Not even close."

"What *are* they like?" Dani asked.

Pierce was quiet for a long moment. "Like rabies," he said at last. "Late-stage rabies, the way you see it in a dog. It renders the victim mindless, aggressive, violent, physically erratic. The parasite affects rage-impulse centers in the brain, to the point that its victims will actively try to kill other people. And they can."

Sam didn't picture a rabid dog. He didn't have to. He pictured the baboon in Station 9, bleeding from the eyes and nose, tearing apart the ruins of that place.

"But no one knew any of this a hundred years ago," Pierce said. "Even with modern science, it took decades to figure out that this was a type of malaria, or that it came from mosquitos and birds. See, the birds would get the disease, but they'd never get *sick* from it. They just carried it. They lived with it, no problem. And the kind of birds that usually got it always nested deep in the jungle, far away from where most people lived. The only people who ever caught the disease were tribal clans who lived far outside of towns and villages, closer to those bird colonies. Even for them, it was a rare thing. For some reason the infections only happened when the weather was unusually hot—maybe at high temperatures the disease lived a bit longer inside the mosquitos. Long enough for them to pass it to humans. Whatever the case, imagine how all of this looked to people who lived in bigger cities in the tropics, along the coasts, far away from the birds. Every few years, when a heat wave comes along, strange people come staggering out of the jungle, attacking and murdering whoever they catch. The infected were usually skin-and-bones by the time they emerged from the forest, after days of rarely sleeping or eating. They looked like corpses. Walking corpses. If you were around back then and witnessed something like that, would you have known any better?"

"I guess not," Dani said.

"No one did. That same misunderstanding happened in every place that was afflicted, all over the world. There's a telling detail: the local people never gave the disease a name, like black plague or spotted fever. They didn't *know* it was a disease. Instead they named the victims, the apparent living carcasses that showed up on occasion to attack them. The Spanish settlers in Central America and the Caribbean called them *los bailarines terribles:* the terrible dancers. They lived in fear of them."

Pierce glanced over his shoulder at the distant barn, where the men were visible as tiny, hurrying specks against the lit-up doorway.

"And that's how it stayed," Pierce said, "until around 1950, when scientists put it all together. Then the governments of each of these countries sent exterminator teams into the jungles, and wiped out the bird colonies entirely. It wasn't hard to do; they nested in huge groups, and there were only so many sites. It might sound harsh, but it was the only way. And it worked. The disease vanished except for a passing occurrence here or there, in which case they just sent in more exterminators. Basically it was under control, and after a while no one thought about it anymore. Except for people who are paid to think about things like that. People like me."

He pushed off from the rail and paced across the deck to the French doors, one of which was still open. He put his hands on each side of the doorway and leaned into the space between, becoming a silhouette against the glow of the buttons on the roll-top desk.

"Weaponizing the disease was my idea. Ten years ago. I called the project Rigel, and I got approval to go ahead with the work, here in Ashland. I'm ashamed now of what I did back then—what I *was* back then—but at the time, I felt it was my job. I was a bio-warfare researcher. I began Rigel with a sample from one of the recent minor outbreaks in Central America. My goal was to make the disease controllable . . . make it something we could store in canisters and deliver in a mist form, like tear-gas or pepper-spray. Take the birds and the mosquitos right out of the equation. Even the parasite itself could be taken out of the equation, if we could synthesize the toxin it produces—the poison it secretes inside your brain when it infects you. If we could create that chemical all by itself, then we would have the disease in its purest form, capable of infecting people almost instantly. The idea was that you'd position it upwind of enemy troops and let it loose on them. You'd infect as many of them as possible, and then *they'd* start killing the rest."

Sam glanced at Dani. In the soft light he could just make out the revulsion in her eyes.

Across the deck, Pierce drew himself back from the doorway. He turned to face the two of them.

"Did it work?" Sam asked.

Pierce nodded. "Perfectly. It never saw combat, but we tested it on primates—and a few human volunteers."

"You *killed* people?" Dani asked.

"No, no. That's the strange part. Neocortical malaria doesn't actually kill its victims—although in the past they've almost always gotten killed anyway, once they started attacking villages. But if they happen to live long enough, they overcome the infection and return to normal. With the natural form of the disease, that took about ten days. With my weaponized version, the timing was different. When you're exposed to the mist, you black out within seconds, stay unconscious for five minutes or so, and then you wake up fully symptomatic—a monster. But because it's just the chemical, without the actual parasite inside you to keep producing the stuff, the body recovers pretty quickly. Three or four hours and you're clearheaded again, like sobering up after too many drinks. It's not very long, but in a combat zone, where you're using it to turn enemy soldiers against each other . . . it would be plenty of time. Enough time for the afflicted to do serious damage."

"The afflicted?" Sam asked.

Pierce nodded. "That's what we always called them, because none of what happens is their fault. The violence, the killing . . . they have no idea they're doing it. They're victims—afflicted—just as much as the people they attack."

Pierce shoved his hands through his hair and shook his head.

"Like I said, I'm ashamed of it now. I was even ashamed of it *then,* by the time I had it working. So I pushed to shut the whole project down. Halt the work. Burn the files. Disinvent it, if possible. Amazingly, the government agreed. I guess they understood how awful the whole thing was. So much more trouble than it was worth. By five years ago, it was officially canceled. Like it'd never existed in the first place. But I couldn't leave it at that. I had to be sure. So I formed a group called Watchdog, made up of old colleagues, people I trusted—people all over the world who could keep an eye on likely outbreak sites as best they could. We knew that anytime the natural disease came back, it would provide a sample of the parasite for someone to restart Rigel if they wanted to. We had to make sure that didn't happen. So we stayed on it. We tried, anyway. I guess we didn't try hard enough."

He stared past Sam and Dani at the bright doorway of the barn. A kind of hate seemed to rise in his expression.

"Who *are* these people?" Sam asked. "The bad guys."

"I honestly don't know," Pierce said. "Back when the project was still going, there were probably two dozen people in D.C. who had access to its files. These guys could be some of them, or even people *hired* by them. Whoever they are, they obviously needed help to get the job done. They grabbed me first, because I had the broadest knowledge of the research. Enough for a year's worth of secret development, down in Station Nine. I'm sure you saw the Cloud Chamber, when you were there. It's one of only a few in the whole world, and it's necessary for developing a fog-based weapon. It's big enough to simulate wide-open space, while also being totally controlled, so you can try different mixtures, different concentrations. There's a lot of trial and error involved. It took most of a year to retrace my work from the original project. It was only after that point, once it was almost done, that they needed Coleman's help. He had the expertise on the finishing touches, including the animal testing. We shouldn't have cooperated with them . . . but they had ways to force us to do it. Those details I won't go into. You really *don't* want to know about that. It's enough to know that they succeeded. As of two nights ago, they have a fully working supply of the disease, in three separate canisters. If they escape with them, they could use them anywhere in the world, or sell them to someone else who will. I doubt it would end up being used in a war zone. More likely New York or London or Tokyo."

A silence fell. Sam thought of the baboon again, and tried to picture a human in the same state. Or thousands of such humans, in some busy public place.

"Christ," he whispered. He started to say more, but stopped himself. He turned his head, listening. At the edge of his vision, he saw Dani do the same.

The sound they had heard was faint—just audible over the wind in the trees. It sounded like a drumbeat, low and flat and very fast.

An incoming helicopter.

A second later all three of them were turning in circles, scanning the horizon. Dani saw it first; she stopped and pointed almost straight north. Sam followed her gaze and saw a blinking red light, maybe a mile away. The chopper was coming in low—practically hugging the ground.

"Air support?" Sam asked.

"I would say so," Pierce said. The relief in his voice was palpable.

The sound of the rotors swelled as the aircraft came in. Within twenty seconds it was nearly above the house. Sam heard the whine of its turbines change pitch—like the sound of a train going by—as it screamed past, maybe thirty yards west of the farmhouse, and no more than fifty feet above the field. It was heading straight for the barn.

Sam dropped to a knee and braced his binoculars on the deck rail again. In the seconds he spent trying to sight in the barn, he imagined what he would see. Without a doubt, the men there would have heard the chopper coming. Maybe they were already scrambling for whatever guns they had, if they were stupid enough to bother with that. Or maybe they would just pile into the car and try to run for it. Maybe they would be so frantic to do that, they wouldn't have time to grab Lauren out of the locked room and take her along. Just like that, every bad possibility would disappear.

It didn't seem like too much to wish for.

Then Sam got the binoculars locked onto the barn.

"What the hell?" he whispered.

Beside him, he heard Dani draw in a breath—she had her own binoculars lined up on the target.

In the magnified field of view, Sam could see the barn door, and the silhouettes of the men in front of it.

Standing in front of it. Calmly. They were just watching the chopper come in. One of them leaned back against the edge of the doorframe and raised a cigarette to his mouth.

"Why aren't they panicking?" Sam asked. "They should be losing their shit, if the military is—"

He cut himself off. He drew back from the binoculars and looked at the chopper, a quarter mile from the barn, already slowing, getting ready to hover and then land.

"It's not air support," Sam said. "It's their ride out of here."

CHAPTER THIRTY-SIX

"No . . ." Dani said softly. "No, no, this is all wrong . . ." She sounded like she was speaking only to herself.

Sam turned to Pierce. "Where the hell is the Army? How can they be taking this long?"

For a second Pierce didn't answer. He stared at the distant chopper, looking as baffled as Sam felt.

Then the man's eyes hardened, and he turned and strode toward the open French door.

"Keep watching them," Pierce said. "I'm going to get someone on the goddamned phone."

He disappeared into the darkness of the house, and a moment later Sam heard a phone handset rattle out of its cradle.

"It's landing," Dani said.

Sam turned back to face the barn. Even without looking through the binoculars, he could see the chopper clearly. The light through the barn door lit it from below, silhouetting the aircraft against the cloud of dust its rotors had kicked up.

Sam knelt again and put his eyes to the binoculars—he already had them braced on the rail and lined up on the barn.

The men on the ground were just visible through the whipping dust. It churned in big sideways swirls, roiling in the space between the chopper and the barn. Within seconds the helicopter settled fully on the ground.

It was big—probably twice the size of the little choppers Sam had seen above L.A. every day of his life. Most of this helicopter's size was devoted to what looked like a cargo bay in the back, a huge space with both its side walls wide-open to the night. Sam could see right through the cargo bay to the barn door behind it.

No sooner had the thing touched down when the men began hustling to load things into it. In a flurry of movement they shoved in the boxes they had carried outside earlier.

At the same time, one of them came out of the barn pushing a dolly, like people used in stores to move heavy appliances. This dolly held a steel canister that looked like a propane tank for a gas grill—only bigger. It was the size of a punching bag, with some kind of valve assembly at one end. The whole thing was painted black; it gleamed in the dusty light.

Two men lifted it off the dolly and struggled with it, shoving it into the chopper's cargo bay. A third jumped up next to it and began securing it to the floor with heavy straps. Already one of the others was rolling the dolly back into the barn.

As Sam watched, he heard Pierce behind him in the

house, speaking just above a whisper. "Pick up. Jesus Christ, somebody . . ."

The men rolled a second giant canister out, and hoisted it into the chopper.

Sam heard Pierce hang up the phone, then lift it again and punch in another number.

"No!" Dani said, all but screaming the word.

Sam could already see what she was reacting to:

Even as the men hauled the third metal canister out of the barn, another of them carried out something else: a person, short and skinny, with long hair, writhing and twisting in the man's arms. It could only be Lauren Coleman.

Lauren's hands appeared to be bound in front of her, maybe with duct tape like Pierce's had been. Her ankles, too. The man handed her off to someone in the chopper.

In the same instant, Sam found his attention drawn elsewhere: the pilot had gotten out of the chopper, and seemed to be arguing with the men who had the third canister. He stood blocking them from putting it in the cargo bay, shaking his head and waving his hands. It was impossible to hear any voices over the distance, but all the same, it was clear the pilot was shouting, and the men were shouting back. For some reason, the pilot didn't want that third canister loaded into the aircraft, though it looked identical to the first two.

At last one of the other men grabbed the pilot by the front of his shirt and shoved him backward, pointing angrily at the empty pilot's seat. To Sam, the meaning was obvious enough: *Get out of our way. Get back in there and do your job.*

The pilot stood his ground for a second or two, then turned and clambered back into the front of the chopper.

The others hauled the last canister aboard and strapped it in, then climbed into the helicopter themselves—some into the cargo bay, others into side doors farther forward. They became a jumble of silhouettes, hard to tell apart from one another, though Sam knew there must be five of them—every man who'd been in the barn. He could see at least two in the bay, buckling themselves into little seats at the back. One of those men had a hold of Lauren by the upper arm. She had stopped fighting. She lay on the metal floor of the bay, curled up.

An ugly thought occurred to him for the first time: Lauren had almost certainly witnessed her father's murder, at the hands—and feet—of these same men.

Maybe she expected the same would happen to her, whenever the chopper reached its destination.

Maybe she was right.

Inside the farmhouse, Pierce cursed and slammed the phone down. His footsteps thudded back out through the door.

"I can't get anyone," he said. "They could already be mobilizing, moving out."

Far away across the fields, the chopper's rotors cycled back up to full speed. By the time Sam turned to look at it again, it had lifted off. It pivoted sharply, climbing away from the lit-up barnyard, heading north again, the direction it had come from earlier. It leveled out around the same fifty-foot altitude it had flown at before—if anything, it was lower.

"Will the military be able to see that thing on radar?" Sam asked. "If it's flying low like that?"

"I don't know," Pierce said. His voice was full of stress.

"We have to do something," Dani said. "Anything. There has to be something you can think of."

Pierce had no answer. His breathing had accelerated; he sounded like he'd just run a hundred yard dash.

The chopper passed by the farmhouse along the same line it had followed only a minute or two before, but again Sam was struck by how much lower it was—nowhere near fifty feet up, this time. Maybe thirty. The engine noise was different, too. The pitch was higher, and it sounded like it was revving over and over. Straining, working hard. That was the impression it gave him. It sped past and continued north, toward downtown and the subdivision beyond.

Dani turned to Pierce. "Try calling someone else."

"I called the only numbers I know."

"Then try *again*—"

Before she could say any more, the sound of the retreating chopper suddenly changed. The scream of its turbines rose in a matter of seconds, like a teakettle hitting the boiling point.

All three of them spun in place and stared after it. At a glance Sam could see that something was wrong: the aircraft had whipped around ninety degrees, its movements erratic, jerky. A second later it spun to face forward again, its nose dipping and then coming right back up—manic, rapid moves, as if something in the machine had failed catastrophically, and the pilot was fighting to keep it airborne.

For maybe ten seconds the aircraft appeared to level out and regain control, still heading north, probably beyond downtown Ashland by now, somewhere near the subdivision.

Then it pivoted again, spinning like a top in slow motion, and descended out of view beyond the low shapes of the storefronts downtown, a mile or more away.

For a long, long moment—time enough for Sam to take a deep breath—nothing happened.

Then a fireball bloomed where the helicopter had disappeared, silent as distant lightning.

CHAPTER THIRTY-SEVEN

Sam heard a sharp little breath from Dani, like she'd been elbowed in the stomach. It was the only sound she made, but after a few seconds he could tell she was crying; he could see her shoulders hitching, at the edge of his vision.

Farther off to the side, Pierce stood with his hands atop his head, muttering something Sam couldn't make out.

Finally the sound of the explosion came—a bass-heavy *whump* like a massive firework, far away in the night. The windows of the farmhouse rattled faintly for a second or two, and then everything was silent again.

The sound seemed to break the trance of the moment; Pierce turned where he stood and sprinted into the house through the open door.

"Stay here!" he yelled.

Sam looked at Dani. She wiped at her eyes, looking awful. She held his gaze for a second and then shook her head, turned and ran after Pierce.

"Where are you going?" she asked, her voice cracking.

Sam followed. Inside, the house suddenly flared with bright light; Pierce had slapped a wall switch on the far side of the living room. Sam squinted, his eyes stinging, but he saw Pierce pull open a door and go through. An instant later the dark space beyond that doorway was also bathed in light, revealing a garage. The lone vehicle inside was a dark green, open-top Jeep.

Ahead of Sam, Dani stepped into the garage, all but running. Pierce was already pulling open the driver's door of the Jeep. He reached in and tilted down the visor, and a set of keys dropped into his hand.

"You're going up there," Dani said.

"Yes."

"We're coming with you. If there's any way she survived—"

"Then I'll help her," Pierce said. "Stay here."

Dani took another two fast steps, grabbed the Jeep's roll bar and clambered into the back seat. Sam did the same, dropping into place beside her.

Pierce stood there outside the open driver's door, staring at them.

"We heard you," Sam said.

Pierce looked at them a moment longer, then gave up. He went around the Jeep's back end, twisted the manual release for the garage door, and hauled the thing up on its rollers. He got back in the Jeep, started it, gunned the engine and reversed out of the garage.

The moment they cleared the north end of downtown Ashland, they saw the crash site. The chopper had gone down in the cornfield, south and west of the subdivision.

Sam stood up from his seat, holding the Jeep's roll bar. Beside him, Dani did the same.

The burning wreck of the aircraft lay maybe two hundred yards from the southwest corner of the suburb—the corner of the sideways rainbow, as it would have appeared on a map. The wind was blowing northeast, hard and gusty, sending the smoke right into the subdivision in a layer that hugged the surface like ground fog.

Sam watched it drift among the houses for only a second or two, and then his attention went back to the crashed chopper and the cornfield around it, brightly lit by the flames.

It was obvious the chopper had not simply hit the ground and exploded. The cornfield had been torn up and shredded in a long furrow that stretched more than a hundred feet. It looked as if the helicopter had come in at a shallow angle, dragging its skids through the corn and the dirt—maybe the edges of its spinning rotors, too. There were also deeper ruts sticking off of the main path of destruction here and there; Sam picture the chopper's tail whipping around and slamming into the ground at those places, carving into the soil.

There was debris strewn everywhere along the length of the furrow: pieces of the aircraft, torn off in the dragging impact. Sam could make out a seat, intact but empty, lying on its side among the corn shoots. There were metal panels of the fuselage, and spearlike fragments of the rotor blades, and heavy-looking steel chunks of what must have been the engine.

And human bodies.

Sam could see three of them already, just in the cleared-out path where the field had been scraped flat. All three lay well away from the burning wreckage.

One of the bodies was much smaller than the other two.

With long hair.

Sam elbowed Dani and pointed, but she was already nodding, her eyes fixed on Lauren Coleman, lying there where she'd been thrown from the crashing chopper.

And then Lauren moved.

There was no mistaking it, even from several hundred feet away. She rolled onto her back and put a hand to her head, pressing it there like someone with a headache.

Dani leaned down and screamed at Pierce in the driver's seat: *"She's alive!"*

Pierce nodded, his attention going back and forth between the crash site and the road ahead; they were now midway up the slope between downtown and the subdivision.

Pierce was just turning in place, as if to reply to Dani, when something near the crash site caught his eye—he jerked his head toward it, and slammed on the brakes.

Sam's chest hit the roll bar hard enough to compress the air out of his lungs; the same happened to Dani beside him. Beneath them, the Jeep's tires bit into the pavement with a long shriek. The vehicle slewed forty-five degrees to the left as it finally came to rest.

Sam sucked in a breath and found his voice. "What the hell was that for?"

Pierce didn't answer. He didn't even seem to have heard. He was staring through the windshield at the wreckage, still a couple hundred feet away. His hands gripped the steering wheel, the knuckles bone-white.

"Hey," Sam said.

"Thirty feet short of the chopper," Pierce said. "Just to the right of the gouge. Look close."

Sam looked. For a moment he could see nothing there; the glare coming off the flames was too bright. Then he heard Dani take a sharp breath, and in the same moment he saw what Pierce was talking about.

Lying in the corn shoots, just off the edge of the scraped-clear ground, was one of the huge black canisters. Its valve assembly must have been damaged in the crash: there was a thick white mist rushing out of it, into the air.

That mist was being pushed sideways on the wind, in the same direction as the smoke.

North and east, hugging the ground in a broad, spreading layer, as it must have been doing for a few minutes by now.

The subdivision was already filled with it.

CHAPTER THIRTY-EIGHT

Sam followed the streaming gas cloud with his eyes, into the streets of the suburb, the sodium lights on the lampposts shining down into it as it drifted past.

Now he saw what he had missed before, when the Jeep had been farther down the sloped road: there were bodies lying all over the ground in the subdivision. They lay sprawled on front lawns, sidewalks, even in the streets.

Sam's mind put it all together like the pieces of a child's jigsaw puzzle:

The chopper crash had been loud enough to wake every single person in the suburb, and the flames had been bright and high enough to be seen from every house.

It was hard to imagine even a single person—man, woman, or child—not going outside to look, or at the very least opening a window to see what was going on.

Nearly the entire population of Ashland had been standing on their lawns when the gas cloud rolled through, indistinguishable from the smoke. They had inhaled it without the slightest idea of what it was.

When you're exposed to the mist, you black out within seconds, stay unconscious for five minutes or so, and then you wake up fully symptomatic—a monster.

"Oh Jesus," Pierce said softly. "This is bad. This is real, real bad . . ."

"Is everyone going to start killing each other when they wake up?" Dani asked.

Pierce stared at the subdivision, thinking it through—maybe envisioning what was coming.

"In the wild, they never did," Pierce said. "The *bailarines,* I mean. The afflicted never attacked each other."

Sam thought of his father—he had to be up there somewhere, probably lying sprawled on the front lawn of the house. But not for long. How many minutes had passed since the chopper had crashed—since the gas cloud had begun drifting through the suburb? Three, at least. Maybe four.

Sam took his eyes off the houses and the yards, and turned them on the crash site again. On Lauren. She was lying nowhere near the ruptured canister, and far clear of where the wind was blowing the gas. There was no real chance she had been exposed. The fact that she was awake verified it.

"Let's just get Lauren and go," Sam said.

He braced a foot on the sidewall of the Jeep and hopped down to the road. Dani was just behind him, about to step down, when Pierce spoke: "Look."

Sam and Dani both turned to follow his gaze to the downed helicopter.

The big canister was running dry. Where there had been a surge of mist coming out, there were now only stuttering wisps of the stuff, like the last coughs of some dying animal. After a few seconds even those stopped. The tank was empty. Sam watched as the wind pushed the last of the mist away, clearing it from the airspace above the cornfield, and then the road and the first yards beyond. The wind was strong; in another minute or two the subdivision would be cleared of the stuff, for whatever that was worth—the damage had already been done.

Dani jumped down to the pavement beside Sam, took two running steps and vaulted across the ditch into the cornfield where the chopper had crashed. She landed without stopping and took off at a sprint.

Sam followed her lead. He'd just landed in the cornfield when Pierce called out behind them: "Hold up!"

Sam stopped. Twenty paces ahead, Dani stopped, too. They both turned and looked back.

Pierce nodded up the road toward the subdivision. "I need to get up there and be ready to talk to the military, when they roll in. If my message didn't get their attention, all this sure as hell will. I need to explain to them what's going on, so they don't start shooting these people when they wake up." He nodded toward where Lauren lay, in the field. "Get your friend and then go someplace where you'll be safe." He was quiet a second, thinking. "You said you've been to Station Fourteen, north of here?"

Sam nodded.

"If you can move Lauren," Pierce said, "take her there. Close yourselves inside, and stay put until I come and get you. You'll be okay."

Sam glanced at the subdivision. The bodies strewn there were still motionless. So far.

"Are *you* going to be okay?" Sam asked.

"I know what I'm doing," Pierce said. "Good luck."

He put the Jeep back in gear and goosed it, accelerating up Truman toward the southern edge of the subdivision.

Sam watched for another three seconds, then turned to Dani, and the two of them took off running again toward Lauren.

They covered the distance in less than a minute, sprinting through the knee-high corn stalks.

Sam could still see Lauren moving, rolling back and forth where she lay.

He also kept his eyes on the other two bodies—two of the men who'd been in the chopper. Like Lauren, they lay far away from where the gas cloud had been. If they were alive, they weren't infected—a fact that made them *more* dangerous, he realized. So far, though, he hadn't seen either of them move.

He caught up to Dani in the last ten yards of the run. He pointed at the two men, then put a finger to his lips: *shhh*. Dani nodded.

They reached Lauren a second later. Dani dropped to her knees beside the girl and put a hand on her shoulder.

"Lauren?" she whispered.

For a moment Lauren didn't seem to even notice her. Then she turned her head and stared up at Dani, and it was obvious the girl was dazed. Maybe outright delirious.

Dani reached down and gently lifted up the hair on one side of Lauren's head, revealing a dark bruise on the scalp there, which had even bled a little.

"She took a bad hit in the crash," Sam whispered. "She's out of it."

Dani nodded, turning again and looking at the two men nearby.

Sam followed her gaze. Both men were still motionless, but up close he could see that they were alive: their chests rose and fell with their breathing.

"Time to get out of here," he whispered.

"Do you think she's too hurt to walk?" Dani asked.

Sam looked at Lauren, considering it. She wore shorts and a T-shirt, and in the light of the flames, her arms and legs looked unhurt. A few scrapes where she'd landed in the soft earth, but nothing bruised or bleeding.

"Let's see," Sam said.

He and Dani each took an arm and lifted. Lauren, though seemingly unaware of her surroundings, managed to get her balance and stay upright. She stood there swaying, looking at the wreckage as if entranced by it.

"Can you walk with us?" Dani whispered.

Lauren blinked and turned to her, and nodded slowly.

"This way," Dani said. She nodded toward the darkness west of the crash site—away from the two unconscious men, and away from the subdivision. Sam stared in that direction: beyond the light of the burning aircraft, the cornfield lay pitch-black and empty. Out there, the three of them would be invisible. They would be home free. Reaching Station 14 would be a cakewalk at that point.

Holding Lauren's arm, Dani got the girl moving. Sam held her other arm, though it seemed almost unnecessary; Lauren was keeping herself upright well enough.

They had gone maybe ten yards when they heard the first scream from the subdivision. A far-off, shrill cry that cut through the night.

Sam and Dani froze in place, turning back toward the sound. Sam's eyes darted over the nearest edge of the suburb—the whole stretch of it that bordered Truman Avenue, the flat part of the sideways rainbow.

Some of the bodies sprawled in the yards were still lying there.

But not all of them.

In the first sweeping glance, Sam could see at least three people up on their feet, moving around, their motions strange in a way that was hard to pin down. He stared, transfixed by the sight.

They're like something you've seen, but . . . what? And where?

It hit him like a shove to the chest—a memory from a few years back, in L.A.

The Cooler Man. That's what all the kids called him. The Cooler Man on Beverly Glen Boulevard.

Sam had been six or seven when he'd first seen the Cooler Man. Sam's mom had been driving, and Sam had been sitting there in the passenger seat, staring out at the city going by. Then they'd stopped at a light, and just like that the Cooler Man was there, standing on the curb six feet away, staring in at him. The cooler in question was a little green-and-white thing, big enough to hold a few sandwiches and a soda can, maybe. The man held it low in his left hand, where it jerked in spastic little twitches.

Ah shit, not this guy, Sam's mom had said. *Don't look at him, he's got a couple gears missing.*

Sam knew what that meant—that the Cooler Man was crazy—but even then, that very first time, he didn't believe it. Sam had seen plenty of crazy people on the streets. He knew what crazy looked like. It was all in the eyes.

But there was nothing crazy about the Cooler Man's eyes. That was part of what made him so scary—the fact that he appeared normal. He looked at you the way a teacher in the hallway might look at you, right before asking if you had permission to be out of class. The Cooler Man would just stand there on the street corner, staring at you like it was the most ordinary thing in the world . . . and then he would move.

He would turn and seem to lose his balance for a second, then throw himself forward in a lunge that turned into a run, fifteen or twenty feet in some random direction on the sidewalk. Pedestrians would flinch and pull their kids out of his way. He would offer a little wave sometimes, like, *Hey, sorry about that.* And then he would jerk to a halt, and get his balance, and look around, and do it all over again. The Cooler Man. He had been a regular fixture on Beverly Glen Boulevard until Sam was ten years old, and then he'd disappeared. Maybe he'd gone off to unnerve people someplace else.

That was how the afflicted moved. Like the Cooler Man. They weren't slow or shuffling or lethargic, like zombies on TV. They lunged. They ran.

As Sam watched, a fourth body on one of the lawns twitched and rolled over and got up on all fours. A man in his thirties or forties, it looked like. He was wearing khaki shorts and a black T-shirt. He hunkered there on the grass like a crouching chimp, jerking his gaze left and right.

Then the man's attention locked onto something: a utility box near the sidewalk, a grey metal structure the size of a big suitcase.

The man in the black T-shirt came up out of his crouch and launched himself toward the thing. He seemed to chase his balance for a few strides, and then he simply ran—about as fast as any grownup could move. He crossed the distance to the utility box and attacked it, slamming his hands and knees into it, caving in its sides, tearing off its top panel and pulling out cables and wires like the entrails of some prey animal.

All at once the man dropped to a crouch again, clutching at a ripped-out tangle of wire, and screamed.

It was like no sound Sam had ever heard a human make. It was animalistic. It was high-pitched and loud, and raw.

And it was enough to wake the two unconscious men near the crash site.

Their bodies jerked, responding to the sound. They

squirmed in the dirt, pushing themselves up and looking for the source of the scream. In a matter of seconds both men were sitting up, their arms braced on the ground, their gazes fixed on the shrieking man at the edge of the subdivision.

Dani reacted in unison with Sam; she flinched and looked around for any visual cover, anything to hide behind before the men turned and saw them.

The only thing big enough, close by, was a long section of the chopper's tail; it rested in the corn shoots ten feet to their left. Sam pointed to it, and Dani nodded, and together they got Lauren moving. They covered the distance and dropped flat behind the tail section, and heard the two men clamber to their feet a moment later.

Already the men were talking—clipped little phrases Sam couldn't quite make out. Then one of them called out a name—Gorman or Borman, something like that—and Sam heard them shoving aside pieces of the wreckage near the chopper.

"They're looking for their buddies," Dani whispered.

Sam nodded, the implication dropping on him like a weight.

"They're going to find us here," he said.

Dani nodded, her eyes huge. She looked at Lauren, lying between them. The girl was still oblivious, holding her head in pain.

"They'll kill her," Dani whispered. "Or they'll take her again. They'll take all of us."

Sam nodded. No denying it.

The sound of the searching came closer—metal fuselage panels being heaved aside, flipped over.

Sam stared out into the darkness they'd planned to escape into. The notion of simply running for it seemed laughable now—they wouldn't get ten feet without the men seeing them, and giving chase.

And with Lauren in tow, he and Dani could not possibly outrun grown men. He doubted whether he could even outrun them by himself, unhindered. Maybe, maybe not. He narrowed his eyes, thinking about that, as the voices and the sounds got closer.

"*Shit* . . ." Dani whispered. She was pulling Lauren against herself, protective.

"I had the record at my old school for the four-hundred meter," Sam whispered. He'd never even tried out for track and field. "I'm going to lead these guys off, and you're going to get Lauren out into the dark."

Dani stared at him. Her eyes were intense, probably seeing right through the bullshit.

"Sam—"

"*Way* out in the dark, until you can barely see to walk, and you'll be good to go. I'll meet you at Station Fourteen. I'll be there."

The men were coming closer. They couldn't be more than ten or fifteen yards away.

Still staring at him, Dani reached out and grabbed one of his hands with both of hers.

"I'll be there," Sam said. "I promise."

She nodded, held his gaze a moment longer, and finally let go.

Sam turned away; he made a fast crawl to the far end of the tail wreckage, and stuck his head out.

The two men were thirty feet away from him, their backs turned, one of them hunched down to see under a big curved piece of the chopper's body.

Sam got to his feet and moved silently, keeping his eyes on the men, using the moment to get as much distance as he could from them—and from Dani and Lauren.

It occurred to him that these guys would have no idea who he was. Would have no specific reason to come after him, if they thought he was just some random kid from the suburb.

They have to chase you. Both of them.

He was still moving, sidestepping and backing away, going south and east from the crash site. It was the direction he meant to run—the best direction to lead the two men, if Dani and Lauren were going to go west and then north to Station 14.

He was fifty feet from the men now, still visible in the bright glow of the flames.

They have to chase you.

He stopped. Took a deep breath.

"I saw what you did!" he screamed.

Both men jerked and spun toward him. Their eyes darted for only a second and then snapped to him like weapon sights.

"At the barn! I saw it!" For good measure he pointed at the southern horizon, in the direction of Echo House and the barn.

He watched them react to the words, caught off guard and confused, but at the same time unable to discount them.

Then the man who was hunched down stood upright and took a step toward him. So did the other one.

Sam took a single step back. *"Stay away!"*

For a second they actually stopped where they were, maybe still trying to work out who the hell he was.

Then the nearer of the two broke into a sprint, and the second followed suit, and Sam turned and ran as fast as he could move.

CHAPTER THIRTY-NINE

They were faster than him.

It was clear within the first twenty seconds.

Sam looked back as he ran, again and again, and each glance brought the two men closer. Not a lot closer—but the fact that they were gaining at all was enough. Enough to shut down every option he had.

His plan, as far as he'd had one, had been to simply lose them in the darkness. He had pictured it working, even if he were a tiny bit slower than his pursuers. If he could stay ahead of them for even thirty seconds, then at some point they would no longer be able to see him. That was how he'd imagined it.

The problem with that plan was clear enough now: in pitch darkness he would be blind, too, and a cornfield full of knee-high stalks and furrowed soil was a hell of a place to try sprinting blind.

If he fell, they would be on him. No question of that. The possibility that one of them might trip instead was no comfort: there were two of them and one of him. His pursuers wouldn't *both* fall.

Hiding in the darkness would have worked just fine,

if he and Dani and Lauren could have gotten there unseen.

Being *chased* into the darkness was an entirely different matter.

He looked back again.

They were forty feet behind him, give or take.

Closer and closer, chipping away at his lead.

Already the field in front of him was too dark for his liking. He could see the shoots and the raised rows of dirt, but only just.

He was still running southeast, moving in a straight line away from the flaming chopper. The only other source of light was the subdivision, ahead and to his left as he ran. He glanced up at it—the smoke from the crash site was still rolling through it, like thick fog under the streetlights, and in the haze he could see the afflicted; they darted through the light cones in spooky little bursts of speed.

He returned his attention to the ground in front of him and flinched—Truman Avenue was right there, ten feet ahead, along with its deep runoff ditches.

"Shit—"

He planted a foot just before the nearer ditch and vaulted over it, almost slipping on his ass when he landed on the gravel shoulder. He kept his balance, kept running, vaulted the second ditch and sprinted into the tall grass beyond—he was now on the slope directly south of the subdivision.

Too dark. He could barely see anything.

He'd gone only a few steps when he heard the men jump the first ditch behind him. Then the second. They were in the grassy field with him now, probably no more than twenty feet back. He risked a glance and felt his stomach give a lurch—they were *much* closer than before.

And still the darkness was deepening. The crash site was far, far behind now, and the subdivision, up atop the rise, was sliding off to his left as he angled away from it.

His foot snagged on something—a shrub or a root—and he cried out as he felt his center of gravity pitch forward, damn near sending him sprawling. He recovered, kept running, but now he could hear the men crashing through the grass behind him, so close he was afraid to look again. He kept his eyes fixed straight forward. And yet—

He could see nothing. Nothing at all. He shut his eyes for a second and found it made no difference. The world was a void either way.

He glanced to his left and saw the lit-up sprawl of the subdivision due north of him. The glow of its streetlights bled out onto the slope to a distance of maybe a hundred yards. He was just outside that glow, still moving southeast, angling farther from the light with each stride.

He found himself beginning to veer back toward that light without consciously deciding to. There was simply no choice in the matter: running in total darkness was asking for disaster. In any case, it didn't hide him from his pursuers—not when they were this close behind him. They could *hear* him. He could damn well hear them.

He made the turn smoothly as he ran—curving to

his left, coming around, until he was running dead-on north, with the suburb splayed out before him at the top of the rise.

It lay 150 yards away from him, the ground directly ahead still deep in the black.

All at once his breathing sounded strange in his own ears. A second later he realized why—it wasn't *his* breathing.

One of the pursuers was that close. Two or three feet back—it couldn't be more than that.

The ragged hissing—in and out, in and out—got louder by the second.

One hundred yards to the subdivision now. The long grass in front of him was just faintly visible again.

Fingertips brushed the back of his shirt, making his heart want to flip up into his throat.

He flailed and leaned forward, like a runner shoving his chest out toward the finish line ribbon.

High up the slope, along the edge of the subdivision, the loping figure of one of the afflicted crossed someone's back yard. It was a man, tall and stocky, wearing an undershirt and jeans. In the glow of a rear patio light, the man dropped to a crouch and looked around, his movements spastic. He was maybe seventy yards away, straight ahead.

At Sam's back, the pursuer's fingertips swiped again, much more than a grazing pass this time. He felt his shirt fabric ripple, the fingers hooking into it and trying to take hold, before they slipped away again.

Next one's going to do the job. He's going to grab a fistful of your shirt and drag you down.

Far ahead, in the lit-up yard, the man in the undershirt was still crouching, swaying forward and back on his haunches.

Sam heard an expulsion of breath behind himself. He pictured the pursuer making a forward lunge, throwing his hand out for that final grab.

Sam sucked in a deep breath and screamed, loud and sharp and sustained.

The result was everything he needed it to be.

Up in the yard, the afflicted man jerked and whipped his head toward the noise.

Two feet behind Sam, the pursuer gasped: *"Fucking hell . . ."*

The words were laced with anger—but also fear. Sam knew the reason:

You guys know all there is about Rigel, don't you? Sure you do.

Sam felt the hand brush his back again, an instant later, but once more it barely grazed his shirt—the man behind him was already slowing. Sam heard him curse again, then heard the guy's feet sliding in the grass, coming to a full stop.

Sam kept running.

Up ahead—fifty yards away now—the crouching man held dead still, staring out on the darkness of the slope.

Sam pictured himself and Dani back in the cornfield, staking out the barn near Echo House. When the men had first emerged from it, he'd counted on their eyes being bright-adapted, unable to see the two of them close by in the dark.

He needed the same to hold true here: needed the afflicted man, with his eyes adapted to the bright lights of the suburb, to see only darkness out here in the weeds.

So far, so good: the man stayed hunched in place, looking around but holding his position.

Still running, Sam looked over his shoulder and saw both pursuers standing there in the tall grass, twenty yards back.

He took another half dozen running strides, then skidded to a halt himself.

He stood exactly centered between the two threats: the men from the chopper behind him, the crouching man in the yard ahead. Sam was a hundred feet from each of them.

The pursuers stared at him, but made no move to come any closer. In the faint light, Sam could see them keeping an eye on the afflicted man, too. Their fear was evident in their body language.

The moment stretched out, wire-tight and surreal, a standoff from out of a fever dream.

And then it fell apart: the man in the yard made a low chuffing sound, like an animal, then turned and loped away into the smoky light of the subdivision.

Sam turned to face the men from the chopper, tensing himself to sprint again.

But they only stood there, watching him—half watching him, actually. The other half of their attention remained on the subdivision.

They still didn't want to come any nearer.

From out of the hazy streets, the screams of the afflicted seeped into the night. Men, women, children.

Sam watched the two men. How long could they stand there? They had to know the authorities would show up at some point. Time was wasting, if they wanted to get out of Ashland before that happened.

Still they stood there, staring at him, pissed off and scared and pumped up on adrenaline from the chase.

If they *were* thinking about their getaway, then one thing must be obvious to them: leaving him alive would make it a lot harder to escape. If Sam told the Army about these two, then there would be choppers hunting them down, out there in the dark fields.

One of the men said something—a quick little sentence, softly spoken. Sam couldn't make it out over the distance, but it sounded like, *What do you think?*

Before the other one could answer, Sam glanced at the nearest back yards along the subdivision's edge. They were empty—for now.

He faced the two men again, and backed up a step, moving toward the suburb.

Then he took another, and another.

For a moment he thought they might rush him after all; there was no doubt they could see what he meant to do.

But they only stood there, their faces going blank as they watched him back away. They were either that afraid to come closer to the afflicted, or that sure he was going to die and save them the trouble. Maybe both.

Sam turned and sprinted into the smoke.

He ran until he was in past the first layer of houses, then stopped and crouched against a shrub in someone's front yard.

The drifting smoke was much denser than it had appeared from outside the suburb. It was heavier than any fog he'd seen in his life.

That was both good and bad. The good was obvious: it helped hide him from the afflicted, especially if he stayed tucked out of sight like this. The bad was obvious, too: it was burning the hell out of his lungs already, the effect made worse by the fact that he was panting from the sprint.

He pulled his shirt up and pressed it over his mouth and nose. It helped a little.

He felt sure enough that it *was* just smoke—that the gas cloud from the Rigel canister had long-since blown away in the wind. The smoke was still rolling through because the crash site was still burning.

Through the haze, the barely human cries seemed to come from everywhere. Other sounds, too: the scrape of running footsteps on asphalt; the clatter of a metal trash can being knocked over; that eerie, doglike chuffing sound again, passing close to the yard where Sam crouched.

You can't stay like this much longer. You're not that *well hidden.*

He continued breathing in and out through the shirt, thinking.

What was the plan, exactly? Make his way across the subdivision and come out on the north side? He wouldn't make it half that distance before someone tore him to pieces.

What options did that leave? Sitting tight somewhere in here? Tucking in and waiting for the military to finally show up and get control of the scene?

Where could he do that? Where could he hole up?

He looked around and found himself considering a tall sugar maple at the edge of the yard. Would the afflicted be able to climb up after him?

Was it worth the risk of finding out the hard way?

He thought of the obvious answer—hiding inside a house—but there were lots of problems with that plan. First, any house might have the afflicted inside it. Second, and more unnerving, any house might still contain traces of the poison gas. The wind had cleared the streets and yards of the stuff, but whatever had blown into houses through open windows could still be inside, if only a little. And a little might be enough.

There was simply no way to be sure, no matter what house he tried—

He cut himself off mid-thought, and stared away into the haze along the street.

Lauren Coleman's house was down there somewhere, not far.

In his mind he saw Dani taking the key from its hiding spot, that afternoon. Saw the two of them stepping inside, the air of the place stale and hot after a week of being closed up tight, no windows open, no air conditioner running.

They had left it that way, too.

CHAPTER FORTY

On a normal night Sam could have sprinted to the house in less than a minute. On this night, the going would be nowhere near as fast.

He moved from hiding place to hiding place—shrubs along the edges of porches, clumps of small pine trees in front yards. Wherever he stopped, he held still and waited, listening for sounds close by in the dense smoke.

He had covered maybe half the distance to Lauren's house now. He ran to a waist-high sprawl of lilac bushes near a mailbox and ducked down. He could hear a low, steady rumbling sound, and realized after a few seconds that it was a car engine.

His mind conjured up an absurd image: one of the afflicted behind the wheel of a vehicle, madly racing up and down the streets of Ashland, taking out any person or thing that got in the way.

But the vehicle didn't sound like it was moving at all. It sounded like it was parked and idling, somewhere close by.

He raised his head above the lilacs and saw it: a

yellow Ford Escort, parked in the next driveway over, right in the direction he was headed. The passenger side faced Sam, but he could see that the driver's door hung wide open on the opposite side. The Escort's dome light shone out in all directions through the smoky air.

From where he crouched, he could see no one inside the vehicle. It seemed to be just sitting there, unattended. All the same, he decided he would steer far clear of it as he went past.

He broke from the low bushes and sprinted diagonally across the road. He darted to the base of a tree, tucked himself into its shadow and listened again.

No nearby movement. He leaned past the tree and studied the street and adjoining yards. Nothing stirred.

He could see the driver's side of the Escort from here. Just outside the car's open door, a big plastic container lay on the driveway. It was white with a red cross on top—a huge first-aid kit, the size of a fishing tackle box. The thing lay broken open, its contents scattered on the pavement.

Sam realized what must have happened. The owner of the car was some kind of medical professional, and had planned on going to the scene of the crashed chopper. He or she had made it only as far as the Escort before breathing in too much of the airborne gas. Sam pictured the driver passing out right at the wheel, maybe just seconds after starting the car; now that same person was somewhere in the neighborhood, wreaking havoc like an animal.

Sam forgot about the Escort and stared ahead along the street again. The Coleman place was probably only three or four houses away now. It was tempting to just sprint to it from right here, without stopping again.

Don't be stupid. Play it safe. You're almost home free.

The thought had barely formed when he heard the strange, doglike panting sound from before. This time it came from somewhere in the darkness behind him.

Sam felt the skin prickle on his forearms. Staying crouched in the tree's shadow, he pivoted slowly in place.

Thirty feet away, at the front corner of the nearest house, was the big man he had seen earlier. The guy in the blue jeans and undershirt.

The man wasn't looking at Sam; his gaze was fixed at nothing in particular, straight ahead of himself in the drifting smoke. He was in the same bizarre squatting position Sam had seen him in earlier, his arms stretched downward and his knuckles pressed to the ground. At this distance, Sam could see details he had missed before: the guy's T-shirt was torn in several places, and the fabric was splotched and flecked with blood. The blue jeans were soaked, too, but with only a single giant stain running from the crotch to the knee—the big man had pissed himself profusely.

From someplace up the street—in the direction Sam had been moving—a woman screamed. The man in the bloody T-shirt snapped his head toward that sound—

And looked directly at Sam.

For a full second, nothing happened; it was long enough for Sam to hope the guy couldn't see him in the tree's shadow, that his gaze only *seemed* to be pointed at him.

Then the deadpan expression twisted into one of almost childlike anger—the face of a toddler throwing a tantrum—and the man lurched forward, straight toward him.

Sam broke from the tree and ran.

CHAPTER FORTY-ONE

In the first second or two, Sam had no thought in his head except to move as fast as possible. He had taken only a few running strides—angling away from the tree and into the street—when he saw the woman.

She was fifty feet away, straight ahead in the direction he was sprinting. She seemed to spot him in the same instant he saw her; she had been loping right down the middle of the road, aimless, but now she faltered, stared at him, and came bolting toward him.

As he took in all of these details—still running—his mind stayed focused on the man behind him.

If you stop for even a second, he's got you.

The woman looked young—late twenties, give or take. She wore pink sweatpants and nothing else. Above the waist, her pale skin was scratched and bloody, not so different from the big man's T-shirt. Sam was still heading straight toward her.

Behind him, he heard the man's footsteps scuff onto the asphalt of the road. *Close.*

The woman screamed, the sound reminding Sam of a chimpanzee's shriek in a nature documentary.

Sam jerked his head to the side and saw the only option he had: the Escort.

It sat there rumbling, its door open like an extended hand, ten or fifteen running steps to his right. He planted one foot mid-stride, pushed off of it and threw himself sideways. He heard the man behind him skid and lose his footing, just for a second, as he changed course to follow him.

To Sam, the sprint to the car took on a feeling that was new to him—and not entirely bad. All at once the world had a clarity that was almost indescribable. A world made of simple and absolute things: the open car door, its inside handle, the little silvery lock button up near the window. Those things were all that mattered on Earth in the next five seconds. There was an exact way he needed to interact with them. A sequence of moves, each one simple and precise—he played it out in his head. He would get it right or else he would be killed, right here on this stranger's lawn in this miserable, fake town.

The woman screamed her chimp scream again. Sam found it had almost no effect on him, this time. He cared about nothing but the geometry quiz coming toward him at sprint speed. Three seconds away. Two. One—

He threw himself across the last three feet of space, pulling his legs up, dropping his head low, twisting in the air, passing through the low-slung shape of the Escort's open door. He grabbed hold of its inner handle as he went by, using his body's momentum to haul the thing shut. It slammed home with a deeply satisfying *thud,* and in the same fraction of a second Sam brought his fist down on the door lock. He pivoted in the seat and leaned fast and hit the passenger door's lock an instant later, and before he'd straightened upright again behind the wheel, both the man and woman collided with the driver's side door. The impact was hard enough to jostle the vehicle.

A second later they were both pounding on the window with their fists, and on the metal roof above it. The tempered glass warped and flexed under each blow, but held—for now.

Sam could already feel the weird, hyper-focused frame of mind leaving him. In its wake was a fear he hoped he could at least keep a grip on.

He looked at the car's controls and tried to see how to put it in reverse. He had never driven anything before, but he didn't need to do much driving right now, either—he just had to get away.

The Escort was an automatic: there was no gear shifter with a knob on top, just a big selector stick jutting up from the center console below the dash. The selector had a lit-up band of letters running alongside it: *P, R, N, D* and *L.* Sam knew what all of those stood for. Right now there was a bright orange indicator line beside the *P,* because the car was in park.

The man's fist came down on the upper corner of the windshield, cracking it in a big spiderweb pattern. Sam could see the glass bowing inward where it had been hit—it stayed intact, but maybe not by much.

Sam tried to picture what grownups did after they

started a car. He was pretty sure they stepped on the brake before putting the vehicle in gear. He found the left pedal in the dark, shoved it hard with his foot, and grabbed the selector lever. It had a side-button you were supposed to push in with your thumb; he depressed it and hauled back on the stick, and was startled by how easily it moved—the little orange indicator jumped downward, right past *R* and *N,* and onto *D.*

"No—goddammit—"

He felt the car try to jerk forward against the resistance of the brake; still holding the selector, he shoved it upward and got the orange pointer onto *R.*

The woman was screaming again, and now the man joined in, the sound deep and guttural. The guy's fist came down on the fractured windshield once more; the spiderweb spread outward, and the impact point sagged deeper in.

Sam was an instant from letting off the brake when a new sound came at him—the shrill scream of a young child, somewhere beyond the passenger side of the vehicle. He twisted in place and saw the newcomer: a boy no older than nine or ten, scrambling out of the smoky darkness toward the Escort. The kid vaulted onto the hood of the car and attacked the windshield on the right side, where the glass was still uncracked. For the moment, his small fists had no effect.

It was the kid's face that grabbed Sam's attention. A chunk of skin the size of a playing card had been torn loose from his left cheek, and hung flapping over the corner of his mouth. A running sheet of blood covered the raw tissue that had been exposed; Sam could make out the cords of facial muscle contracting and tensing as the kid screamed.

Even as Sam reacted to that sight, something thumped hard against the car's back end. He looked over his shoulder and saw a bald man, maybe in his fifties, clambering onto the big hatchback window above the rear seat. In the same moment, at least two more of the afflicted pressed into position outside the driver's door, their hands and arms spastically pawing at the glass. The crush of bodies shoved the young woman in the pink sweatpants tightly against the window. Sam caught a glimpse of one soft breast mashed onto the glass, six inches from his face, and then the woman was shoved aside and a red-haired man with a shaggy beard was right there, shrieking at him and attacking the pane with his bare knuckles; their skin burst and bled with each impact.

The afflicted were coming in from all over the place. Sam could see a dozen or more now, emerging from the smoke haze at a shambling run, drawn by the screams and the commotion.

Like seagulls to a handful of bread crusts, he thought, and the crazy image broke his paralysis. He gripped the wheel, took his foot off the brake and shoved it down on the accelerator.

The Escort leapt backward, faster than he had expected. He hit the brake again, and the bald man atop the hatchback window cried out and fell away. Sam heard him land in a heap, right on the concrete behind the car.

Oh shit.

The realization came to him even as new arrivals continued bunching up around the vehicle.

He couldn't back up again—not with someone lying on the ground back there. None of these people were actually responsible for what they were doing right now. It went without saying: absolutely none of this was their fault.

If you kill one of them, it's murder. Plain and simple.

Even as Sam watched for the bald man to get back on his feet, a younger man appeared at the rear bumper, pounding on the sloping hatchback window.

Sam turned and studied the space ahead of the car. While the kid with the ripped-open cheek was still on the hood, there was nobody actually in front of the vehicle.

He considered the space between the car's front end and the house: a distance of twenty feet.

Behind him, the hatchback window finally cracked and spiderwebbed—the safety glass stayed intact like the windshield, but the whole thing sagged in its frame.

The vehicle was rocking and swaying now. There were people bunched up at both sides, their faces pressed to the glass, their screams drowning one another out. Sam had never experienced claustrophobia before, but he imagined this was what it felt like.

Right against the driver's side window, the red-haired man with the beard suddenly spoke:

"Kill you."

The words were more hissed than shouted; they were just loud enough to discern under the screams.

Startled, Sam turned and looked into the man's eyes. He saw nothing in them but dumb, animal rage. The face of some dimwitted, starving predator.

"Kill you," the man hissed again.

"Fuck you," Sam said, and dropped the selector into drive.

He took his foot off the brake pedal, cut the wheel all the way left, and stepped on the gas.

The Escort shot forward and to the left, in a tight arc. The people pressing against it were momentarily yanked off balance, pulled along with it, and then they were gone, falling away in a chorus of furious screaming. The kid on the windshield was instantly thrown sideways by the centrifugal force of the turn. He made a frantic grab for purchase, his fingers scrabbling over the right-side windshield wiper, and then he was gone too, tumbling away off the hood.

Sam held on to the wheel and kept the gas pedal down, and watched the house's front porch come at him on the right. It slid by the passenger side of the car, and a second later the Escort was on the grass, pointed back out at the street and accelerating. Sam cranked the steering wheel hard to the right and straightened the vehicle out. He snapped his gaze in both directions along the road, hoping one of them would be clear of lurching bodies.

Neither was.

Sam held the wheel straight as the car launched itself across the road and onto the opposite lawn. Ahead of him loomed a pitch-black gap between adjacent houses. He had no idea how to turn on the vehicle's headlights—was pretty damned sure they would have only lit up the smoke, anyway.

An instant later he was into the gap, the two houses rushing past, falling away behind him, the deep void of their back yards swallowing him up.

The seconds that followed were surreal. He could see the lampposts of the next street, maybe two hundred feet ahead of him, and the silhouettes of houses over there, but everything closer than that was invisible: a formless dark through which he was driving at thirty miles per hour.

Something blurred past the driver's side window—maybe a wooden play set. He had hardly processed this thought when another shape rose up straight in front of him. He slammed his foot on the brake, felt the Escort's wheels lock up and slide on the grass, and held on tight to the steering wheel.

The impact jolted the car. Sam was thrown forward, his hands slipping off the wheel. Then his body pitched backward—he found himself sagging into the seatback, as if the car were pointed nose-up on a steep, steep hill.

Silence, except for his heartbeat knocking in his chest.

Then another sound: distant screams outside, in the darkness behind the car.

Move. Right now.

He took a deep breath and forced it back out. He felt for the door release handle, pulled it and shoved on the door with his elbow.

The door moved—but only a little. There was some kind of resistance pushing back against it.

For a second he was sure it was jammed against something—a heavy shrub, maybe. Then he pushed it farther, and realized what he was feeling: there was nothing pressing against the door; the thing was just heavy. Because of the car's strange upward tilt, the door needed to be pushed *up,* not *out*.

Sam braced himself and shoved the door with all his force. It swung upward and open, and he leaned out and fell three feet, hitting the ground with his shoulder.

Above him in the dark, the door fell shut again with a resonant *thud* and *click*.

Sam got his hands and knees under him, and got to his feet. He stepped back from the car, and in the faint light he could see what had happened.

He had run over a small pine tree—one that was just big enough to stop the car and force it upward at the front end. The tree itself, two inches thick across the trunk, had bent under the vehicle's weight—but hadn't broken. The car was just hanging there now, angled upward, while the tree strained beneath it like an archer's bow under tension. Sam took a step back from it; there was no telling how much longer the tree would hold.

The far-off screams grabbed his attention again; he turned toward them. A hundred feet away, in the gap between the two houses, half a dozen silhouettes were visible. And coming toward him.

Sam turned fast and considered his options. He was in the center of a long, dark channel formed by the row of back yards. That channel ran parallel to the street he had been following earlier—the way to Lauren Coleman's house.

Sam ducked around the crashed Escort and sprinted away into the darkness.

Sixty seconds later he sat crouched beside the front corner of a house. Straight ahead of him, across the street, stood the Coleman place. He scanned the street in both directions and listened.

Nothing there.

Four houses away, he could hear the afflicted—a whole cluster of them in the back yard where he'd left the car. For now, at least, that commotion had drawn them all together like a magnet.

He watched the street for another ten seconds, then broke from cover and ran.

The key was where Dani had left it—inside the fake rock next to the porch. Sam scooped it up mid-stride, popped it open, shoved the key into the lock. He turned in place and scanned the night around him, watching for any movement in the smoke.

Still clear.

He unlocked the door and slipped inside.

Hot, stale air—but at the moment it seemed as fresh as a spring breeze. He closed and locked the door, then stood there sucking in lungful after lungful of the air, clearing the acrid taste of the smoke from his throat.

He moved through the entryway into the dark space of the living room, and lay down on his back on the carpet. He got his breathing under control. Long, slow breaths instead of frantic ones.

You're safe. Relax. Lie here for an hour if you want to.

He wanted to.

He shut his eyes and listened to the distant screams outside, the sounds dampened by the walls of the house. Compared to what it had sounded like out there, this was close to a lullaby.

His breathing slowed almost to normal.

His arms and legs, flat on the carpet, felt pleasantly light. The adrenaline rush of the past ten minutes was fading out. He didn't feel tired, but his body had never been so exhausted. He wanted nothing more than to keep his eyes closed and lie here doing nothing at all.

He thought of Dani and Lauren, somewhere out in the darkness of the cornfield, heading north for Station 14. Dani would worry when he didn't show up there right away, but she would understand later, when he explained. Hell, if she knew the circumstances, she would insist he stay right here for now. In the meantime, she and Lauren wouldn't have to wait alone: Pierce would meet them there soon enough.

A thought made him smile: *Remember to ask Lauren what the darts were all about.*

What the hell *were* they about?

Dani's assessment came back to him now: *Belly buttons and a pool table. If there's a connection, I'm missing it.*

He thought about it for another few seconds and then let it drift away.

He let everything else drift away, too. All the sounds. All the worries. Everything was good now. Everything was just—

His eyes opened and he flinched as if someone had kicked him in the side. He swiveled his head and stared across the floor at the steps leading down to the rec room.

"The darts," he whispered.

He sat up fast, got to his feet, crossed to the stairs and descended them three at a time.

The rec room was dark, like the rest of the house, but his eyes were adjusted well enough. A narrow shaft of streetlight glow shone through a little window on the front wall, up near the ceiling—the side of the basement that faced the front yard.

On the room's end wall were the movie posters. Superman and Rambo still had the darts stuck into their navels. Sam went past them to the pool table, centered in the space of the long room.

He went to the table's nearest corner, leaned over it, and stared straight down.

In the faint light he could see the dart there, deep inside the opening.

If there's a connection, I'm missing it.

He'd missed it, too.

Because the darts weren't just hidden in the pool table.

They were hidden in its pockets.

Navels and pockets.

And there sure as hell was a connection there, wasn't there? A simple one. The kind Lauren could have come up with in the minute or two when she'd been down here, listening to her father confront the kidnappers upstairs. The minute or two that she'd had in which to write a message, hide it, and point the way to that hiding place for anyone who came looking later on.

Navels and pockets.

Sam turned away from the table. He went to the laundry room below the stairs, its interior just visible in the indirect streetlight glow.

He and Dani had checked the washer and dryer as part of their thorough search.

A little more thorough and they would have found the note anyway.

Sam stepped into the room and knelt in front of the dryer. He took hold of the small plastic hatch just below the big door on the front.

The hatch for the lint filter.

He pulled it open and saw the note flutter down onto the floor. He picked it up and brushed it off, stepped back out of the room, crossed to the shaft of streetlamp glow. The light was more than enough to read by:

3 MEN KIDNAPPING US

MY DAD CALLED ONE OF THEM

ELLIS PIERCE

PART SEVEN

THE TUNNEL

JULY 1989 / SEPTEMBER 2018

CHAPTER FORTY-TWO

SEPTEMBER 2018

"What is it?" Danica asked. "What's happening?"

Dryden couldn't answer. He had no idea.

From far away to the north, somewhere lost to sight in the forest, came another burst of autofire. Then more screaming, from the same man they had heard just seconds earlier. The cries had an animalistic quality to them—it sounded like the guy was tearing the lining of his throat with the force of those screams.

Dryden glanced at Danica, then down at the unconscious body of Jack Grace sitting between them, his back propped against the rotted picket fence. Dryden held Grace's shoulder microphone in his hand, the cord stretching down to the receiver unit that was still clipped to Grace's belt. In a single quick movement, Dryden stooped and detached the radio from the belt, and fixed it to his own. He looped the shoulder mike's cord around his own neck and let it hang there, ignoring it for the moment. He took the Glock that was holstered at Grace's hip, aimed it at the ground, and pulled the slide partway back. He saw a round already in the chamber, and let the slide rack itself shut again. He stood and held the weapon out to Danica.

"That's ready to fire."

She nodded, tense but unflinching. She took hold of the gun and held it low at her side.

Dryden crouched once more and picked up Grace's M4 carbine. He checked for a chambered round, then flicked the safety off and set the fire-select switch to single-shot. He stood again, keeping the rifle pointed low but ready, and returned his focus to the trees off to the north.

He could see nothing there yet, though at that moment he heard another burst of autofire, this one from much closer than the earlier shots had been. There were at least two shooters—and judging by the cyclic rate, they were both firing M4s.

Which didn't tell him much, because right now the woods were littered with M4 rifles, a hundred or more for the taking. There was still no way to know who was shooting, or what they were shooting at.

Dryden considered the position he and Danica were in—fully exposed, like targets on a firing range. Then he looked around at the FBI agents he could see from this spot: a dozen at least, lying as they had fallen, alive but defenseless.

"We can't just leave them like this," Danica whispered.

Dryden nodded; it simply wasn't an option.

He turned toward the house that went with the picket fence, fifty feet behind them. It had wooden siding and sheathing, much of which had rotted away, leaving empty horizontal slats between boards. Through those gaps, the dim interior of the house was visible; the drywall and insulation behind the exterior had long since fallen away.

"Come on," Dryden whispered.

He nodded toward the house and ran for it. They crossed the yard in a few seconds and clambered over the sill of an empty window frame. Inside, it took only a moment to find a wall section that was mostly intact, with open slats close to eye level. They stood there, staring north through the trees. They could still see Grace and the others; they would be able to defend them, if it came to it.

Another scream from the woods—it had the same ragged intensity as before, but the voice was different, lower-pitched. There were now at least two people making those sounds.

Danica turned to Dryden, her eyes asking the question again: *What the hell is this?*

Dryden felt for the collar microphone and keyed it.

"Dryden to air, are you seeing anything happening in the northern part of the subdivision? Any activity in the woods up there?"

Three seconds passed, and then the pilot's voice came through the speaker: *"Negative, but we've got no visual at all through the trees. We can't see the ground. What are we looking for?"*

"Shooters," Dryden said. "And—" He cut himself off, unsure of how to even describe the rest of it. He keyed the switch again. "I need to know if anyone else could have entered the woods after the gas attack. Do you have a good enough look at the surrounding area to rule that out?"

"Yeah, spotters couldn't have missed that. We've got clear sightlines and five hundred yards of open land around the woods. Nobody else went in."

Dryden considered that, his mind already trying to fit the pieces together. The FBI agents were all down, and there was no one else in the forest who hadn't already been there before the gas clouds came through.

What explanation did that leave? Bad guys with respirator masks, who had been hidden away somewhere in the houses? In the attics? People who'd been in place, ready to spring their attack once the gas had taken effect?

Something like that might account for the shooting they were hearing now, but it still wouldn't explain the screams. What the hell *could* explain those—

Danica grabbed his arm, cutting off the thought. She pointed to something outside and far to the right:

Out in the dead leaves, the female agent with the short black hair was moving. She had already rolled onto her back, and now her head was turning side to side, slowly. She brought up one hand and rubbed her face. The movements of somebody in a stupor, slowly coming around.

Somewhere off to the north, another long burst of autofire echoed through the woods. Dryden heard the stream of bullets cutting through foliage close by.

Now, as he listened, he could hear at least three different voices screaming, somewhere up near the shooting, still out of view.

The female agent drew her knees up, her feet pressed flat to the ground.

Dryden slung the M4 on his shoulder by its strap, and went back to the window. He paused and looked back at Danica. "I'm going to bring her in here. Keep watching for anything—"

A new scream ripped through the forest, from somewhere very close to the house. Dryden spun to face the sound—

And stopped dead. He stared.

It was the female agent screaming. She had her hands jammed against the sides of her head, and her mouth open, and her face contorted in rage. The scream, wild and raw like the others, went on for another five seconds, and then she sucked in a deep breath and did it again, still lying there.

Dryden withdrew from the empty window frame and went back to where he'd been standing, at the narrow, eye-level slot in the wall. One of Danica's hands, holding on to an upright two-by-four of the wall, had gone bone white with the tension of her grip.

Outside, the black-haired woman finished screaming and rolled onto her front with a convulsive movement. She got her hands under her and shoved herself upward into a squat, her palms to the forest floor, like an animal on its haunches. Her breath went in and out in fast spurts.

Then she moved—she took half a dozen scrambling steps, caught her pant leg on the jagged corner of an old Volkswagen, and went sprawling on her hands in the dead leaves.

Her reaction was almost inhumanly fast; she pushed up again, turned and attacked the car with a kind of savage energy. She pounded it with her fists and her knees, denting the panels, smashing a lone intact window on the passenger side. Within a few seconds, her fists were leaving bloody smears on the powder-blue paint; she seemed to neither notice nor care.

Watching her, Dryden caught movement at the left edge of his vision. He turned and saw two of the other fallen agents moving on the ground, rolling, getting themselves upright. One of them, a man in his forties, absently held on to the M4 he'd been carrying when he fell. He got up on his knees, took hold of a small tree and pulled himself to his feet; he stood there swaying.

Then he let loose one of those impossible, throat-ripping screams, and clenched his hand tight on the M4's grip—pulling the trigger in the process.

The weapon opened up on full-auto, the firestream chewing apart leaves and dirt at the man's feet. It went on for three seconds and then the rifle's magazine ran dry. A second later the man took the gun by the forestock, the way he would have held a baseball bat, and attacked the tree he had pulled himself up by.

"Look," Danica said, her voice hardly above a breath.

Dryden followed her gaze—to Jack Grace.

The man still sat where he'd passed out, against the fence, but his eyes were open, staring at the ground near his feet. His hands were clenching and unclenching, slowly.

"Rigel," Danica whispered. "This is what it does."

Dryden stared at Grace and the others, letting it sink in. He took in their screams and their frenzied movements, and tried to imagine the kind of mind that would have invented a chemical weapon like this. That wanted to sell it. That wanted it to be used against civilians by the thousands.

And it would be—next week or next month or next year. There would be no stopping it, once it got out to the buyers.

Now the question that had plagued him for hours returned:

We saw this stuff used against a whole town when we were kids, but that's not why the military wiped our memories. What did we see that was even worse than this? What was a bigger secret than this?

Across the yard, Grace had gotten himself up in a crouch, rocking in place, his breathing fast like the black-haired woman's had been. Behind him, scattered across the stretch of forest that Dryden could see, all of the other agents were either moving or fully upright. The more distant shrieks, coming from unseen others in the woods, were too many to count now—and every few seconds there came another sporadic rattle of gunfire.

Dryden stepped back from the gap in the wall. "Time to go," he said.

Nodding, Danica moved back with him. They turned and picked their way over the floor toward the south side of the house, watching for holes and rotted boards. They had almost reached an empty window frame on the far wall when Danica froze in place; she was staring at something just out of Dryden's view past the window's edge. He went dead still beside her.

Then he heard it: the scrabbling of hands and feet, pushing dry leaves around, right outside somewhere. A moment later the figure staggered into view: an agent no more than twenty-five, with close-cropped hair. He took another step and then stumbled and fell, and as he got back up, his holstered Glock fell free and landed in the dirt. For whatever reason, the weapon drew the man's attention. Maybe there was just enough brain function to recognize the gun as something important. The guy stooped and got a hold of the thing, his hand going habitually to the grip—and his finger touching the trigger.

When he stood upright again, he was directly in front of the window frame, facing sideways down the outer wall of the house. All he had to do was swivel his head, and he would see them. They were less than ten feet from where the man stood.

For maybe five seconds the moment lingered. Dryden mentally rehearsed raising the M4 and drilling the guy through the head—the safest move against someone already holding a live weapon.

He would take the shot if he had to. There was no question of that. But—

But holy hell, the morality of it was impossible to square with. He didn't want to think about it.

For another long-held breath, the man just stood there, reeling in place. Then his balance faltered and he jerked forward, and like that he was out of view past the window's edge. Dryden listened to him shambling away down the outside wall.

Danica exhaled slowly, the sound of it carrying a tremor. She turned to Dryden—and flinched hard at something in her peripheral vision. She jerked her head toward the front of the house, where they had stood earlier. She only just stopped herself from screaming.

Dryden turned fast, the rifle coming around, the stock going automatically to his shoulder.

Jack Grace stood outside the empty window frame on the north wall, his eyes wild and locked on the two of them. In one violent move he lunged through the window frame and landed inside on the flooring, already throwing himself forward toward them.

Dryden could feel the situation playing out in each of its awful details, fractional second by fractional second. The feeling was old and familiar to him; in his former line of work he had experienced it a thousand times.

He saw it all, not in slow-motion but in perfect clarity:

Grace pounding toward them across the rotted wood.

Danica pulling back, her expression full of pain because she knew what was coming—what *had to be* coming.

The M4 rose in Dryden's hands, all but aiming itself by muscle memory, pointing exactly where his focus had already gone.

Dryden fired.

He felt the rifle kick against his shoulder, heard the shot like a thunderclap in the closed-in space of the house—

—and saw Jack Grace's right ankle explode inside the cuff of his pant leg.

The man screamed and pitched forward, reaching as he fell, missing Dryden and Danica by only inches as they jumped back.

Even as Grace hit the floor, he was already lurching forward, pushing with his remaining foot, coming at them like a monster in a horror flick.

Next to Dryden, Danica pivoted and threw herself out the empty frame of the window. He followed half a second behind her, turning as he passed through the opening, looking for the young guy with the Glock—but there was no sign of him now.

The two of them hit the ground at a sprint, running south into the trees, away from the gunfire and screams that filled the woods.

They ran until all the sounds were far behind them—three hundred yards or better, past houses and streets and more houses. By the time they stopped, they were close to the southern boundary of the subdivision again; they stood on the cracked remains of the last street, facing the homes that made up the outer edge.

Catching their breath, they turned in place and stared back in the direction they had come from. Nobody had followed them.

Dryden keyed the collar microphone again. "Dryden to air, are you guys seeing any of this yet?"

The speaker on his belt crackled. *"We're seeing it. Christ . . . They're attacking the parked vehicles, smashing out the windows. What the fuck happened to them?"*

Dryden ignored the question. "Listen to me. Get in touch with your field office right now, and have them call off the emergency responders. If regular cops and paramedics show up here, it's going to be a nightmare. The FBI needs to get its own personnel in here and get control. These people need to be contained, and then they need treatment—with what, who the hell knows?"

"Copy that. Right, we'll get on it—" The pilot cut himself off; Dryden could hear someone else in the chopper talking to the guy, the voice fast and frantic. *"I know, I know,"* the pilot said.

Dryden keyed the mike again. "What's the problem?"

"We're down to our reserves on fuel. We need to bug out. We can pick you up south of the woods, if you can get out in the clear right now."

Dryden thought about that. He turned to Danica and spoke. "If we can pin down who's behind this, it really can be over with. We can get our lives back. There's something here they're terrified to have us see. The way they've been after us, it's like every play has been a blitz. I think it tells us something. They don't just *think* we'll find something important here. They're acting like they *know* it. I want to see that underground complex."

Danica nodded.

"But if you want to get out of here," Dryden said, "I understand—"

"I want to do what I came here for," she said. "I'm not leaving yet."

Her tone invited no debate.

The radio crackled again. *"Dryden, you still there?"*

"We're here. Give me the location of those underground stairs you found."

It took the pilot thirty seconds to describe the spot, two miles north and just west of the road, near the ruins of a farm.

Dryden asked if there was an emergency kit aboard the aircraft, containing a flashlight. The pilot confirmed it, and Dryden asked him to drop it in the weeds beside the access stairs.

A moment after they finished speaking, the sound of the distant rotors began to fade; the chopper was moving off to the north.

Dryden thought of the underground stairs, and what sort of barrier might be waiting at the bottom of them. There was only a small chance he and Danica would actually get inside the complex; Jack Grace had been counting on heavy equipment to bust through the door.

Oh you'll get in. You'll wish you hadn't, but you'll get in.

The absurd little thought had risen out of nowhere, taking him off guard. In the autumn morning air, he shivered—just once, and then the feeling was gone.

"We'll go south out of the woods and make a wide circle around the north end," he said. "We can keep plenty of space between us and the FBI people—"

He cut himself off: Danica was staring raptly at a house two doors down the street.

Dryden followed her gaze; the house had vinyl siding, plain white under green asphalt shingles that had mostly fallen away. It stood on the outer curve of the subdivision, facing south, like the place they'd gone into earlier.

"That's where I lived," Danica said.

They entered through a big rotted opening in the back corner of the place, into what must have been Danica's bedroom. A twin mattress lay in tatters atop the collapsed wreck of a bedframe. On the opposite wall stood a dresser and a small desk. The elements had played hell with all of it: every wooden surface was cracked and warped. A dense covering of moss had scaled the front of the dresser, fusing the drawer fronts together. Dryden pulled them open one by one; there was nothing in any of them but misshapen lumps of old clothing, colonized by decades' worth of fungus and mold.

Danica crouched beside the dresser and put her eye to the gap behind it.

"There's something back here," she said.

They slid the dresser out and found three picture frames that had fallen off the top of it, down to the baseboard. Each of the frames still had its glass intact, but all three pictures inside were ruined anyway: twenty-nine years of winter frost and summer humidity had caused a reaction in the photo paper. All three images had darkened until they showed only phantom-like outlines of the people in them—presumably Danica and some of her friends, but they could have been anyone.

"Ashland's no place for memories to survive," Danica said.

She turned and studied the room itself. The interior walls were like those they had seen everywhere else: discolored, mostly fallen away from the studs. Rot-blackened insulation clung to the uprights here and there. None of it could possibly be recognizable.

Danica went to the doorway that led deeper into the house.

"Hold up," Dryden said.

He crossed back to the rotted opening in the exterior wall. He stared out into the woods, north toward the distant sounds of screaming. The occasional burst or crack of gunfire still filtered through the trees.

It all sounded far away yet, way up at the north end of the forest.

Dryden scanned the nearer trees anyway. He watched and listened.

Nothing coming toward them. Nothing moving at all.

So far.

"We're good," he said. "But let's not push it."

They made a quick survey of the next bedroom—the master. The walls and furniture were in the same condition as in the previous room. Nothing left to jog a memory.

They looked into a small bathroom off the hall, then

continued past it. In front of them the hallway ended at a corner, beyond which could only be the living room and kitchen. They rounded it—and stopped.

There was a blue camping tent pitched in the middle of the living room, crisp and clean against the backdrop of decayed carpet and furniture. It looked as if someone had bought it brand new yesterday.

"What the hell?" Danica whispered.

"The FBI sweep didn't find this," Dryden said. "I don't think they made it this far south."

The tent's front flap hung inward, unzipped. Dryden could see a sleeping bag inside, on an inflated air mattress, and a bag of trail mix held shut with a clothespin. Tucked under the mattress's edge, just visible, was a red leather wallet.

Danica went to the tent, leaned in and picked up the wallet. But before she could open it, there came a sound from the nearby kitchen: a muffled *thump,* as if from inside a closed container.

Dryden turned and raised the M4. He took a step toward the kitchen; the bulk of its space lay out of sight past a dividing wall. Another step brought the room fully into view: it was every bit the shambles they could have expected, with one added touch—someone had thrown the contents of the refrigerator out onto the floor, including the shelves. The fridge itself was closed at the moment.

It had happened recently.

Maybe *very* recently—there were things among the debris that could not have been lying there for long, like loose scraps of aluminum foil and plastic wrap, some of them already skittering in the breeze that filtered through the house.

Dryden traded a look with Danica, then raised the rifle and trained it on the refrigerator door—finger outside the trigger-well, but ready. He spoke in an authoritative voice, not loud, though hard and clear:

"Whoever's in the fridge, show me your hands first, and come out very slowly."

Before he'd finished speaking, someone moved inside the appliance—Dryden pictured somebody flinching, banging an elbow into one of the interior walls.

"Do it right now," he said. "Hands first. Slow."

Three seconds passed. Then the door jerked open, and the hands came out at the same time as the face—a woman's face. Dryden had just a second to get a sense of her features—blond hair, green eyes, probably around his age—and then the woman saw the gun pointed at her, and her expression flooded with panic. She fell out of the refrigerator screaming.

The sound of it seemed to cut through the air—seemed like it would carry a thousand yards outside the house.

Dryden lowered the rifle and waved his hands. *"Quiet, quiet, stop it!"*

The woman couldn't hear him. She was clambering over the discarded shelves and the putrid debris from inside the fridge, banging into its open door, scrambling away—and all the while still screaming, a jumble of *No* and *Please* and *Don't.*

"Hey!" Dryden said it just loud enough to get through to her.

The woman stopped screaming; she had pushed herself backward into a corner of the room, where the cabinets met the wall. She sat there, her knees drawn up and her forearms in front of her, defensive.

"Don't shoot me," she whispered. *"I'm sorry—"*

"We're not going to hurt you," Dryden said. "Look."

The woman blinked and managed to raise her eyes toward the two of them. Dryden had his open hands out in front of him, the rifle already slung on his shoulder again.

"Who are you?" Dryden asked. "What are you doing here?"

The woman didn't answer. She just sat there, looking overwhelmed, her focus going back and forth between them.

"Hey," Danica said. She was addressing Dryden.

He turned and found her holding the red wallet out to him—open now.

Dryden took it. He saw a Maryland driver's license in the wallet's plastic sleeve. The photo in the corner was unmistakably the woman in front of them now. Her name was Lauren Coleman.

CHAPTER FORTY-THREE

JULY 1989

Sam stared at the note from the lint trap. He held it dead still in his hand. No muscle trembled. No part of him seemed to move at all. For five seconds he didn't even breathe.

Ellis Pierce.

Sam thought of Lauren's father, dying on the floor in Station 9, trying with his last breath to tell Dani the name of the insider. He'd gotten half of it out—just not the half Dani had thought he meant.

Ellis Pierce.

Five seconds, motionless as a statue, nothing moving but Sam's focus, back and forth over the three scrawled lines.

Pierce.

Not Dani's father.

Pierce.

In on it.

Behind it.

The whole time.

Pierce.

Five seconds, staring, thinking, trying to get his mind even halfway around it.

Then he thought of Dani and Lauren, heading for Station 14 right now, and his brain screamed, *Think while you run.*

Sam dropped the note. He ran.

He vaulted up the stairs in three steps, reached the front door in a few seconds and yanked it open. He spared only a glance for any afflicted that might be nearby—none in sight—and a moment later he was around the corner of the house, sprinting for the back yard and the cover of darkness beyond.

He crossed into the tall grass without slowing. He gave little thought to the two men who had chased him earlier; if they were dumb enough to still be out here somewhere, he would just have to deal with them. It was time to put speed above every other worry. Nothing else mattered if he didn't reach Station 14 before the girls did, because—

Because Pierce is there right now. He went straight there as soon as he left us. He never contacted the military at all. He's waiting there near those stairs in the cornfield, at this very moment, and when Dani and Lauren show up—

Pierce would kill them.

Simple as that.

The girls were going to walk right up to him, Dani relieved to see him, Lauren probably still delirious, and they weren't going to have the slightest warning of what was coming.

Maybe Pierce would knock them both unconscious

and then strangle them. Or beat them to death with the Jeep's tire iron. Or whatever else he could think of to get the job done fast.

But one way or another, it would happen. The moment Dani and Lauren got there, it would happen. If Sam didn't get there first.

He ran. Straight out from the suburb. The houses and the streetlight glow fell away behind him. He sprinted to the farthest point at which he could still see in front of him, and then he turned, following the edge of the light—following the outer curve of the subdivision, east and north. That curve would take him all the way up to Truman Avenue, at the far north end of the suburb. From there he could simply follow the road, the same route he and Dani had taken when she first showed him Station 14—two days ago almost to the hour.

Around him, the night was still full of smoke, though it wasn't as thick out here, farther from the crash site. Still it burned his throat. He breathed it deep anyway and kept running.

He found his thoughts going back over the preceding hours—back to the barn, and the stakeout, and everything that had followed. Every fake detail of it.

From the moment Pierce had been dragged out of the barn, bound with duct tape, the whole thing must have been an act, as absurd as that seemed. It made no sense, unless—

Unless they knew we were out there, watching the place.

He spent about a second wondering how that was

possible, and then felt stupid: there were lots of ways. Night vision was an obvious one. Or thermal vision. The kind of people who could afford a helicopter could probably drop a few thousand dollars on a camera system, to secure the location where all their work would be on the line. Where their own lives would be on the line, if they got caught. In hindsight, it would have been strange if they *hadn't* set up some system to watch over the place.

So what would Pierce and his men, there inside the barn, have thought when they saw two kids with binoculars surveilling the location, an hour or two before the main event?

What the fuck is this? That's what they would have thought.

Sure, but then why hadn't those men done the obvious thing, which was to run out and grab the two of them right there? Why not drag them back into the barn and make them talk?

But the answer to that was pretty obvious:

Because it wouldn't have worked.

If the men had tied them up and questioned them—*Who are you? How did you know about this place?*—there would be no way to know if the answers were true or not. Or if the two of them were leaving things out. If all you did was threaten or torture someone, you'd never know if they'd actually told you everything.

Sprinting, Sam replayed the spectacle in the barnyard again. The men dragging Pierce out to the grave, then leaving him there unguarded for those fleeting moments. Then the rescue, the frantic escape into the darkness and the ditch, he and Dani helping Pierce out of the tape, and all the while . . . talking. Just talking and talking, answering every damned question he asked them.

And once that part was over with, once they'd told him everything they knew, and he had them inside the farmhouse a mile from the barn—

There's a secure bunker downstairs, Pierce had said. *It's not much bigger than a closet, but it's safe. I'd like both of you to wait in there until this is over with.*

Had he really not wanted to kill them, at that point? What if he'd had some other idea in mind, then? Like leaving two witnesses alive who would swear forever that he had been an innocent prisoner. Maybe. That wouldn't have worked if Lauren survived to tell her side of things, but maybe her captors had never intended to let her live—whatever her father had believed.

And none of that mattered now, anyway; the chopper crash had changed everything. Pierce and his people—the ones that weren't dead—would be on the run now with no money, and no head start. All bets were off, and the only certainty was that Pierce wanted all three of the kids to meet him at Station 14, a place where bodies could probably go undiscovered for decades, if they were ever found at all.

Sam was running north now, already making the long curve back toward Truman Avenue—toward the little park where he'd first met Dani.

He pictured her and Lauren, somewhere farther north on Truman at this very moment, heading up that road toward Station 14. Did he have time to catch up to them? Could they almost be there? They had a big lead on him, that was for sure; he had lost so much time playing cat-and-mouse in the suburb.

Still, it was two miles up to Station 14, and Lauren's injury would have to slow them down at least a little. Maybe there was still time to overtake them.

Assuming they went up Truman at all, and didn't go some other way.

The thought sent chilly little waves over his skin.

Jesus, what if Dani knew a different route to get there? Some other road or two-track that led north, maybe on the other side of that cornfield where the crash site had been. If there were another route like that, Dani would know about it; she and Lauren had been snooping around Ashland for months, learning its secrets.

Shit.

In that case, there would be no certain way to head them off before they reached Station 14.

What could he do, then?

He thought about it as he ran. He could see the park far ahead, where the curve of the subdivision ended at the road—and where the road itself led north into darkness.

Everything hurt. Everything burned. He kept running.

The cornfield near Station 14 lay black and cool in the night. Ellis Pierce could hear the everywhere-at-once hum of insects coming from all over it.

He stood leaning against the Jeep, his eyes closed and his head lowered.

Just get it done. One-two-three, literally.

He breathed out sharply. He guessed it might have sounded like a laugh, if anyone had been there to hear it. It was very far from a laugh.

This business was always going to get people killed. Even little kids. Would it have been any better if it were kids in some war-fucked backwater in sub-Saharan Africa?

Well, all those kids were safe now, whoever and wherever they were—safe from Rigel, anyway.

What were three little deaths, compared to all those?

He opened his eyes and pressed the night-light button on his watch. He'd been here twenty minutes—long enough to have already gone down the stairwell, and through the left-hand door at the bottom.

The door that opened to the tunnel.

Several hundred feet long, the tunnel led away from Station 14. The place at the far end, Station 17, was one of the active ones, but it was vacant at this hour of the night. Pierce had gone there, made all the preparations for what he needed to do now, and come sprinting back.

He pushed off from the Jeep and stood upright. He paced in the dirt behind it, watching the dark field and listening for voices.

One-two-three. Get it over with and get out of here.

CHAPTER FORTY-FOUR

SEPTEMBER 2018

Dryden stared at the blond woman—Lauren Coleman.

The name from the blue binder.

The woman Danica's father had apparently lost track of, after the incident here in 1989—whatever connection he'd had to her before that. He had written, *What happened to her?*

Except she hadn't been a woman back then. Couldn't have been.

Dryden glanced at the birthdate on the driver's license: 01-26-1977.

Lauren Coleman would have been twelve during the summer of '89, just like himself and Danica.

He looked at Lauren again. She was still sitting there in the corner, staring up at the two of them with wide eyes.

To Dryden, it felt as if someone had just dumped half a dozen new ingredients into the mix, each one of which wanted his full attention right now. A whole cluster of sudden questions competed for his focus:

What was she doing here?

How was she involved in all this?

How much did she know?

At that moment Lauren cocked her head, reacting to a sound. Dryden realized it was the distant chorus of human screams and intermittent gunfire, still far away in the woods.

The effect on Lauren was instant—the fear in her eyes intensified, and her gaze darted back and forth between Danica and Dryden, full of her own questions: *What is this? What's happening?*

Which told Dryden at least one thing for sure: Lauren Coleman didn't know what Rigel was. She had closed herself inside the fridge when she saw the gas cloud coming, but right now, listening to the chaos that the gas had created, she was clueless.

Dryden flipped the wallet closed, stepped forward and held it out to Lauren. For a moment she only stared at it, blinking, and then she grabbed it from him and clutched it close to herself.

Still standing there with his arm extended, Dryden offered a hand to help her up.

"We need to talk," he said. "But first we need to move. Will you come with us?"

Lauren Coleman held his gaze, her breathing still fast and scared.

But she nodded and took his hand.

They left the house through a collapsed section of the living room wall, and a few seconds later they were clear of the woods, moving south onto the grassy slope that led toward downtown. Three hundred yards out, they turned east toward a pocket of scrub brush. There were dozens more thickets just like it, farther away; if they needed to get more distance from the woods, they could do so without the stricken FBI personnel seeing them. The tall grass itself offered good cover, as long as they stayed low.

From the stand of brush, they watched the south edge of the subdivision. Dryden could just make out the screams now, and the gunfire had tailed off almost to nothing.

In the sunlight, Dryden noticed something about Lauren Coleman that he'd missed in the dim space of the house: her left arm had lines of thick, hardened scar tissue running from her bicep to her forearm, crisscrossing and snaking everywhere. The marks of some horrible injury in the past. The elbow, in particular, seemed to have taken the brunt of whatever happened: faded but still visible depressions in the skin hinted at surgical pins and rods, long since removed. It looked like someone had taken a jackhammer to that arm, and then a battlefield surgeon with sweaty hands had bolted and screwed and stapled it back together—years or even decades ago.

The woman's composure was better than before, though she still looked badly rattled.

Dryden turned to her. "My name's Sam Dryden. This is Danica Ellis. Do either of those names mean anything to you?"

He watched Lauren Coleman's reaction to the question. Saw her eyes narrow, not only with lack of recognition, but with confusion as to why he was even asking it.

It couldn't have been clearer: she had never heard of them.

Dryden traded a look with Danica, but before he could say anything more, Lauren spoke up:

"You're FBI agents?"

The question caught Dryden off guard. For a second he couldn't imagine where it had come from—and then he remembered the windbreakers. He hadn't given them a moment's thought since he and Danica put them on.

"Oh," Dryden said. "No, we're not with them. We just came with them. We'll explain that with the rest of it."

But the damage was done. He could see it in Lauren's expression. That momentary confusion on his part—that momentary lapse—had come across as the faltering manner of a liar.

Lauren Coleman took an involuntary step back from them, folding her arms. Just like that, she looked scared of them again.

"Wait," Danica said. "Look, this is strange for all of us. Let's just talk. Can we do that?"

Lauren stared at her a long beat, then nodded. Still, she was the picture of distrust.

"Good," Danica said. "Can you tell us why you came here? Like, what happened that made you come here now? Are people after you?"

Lauren's reaction to that was complicated: surprise, fear, interest.

"How can you know about that?" she asked.

"They're after us, too," Danica said. Then: "Did you live here when you were a kid? Maybe just for a little while?"

For two or three seconds Lauren only stared at Danica, still unnerved and worried. Then she nodded. "Yes, I lived here—I mean, my family said I lived here. I don't remember."

"Were you drugged?" Danica asked. "Back then, the summer of 1989? Did they use the memory drugs on you?"

At this Lauren looked merely confused. Her eyes narrowed and she shook her head. "I don't know what you mean by that."

Danica looked at Dryden, then turned back to Lauren and spoke as if playing a hunch: "Were you in a coma that summer? Did you lose a few months' worth of your memory because of it?"

Lauren Coleman's arms uncrossed themselves. One hand rose to her mouth, which had fallen partly open.

"How do you know all this stuff?" she asked—her voice had softened to almost a whisper. "There's no way . . ."

Danica took a step toward her. "*We* were kids here in 1989. *We* had those drugs used on us. We're trying to figure it all out too. Hell, maybe we knew you back then. Maybe we were friends."

Lauren blinked a few times, her eyes just noticeably filming with moisture. She looked back and forth between the two of them, some kind of fragile hope in her expression.

Dryden spoke gently. “We still don’t remember much of anything about Ashland. Someone else filled us in, and then the FBI brought us here. Can you tell us how *you* knew about this place? How you got here?”

Lauren wiped at one eye, took a fast breath and nodded. “My family. I mean, there were letters my dad sent them back then, when he and I lived here. Just ordinary letters, but they had the name of the town, and—”

She stopped. Something changed in her eyes. A kind of hardening—like a heavy door falling shut.

“What’s wrong?” Danica asked.

“I’m sorry,” Lauren said. “I want to trust you. I just want to trust *someone* at this point, but . . . I don’t. The things that have happened to me in the last twenty-four hours . . . you wouldn’t believe it.”

“We might,” Dryden said.

Lauren wiped at her eyes again. “I don’t want to talk. I want to go to the authorities. You said you came with the FBI. Can you take me to them? I’ll talk to them.”

Dryden glanced at the tree-choked subdivision.

“Probably not the best time for a conversation with them,” he said. “Backup’s coming, maybe an hour away. They’ll talk to you.”

Lauren nodded. “Okay. Can we just wait here?”

“There’s a place we need to go see,” Dryden said. “It’s not far. You can come with us, if you want to.”

Lauren stood there, looking unsure. Looking lost.

“You don’t have to,” Dryden said. “But if you don’t, you shouldn’t stay right here, either. I’d get a long ways from that subdivision, and wait for the backup to get here. Either way, it’s up to you.”

Lauren turned an ear toward the woods atop the slope. The wind, rolling at them from that direction, carried the distant screams.

"Where are we going?" Lauren asked.

The underground staircase was invisible until the moment they were standing over it. It lay in the middle of a dense clutch of brush and scrubby trees, surrounded by the waving ocean of autumn weeds. Even from the air, the spotters in the chopper must have barely seen the thing.

Dryden stood next to Danica and Lauren, staring down into the black depths of the staircase. For just a second it gave him the impression of an open grave; he shoved the thought away and focused on what he was seeing—which wasn't much. Between the low-angled morning sun, and the thick screen of foliage casting shadows, he could resolve only the first few stairsteps clearly. Beyond that, in the deep murk, he had only a vague impression of a door at the bottom.

For a long moment no one spoke. Or moved.

"The other thing we witnessed," Danica said softly. "The thing that was worse than the accident. I think it happened down there." She turned to Dryden. "Don't you?"

Dryden nodded. He had no idea why he believed it; there was nothing rational behind the feeling. Still, there it was.

He stared into the dark a moment longer, then stepped away and scanned the tall grass for the hard-case emergency kit from the chopper. He found it at the edge of the scrub, ten feet away, and brought it back to the stairs.

Inside the case, set into cutouts in the foam interior, were four marker flares, four emergency Mylar blankets, and four Maglite flashlights. Dryden took one Maglite out and tested it; the beam shone brightly. Danica and Lauren each took another, and a moment later the staircase lay flooded with light.

The door at the bottom was metal, its surface almost entirely covered with rust, save for a few tiny chips of black paint clinging to it. Against the foot of the door, a two-foot-high drift of dead weeds and twigs had accumulated, blown in from the field above.

The door had a steel handle instead of a knob, and above it there was a twelve-button keypad—probably entirely mechanical, given how old it had to be.

Even at this distance, the keypad struck Dryden in exactly the same way as Echo House—more intensely, even. At the same time, it was like looking at those darts in the pool table's pockets. There was more than just recognition here, there was—what, exactly?

Something to remember. Some specific piece of knowledge. Something they had known back when—

Danica suddenly drew a quick breath. She looked at Dryden, then Lauren, and without a word she stepped over the edge and descended the steps at a run. Dryden followed, Lauren coming along behind.

By the time Dryden reached the bottom, behind Danica, she had her hand poised in front of the keypad, her fingertip six inches away from it.

It hit Dryden half a second before her hand moved.

Five sevens in a row.

Danica punched in the sequence. There was a heavy *thud* from inside the door, and she took hold of the handle and pushed.

It'll be rusted shut, Dryden thought, but he saw almost at once that he was wrong. The door budged open under Danica's effort, and he stepped forward and leaned into it with her. The door was solid steel, and heavy. Together they shoved it open, dead weeds spilling in around their feet. Lauren followed, raising her light, and a few seconds later all three had slipped through the opening.

The space beyond was small: a short corridor lined with grey ceramic tiles. It had the entry door at one end, and at the opposite end, maybe ten feet away, a door with a handle but no keypad.

All three flashlight beams gravitated to one of the side walls, where four lines had been stencil-painted in black over the tiles:

UNITED STATES D.O.D.
ASHLAND-STATION 14
LIMA 4 CLEARANCE REQUIRED
BEYOND THIS POINT

Staring at the words, and looking around at the tiles, Dryden thought back to the story of Kurt Reyher visiting the Bode Museum in Berlin, decades after defecting. Walking the rooms. Seeing the architecture. Things that looked exactly the way they had in his lost memories.

Here in Ashland, the houses had rotted and the streets had been torn up by weeds. Even Echo House was full of animal nests and invading plants—probably far more so than it had been in 1989.

But this place—this place could not have changed at all. It had to be identical to its past self, down to the color of the grout-lines.

All of which mattered.

Because he felt more than just déjà vu here. More than just passing recognition.

He felt the pull of connected memories, at last. They were right there, under the surface, straining upward. He looked at Danica and Lauren; they were reacting to the small room the same way he was.

Danica turned to the door at the other end of the room, shining her light on it. "There's a stairwell on the other side of that. A hundred and twenty steps down."

Every word of it sounded right to Dryden, his mind confirming it in a way that felt sure and spooky at the same time. He saw Lauren nodding, too.

Danica led the way to the far door. She pulled it open. The stairwell beyond stretched down into darkness.

As the three of them descended, an image of the space at the bottom swam into Dryden's head.

Two doors: one with just a handle, and one with another keypad lock.

The five sevens don't work on that one. We won't be able to get past it.

Then he rounded the final landing and saw that he

was only half right. One of the doors at the bottom did have a keypad lock—but they would certainly get past it.

Both doors were lying flat on the concrete floor of the stairwell, their hinges blackened and warped by the flame of a cutting torch. Across the foot of the stairs, two lengths of red plastic ribbon had been stretched, forming an X. Where the ribbons crossed, a sheet of paper had been stapled in place, bearing a message in plain black text:

ASHLAND SITE ACCIDENT INVESTIGATION
SURVEYED 1989 JUL
NO ACCESS BEYOND THIS POINT
WITHOUT WRITTEN AUTHORIZATION

Standing three steps up from the bottom, Dryden shone his light beyond the paper sheet and the torched-off doors. The stairwell floor was probably fifteen by fifteen feet, with the two empty doorframes facing each other across it—one on either of the side walls.

A left door and a right door.

Dryden shone his beam through the right-hand frame first. From where he stood, he could see nothing beyond the doorway but a broad concrete floor.

The room past that doorway is enormous. So big you feel like you're outside, once you step away from the wall.

He felt certain of that intuition. He also felt no emotional response at all about that giant room—none of the dread that had struck him when he'd first looked down the stairs.

Then he swung his beam to the other doorway, and felt his breathing speed up.

"Try the left one first?" Danica asked.

No. Never. We should turn around right now and go back.

"Yeah," Dryden said.

CHAPTER FORTY-FIVE

JULY 1989

Sam crawled the last hundred feet through the corn stalks, his eyes just above their tops. His vision was about as dark-adapted as it could get; he could see the Jeep fifty feet north of him, parked beside the tangle of weeds and undergrowth that marked the stairway down into Station 14.

Pierce was there, pacing back and forth behind the vehicle, stopping every few seconds to listen to the night.

Sam listened, too. He heard crickets and frogs, and corn shoots moving in the wind. Nothing else. No sound of Dani and Lauren. Not yet.

It was hard to make out much detail of Pierce beyond his shape. Hard to see if he was holding any kind of object as a weapon. There was just no way to tell.

Sam settled back into a crouch, his feet braced in the soft soil, ready to run toward the girls as soon as he heard them. That was all he had, for a plan. Just get to them first. Get to them and turn them around, and get them the hell out of here. Run away into the dark, before Pierce could murder all three of them.

This isn't going to work. You won't hear them coming any sooner than he will. It's a toss-up.

He ignored the doubt as best he could. Maybe it would work, and maybe it wouldn't. What else could he do but try?

He thought about that.

Was there something more he could do?

He pressed his hands into the soil, moving them through it slowly, silently. He felt the wide, spreading roots of the corn stalks, and the stems of weeds growing around their bases, and the hard, smooth surfaces of rocks embedded in the earth. Most of them were pebbles. But not all of them. Some were a lot bigger than that.

Dani saw the Jeep a hundred yards ahead in the darkness. She was guiding Lauren through the cornfield, moving east—they had followed an old tractor lane north through the woods, after walking several hundred yards west of the burning chopper and the lit-up space around the subdivision. Past the forest now, they were coming up on Station 14 from the opposite direction they usually approached it from.

Lauren's state of mind had improved only a little since they'd left the chopper. She seemed capable of understanding basic instructions like *Walk* and *Stay with me,* and she was keeping her balance well enough, but her dazed condition remained. She almost certainly had a concussion. She needed medical help as soon as possible.

At fifty yards, Dani cupped her hands to her mouth and shouted: *"Mr. Pierce!"*

Pierce turned toward them.

"Dani?"

Before Dani could answer, Lauren flinched beside her and came to a stop. Dani, holding on to the girl's arm, was jerked to a halt with her.

"Who?" Lauren said. The word was badly slurred, but audible.

"I'll explain later," Dani said. "Come on."

Lauren didn't move. She stood there, slowly shaking her head, as if confused.

"Lauren, come on."

Across the rows of corn, Pierce called out, "Is it all three of you?"

"No," Dani said. "Isn't Sam here already?"

Pierce was silent a few seconds. Then: "He's not with you?"

Dani heard concern in the man's voice—to a degree that was almost strange. He was moving now, striding through the shoots toward them, thirty yards away. Dani was staring at him, opening her mouth to reply, when she caught a hint of movement in the darkness, forty or fifty feet away from the man. A low shape lunging upward, and then something—an arm, she guessed—swinging fast. A fraction of a second later, something collided with Pierce's head. It slammed into it with a dull, heavy *thud,* knocking the man forward a step. He staggered and fell to his knees.

Then the low shape in the darkness started moving

again—coming right toward her and Lauren, fast. She realized it was Sam in the instant before he screamed: *"Run!"*

Pierce was still on his knees, his hands groping at the side of his head. Watching him, and watching Sam run toward her, Dani felt a moment of logical paralysis; nothing she was seeing made sense.

Then Sam reached her, barely slowing, grabbing both her and Lauren and turning them, propelling them away through the corn, and at the same time she saw Pierce drop his hands from his head and grab something from his belt.

The first gunshot sounded like a wooden stick being snapped—a flat *crack* that ripped through the air. Dani saw the muzzle flash, and heard the bullet cut through the corn stalks somewhere off to her left. By then she was turning away, allowing Sam to drag her along, getting her feet moving under her, running to keep up.

A rapid series of gunshots followed, so close together it would have been impossible to count them. She heard the bullets passing behind her—behind all three of them as they ran.

Then silence, only for a moment, before she heard Pierce far back in the darkness, cursing and trying to reload the gun. There were metallic clicks and scraping sounds. He swore again, the sound full of frustration.

"Keep going," Sam hissed, barely whispering. *"Far away as we can get."*

"What is this?" Dani asked.

"He's one of them. Tell you later."

"What are you talking about?"

Before he could answer, the cornfield around them flared to life with faint light. Dani turned her head and looked back, in unison with Sam.

Pierce, two hundred feet behind them, had turned on a flashlight. For the first second it shone straight down at the ground; then it jerked upward and began sweeping over the tops of the corn shoots.

"Down," Sam whispered.

Dani threw herself flat, pulling Lauren down with her. All three of them landed in the soft soil half a second before the stalks above them lit up. The beam swept over them very slowly, a searchlight taking its time. Even after it had gone past, Sam shook his head.

"Don't move yet."

No more than three or four seconds had passed before the light swept back above their position, creeping as slowly as before. It slipped away, then came back a third time, moving faster now.

Then it was gone—pointed somewhere else, at least. Dani could still see its peripheral glow on the highest leaves.

She counted to five, turned and met Sam's eyes; he stared back, then nodded and poked his head up above the stalks. Dani did the same.

Pierce was still standing where he'd been, two hundred feet behind them. He was shining the light all over the ground in front of him, darting it back and forth in sharp little arcs.

Then it froze. He stared at whatever he'd found with it.

And started walking.

"He sees our footprints," Sam whispered.

"We need to run," Dani said.

Sam shook his head. "He'll hear us. And he'll chase us. Hell, with a gun he doesn't even have to catch us."

Pierce was moving slowly, stopping every few feet to be sure he could still see the tracks, but as Dani watched, she found herself waiting for the inevitable: any second now, the man would simply break into a sprint along the straight-line path the footprints formed.

"Shit . . ." Sam whispered. No doubt he'd drawn the same conclusion.

"Sam, we *have* to run."

For a few seconds Sam didn't answer. He was staring off to the east, toward the big clump of weeds that concealed Station 14's access stairs—fifty yards away, maybe. Dani's mind automatically put together the geometry of the scene: three points that roughly made a triangle. She and Sam and Lauren formed one of the points; Pierce was another; the access stairs in the weeds were the third. If they ran toward the stairs, they wouldn't be moving away from Mr. Pierce, but they wouldn't be moving toward him, either. They would be traveling sideways across his field of view, almost like—

Don't think of it. Don't—

—mechanical ducks in one of those target-shooting booths at a carnival.

Sam looked at her, and nodded toward the stairs. "It's all we've got."

"We'll be trapped down there. That big room—there's no way out except the way in."

"Lots of places to hide in there," Sam said. "It's better than out here."

Dani turned and watched Pierce. He'd advanced maybe ten feet, still probing the soil with his flashlight.

Then he stopped.

"He's got us," Sam said.

A second later the beam swung up, shining right into their eyes, blinding. Dani had time for one panicked thought—

Where the light points, the gun points—

—and then Sam was yanking her to her feet, and Lauren too, hauling them forward, all three of them running, the light beam jittering and flickering in the space around them.

She felt the first bullet pass by, an instant before she heard the gunshot. The space right in front of her nose suddenly popped with a little wave of heat, and a rush of air as if someone had swept a hand past her eyes. She didn't stop. She dug her feet into the furrowed soil and kept running, as the *crack-crack-crack* of more shots filled the darkness.

"Picture the keypad!" Sam shouted.

"What?"

"It's going to be pitch-black down by the door! You'll need to punch in the code by feel! Picture it now, so you can do it fast!"

They were halfway to the clump of weeds, sprinting hard, the light still stabbing at them though the bullets had finally run dry. Dani pictured the keypad—tried to picture it. For a terrible second she couldn't remember whether the numbers started from the bottom or the top. Were they like the keys on a computer keyboard, with the 1 at the bottom, or were they like a telephone touch pad, with the 1 at the top?

It's like a phone. Start from the top and count across and down.

She saw it in her head as she ran. Seven would be—

Third row. First button on the left.

She hoped.

Somewhere far to the side, Pierce was screaming, and no doubt sprinting toward them. The flashlight beam swung wildly as he ran.

Thirty feet to the stairs now. Twenty. Ten.

"Go first!" Sam shouted.

He wrenched his arm forward, pulling her ahead, almost dragging her right off her feet into a sprawl. Then she caught up with her balance and took the lead, vaulting over the near edge of the weeds and landing two steps down inside the recessed staircase. She caught herself against the side wall with her hands and forearms, pivoted and took the stairs down into the darkness in a few falling strides. Above her, she heard Sam helping Lauren into the staircase, and somewhere behind them, Pierce's voice, screaming something incoherent.

She hit the door with her shoulder—its massive steel bulk barely registered the impact—and found the keypad with her right hand. Felt out its edges with her fingertip. Got her bearings on it.

Third row down. First button on the left.

She pressed it five times, heard the lock mechanism

thud open inside it, and shoved on the door with all her weight. As she did, she felt Sam come to a stop behind her. His hands fell into place beside hers on the door, and together they pushed it inward.

All at once the darkness behind them came to life in spastic pulses of light. Little bursts of reflected glow off the concrete walls of the stairwell, as Pierce covered the last sprinting yards above.

"I'm holding it," Sam said. "Get her through."

Dani had already turned and grasped Lauren's hands. In the frenzied light, she could see the girl's silhouette against the stairs. Dani leaned back and hauled her through the doorway, and Sam pivoted through after them, turning and getting his hands onto the door from the inside. He heaved his weight against it, and in the last second as it swung toward its frame, Dani heard Pierce shriek like some kind of animal, no more than five feet away on the other side. Then the door slammed and latched shut, and the space around them went black—as perfectly dark as anything Dani had ever experienced.

"Don't stop," she said. *"He'll be through it right behind us."*

She blundered forward through the void, keeping hold of Lauren. She heard Sam's footsteps scuff the floor, passing ahead of her, then heard him open the second door. He reached out to her, guiding her and Lauren through.

"Stairs are right here," he said.

She felt for the metal railing, got a hold of it. Felt

for the edge of the top step with her leading foot. The slow going made her nerves want to vibrate right out of her skin.

Why isn't Pierce already through the door? He must know the code.

The answer flashed across her mind an instant later:

He's reloading the gun.

She regripped the rail farther down, and took the stairs as fast as she dared.

They were three flights down when they heard the outer door lock disengage again. Though Dani had been expecting the sound, it made her body jump.

"I see light below us," Sam said.

Dani realized she could see it too. A faint glow from somewhere at the bottom of the stairwell, just bright enough to rim the edges of the stairs up here.

"Lauren, can you run with us?" Dani asked. "Can you hold the rail and run?"

For a second, as they continued downward, the girl didn't answer. Then she murmured, "Think so."

"Then run," Dani said.

At that moment Pierce wrenched open the second door, above them in the stairwell, hard enough to slam it against the tiles in the entry hall. The glow of his flashlight beam, indirect and wild, began sliding over the walls.

"Run," Dani said again, and Lauren got moving, sprinting downward even as she held on to Dani's hand. Sam followed as they went, flight after flight, throwing themselves toward the bottom of the shaft.

They saw the light source as soon as they rounded the final landing. Below them lay the square space with the two doors—one on the right, leading into the massive test chamber, the other on the left, leading somewhere they'd never seen; they'd never had the code for it.

That door on the left stood open now.

Wide open, with light shining through from the other side.

From above them came the clatter of Pierce's footsteps, no more than two or three flights up.

The three of them took the last set of stairs in a few seconds, their momentum carrying them straight to the open door. They turned and stared through it.

Beyond lay a narrow corridor—a tunnel, really: three feet wide, its walls and floor made of poured concrete, the ceiling a metal gridwork held up by steel beams running across it. At the top of one wall, dim white lights were set into the surface, forming a line that stretched away into the distance, straight as a tightrope.

There was no way to tell what the tunnel led to.

"Try it?" Dani asked.

"It's one more door we can shut," Sam said.

It would buy them a few seconds, Dani thought. No reason to waste those same seconds deciding. She shoved Lauren through the doorway and followed after her, with Sam at her back. He pushed the door shut behind them, and they ran.

CHAPTER FORTY-SIX

SEPTEMBER 2018

Dryden stood in the doorframe and stared at the place from his nightmare.

The tunnel.

Three feet wide.

Poured concrete walls and floor.

Metal grid ceiling held up by steel beams crossing it from side to side.

There were small light bulbs set high in one of the walls—dark and dormant now, but once upon a time they had shone dimly white.

Dryden stared down the tunnel's length; the flashlights could illuminate only a few dozen yards of it, but he knew it stretched much farther than that.

He felt the breath want to lock itself in his lungs. It took effort to keep it going in and out.

On either side of him, Danica and Lauren stood staring, too.

"I've dreamed about this," Danica whispered.

Dryden could hear the just-controlled fear in her voice.

"The lights were on in the dream," Dryden said. "Right?"

Danica nodded slowly, then looked at Lauren. "How about you? Have you dreamed this?"

"I don't know. Maybe."

Dryden thought she sounded every bit as rattled as himself and Danica. He glanced at her and saw a sheen of sweat on her forehead.

Danica said, "In my nightmare, I never reach the end of it. I just know I'm moving toward something bad. Really bad. And when I wake up, I think . . . I don't get to the end because I know I can't handle it."

"No choice this time," Dryden said.

Danica took a deep breath and forced it out. "Let's go."

Dryden stepped through the doorway into the tunnel.

They watched the walls and floor slide into view ahead of them, yard by yard in the flashlight beams. Dryden listened to the strange acoustics of the place, the echoes of their footsteps seeming to race away in front of them and behind them.

Far ahead, something glimmered on the left-side wall, just catching the glow of the Maglites.

They came to it thirty seconds later. The three of them stood staring at another block of stencil text in black paint:

STATION 14 - 450 FEET LEFT
STATION 17 - 350 FEET RIGHT

Strangely, Dryden found the words struck no chord in his memory. Not even the vague feeling some of the places above ground had given him.

That didn't make sense; he had to have seen this writing before. He must have gone right past this spot—

Yes, at a dead sprint. You weren't stopping to smell the roses last time you came this way.

The intuition chilled him. He thought about it for another second, then he and the others turned and kept going—toward Station 17, and whatever ghosts might be waiting there for them.

On the occasions when he had wondered about the tunnel in his nightmares, and what might lie at the end of it, Dryden had never actually envisioned anything.

Now he saw it for himself:

It ended by opening into a space that measured probably thirty feet by thirty. A big square chamber with the same concrete floor and walls as the tunnel itself, and the same metal gridwork ceiling.

On the far wall, opposite the tunnel's mouth, were four doorways, evenly spaced apart. Each one had its corresponding door lying flat on the concrete in front of it, its hinges cratered out by a cutting torch like those back in the stairwell.

Dryden aimed his flashlight from one empty doorframe to the next. There were glimmers and vague shapes beyond each, but nothing he could clearly discern.

His mind was already numbering the doorways—one through four, left to right. His light beam settled on number one, at the far left; he crossed toward it. Even as he did, another of those spooky, sourceless thoughts came to him:

Inside door number four is a doozy. Hold on to your hat for that one.

The notion was there and gone in a beat. Nothing followed on its heels. Dryden let it go as he stepped through the first doorway.

The room beyond was the size of a two-stall garage, containing a machine that took up more than half the space. At a glance Dryden guessed it was a furnace; there were huge metal ducts going in and out of the thing, disappearing into the concrete wall behind it.

There was a hatch on the front of it, the kind that might be used for shoveling coal into a burner—except it was a bit large for that, and anyway the unit had a gas line running into it on the right side. It didn't burn coal at all. So what was the hatch for?

Dryden's flashlight beam caught something at the bottom edge of the hatch's steel door. He went closer, Danica and Lauren following. The three of them crouched low and concentrated their beams on what he'd seen.

It was a tuft of fur, stuck to the metal frame that the door closed against. The fur seemed to have been caught on the edge of the hatch's opening.

"Cremator," Dryden said softly.

He stood upright and gave the space a last once-over with his beam.

"I don't think I was ever in this room," he said. "I get no reaction to it at all. How about you?"

"Nothing," Danica said.

Lauren just shook her head.

They returned to the larger room outside and went to the next doorway.

The purpose of the second room was clear at once: it had been a weapons cache. The space was small—not much larger than a walk-in closet—and its walls were lined with gun racks for firearms of every size. All those racks were empty now, though the room had been fully stocked at one time: Dryden could see faint outlines where oiled metal and wood had once rested against the wall surfaces behind the racks.

Like the first room, this one gave Dryden no hint of familiarity. He had never seen the inside of it before.

The third room was a different matter.

Just inside its doorway was a narrow entry channel, stretching fifteen feet in. That was necessary because the room itself would not have fit between the two on either side of it: it was twice the size of a high school classroom.

The three of them reached the end of the throat-like entry and simply stood there, staring at the room. For thirty seconds, nobody made a sound. The light beams played over the space in a kind of spectral silence.

The floor was strewn with dead animals—almost certainly chimpanzees. They lay scattered here and there, no rhyme or reason to their positioning. They'd simply fallen where they'd died—where they'd been shot. The bullet holes—punched into abdomens and chests and heads—were still visible because the corpses still had their skin. They had not decomposed as they would have in a normal setting. None of nature's usual means for clearing away the dead—predators, scavengers, parasitic insects—had been available to do the job down here. The bodies appeared to have moldered and dried and caved in on themselves, like tanned hides draped over bones. Every visible face seemed to be grimacing in pain—lips and gums had withered and retracted from exposed teeth.

Dryden moved his beam over the long walls on either side of the chamber; they were lined with cages, all of which stood open. Elsewhere in the room, random things had been left behind: a few metal chairs, a dry-erase board on the wall, with nothing written on it. There was a big steel flatbed cart, with a raised handle on one end; it looked like the kind they had at Home Depot, meant for hauling bags of cement mix and cinderblocks.

Next to Dryden, Lauren had her shirt collar pulled up over her mouth and nose. She had done that reflexively within seconds of seeing the bodies, though in fact there was no reason for it—the room smelled no different than the tunnel had: stale and dry. With every door in the complex torched off, all the air had mingled and intermixed completely, even without the benefit of fans or cross-breezes to move it around. Twenty-nine years of shared stillness had been enough.

"How would this happen?" Danica asked. "Did the people in charge of shutting down Ashland just . . . kill them? Why the hell would they do it this way? They could have left them in the cages and given them a shot or something. Jesus Christ . . ."

Dryden had no answer. This space seemed to pull him in two different directions: the room itself set off every recognition alarm in his head—he had been here, no question about it—but the carnage didn't. However this massacre had happened, he had not watched it unfold.

"I don't know," he said softly.

The last thing his flashlight settled on was a standalone cabinet against the back wall of the room. It was seven feet tall and just as wide, like a doubled bookcase with doors. The thing was made of cheap particle board with cracked melamine veneer. The big doors stood wide open, revealing a bare interior. Dryden took a few steps closer to it, mindful of the bodies. He shone his light into the cabinet, scrutinizing it.

It didn't quite fit the room—not his rough memory of it, anyway. It looked wrong. He stared at it a moment longer, then chalked it up to the thing's emptiness—it would have been filled with supplies in 1989.

Dryden turned and crossed back to where the others stood.

"One left," Danica said.

Dryden heard an edge of fear in her voice.

"You get a bad vibe about that one, too?" he asked.

She nodded, and—he was sure he saw it—shivered just noticeably.

Dryden glanced at Lauren. "What about you?"

Lauren nodded fast, and Dryden saw that she was still sweating—more than before. He had the impression her nerves were lit up and humming.

What the hell was in that last room?

He raised his light and stepped past them, leading the way back out through the entry channel.

Ten seconds later they were back in the open space at the end of the corridor. They stood facing the fourth doorway, though none of them had shone a light into it yet. The darkness on the other side was perfect, a kind of deep night that belonged to that room alone.

"This is where it comes back, isn't it?" Danica said. "I can feel it. It's right in front of us."

You're wrong, Dryden thought. *It's behind us. It's chasing us.*

CHAPTER FORTY-SEVEN

JULY 1989

Sam was sprinting with Dani and Lauren in the tunnel, bringing up the rear. He kept his attention on Lauren—tried to be ready to grab hold of her if she stumbled. If she tripped and fell now, the seconds they lost would be the ones they couldn't afford.

They had gone maybe a hundred yards when he heard the door click open behind them. He heard Pierce's running footsteps a second later, like a fast drumbeat—faster than theirs.

They ran on.

Some kind of stenciled text went by on the left-side wall, gone in a blur before he even registered it. Behind them, Pierce's footfalls seemed to get louder and clearer by the second.

Up ahead, the line of white lights ended. It was hard to tell what lay beyond—the tunnel seemed to open up into some wider space there.

At fifty feet, Sam saw that the chamber at the end had doors on its opposite wall. Two of them—no, four.

They sprinted through the last dozen yards, entered the open space without stopping. By then Sam could see that all four doors had keypad locks. There was enough time for an ugly hunch to grip him: the five sevens wouldn't work on these doors—not if this lit-up part of the station wasn't abandoned.

He shouted, *"Try the two on the right, I'll try the left!"*

Dani broke to the right before he'd even finished saying it. She crossed the square space toward the door just right of center; Sam lost sight of her as he focused on his own door, the nearest one on the left. He slammed to a stop against it, put a finger to the seven key and stabbed at it—*one-two-three-four-five*—

Nothing.

He threw himself sideways to the next door, the one at the left end. For a fleeting second before he punched the keypad there, he caught a sound coming through that door—a steady rumble, almost like a jet engine cycling up. He felt something, too: a trace of heat coming off the metal of the door itself. Coming *through* the door.

He punched in the five sevens.

Nothing.

He turned and looked along the row of doors, and found Dani looking back at him from the farthest one down. No hope left in her eyes—just panic.

He saw Lauren in between them, a few steps back in the space of the room.

His eyes returned to Dani. Her own seemed to be asking, *What do we do? What do we DO?*

Before he could think of anything, he heard Pierce's footsteps click to a stop at the mouth of the tunnel.

CHAPTER FORTY-EIGHT

SEPTEMBER 2018

Dryden stepped across the threshold into the fourth room.

There was nothing interesting inside.

Nothing at all.

It was a simple, medium-sized storage room. Plain metal shelves lined the walls on all sides.

He swept his flashlight over them, one by one.

Empty. All of them.

Yet every detail of the room seemed to heighten Dryden's fear—that irrational panic he'd felt before entering the tunnel in the first place.

He knew the feeling all too well: it was the exact sensation the nightmare had given him, all his life since he was twelve years old.

This room is the thing at the end of the tunnel. This room is what makes the dream a nightmare.

But why?

And how?

There was nothing here. Even when the room had been stocked full, as it probably had been in 1989, what would it have held? Food for the chimps? Boxes of cleaning chemicals? Random tools? It was a glorified office closet.

He watched Danica and Lauren take it all in. Watched their eyes in the backscatter glow from the flashlights. Wide eyes—like his own, no doubt.

Danica turned to him. Shook her head. *I don't understand.*

CHAPTER FORTY-NINE

JULY 1989

"Look at me," Pierce said.

For a moment Sam considered disobeying him. Why let themselves be ordered around if they were about to die, anyway? Maybe *Go fuck yourself* was the proper response.

What did any of it matter, though? Nobody was going to learn about any bravery of theirs down here. Maybe no one would ever know what had happened to them at all.

He turned, along with Dani. Lauren stayed facing forward, away from Pierce—she was holding her head again, her eyes focused on nothing in front of her. She seemed barely aware of what was going on. Dani went to her side, took hold of one shoulder and gently turned her toward Pierce. By then Sam had crossed back to where they were; the three of them faced the man as he came forward.

Pierce stopped ten feet away, the gun held level but aimed at no one in particular. He pointed at the fourth door along the opposite wall.

"Open that," he said to Sam. "Zero zero three one five."

Sam shook his head. "If you're going to kill us, just . . . fucking . . ." He wanted to sound hard, but he couldn't make it work. All he sounded like was a scared kid. He felt as if he were about a breath away from losing control and crying. He had never been half this afraid. Or angry.

It occurred to him that Pierce didn't look very hard, himself. The guy's lower jaw was shaking as if he were freezing, though the air down here was room temperature. Pierce's eyes were wide and darting over the three of them. If not scared, he looked deeply uncomfortable, at least.

"You don't really want to do this," Dani whispered. "You don't, I can tell. And you don't have to."

Pierce pointed the gun at her. "You open it." He repeated the entry code.

"Mr. Pierce, please don't do this," Dani said. Her voice cracked and trembled. She could barely say the words. "Don't do this to us. You don't have to do this—"

"*OPEN THE FUCKING DOOR!*" Pierce screamed, making all three of them jump.

Dani turned and ran to the fourth door, her breath hitching in sobs that echoed off the walls. Sam heard the metal keys clicking as she pressed them.

CHAPTER FIFTY

SEPTEMBER 2018

Dryden crossed to the shelves opposite the entry door. He moved his flashlight beam over each level, slowly and carefully. On the metal surface of each shelf were faint outlines of what had once been stored there. The bottoms of boxes and cans and plastic bags had left their impressions behind: clear shapes surrounded by the sparse dust that had once settled around them. Those outlines remained because there had been no *new* dust here in twenty-nine years. No people walking around, running hands through their hair, brushing their shirtsleeves against their sides.

Dryden studied the shapes, one shelf after another.

Nothing jumped out at him.

He crouched and put his face almost down to floor level, and shone his beam into the four-inch gap beneath the lowest shelves. Nothing of interest there, either: a wadded tissue paper, a crushed foam cup, a nickel resting in a layer of dust much thicker than what lay on the shelves above. Whatever mop-up crew had been assigned to empty this place, after the accident in 1989, they clearly hadn't worried about any white glove inspection happening afterward.

Dryden stood again, turning in place, taking it all in. The walls. The ceiling. The doorway, where Lauren still stood, tense and rigid.

Dryden completed the turn and let the flashlight fall to his side, the beam lighting up the floor in the middle of the room. His gaze settled on that surface—

—and froze on it.

As did Danica's. She came up beside him, staring down.

A huge, rust-colored stain covered the concrete in front of them.

Dryden was struck by the feeling he'd had a moment before: that the lost memory was chasing them down the tunnel outside. Accelerating now. Surging like water through a conduit. Like blood through an artery. Like—

CHAPTER FIFTY-ONE

JULY 1989

The room behind the fourth door had metal shelves along the walls, and random supplies stacked all over them. Sam guided Lauren in through the doorway; Dani was already inside, still crying, pawing at her eyes and trying to get control. Her gaze locked onto Pierce as he came through the doorway behind Sam and Lauren.

"We're twelve years old," Dani said. Her voice was breaking, as before. "Don't do this. Please just don't do this."

Sam could feel his own eyes burning. The room started to swim. He blinked a few times and got it clear again for the moment.

Only Lauren seemed unaffected. Unaware, even. She wandered to the shelves along the side wall, took hold of one and leaned against it for balance. She touched the bruise on her head, winced in pain, and sat down hard on the concrete.

Pierce shoved Sam by the shoulder, sending him stumbling across the room to where Dani stood. Sam turned and faced the man, side by side with Dani, and took hold of her hand. She interlaced her fingers with his and squeezed.

Pierce stood there, still looking rattled, still holding the gun on them.

"We thought we were saving your life," Sam said. "At the barn. We thought we were risking ours. We did that for you."

The words seemed to have a real effect on Pierce. Through the anxiety of his expression, something like consideration showed—it flickered there for a second or two, then disappeared.

"Quit talking," Pierce said. He swallowed with difficulty. He took a deep breath and let it out. And again. To Sam, he looked like someone psyching himself up to jump off a high-dive board.

Then, behind Pierce and off to the side, Lauren moved. She pivoted where she sat, and stared up at the man's back, her body language entirely different than it had been a moment before.

She no longer looked dazed and unaware. She looked lucid as hell.

Sam pictured her in the stairwell earlier—running, hitting every tread, keeping her balance. Then the sprint through the tunnel—again, keeping pace just fine. Sam remembered thinking she must be mostly back to her wits, at that point, right up until he'd seen her looking confused again, in the chamber outside this room.

Looking confused.

Sam willed himself to keep his focus on Pierce's

gun, and off of Lauren. To keep his eyes from giving her away. It took all the willpower he had. Off-center in his vision, Lauren rose up onto her knees, turned silently and studied the shelves beside her.

Pierce took another deep breath. His lower jaw was still shaking. He clenched his teeth together to get control of it.

"Please," Dani said again.

Pierce's eyes centered on her, narrowing a little. Hardening.

Behind him, Lauren reached out of sight between two large boxes, and when her hand came back out it was holding a fire extinguisher. A medium-sized one, like some people kept in their kitchens or near their furnaces.

Pierce was still focused on Dani. Sam could hear the man's breathing speeding up. Could almost see the thought cycling behind his eyes: *Do it, do it, do it.*

Lauren pressed her free hand to the concrete floor, pushed herself up from where she knelt, and stood. She gripped the fire extinguisher with both hands at one end, as if the thing were a short, squat club.

She turned to Pierce and took a step toward him. Just like that, she was in striking distance. She drew the extinguisher into a backswing—

—and faltered, her balance betraying her just for an instant. She took a fast step backward to correct for it. As she did, the sole of her shoe scraped the concrete.

Pierce reacted as if slapped. He jerked, spun in place, swung the gun around as he turned.

And fired.

The sound was like a hammer blow to Sam's eardrums.

The bullet hit Lauren just above the right eye, and blew the back of her head apart in a ragged cloud.

CHAPTER FIFTY-TWO

SEPTEMBER 2018

—a bullet through a gun barrel.

The memory crashed into Dryden with almost physical force, making him flinch. He saw Danica do the same, the whole thing coming back to her in that single moment.

"Wait," Danica said—it was more a sound than a word. A primal expression of confusion, reflexively shaped into letters.

Dryden could do no better. For a full second his mind tried to reconcile the two realities.

In that same second he saw a burst of movement across the little room. His focus—and the beam of his flashlight—had still been directed at the bloodstained concrete. Now he jerked both of them upward; he saw the woman who'd called herself Lauren Coleman reaching up, grabbing something off the topmost shelf beside the door. That shelf was seven feet high; anything lying flat on it would have been invisible until now.

The woman yanked her hand back down, spinning as she did, leveling her arm toward Dryden.

She held a Beretta M9. It was steady in her hand, centered on Dryden's face from eight feet away.

He took note of her posture—the modern isosceles shooting stance, right down to the position of her shoulders. It looked second-nature, ingrained by hundreds of hours of range time. Whoever and whatever she was—ex-military, ex–law enforcement—she had logged years at it, and was still in her prime.

Dryden stared at her finger, tight against the trigger. He had the M4 rifle slung on his shoulder, easily two full seconds from being aimed and ready to fire. Next to him, Danica had the Glock tucked into her rear waistband. Dryden rehearsed a sequence of moves in his head: pitch himself sideways, shove Danica down, grab her Glock in the same movement, level it on the doorway and fire.

It would take less than a second.

Which still wouldn't be fast enough.

They would both be dead before he could even free the weapon.

"Who the fuck are you?" Danica whispered.

"Not your friend," the woman said.

The blonde took her left hand off the gun and banged her palm down on the shelf beside her. She did it five times in a fast sequence, a loud drumbeat that rebounded off the walls and out into the space at the end of the corridor.

A second later, Dryden heard a clamor somewhere out there. It sounded like wood crashing down onto concrete.

In his mind he saw the cheap melamine cabinet

in the third room—the thing that hadn't fit with his memory.

He thought he could guess the reason now: the cabinet hadn't been there at all in 1989. It was only there now because—

Dryden cursed under his breath.

The cabinet was there to hide a doorway. The damned thing was more than large enough.

He heard footsteps a moment later—lots of them, running and scuffing the concrete. Behind the blond woman, the dark space of the corridor's end chamber suddenly flickered with light. Multiple flashlight beams swinging and pointing.

"In here!" the woman yelled; her eyes stayed locked on Dryden, as did the Beretta.

The newcomers shouldered their way into the room: first came a big man with short black hair and a beard that went to his collar. Five others pushed in behind him, fanning out—every one of them had the hardass look of high-end private security. They carried MP5 submachine guns, leveled and ready. Their flashlights were mounted under the barrels of the weapons.

"Turn around," the man with the black hair said. "Both of you, slow, hands out from your sides."

Dryden looked at Danica. "It's okay. Do what they say."

They turned around. Dryden heard someone shuffle forward, felt the M4 unclipped from its sling and taken from his shoulder. Then hands patted him down, fast and thorough. They took his wallet, then the Maglite he held. Finally someone grabbed his wrists, pulled them tightly together and bound them with a zip-tie. Three feet away, the same happened to Danica.

Someone said, "Clear."

The feet shuffled away again.

"Face forward."

They turned back toward the gunmen; by then Dryden could hear a final set of footsteps coming. They ticked softly on the concrete outside the room, closer and closer. The woman and the six men parted from the doorway.

The man who stepped through it had to be seventy years old. He was tall and slim, with short-cropped grey hair. The features of his face were severe—

—and familiar.

Dryden recalled the first moments between himself and Danica, in the basement of that house in Thousand Oaks; neither of them had recognized the other. It made sense, he supposed: a lot happened to a face between age twelve and forty-one. The three decades *after* forty were another matter: there was plenty of wear and tear, but no real structural change.

Not enough, anyway. Not in this case.

Dryden spoke the words even as they surfaced in his head: "Ellis Pierce."

CHAPTER FIFTY-THREE

JULY 1989

In the fractions of a second that followed the gunshot, Sam experienced the same surreal clarity he'd felt earlier—it was the race for the Escort all over again. The space around him suddenly broke itself down into simple things: the ones that mattered.

He saw Lauren's body drop where she had stood. There was no longer anything telling her limbs what to do. She was gone.

He saw Dani screaming, stumbling backward into the metal shelves behind her, her eyes full of shock and fear.

He saw Ellis Pierce, still holding the gun. Sam could see only an edge of the man's face, from behind and to the left, but it was enough to see shock there, too. The gun itself hovered in place, shaking in Pierce's hand, still pointed in the direction it had fired.

There was a second in which it all seemed to hold still—Dani and the fallen body and the outstretched gun—the whole room poised like a teetering vase.

Then everything happened—fast.

Pierce moved. He pivoted, swinging his arm through another 180-degree arc, the gun whipping around—

—and pointing at Dani's face.

By then Sam was moving, too, throwing himself forward across the five-foot distance to the gun.

He wasn't fast enough.

He saw Pierce's fingertip compress against the trigger. Saw the man's whole grip on the gun tighten with it, the hand going white with the force of the pull.

Nothing happened.

In the instant before Sam crashed into him, he saw Pierce's face register confusion, his eyes darting down to the gun.

A tenth of a second later Sam got his right hand on the gun's barrel, then collided with the man at something close to sprint speed.

Pierce was a head taller and fifty pounds heavier than Sam, but he was not balanced to take a hit, and he wasn't expecting one. The impact sent him—and Sam with him—toward the shelves on the side wall of the room. They took three lurching steps and crashed into them, Pierce hitting first. At no point did the man's grip on the gun weaken.

That sense of absolute clarity was still there, even in Sam's thoughts. They came through as sharp, concise little sentences, like bullet points:

He was *not* going to win a fight over the gun itself.

Not against an adult.

Even now, Pierce was reaching to put his second hand on the weapon, because—

Because he thinks you are *fighting for it.*

Which you can take advantage of.

The man's other hand closed over the pistol, right beside Sam's.

The doubled force was too much to handle; Sam could feel the metal twisting, slipping away in his grip.

He held on as best he could with just his right hand, and pivoted his body while shoving himself inward toward the man. The resulting position put Sam almost in front of Pierce, with his back to him; Sam's left side was now tight against both of the guy's arms.

It also put Sam's left elbow twelve inches in front of Pierce's face.

Pierce's undefended face.

Sam stopped thinking any of it through, and simply exploded. He slammed his elbow backward, as hard and as fast as he could, over and over.

Every blow connected somewhere. There was nothing Pierce could do to move his head out of the way. Sam felt the hard point of his elbow hitting teeth, an eyeball, skipping under the jaw and hitting the throat. He heard Pierce grunting, seething—but still the man's two-handed grip on the pistol held.

Then Sam's elbow struck Pierce's nose. He saw the impact at the edge of his vision, felt the cartilage crunch and deform, and the sudden hot rush of blood onto his arm.

He saw Pierce react instinctively, turning his head sideways to spare his nose another hit.

Sam's next blow went into the side of the man's neck, an inch beneath the ear.

Whatever he hit—something thick and ropy, a cord of muscle tying into the base of the skull—it worked. Pierce's hands didn't just loosen on the gun; they let go. The man's breath rushed out and he stumbled back and landed on his ass, one shoulder against the shelves beside him.

Sam spun toward him, stepping back to get even more distance from the guy. As he did, he got his left hand around the gun, then grabbed it properly with his right. His finger settled in place on the trigger.

Pierce was sitting there, eyes shut in pain, blood streaming from his broken nose. He was conscious but dazed, like a drunk trying to figure out where he was.

He's not down for long. Do it.

Sam raised the pistol, locked his arm straight, lined up the sights on Pierce's face from ten feet away.

He realized he could hear himself breathing—Dani's screams had gone silent.

Sam turned and looked at her.

She was watching him, her eyes bloodshot and wet. Then she looked at Lauren's body, and finally at Pierce.

She returned her gaze to Sam and nodded.

Sam looked down the sights again, took a deep breath—

—and pulled the trigger.

Nothing.

He tilted the gun and stared at it.

There was a shell casing wedged in the little slot on the side—the casing that should have come out after the last shot.

Sam pulled the weapon closer to himself, careful of where he pointed it, and studied the problem.

He had never held a gun before. He had seen plenty of them in movies, and he knew this was the type where you pulled back the slide on top to get it ready—at least that was what characters did on-screen, normally. But how did you fix a jammed gun? Had he *ever* seen that happen in a movie?

Then Pierce's foot slid hard on the concrete, and Sam flinched and looked.

The man's eyes were open and staring up at him, still dazed but at least focusing—and angry. The guy made a weak grab for the nearest shelf, missed it, tried again and got a grip on it.

Coming around. Fast.

Sam turned to Dani, saw her chest rising and falling, the fear coming right back.

He gave the gun one last good look. Maybe he could fix the jam by just pulling on the wedged casing. He rotated the weapon, got a hold of the little brass cylinder with his left fingertips, and pulled.

The casing didn't budge.

Pierce gripped the shelf and tried to pull himself up. He got six inches off the ground and then fell back, blinking, shaking his head.

It occurred to Sam that he might just rush the guy and kick him in the throat. Get him down and then just *beat* him with the gun, over and over until the skull fractured. It would be self-defense. *Anything* counted as self-defense now.

Then he looked at the man again and saw his eyes

clearing rapidly—the lights were coming back on inside his head, for sure.

If he attacked Pierce now, the guy might just grab him and drag him down—and get the gun back.

All at once the man pressed his hands to the floor and heaved himself upward, getting onto his knees in a single movement.

Sam backed away and sidestepped, grabbing Dani's hand again. The two of them circled around Lauren's body, toward the door out of the room.

"Little fuckers," Pierce hissed, his eyes tracking them. He raised a leg and planted his foot flat beneath him.

Sam and Dani, still facing him, reached the doorway. Sam pushed Dani behind himself, out of the room, and followed. The last thing he saw, before he pulled the door shut, was Pierce rising up onto both feet. Then the door slammed and latched.

"Back down the hall," Dani said.

Sam shook his head. "We had a big head start before. This time—"

The door was suddenly buffeted in its frame—Pierce had already crossed the room and collided with it.

Sam turned toward the nearest other door, six feet away along the wall. Still holding Dani's hand, he bolted toward it.

"Do you remember the combo?" Sam whispered.

For a second Dani only stood there, wet eyes narrowing.

"Oh shit . . ." she said.

"It started with two zeroes, right? And then—"

Her fingertip shot forward to the keypad. He saw her stab the two zeroes and then he lost track of the rest. The moment she finished, the lock disengaged with a heavy *clack* inside.

The two of them threw their weight against the door and shoved it inward, even as the fourth door's latch clicked—Pierce had not needed to enter the combo to open it from inside.

In the last instant before Sam followed Dani through the third door, he saw Pierce burst out into the open, turning, furious, lunging at them.

Sam slipped through the gap, turned fast and slammed the door shut. Even through the thick metal, he could hear the man scream in rage.

Sam kept his eyes on the door as he backed away from it. Dani was somewhere behind him, farther into the room. Whatever this place was, it had its own little hallway just inside the door. Sam had not yet turned around; had not seen the room itself.

He kept the gun raised, leveled on the door, though the weapon remained useless at the moment. He could still see the empty bullet casing wedged in place.

Around him, the narrow passage of the entry hall kept sliding by as he backed up. How long since he and Dani had entered? Five seconds? Ten?

Why wasn't Pierce already coming through the door after them? He obviously knew the code.

The answer—the guess, anyway—came to Sam like a wave of nausea.

He looked at the gun and considered an obvious question for the first time:

Where the hell had Pierce gotten it?

He had not been carrying it when they last saw him in the Jeep, right after the helicopter crash. Where had it come from?

Maybe somewhere in this complex.

Maybe one of those two other doors right outside this room.

If so, it would explain this delay right now.

"Fuck," Sam whispered.

If Pierce could get another gun, it would be game over any second now—a fully working gun vs. one that was jammed and worthless.

Ten feet from the door now. Still moving backward. The narrow entry channel still boxing him in on both sides.

He looked at the gun again. He focused on the wedged casing, gleaming in the dull light of the room, and the gun's slide, pinching the casing in place by some spring mechanism inside.

Sam took hold of the slide with his left hand, and gripped it firmly.

Could he fix it by just—

It happened so easily it startled him. He pulled back on the slide, and the brass cylinder fell free immediately. It bounced off his arm, pinged loudly against the wall and settled on the floor with a ringing clatter.

Still holding the slide, he pulled it back as far as it would go. Through the open slot on the side, he could see into the gun's inner workings. Could see where the bullet magazine fed up into it from below.

When the slide came to a stop, all the way back, a

live new bullet clicked upward into that space inside the gun.

Sam eased the slide forward again, saw it grab and drag the new bullet, pushing it smoothly along—

—right into the gun's barrel from the back end.

The slide closed with a metallic *click* that sounded right—exactly right. He leveled the gun on the door again.

His next backward step took him out of the narrow entry passage, into what seemed to be a big room; to his left and right, the wall stretched fifteen feet in each direction.

Another step, and he bumped into Dani; she'd gone still for some reason. Sam risked taking his eyes off the door for a quick glance at the room.

It was full of cages.

With chimpanzees in them.

The cages lined each of the two side walls. Big cages—bigger than the ones in Station 9. And their occupants were alive.

From inside each enclosure, a pair of deep-set eyes stared out at the two of them. Leathery hands gripped the bars.

For another second, a weighted silence held. Then one of the chimps uttered a short, deep-throated sound, like a dog's bark, and all the cages erupted with screaming.

Sam swept his gaze around once, taking it in—the chimps were slamming their bodies back and forth in the cages, grabbing the doors and shaking them, jumping up and down and shrieking with their teeth bared—huge fangs half as long as human fingers.

Sam noted the difference between this behavior and the mindless, destructive rage of the baboon in Station 9.

This is what ordinary pissed-off looks like, he thought. Then: *Still pretty goddamned scary.*

He saw all that in a second, then locked his eyes on the door again, the gun raised and ready to fire.

That notion stopped him where he stood:

Was it *really* ready to fire?

Was he absolutely sure?

He tried to focus on what little he knew about guns like this. He was almost certain that once you fired the first shot, you could just keep pulling the trigger and shooting. But *before* that first shot, like when you reloaded it, there were steps you had to take, to get it ready.

When he had pulled the slide back, a few seconds ago, had that been the same thing as reloading?

As in, was there still something he needed to do, right now, before this thing would actually fire?

He didn't know. Just simply didn't.

"Shit . . ." he whispered, the sound lost under the cacophony of animal screams.

He turned the gun in his hands just enough to look closely at its details.

There was no hammer to pull back, but there was a little inset button on the grip, right behind the trigger.

Was that a safety? It wasn't *labeled* safety, but maybe not all guns had a label for that.

Then he saw a metal tab on the left side of the barrel, just where the slide met the gun's frame. It was right above the trigger, and it looked like something you could push down with your thumb.

What the hell was *that* for?

None of the writing engraved into the weapon was any help. He saw the word *GLOCK* on the side, up near the end of the barrel, along with the number *17.* There were other words and numbers here and there, but nothing like *safe* or *fire*. None of it told him what to do. You were supposed to already *know* what to do, if you were holding a gun.

He stood there, all at once feeling like nothing more than a kid. An overwhelmed kid who just didn't know the things he needed to know.

Maybe the gun would fire, and maybe it wouldn't.

If Pierce came through that door in the next second, *his* gun would be ready, no question about it.

The feeling of helplessness seemed to burn under Sam's skin. Shame and fear and anger, all mixed together. He felt it right down to the bone.

He just wasn't ready. His opponent was bigger and smarter, and he was coming any second now.

Sam clenched his teeth and held the gun steady on the door, and waited.

We'll just see, I guess.

How long had it been, now? Twenty seconds since they'd come in here? Thirty?

He was thinking about that when Dani's hand slapped his shoulder, fast and urgent.

Sam turned his head, keeping the gun leveled at the

door. He saw Dani pointing somewhere straight behind him, and craned his neck to look.

There was another door, on the far wall of the room. It was shut, but it had only a simple lever-knob, no key-pad lock. Maybe its keypad was on the other side.

There was no telling where the door led—somewhere deeper in this complex, anyway.

"He'll just follow us," Sam said, loud over the sound of the chimps. "We have to deal with him somewhere."

"I wasn't pointing at the door," Dani said.

Sam stared at her, confused, then followed her gaze again to the far side of the room.

There was a big metal panel on the wall right next to that door. It had a familiar, stylized logo across the top of it: ELECTROBOLT. Lower down, there were rows of buttons with paper labels on them, just like the setup in Station 9.

And above those was a big red button all by itself—covered by a clear plastic dome, so nobody would accidentally push it.

Also just like Station 9.

Sam turned and moved his gaze along the rows of cages on each side of the room. Every lock bore the ElectroBolt logo.

He met Dani's eyes—they were still bloodshot and wet and miserable, but at the moment they also looked hard.

CHAPTER FIFTY-FOUR

SEPTEMBER 2018

To Dryden, Ellis Pierce's expression looked like Russell Moss's, staring across that campfire in Somber Valley. The face of a man trying to compare memory with the present.

Pierce stood there, just inside the storage room, flanked by his gunmen and the woman who wasn't Lauren Coleman.

"You couldn't have planned this," Dryden said. "I don't care how smart you are. Too many variables. Too much left to chance, for a plan."

"For *a* plan," Pierce said. His tone was soft, matter-of-fact. "But if you're smart, you make twenty plans. Abducting both of you the other day would have suited me fine, if it'd worked."

Pierce turned to the man with the black hair. "Bring the cart."

The man nodded and disappeared out the door. Dryden heard his boots on the concrete, running footsteps fading away into the next room.

"What are you going to do with us?" Danica asked.

"We're going to go somewhere and talk," Pierce

said. "Just need to know who you've spoken to, how much you remember, what you told Grace and his guys. I know I won't get everything out of you, but . . . I'm thorough. I'll get as much as I can, within reason."

His tone was devoid of anything like gloating. He sounded like a dentist saying, *This shouldn't hurt much, might just feel some pressure*.

"And then you'll kill us," Danica said.

"It'll be quick," Pierce said. "I'm not a sadist."

Dryden ignored the guy and studied the layout of the situation. The room, the people, the hardware, the firing angles.

None of it looked good.

The five gunmen still in the room had their MP5s trained and level. The blond woman still had her Beretta leveled, too. Pierce himself had no weapon in hand, for what it was worth, which was nothing.

There was no move to be made against these people.

Not here and now, at least.

From far away outside the room there came a rumble, deep and resonant. Heavy-duty wheels on concrete. A metal surface vibrating and thrumming and bouncing. Dryden pictured the big flatbed cart he'd seen earlier. The one that belonged in a Home Depot.

"No maps of Ashland left, you know," Pierce said. "Not even for the FBI. No schematics to show how far these underground complexes actually go. Or the old service tunnels for plumbing and wiring. You'd be surprised where some of them lead to."

Pierce nodded through the wall toward the unseen

third room, where the melamine cabinet had concealed a doorway.

"Past that animal containment, there's another corridor, then one more empty complex at the end of it. Then there's a service tunnel running to an old power substation two miles outside the boundary fence. When they shut Ashland down in 1989, the Army filled the last twenty feet of that tunnel with concrete, out there at the substation. And then . . . the records got shredded with everything else tied to this place. These days nobody knows about that tunnel at all. Things in Ashland just have a way of being forgotten."

Pierce wandered to the doorway and turned an ear toward the sound of the distant cart.

"That old tunnel is how we came in," he said. "And how we're going back out. We'll have you a thousand miles from here before they figure out what happened."

Dryden took a last sweeping glance at the guns and then looked away.

Pierce came forward again from the doorway and stood watching the two of them. Dryden looked up and met his gaze.

"How the hell could you count on us getting away from the gas?" Dryden asked. "It was one in a thousand we could've done that."

"Probably not even those odds," Pierce said.

Dryden waited for him to go on.

Outside the doorway, the rumbling cart sounded much louder now.

"If the gas had gotten you," Pierce said, "we would have come into the woods in force, tranqed you both and dragged you back here. We figured we'd have to kill a third, maybe half the afflicted FBI agents by the time we found you. We ran it through scenarios. Drilled for it. It was manageable. Some approach always is."

Behind Pierce, the black-haired man pushed the flatbed cart into the room.

"Let's go," Pierce said.

The two gunmen closest to the cart reacted in unison—maybe they'd drilled for this, too. They handed their MP5s to the men beside them, then came forward and grabbed Dryden by the shoulders. They dragged him to the cart and shoved him down onto it, face up, his bound wrists contorted painfully beneath him. They did the same with Danica, and a moment later the cart was rolling again.

CHAPTER FIFTY-FIVE

JULY 1989

Even through the closed door, Pierce could hear the chimps screaming. He'd been in that room once or twice before; he could picture the big cages lining the walls on both sides. The screams were getting on his nerves now, but otherwise he ignored them. He had the new pistol in his hand, a round chambered and ready, and three full magazines in his front pocket.

It had killed him to lose time getting the stuff—half a minute, maybe more—but there had been no choice: if the fucking kid managed to clear that stovepipe jam in the first gun, the weapon would be all set to go. The kid might be standing there right now, with the sights lined up on this door.

That, or else the two of them had run for it, through the second door and into the long corridor beyond.

Which was the nightmare scenario, of course. Because at the end of *that* corridor was one more locked door, and though the kids would not have the code for it—

They won't fucking need it, Pierce thought.

No, not for that door.

Pierce cursed to himself and rested a fingertip against the zero button on the keypad.

He paused then, and mentally ran through his course of action one last time:

Crack open the door and stick the gun through.

Fire four shots in a sweep pattern.

Rush in—fast.

That last step was the key: not just getting into the room, but getting through that slim entry channel as quickly as possible. Every second spent inside of it was courting death. The thing was like the Thermopylae Pass, but in reverse: a choke point that gave him only disadvantages. No matter where in the room the kid might be, he would know that Pierce had to come through that narrow passage.

Unless Pierce could get past it while the kid was still flinching and running from the first four shots.

He sucked in a breath and expelled it, and punched in the code.

The lock disengaged.

He shoved the door open six inches.

He stuck the gun through and fired—*one, two, three, four*—and heard the chimps go silent.

He put his shoulder to the door and heaved it all the way open, already sprinting, leaning forward, hurtling down the channel, because all that mattered now was—

Pierce stopped with a convulsion that hit his body like a seizure.

One foot slipped, almost went out from under him, then caught and held on the concrete.

He was standing right at the end of the entry passage, where it opened to the room.

The momentarily silent room.

Somewhere behind him, the door fell shut and latched with a *click*.

Three hundred feet away, in the tunnel beyond that room, Sam and Dani heard the man scream. From far behind them, even over the noise of their running footsteps, the sound of it came through: high-pitched and saturated with fear.

They had heard the four gunshots a second or two before—had heard the chimps go silent at that instant. Then had come a weird, quiet little moment. And now Pierce was screaming like a terrified child.

Then the shrieks of the chimpanzees started up again, drowning the man out, and on the heels of that sound the gun started firing once more, fast and sporadic, over and over. All of these sounds grew fainter by the second, as the tunnel fell away behind the two of them.

Sam glanced at Dani and saw new tears in her eyes. She blinked and wiped at them, not slowing down.

"We had to," Sam said. "We had to let them out. He would've got us if you hadn't thought of that."

If the words made her feel better, she didn't show it.

Sam faced forward again and watched the tunnel.

They reached the end of it thirty seconds later. Like the other tunnel, it opened up into a square space at the end, though this one was far smaller—about the size of an average bedroom. It had just a single door centered on the far wall, with a keypad lock.

The only other feature at the end of the tunnel was a set of metal shelves, snugged into the right-hand corner of the end wall. It was a single upright unit, just like the dozen or more that had filled the storage room. Someone had stood this one out here by itself and left the same kind of random clutter on it: tools and boxes and cans, in no obvious order.

Dani went to the door and put her hand to the keypad. She punched in the code that started with two zeroes.

Nothing happened.

She traded a look with Sam, then pressed the seven key five times.

Nothing.

The two of them turned in place and stared back down the tunnel. They held still and listened.

No more shooting. No more chimpanzee screams.

Which might mean anything. Pierce could be dead—or all the chimps could be dead. The tunnel was silent on the matter.

Then Sam cocked his head—he *could* hear something, but it was—

—behind them.

He saw Dani react to it at the same time, and together they turned back to face the locked door. The new sound was coming from the other side of it.

Dani's eyebrows drew closer together, in confusion.

"What *is* that?" she said.

CHAPTER FIFTY-SIX

SEPTEMBER 2018

One of the flatbed cart's wheels had a raised bump on it, or maybe a depression. Whatever it was, it made a thudding sound once per revolution, like a drumbeat marking time.

Dryden listened to the cadence of it, watching the ceiling of the tunnel go by.

The tunnel lay beyond the room with the open cages and the dead chimps. It looked exactly like the other tunnel, the one he had dreamed about for twenty-nine years. Poured concrete walls, metal grid ceiling supported by crossbeams, small inset lights high on one side.

As in the first tunnel, the lights were off. They gleamed and winked in the harsh flashlight beams of Pierce's men.

The group had fallen into a rough formation, moving along the tunnel: five were up ahead of the cart, three behind it. Of those three, one was pushing the cart by its handle, and two were watching the prisoners.

The watchers were doing an effective job of it, though not quite a perfect one. The tunnel's three-foot width didn't allow three adults to walk abreast, which meant the watchers had to be a step behind the pusher. That made it awkward to point their gun-mounted flashlights down onto the cart. What they did instead was aim them at the side walls of the tunnel, so the light bounced back and cast a scattered glow on everything—the cart, the people ahead of it, the prisoners. Not a bad solution. It kept things visible, if not glaringly bright.

More important was what the watchers were doing with their eyes—which was a little of everything. They were glancing down at Dryden and Danica every few seconds, but mostly they were keeping their gazes ahead, roaming over the group and the space far in front of it. It looked like the careful attention habit of personal bodyguards—watching for threats from all corners. No doubt these people *were* Pierce's bodyguards, among other things. They were sharp and efficient and professional.

But these two were doing a lot wrong. They weren't on security detail; they were on prisoner detail. They should have glued their eyes to their targets and not blinked. The guy on the left should have said, *I'll watch the left one, you watch the right one*. They should have pretended both captives had their hands free, and a belt of grenades around each of their waists. They should have been that paranoid and vigilant. And they weren't.

It reminded Dryden of something one of his instructors had told him about, long ago. The concept of *danger in numbers.*

Most people thought in terms of safety in numbers—being part of a big group was safer than being alone.

Which it was. The problem was that it made you *feel* safe, and that took the edge off your focus—if you let it. That was the danger in numbers. Dryden and his guys, back in the day, had trained against it continuously. It was one of a thousand human biases you had to work around.

Pierce's men were good, probably even great—but a long way from perfect.

And none of that mattered.

Not in the least.

The math was still two against eight, and the two were bound and unarmed, and the eight had seven guns among them.

Pierce's guys could have been stumbling idiots and it still would have been no contest.

Dryden listened to the thudding drumbeat of the cart. He felt it, too, each tiny impact transferring through the metal deck into his shoulder blades.

He watched the tunnel go by, yard by yard. The tunnel that was just like the last one.

More like it than you think.

It was another of those spooky intuitions, the same as before. A stir of lost memory just below the surface, working its way up.

There were things to remember at the end of the first tunnel. There's something to remember at the end of this one, too. Something important happened there.

What the hell did that mean?

And what did it matter?

So what if something had happened in this tunnel in

1989? How could remembering it make any difference now?

There was no intuition in response to that. Nothing but his own confused thoughts trying to make sense of it all.

Yet the memory was certainly there, trying to come back to him. *Fighting* to come back. It was right at the threshold. It was—

It was all he could do not to gasp, when it hit him. It came to him all at once, the understanding and the mental picture and everything else about it. The whole memory of what had happened at the end of this tunnel, fresh and clear as if he'd lived it five minutes ago.

And it mattered.

It mattered right now.

He kept his breathing steady. Kept his body still, and his face slack. This was not the time to start drawing attention.

He was lying on his back, with his zip-tied wrists beneath him. He was on the side of the cart closest to the tunnel's right wall, and he didn't quite fit; his shoulder and hip hung over the edge by an inch, just missing the wall as it grazed by.

Through his clothing, he could feel the sharp, machined edge of the cart's flatbed deck. Nothing fancy or rounded over. This thing had not been built for toddlers to sit on while their parents shopped for groceries. It was solid and rough and utilitarian. It was industrial equipment.

Dryden arched his body just enough to ease the

pressure between his lower back and his bound wrists. Enough to *move* his wrists. He shifted them sideways, an inch, three inches, six inches—he stopped, feeling the sharp edge beneath his hands. He turned his wrists until he was sure the band of the zip-tie, stretched between them, was pressed against that edge.

None of it would be visible to the three behind the cart; his body concealed everything.

He slid the zip-tie against the edge. Small movements. An inch forward and back, slow but with heavy pressure—all the weight he could bring to bear on it.

Time's almost up.

It wasn't intuition telling him that. Just simple perception: the drumbeat of the rolling cart had begun to slow down. The group was coming to the end of the tunnel.

A second later, the narrow ceiling above him gave onto a wider one. A square space at the end of the passageway. From where he lay, looking straight up, he could see the gathered group ahead of the cart. Could see a single doorway on the wall at the end, where the group had bunched up for some reason. He saw four or five of them crouch and reach down for something, and heard the grind of some heavy object sliding and then being lifted.

It had to be the door. Like all the others in the complex, it had been torched off its hinges and left lying there, right in front of the open frame. Pierce and his men, having come in by this route, would have stepped right over the door the first time. Now, with the cart in tow, they had to move it out of the way.

It would take ten seconds at most.

Still working on the zip-tie, Dryden turned his head twenty degrees to the side. He made the movement look slow and lethargic—a hopeless man letting his head roll. He darted his eyes farther in that direction, and saw the shelving unit in the corner, exactly where it had been in 1989.

The shelves had been full then; they were empty now, as he'd expected.

He let his head turn another ten degrees, and took in the very bottom of the shelf stack—not the lowest shelf, but the four-inch gap beneath it.

Dryden centered his head again, pointed his eyes straight up at the ceiling. He took in the room one last time, making a fast mental map of each person's position in it—a skill he'd used over and over in his former career.

Behind the cart, the pusher stood idle, staring off at nothing while he waited. Flanking the man, the watchers kept watching—their eyes continued moving, taking in everything for no good reason.

No one person was focusing solely on the prisoners now.

Danger in numbers.

Then the people lifting the door set it down again, and in the same moment the zip-tie snapped with an audible *twang.*

Dryden didn't wait to see anyone's reaction. He pitched his body sideways into a roll, off the cart and onto the concrete floor. He landed on all fours and lunged for the empty shelf unit in the corner.

CHAPTER FIFTY-SEVEN

JULY 1989

"It's music," Dani said. She had her ear almost touching the metal door now.

Sam did the same. He could hear a guitar, sharp and resonant, like it was playing in an echo chamber. Then a man's voice, singing; he recognized it at once.

"U2," Sam said.

Dani nodded. "Heartland."

For a second, Sam saw the two of them on the swing set again, the morning he'd met her. Those amped-up few minutes, when they were first talking. The way he couldn't stop looking at her eyes, and hoped she wouldn't notice. The way they kept finding new things they had in common, each one like another room to explore in some giant house.

They hadn't gotten around to talking about music, but if they had, he would have told her U2 was his favorite band. He had bought *Rattle and Hum* the day it came out last fall, and listened to it three times straight through when he got home.

To have recognized Heartland, Dani must have the album, too. That song had not been released as a single.

For just that moment, Sam felt like talking about it. Talking about albums they owned and songs they liked, the way kids talked everywhere. That was what they should be doing right now. They should be lying on that picnic table out on the grassy slope, under the stars, with a bag of chips and a six-pack of soda. They should be watching for satellites and talking about U2 music.

Sam let the thought go. They were not lying under the stars. They were leaning against a locked door, 120 feet underground, and there might still be someone coming to kill them.

He turned again and stared down the tunnel, its row of white lights leading away into the darkness.

Pierce could be in that tunnel right now, heading toward them. He could have killed every animal in that room, shut off the lights, and opened and closed the door without letting it slam.

He could be a hundred feet away at this moment, walking fast and quiet, coming this way.

Sam turned back toward Dani and the metal door.

"If there's music, there's people," he said.

He made a fist and pounded the door with the base of it, half a dozen good, loud hits. A second later, the song shut off.

The two of them stood there waiting. There were voices beyond the door now. A woman's voice and at least two men's voices, coming closer. Sam couldn't quite make out the words.

He glanced back over his shoulder into the tunnel. No sign of Pierce yet.

Maybe the people beyond the door would be armed soldiers. It didn't seem like too much to hope for; this was a military base.

On that notion, something obvious suddenly occurred to him: he was still holding the gun.

Probably not the smartest thing to be doing, if soldiers with rifles were about to show up. Probably a damn good way to get shot, actually.

At that moment someone disengaged the door's lock from the other side. The heavy latch mechanism clicked and thudded.

Sam turned fast, looking for any place to ditch the weapon. His gaze locked onto the only thing in sight: the metal shelf unit in the corner.

He sprinted toward it, dropping into a crouch and then down on all fours. There was an open gap beneath the very bottom shelf: a few pitch-black inches of space between the concrete floor and the shelf's underside.

Sam gave the gun a shove and let go, and watched it slide barrel-first into the gap. He heard it click softly to a stop against the back wall.

CHAPTER FIFTY-EIGHT

SEPTEMBER 2018

Dryden's lunge put him right at the foot of the shelf unit, with his right arm drawn back like a coiled spring. In the instant it took to launch his hand into the gap under the bottom shelf, there was time to imagine the worst. Like maybe the mop-up crew had been more thorough with these shelves than the ones back in that storage room—maybe they'd actually bothered looking underneath this unit. Or maybe the gun would be there, but simply wouldn't fire after all this time.

On that score he felt more confident: the stale, dead air of this place was bone dry, like one of those desert Army posts where they mothballed old equipment for spare parts. It was no different than keeping a pistol in a sealed case for thirty years—and Dryden had fired plenty of guns and ammo like that.

If it doesn't work, I promise not to bitch about it for long.

A hundredth of a second later, Dryden's hand closed around the grip of the pistol.

In that moment he saw himself holding the thing—a Glock 17—all those years ago. Standing with the weapon pointed at a door, his hand shaking, and his head full of doubt about whether it would fire. In that memory, he had just cleared a jam and chambered a new round.

A Glock with one in the pipe. No safety. Ready to rock.

For Danica, it unfolded so quickly there was hardly time to react.

A second and a half earlier, Dryden had been next to her on the metal cart. She had seen his head roll to the side and then back. For whatever reason, that body language had seemed like the picture of resignation. Of defeat. In its own way, it had unnerved her more than even the guns had.

Then had come that snapping sound—Dryden's zip-tie, it had to be—and he was gone, rolling into the dark, his elbows and hands scrambling on the concrete, a rush of crazed motion and sound.

Now she could see Pierce's security people reacting, their heads turning, their bodies and flashlights pivoting. From Dryden's direction there came a scrape of something metal on the floor, and an instant later the room exploded in gunfire—all of it from Dryden's position.

Danica flinched and tried to cover her ears, but her wrists were still bound beneath her. She saw the flashlights in the room suddenly jumping and jerking, swinging wildly in random directions. She saw bodies falling, collapsing into one another. Others were looking around, frantic, bunching together as if for safety—

but they were hit too, all of them going down in a tangle of limbs.

She saw Dryden come charging forward in a crouch, dropping a handgun with a clatter on the floor, grabbing the machine gun from one of the fallen men, rising up and shouldering it and firing fast little bursts into the pile of bodies on the other side of the cart. He was taking aim, shining the light from one to the next, shooting and moving on, shooting again. Now he dropped the machine gun and picked up another, and just stood there shining the light from body to body, making fast but thorough moves.

He stopped on someone. Danica turned her head on the cart, and in the flashlight glare she saw the blond woman, sprawled with the bodies of two men—tangled up with them, pinned down by their dead weight.

But she was alive. She stared up at Dryden, squinting into the beam of the flashlight.

"Show me your hands," Dryden said.

One of the woman's hands was already visible, empty. The other was out of sight beneath one of the bodies that held her in place. She glanced down at that hand, then back up at Dryden, her expression betraying some desperate calculation.

Dryden fired a burst into her forehead and she flopped backward, out of Danica's view behind the dead men.

He made one last sweep with the light, and finally seemed satisfied. Still, he kept the gun in his hands—kept it leveled on something Danica couldn't see from her angle.

He stooped quickly over one of the bodies and unclipped a knife from its waist. He stepped past the corpse and knelt down beside Danica.

"Roll on your side," he said.

She twisted her shoulders and got herself up onto one of them, exposing her bound wrists to Dryden. A second later the zip-tie parted with the same snapping *twang* she'd heard earlier.

She pushed off the cart's deck and sat up, blinking, still disoriented by what had happened. Her ears were ringing, and the air was thick and acrid with the smell of spent gunpowder.

Danica saw Dryden still pointing the machine gun and its light at something out of her field of view—something behind her. She turned and looked over her shoulder.

Ellis Pierce sat upright, his back against the wall beside the doorway. He was shot and bleeding, but still alive.

CHAPTER FIFTY-NINE

JULY 1989

Sam drew back from the shelf unit, stood up and turned, and saw the metal door swing inward. He went back to Dani's side.

A woman stood in the open doorway, maybe thirty years old. She had on a military uniform—not the dressy kind that people wore to official ceremonies, but the casual type you saw in movies most of the time. This woman's uniform also had a red cross emblem on the left side of the chest. She was some kind of medic.

Behind her were the two men Sam had heard; they wore the same uniform as the woman. The room they stood in was brightly lit, far more so than the tunnel. Sam could see rolling carts of equipment with the same big red cross on them, and there was a wide corridor leading away, with doorways every twenty feet. The doorways had clipboards hanging on the walls outside them, and farther down the hall stood a rolling gurney.

This station was a hospital—a medical quarters, anyway.

The woman and the two men stood staring at Sam and Dani, confused. Then the woman stepped forward, leaned through the doorway and looked around for anyone who might be accompanying two random kids in this tunnel.

Seeing no one else, she stepped back again and stared at them.

"What the hell is this?" she asked.

Sam glanced over his shoulder, into the dim reach of the tunnel, then turned to face the woman again.

"Can you lock this door so even the code won't open it?" he asked.

"Who *are* you?"

"Yes or no?"

As he said it, he looked behind him again, just for a second. The woman opened her mouth as if to repeat her question, then stopped. She leaned to the side and looked past him and Dani, staring into the tunnel herself. Though she didn't seem to see anything, she was clearly spooked.

"Yes," she said. "We can hard-lock it."

"Please let us in," Sam said. "We'll tell you why."

She hesitated another second, then seemed to shake off whatever rule or regulation was holding her back. She stepped aside and waved them forward. "Get in here."

The moment they passed through the doorway, everything inside Sam seemed to change. He looked at Dani and knew it was the same for her. It felt as if some kind of internal structure had kept them on their feet for the past several minutes—the need to stay alive, the knowledge that they were on their own. Now as the woman shut the door behind them, and gave the latch a twist that locked a bolt into place, that inner strength evaporated like something from a dream. They just didn't need it anymore.

Sam felt the hitch in his chest just before the sobs overwhelmed him. He saw Dani and everything else around them ripple and swim, and then both of them were crying aloud, unable to keep it quiet. Dani grabbed onto him and they sat down, right there on the concrete in front of the medics. Sam held her tight against himself and shut his eyes and didn't try to stop the tears.

"You're safe now," he managed. It was all he could get out through the spasms in his throat.

But the thought cycled again and again in his head:

It's over.

We're safe here.

We're safe, we're safe, we're safe.

CHAPTER SIXTY

SEPTEMBER 2018

Dryden kept the MP5 and its flashlight beam centered on Pierce. There was no sign the man had a weapon: his shirt was tucked in, with no holster visible on his waistband. No ankle holster, either; his seated position against the wall had drawn his pant cuffs upward, showing nothing but socks. All the same, Dryden kept the sights on him, and his finger on the trigger.

Pierce had taken a single shot through the abdomen—Dryden was sure it had happened during the initial volley with the Glock. The round had caught him dead center, and must have nicked the thoracic artery; there was a huge amount of blood running out of the guy, streaming between his fingers, saturating his clothes below the bullet hole. He was going to lose consciousness in another sixty seconds, and be dead within a couple minutes, but at the moment his eyes were open and blinking.

Dryden shone the light into the man's face and spoke with authority. "Is there another attack coming today? Tell me."

Pierce looked up into the glare.

"Is there another Rigel attack?" Dryden demanded.

Pierce shook his head, the movement requiring effort.

"Where are your stockpiles?" Dryden asked. "Where were you based?"

The man only shook his head again. "They'll find it all. They'll start with me and . . . they'll figure it out."

Dryden heard the metal cart shift as Danica stood up from it. She stepped over the nearest bodies and came to Dryden's side, staring down on Pierce.

Dryden looked at him again. "How did you get away? After that night. We must have told the military all about you. They would have come after you like an escaped convict. How the hell did you get away?"

Pierce's mouth had gone dry. He tried to wet his lips with his tongue, then spoke thickly. "I didn't."

Dryden stared, waiting for more.

The old man leaned his head back against the wall. "They liked what they saw," he whispered.

"What are you talking about?" Dryden asked.

"That night . . . after you got away from me . . . I tried to leave town. It was too late. You'd talked by then. Talked to the medics. Security teams were locking down the borders outside Ashland." Pierce shook his head. "I couldn't get out."

"Then why weren't you arrested and charged? You should have gotten the chair. Or you should have rotted in a cage the rest of your fucking life."

Pierce lifted his focus above the flashlight beam, meeting Dryden's eyes.

"They liked what they saw," he said again. His

voice was losing all power, but for the moment it remained audible. "The people in charge here . . . they'd seen Rigel in action—finally."

Pierce seemed to find something funny in that last statement. Though he didn't have the breath to laugh, his face went through the motions.

When he spoke again, there was an edge of delirium in his tone. The blood pressure in his brain had to be crashing.

"Rigel was mine," the old man whispered. "I wanted it for me, not for them. Wanted to sell it. My baby. Way back, I told them to kill it off . . . told them it was too dangerous. And they did. Then I made it again, just for me . . . and watched it all go to hell that night. Down in flames. But . . . the Army finally saw it. Saw what it did to Ashland. They decided they wanted it after all."

The powerless laugh had faded from his expression, but something like a smile settled into it now. A look of pride, Dryden thought.

He considered Pierce's words, and the implications that came with them.

"Jesus Christ," Dryden said. Then: "They cut you a deal. You'd stay out of prison if you gave them Rigel. You had it all in your head. They needed you, if they wanted that weapon."

Pierce nodded, blinking slowly.

Dryden said, "That's why they scrubbed our memories. Because we saw you murder Lauren Coleman. And if they were going to make a deal with you, they couldn't have us out there somewhere, knowing what you did."

Another nod, just perceptible. The man was fading fast. Still that look of satisfaction held—some twisted version of a father's pride. It was going to be the last face he ever made.

Then Danica stepped forward and crouched down, eye level with Pierce.

"What happened to Lauren Coleman's body?" she asked.

Wasting your time, Dryden thought. *They shoved her into that cremator down the hall, then dumped her ashes up in the cornfield. Or maybe they left the ashes in the machine, like they left the chimps to wither away in that room.*

Pierce stared at Danica, his eyes going blank. For a second Dryden thought he was gone already.

Then Danica grabbed a fistful of the man's hair, right on top, clenching it tight.

"Tell us," she said. "You're dead anyway, it's nothing to you. Tell us where they put her."

No response. Just the glassy stare.

Danica slapped Pierce's face with her other hand, rocking it sideways even as she held on to his scalp.

"Tell us!"

"Potter's Field," Pierce said softly. "Somewhere in Des Moines. You have the date."

It was his last breath. It hissed out on those words, and didn't go back in. Danica let go of his head and let it thump dully into the wall behind him.

Silence, as dead as any Dryden had ever known.

He swept his gaze over the little room. The gun-mounted flashlights still shone everywhere, pointed up at random angles from the sprawled bodies. In the confining dark they looked like spotlights—like some nightmare rock concert frozen in time.

"Let's get the hell out of here," Danica said.

Epilogue: FRAGMENTS

The Spanish villa in Malibu was a long way from being finished, but at least the cleanup was done. The stale air and the odor of dry rot were gone, replaced by the smell of new lumber and sheetrock. Tonight the house mostly smelled like the pine forest outside; Dryden had the windows open.

It was the tenth of April, 2019. He had finalized the purchase of the house in November, two months after the events in Ashland, Iowa had run their course. Those autumn weeks, right after it all happened, had played out like an IRS audit and a plague quarantine rolled into one.

For starters, he and Danica had been dumped into a kind of custody limbo—free to go, but strongly encouraged to stay in FBI hands. Early on, there were practical reasons for that—security reasons. While everyone agreed that Ellis Pierce was indeed the arms dealer Whiskey Four, his death did not immediately remove the threat posed by his organization. For close to a month, Dryden and Danica lived in an FBI safe house in the San Fernando Valley, half the time playing board games with their protective detail, the other half answering questions for random investigators who dropped by.

It was mid-October before the Bureau felt confident the danger had passed. Whiskey's network of associates had been *nullified,* as one agent phrased it. Dryden liked the word. It was a neat way of saying *hung upside-down in the bilge compartment of a ship and used for a punching bag until you started talking.* Whatever the case, those people were out of the picture for good.

The FBI had let him and Danica go home then, but only after a long, unpleasant talk about discretion, and how it wouldn't be helpful if any of this got out into the public sphere. None of it had made the news so far—not even the attack on the FBI personnel in Ashland. The Bureau seemed eager to keep it that way.

I'm sure you can appreciate our stance on this, an agent had said. *I mean, you've got the same incentives we do. Who wants the hassle of dealing with reporters, right?*

I don't know, Dryden said. *It's kind of a shame not to tell this story. Think of the endorsement deal I could get from Glock.*

The agent stared at him, unsure whether that was a joke.

If you really want to shut us up, Dryden said, *there's a drug cocktail they used to make. I'm told it's safe—they've even used it on kids.*

That's not funny, Mr. Dryden.

I'm not laughing.

The agent frowned and said, *You seem to be bargaining for something.*

I seem to be.

Okay, are we talking about money? Because we don't really—

No, we're not talking about money.

What, then?

At which point he and Danica had told him what they wanted. The agent leaned back and rubbed his eyes and said, *That's going to take time.*

Take all you need. Just get it done.

Outside the villa, the night wind off the ocean picked up. Dryden listened to it coursing over the barrel tiles on the roof. He stood in the master bedroom, which overlooked the motorcourt from the second floor. The room was dark and the French doors to the balcony stood open. He stepped out onto it, crossed to the rail, and wrapped his arms around Danica's waist.

She turned her head and kissed his cheek, and for a long time they stood staring over the treetops at the Pacific. The night was clear; they could see the lights of the Channel Islands on the horizon.

Then came the sound of an engine, and the glow of headlights through the trees—a vehicle winding its way up the switchback road. It pulled up and stopped on the paver bricks in front of the house: a black SUV with federal plates. The back door opened, and Jack Grace stepped out—on one shoe-clad foot and one metal prosthetic.

They gave him a tour of the place; he had a cane to go with the artificial foot, but he mostly got by without it. He'd been fitted with the prosthetic in December, and was using it continuously now.

The three of them sat at the makeshift table in the dining room: a sheet of plywood on sawhorses, surrounded by lawn chairs. The house was not officially certified for occupancy, but there was no law against sleeping in your own construction site; in the past few weeks, Dryden and Danica had spent most of their nights here. The rest of the time, they stayed at Dryden's place in El Sedero.

In spite of the month-long absence from her classes last fall, Danica had finished the semester with passing grades. After that she'd begun the process of transferring her credits to UC Santa Barbara; Dryden had convinced her, without much arm-twisting, that he needed someone to handle the business side of flipping houses.

There was pizza in the jobsite fridge in the kitchen, and a microwave on the chipboard countertop, but Grace passed; he'd eaten on the way. He accepted a beer from the fridge, and the three of them sat talking as the breeze rolled through the old house.

They talked about Rigel—as much as Grace had heard from the higher-ups. From the sound of it, Ellis Pierce had kept everything in a single secure location: his stock of the gas, the ingredients and tools for making it, the written knowledge that amounted to the recipe.

When the authorities had finally located that site and cracked it open, there was no sign anyone else had been into it since Pierce died. No reason to think any sample of Rigel, or any copy of that recipe, had gotten away when Pierce's network scattered. All of it was in the government's hands now.

"That'll help me get to sleep," Danica said.

"It's the best we could have asked for," Grace said. "They're not big on disinventing things. Christ, they've still got smallpox in a vial somewhere, for some kind of rainy day."

"These people need to pick up a hobby," Danica said. "Desperately."

Dryden stood and went to the window. He could just hear the hiss of traffic on the Pacific Coast Highway, far below through the trees.

"There are parts of it I still don't get," Dryden said. "Pierce told us he made a deal with the military, back in '89. No punishment for Lauren's murder, or for anything else, if he gave them Rigel." He turned from the window. "Have the investigators confirmed that?"

Grace was quiet for a moment. He glanced down at his hands, resting on the plywood. "Yes. The deal happened. Rigel for clemency."

Danica shook her head. "There's no way an agreement like that could have been official. Or legal."

"No," Grace said. "But the people overseeing Ashland weren't exactly sticklers for the law. And they were very, very interested in acquiring that weapon."

"But that's the part that doesn't tie together," Dryden said. "The military made the deal to get Rigel . . . but they *didn't* get Rigel. Last fall, when you were still trying to find out what that project was about, the Pentagon didn't even have it in their computers. Nobody there had ever heard of it."

"I wouldn't think so," Grace said.

Dryden waited for him to go on.

Grace finished his beer and leaned back in his chair.

"When the accident happened in 1989, the government moved pretty fast to shut Ashland down. All the risk, all the potential embarrassment—they wanted it sealed up and buried and forgotten. The people they put in charge of doing that were the same people who'd been running the place all along—who else were they going to use? And we're not talking about a huge group, either. It wasn't the rank and file, the people who'd lived and worked in Ashland. It was just the senior controllers, a handful on-site and another handful in D.C. That's who was in charge of buttoning it all down. The government wanted the smallest group that could still get the job done—we think it was no more than a dozen people. Everyone below them was following blind orders, and everyone above them wanted deniability. *It's your mess, you clean it up, I don't want to know the details.* And that skeleton crew in charge . . . that's who Ellis Pierce made his offer to."

"Oh shit," Danica said softly.

She looked at Dryden. He nodded; he could see where it was going.

"Yeah," Grace said. "It was kind of a perfect storm. These were high-ranking, well-connected people who'd spent their lives dealing in dangerous military secrets. And on the night they were ordered to shut down the place they'd built their careers on . . . one of its ghosts walked in and said, *Let's make a deal.*"

"So these guys set up, what, some kind of side business?" Dryden asked. "They kept Pierce's name out of the reports, kept him tucked away safe somewhere, and he gave them Rigel? What were they going to do, sell it on the black market?"

"From what we've learned," Grace said, "they ended up sitting on Rigel, even after Pierce re-created it for them. These guys were smart. They would have realized, at some point, how damned hot the thing was, how much attention it would bring. They decided not to risk it. But there were lots of other things Pierce could make for them. He was a chemical engineer with all sorts of ugly knowledge in his head. Old school nerve-toxins, bio-agents, things that were safer to bring to market."

"Their definition of *safer* is different than mine," Dryden said.

"Anyway," Grace said, "that's how it started, and how it went for years. They stayed as low-profile as they could. They were selling very bad stuff all over the world—but only so much, only so often. In time, when those guys started getting old, dying off, Pierce ended up in charge of things. By then he knew the game—he had contacts everywhere in the government, and he knew how to compromise people so they'd work with him. And somewhere along the way, we think he got tired of staying low-profile. A genius like him, he could afford to play the big game. That's when he became something new."

"Whiskey Four," Dryden said.

Grace nodded. "The kind of player who could finally sell Rigel. His baby."

A long silence followed.

"And none of this is what I came here to tell you," Grace said. "It's not the thing you bargained for."

"No it isn't," Danica said.

Grace reached into his shirt pocket and withdrew a folded piece of paper—a printout. He opened it and handed it to Danica. Dryden came back from the window and read it over her shoulder.

(07-26-1989)
DES MOINES—WARD III—OFFICE OF MEDICAL EXAMINER
NAME: **N/A (JANE DOE 1989-07-A)**
SEX: **F**
AGE: **13 (APPROX.)**
RACE: **C**
CAUSE OF DEATH: **CRANIAL GSW (FRONTAL / PARIETAL)**
FINGERPRINT MATCH: **N/A**
DENTAL MATCH: **N/A**
INTERRED: **CEDAR BANKS MUNICIPAL CEMETERY, MARKER 1732**

Danica held the page for a long moment, then set it gently on the makeshift table.

She said, "And what we discussed?"

"The paperwork is going through now," Grace said. "We can move her anyplace you decide on. Just let me know."

Danica's eyes hadn't left the printed words.

"We will," she said.

Long after Grace had gone, they turned off every light in the house. They took a six-pack of Diet Coke from the fridge, and a bag of Ruffles from the counter, and went out through the rear slider in the living room. The back yard lay in pitch darkness.

Two weeks earlier, browsing outdoor furniture in a landscaping shop, they had happened upon something they both loved: a big metal picnic table, its top measuring six feet by six. It looked gaudy as hell, and in no way did it match the Spanish villa; they purchased it on sight.

It was a sort of intuition they'd both experienced, over and over, since those few hours in Ashland. The daisy chain of memories—even if only fragments sometimes returned. They took them all as they came.

Dryden felt his way in the dark, until his hand brushed the surface of the table. A moment later they were lying atop it, side by side, the sky full of stars above them. There were probably better places for this than Malibu, but it was dark enough for shooting stars—dark enough to spot the occasional satellite, even.

Every clear night these past two weeks, they had done this for hours. There was something about it that was hard to pin down—some feeling that transcended age, Dryden thought. Under the sky on a night like this, maybe everyone was still twelve.

His focus went to a bright star almost straight overhead.

Vega? Deneb?

Those two names kept coming to him—it had

happened last night, too. He didn't know why, and had no idea if either of them was right. He had only a passing knowledge of astronomy.

"I remember something," Danica whispered.

Dryden heard a mix of emotions in her voice: pain and wonder at the same time, somehow. She took hold of his hand, interlaced her fingers with his. He could feel a tremor in her grip, her body tense like a wire.

"I remember her laugh," she said.

ACKNOWLEDGMENTS

It would be impossible to fully thank the people who made this book happen. Their work, encouragement, and patience (a whole lot of patience, this time around) made all the difference. Thank you to my agent, Janet Reid, and my editor, Keith Kahla, who each read several drafts of this one—and whose input improved it greatly at every pass. Thank you to Alice Pfeifer, and so many others (more than I'll ever know, I'm sure) at St. Martin's Press and Minotaur Books: Sally Richardson, Jennifer Enderlin, Andy Martin, Kelley Ragland, Paul Hochman, Hector DeJean, Rafal Gibek, Lauren Humphries-Brooks, and Joe Brosnan.